MW01641370

The loudspeaker blared: "Incoming wounded! All reception personnel report to loading pads!"

Sybil barely had time to change into a surgical suit when the first ambulance arrived. The wounded were laid out on gurneys and the emergency crew swung into action.

The first patient had a poncho over him. Pale, with clammy skin, he kept asking what time it was. Sybil pulled the poncho open and, despite her experience, blanched. The soldier's right leg was a jagged stump.

"Let's get an IV over here! This one's going into shock!"

The afternoon turned into a long one, preparing the bloodied wounded for surgery. Sybil was exhausted. She wanted to cry, to scream—but she had to remain calm and composed. This was war. She had a job to do and she would do it. She had no choice. She was a

VIETNAM NURSE

ZEBRA BRINGS YOU EXCITING BESTSELLERS
by Lewis Orde

MUNICH 10 (1300, $3.95)

They've killed her lover, and they've kidnapped her son. Now the world-famous actress is swept into a maelstrom of international intrigue and bone-chilling suspense—and the only man who can help her pursue her enemies is a complete stranger . . .

HERITAGE (1100, $3.75)

Beautiful innocent Leah and her two brothers were forced by the holocaust to flee their parents' home. A courageous immigrant family, each battled for love, power and their very lifeline—their HERITAGE.

THE LION'S WAY (900, $3.75)

An all-consuming saga that spans four generations in the life of troubled and talented David, who struggles to rise above his immigrant heritage and rise to a world of glamour, fame and success!

DEADFALL (1400, $3.95)

by Lewis Orde and Bill Michaels

The two men Linda cares about most, her father and her lover, entangle her in a plot to hold Manhattan Island hostage for a billion dollars ransom. When the bridges and tunnels to Manhattan are blown, Linda is suddenly a terrorist—except *she's* the one who's terrified!

Available wherever paperbacks are sold, or order direct from the Publisher. Send cover price plus 50¢ per copy for mailing and handling to Zebra Books, 475 Park Avenue South, New York, N.Y. 10016. DO NOT SEND CASH.

VIETNAM NURSE

EVELYN
HAWKINS

ZEBRA BOOKS
KENSINGTON PUBLISHING CORP.

This book is a work of fiction. Any similarity between its characters and actual persons, living or dead, is coincidental and unintentional.

ZEBRA BOOKS

are published by

Kensington Publishing Corp.
475 Park Avenue South
New York, N.Y. 10016

Copyright © 1984 by Evelyn Hawkins

All rights reserved. No part of this book may be reproduced in any form or by any means without the prior written consent of the Publisher, excepting brief quotes used in reviews.

First printing: October 1984

Printed in the United States of America

To Julie Stensland Andrews

Special acknowledgment to
Patrick E. Andrews

'Twas the tears and the valor that sustained us throughout the dreadful ordeal.

—Remark attributed to Lady Daphne Warrenton following the end of the Siege of Rochester Castle in 1088.

Chapter One

South Vietnam, 1966

The sun, a white blurry disk in the bleached sky, radiated its heat downward in angry waves. The torrid intensity boiled the moisture out of the ground in imperceptible clouds of steam, and the reflection off the concrete helicopter-landing pads made the people standing around them almost gasp in discomfort. Several, beginning to show adverse reactions to the high temperature, were taken to the questionable comfort of the shade afforded by the ambulances parked around the area.

Second Lt. Sybil Watkins wiped at the perspiration on her forehead. Her jungle fatigue uniform, a two-piece affair with jacket and trousers boasting large pockets, was wilted. It clung to her in the most uncomfortable places. She sighed aloud and licked her dry lips. "Why didn't somebody think to bring enough water along?"

Connie Montaldo, a fellow nurse and her best friend, slowly shook her head. "We weren't supposed to be out here this long, *amigita*."

Both young women turned and looked longingly at their unit's billets only a few hundred meters away. The view of the Quonset huts appeared blurry in the heat waves that danced across the Long Binh garrison's expanse.

Sybil could feel the perspiration trickle from the baseball style fatigue cap she wore, through her short hair, and down between her shoulder blades. "Couldn't we send somebody—"

"You know better than that," Connie interrupted. "Mother Moorehead was most explicit. She said everyone had to stay out here until the choppers arrived."

Sybil gave the billets another longing look. "Think of all the cool drinks over there. Fruit juices, soda pop, water, and even some beer."

"There's wounded coming in," Connie reminded her. "We have to be here to meet them. It'd be a pretty sad situation if they showed up and there weren't enough people around to take care of them because we got thirsty."

Sybil's thoughts turned to the injured soldiers. "I can see Mother Moorehead's point. There's no denying our discomfort is nothing compared to what some of those wounded boys will be going through."

Connie's expression turned grim. "You're right about that."

Their unit, the 555th Field Hospital, dubbed the Triple-Nickel by its inmates, was a permanent part of Long Binh. They were tasked with a twofold requirement of providing medical care for temporary concentrations of troops in the immediate area, and taking care of any influx of combat casualties flown in from the field. The work was either feast-or-famine with long periods of boring, tedious duty broken up by organized chaos from time to time.

The Triple-Nickel was preparing for the latter situation at that particular time. Elements of the First Cavalry Division had been engaged in a search-and-destroy operation several hundred kilometers to the north. The situation had turned nastier than expected and the unit had sustained heavy casualties. Arrangements had been made to fly the numerous wounded troopers into the Long Binh for initial medical treatment. The word had arrived at the Triple-Nickel early that morning. The medical teams had formed up and rushed out to meet the incoming aircraft and their injured burdens.

Sybil and Connie, assigned to one of the convalescent wards, were always listed for the reception details. They, the other nurses, and enlisted medical corpsmen of that particular part of the Triple-Nickel, were more easily spared for extracurricular activities than the personnel in the surgical and intensive care units.

Their job was to meet the newly arrived patients to give the injured hasty preliminary examinations. This was to see that they were taken to the correct areas for further and more extensive medical care.

That day was a typical hurry-up-and-wait army situation. The medical teams had been standing by in the vapory heat for five hours.

Sybil moaned again. Her feet, encased in wool army socks and leather boots, felt as if they were in an oven. She was young, only twenty-three years of age, and had less than a year's service as an army nurse. Not quite petite, Sybil was five feet, three inches tall with a rather athletic-appearing figure that didn't detract from her femininity. She displayed an attractive schoolgirl quality. Even in the fatigue uniform with its baseball style cap she was cute. Blue-eyed, with soft brown hair cut in a short style, she had a scattering of freckles across her small nose. Her voice was soft, almost demure, and complemented somewhat by the slow drawl indigenous to her native Oklahoma. It added a bit of southern charm to her personality.

Connie winked at her. "Hang in there, kid. They'll be here soon."

"You're used to heat," Sybil said with a near accusatory ring in her voice. "Being born and raised in the Arizona desert should make you feel right at home."

"It's the great Sonoran desert," Connie corrected her. "And the heat in Tucson is nice and dry. Not this steamy crud like they have over here."

Connie was Sybil's temperamental opposite. Vivacious, blunt and vociferous, her Latin emotions could run wild at times. But she had the capacity to display a quiet stoicism during trying circumstances. Connie took Sybil's arm. "Let's go over by the ambulance."

"It's just as hot over there," Sybil said.

"We'll talk to Ernie. Maybe the runt will cheer us up."

"Okay."

The two nurses walked from the landing pad across the short stretch of grass where a G.I. ambulance, a large white square sporting a red cross painted on both sides and top, stood. Officially designated as *Truck, Ambulance, 1¼ Ton, M792,* its squat impersonal appearance belied its basic humanitarian task—the transportation of maimed, suffering men.

The back doors were open, and a young medical corpsman sat in the questionable comfort of the vehicle's interior.

"How you doing, Ernie?" Sybil greeted him.

"It's fuckin' hot."

Connie whipped her fatigue cap off and slapped him hard with it across the shoulders.

Smack!

"Ow! What's'a big idea, huh?" he complained. "That stung, Connie."

"It was supposed to," Connie said angrily. "I told you to stop saying that word."

"Ever'body says it," Ernie said. "This is the army fer Chrissake!"

Sp4g. Ernie Kaznowski was a nineteen-year-old kid out of Chicago's Polish-American community. Undersized and skinny, he made up for his lack of physical impressiveness with a mouth big and brash enough to get him more than his share of trouble. Ernie had a friendly, open face with blue eyes that did little to hide his cocky belligerence. His blond hair, despite the short G.I. haircut, always appeared wild and unkempt.

"You say that word more than any ten other people combined," Connie said.

"So?" He rubbed his shoulder.

"It's not supposed to be a swear word," Sybil interjected. "It's an act of deep love and affection between man and woman."

Ernie leered. "You ain't been down to Juicy Lucy's, have you?"

"Of course we haven't," Connie said. "And you'll stop going down there if you know what's good for you."

"Well, I guess I don't know what's fuckin' good for—"

Smack!

"Ouch! Goddamnit, Connie. That hurt!"

"Then stop saying the 'F' word," the Chicana warned him.

"Fuckin' this and fuckin' that," he said with a defiant smirk.

Smack!

"Fuckedy-fuckedy-fuckedy—"

Smack! Smack!

"All right, all right already," Ernie said wincing. "I won't say it no more."

"*Any*more," Sybil corrected.

"'Anymore—I won't say it anymore. Jeez, you two are worse than my ma."

"Look at it this way, kid," Connie said replacing her cap. "You'll be a better person from having known us."

"I'll be a blacker and bluer person, that's what I'll be," Ernie said. "You two broads—"

Smack!

"Ow! You two ladies have got to lighten up or you'll turn me into a sissy."

Connie treated him to a particularly disapproving glare. "You have such a nasty mouth, I can't believe you eat with it."

"Aw!" Ernie protested.

"Just mind your p's and q's," Sybil said.

"Whatever you say, lieutenant." Ernie reached under the stretcher rack and produced a canteen. "Anybody want a drink o' Kool-Aid?"

"Kool-Aid?" Sybil exclaimed. "Where in the world did you get that?"

"My ma sends me packets of the stuff," Ernie answered unscrewing the lid.

Connie snatched the canteen from him. "Why didn't

you tell us you had something to drink?" She took several greedy gulps. *"Ay Dios mio! Es delicioso!"*

"Hell, I figured if you got thirsty you'd come over and ask for somethin'," Ernie said.

Connie handed the container to Sybil. "It wouldn't have hurt for you to make mention that you'd brought this along y'know."

"I always take care o' you two, don't I? It don't matter how much older you are or how much more schoolin' you got than me. Broads needs—"

Smack!

"—women need men to look after 'em." He glared at Connie, then turned his attention to Sybil. "Hey! Don't drink it all, huh?"

Sybil handed the canteen back. "My God, that was good."

"Yeah," Ernie said. "I never could make it through a hot summer's day without gallons of the stuff. My ma always kept a big pitcher in the icebox for us kids." He treated himself to a couple of swallows. Suddenly he stopped. "Listen!"

At first there was only the whisper of steamy breezes that wafted and died in the hot afternoon air, but after a few moments passed there was a definite chopping sound from afar.

Ernie tossed the canteen inside and leaped to the ground. "It's the choppers, ladies. Let's get ready."

They went over to the helicopter pad. Another medic, a black kid named Joe Sampson who had been teamed up with Ernie, left an ambulance where he'd been playing cards with a couple of his cronies and joined the trio.

"Ever'body ready?" he asked.

"Let's get those poor guys—and us—out of this heat as

quickly as possible," Sybil urged.

Joe, his ebony face streaked with rivulets of sweat, nodded his agreement. "Right on, lieutenant."

The aircraft appeared as numerous dots in the distant sky. The chopping sound of their engines grew louder as they formed into the proper echelon to come into the available landing areas. These were UH-1C Hueys, each carrying two wounded.

Ernie and Joe, well trained and practiced, directed the first helicopter down. The pilot settled his craft to the ground in a smooth, expert descent. As soon as the skids made contact with the concrete, the two young medics rushed forward. They took the first stretcher off and carried it over to the grass and sat it down. After repeating the procedure with the second, they waved the all-clear to the pilot. The airman twisted the throttle and applied upward pressure on the collective to make the helicopter climb back into the blazing sky.

The two nurses each went to a stretcher. Sybil hoped there would be none of the patients that she would have to classify as expectants. An expectant was a casualty so badly injured there was no hope for survival. These were set aside so that those with hope could be treated first.

Sybil was pleased when the young soldier, his face blanched and teeth clenched, looked into her face. "Howdy, ma'am."

"How're you doing?" Sybil said. She checked his casualty tag and noted that he'd taken shrapnel in the left leg and buttock. His unit aidman had also administered a tetanus shot.

"I'm hurting, ma'am."

Sybil was more concerned with shock and bleeding at that particular moment. "We'll have that taken care of right away." She worked rapidly, inspecting his bloody bandages, then gave his pulse a check while noting his appearance and respiration. A tough young paratrooper, she decided, who would heal quickly.

Ernie and Joe Sampson had only time enough to load the wounded men into the ambulance before the next helicopter hovered in. The team of medics again took a stretcher out and carried it to a spot by their vehicle. They set the first man down for Connie to examine, then rushed back for the next injured soldier.

Sybil watched as they pulled the burden free of the fuselage. Then she noticed a look of alarm play across Ernie's face. He and Joe broke into a run, rushing toward her with the man bouncing on the stretcher between them. Ernie shouted something, but his voice was whipped away by the roar of the helicopter engine. Within seconds he reached her.

"This guy's choking, Sybil!"

They set the litter on the ground and Sybil quickly dropped down to examine the patient. It was impossible to determine if it was a young kid or an older officer or sergeant. His lower face was completely covered by a couple of OD field dressings and surgical gauze. He'd obviously suffered a facial or neck wound in the throat area. Sybil noted the man's face was purpling and, now that the helicopter had soared away leaving the area silent, she could hear the strangling, coughing sounds he was making.

"Give me your switchblade!" she said to Ernie.

Ernie wasn't thinking fast. "Wh—what?"

"I said give me your switchblade," Sybil repeated. "I know you have one, you little hood!"

Ernie reached into his fatigues and produced a long

knife with an imitation plastic mother-of-pearl handle. He pushed the button and flipped the blade open.

Sybil took it and made a deft cut in the wounded soldier's throat at the base of the neck just above the collarbone.

Joe Sampson watched her, his concern evident. "Is he gonna die, lieutenant?"

"Not if I can help it," Sybil said pushing out her ballpoint pen and quickly dismantling it. She threw away the writing innards, then pushed the hollow stem into the wound.

There was a sudden sound of air being pulled through it in time with the wounded man's heaving chest.

"Get him into the ambulance."

"He's breathing," Ernie announced unnecessarily.

Joe grabbed his end of the stretcher. "Let's go, Ernie."

Sybil stayed at her patient's side as they lifted him up and put him in the back. "Get the other wounded man in here and don't waste a second. I want this guy back at the surgical hut as quick as you can drive over there."

Within a scant two minutes the vehicle raced toward its objective. Connie, who had leaped into the back, looked over Sybil's shoulder. "How's he doing?"

"Breathing steadily," Sybil answered holding her makeshift instrument in place.

"I would call that a classic emergency tracheotomy," Connie said. "I'd say you saved his life."

"That was the idea."

Ernie, up in the driver's seat, braked the vehicle. Leaving the engine running, he leaped out. Joe Sampson did likewise and the two raced around to the back.

The litter, with Sybil walking beside it, was taken through the door of the operating hut. The young nurse was concentrating so intently on her patient that she didn't notice the sudden coolness of the air-conditioned interior of the building.

The surgical team, already set up and waiting, sized up the situation immediately and relieved them of their burden. The three vacated the room and went back outside where Connie waited for them.

The other three wounded were being unloaded by medics from the surgical detachment. "Nice goin', Lieutenant Watkins," Joe said, watching her put her pen back together. He looked over at Ernie and grinned. "You better hide that blade. If Sar'nt Major Rafferty finds out about that, you'll be dancin' the stockade shuffle."

Ernie smirked. "What blade?"

"Don't fret yourself. *I* ain't gonna tell nobody about it," Joe said with a reassuring wink. "Hey, I'll turn the ambulance in, okay?"

"That'd be a good idea, Joe," Ernie said, "'specially since you're the one that signed out for it."

"That don't mean I have to turn it in," Joe said. "I ain't no NCO. I'm just a plain ol' speedy-four like you. I'm only doin' it so the lieutenants don't get no hassle."

"Hell, yes, you gotta turn it in!" Ernie insisted. "What the hell you think, you can just park it somewheres and forget about it?"

"Hey, Ernie," Joe said angrily. "Don't give me no shit, huh?"

"Well *I* ain't turnin' it in!" Ernie snapped.

Connie grew tired of listening to them. "Ernie, be quiet. Joe said he'd turn it in, didn't he?"

"All right, all right!" Ernie said. "See you later."

The black soldier got into the vehicle and started it up. He slipped it into gear and drove away toward the motor pool. Connie took a deep breath. "Well, that's over. We waited five hours to do ten minutes' worth of work."

"That's the way it is in the Triple-Nickel," Ernie said. He gave Sybil a friendly nudge. "Say! I'll bet Mother Moorehead gives you a few good words out of today's action."

"Don't count on it," Connie said testily. "You could've used your nail file to perform a faultless, emergency appendectomy on the guy during the run over here and she wouldn't say a thing about it."

"You're right," Sybil said. "You have to screw up to get Mother's attention or personal comments."

Ernie checked his watch. "Hey, we go off duty in another hour. What say we drop over to Lucky's for some cool ones, huh?"

"Ay Dios!" Connie said. "The thought of a cold beer is positively sensous."

"And a shower and change of clothes," Sybil added.

"Yeah," Ernie agreed. "But remember we got another hour before our shift is over. In the meantime we gotta get back to the fuckin' ward."

Smack!

Chapter Two

Connie was already in the shower while Sybil slowly undressed in the room they shared in the nurses' billets. She glanced in the mirror mounted on her wall locker door and winked at her reflection.

"What's a nice girl like you doing in a place like this?" Sybil asked herself. Then she answered, "Why, I'm off to take a shower after a day of devoted, selfless service to humanity."

She got her shower gear and headed for the door. "What else?"

Sybil Mae Watkins was born in Oklahoma City, Oklahoma, at the end of World War II. Her conception was the result of her father's inebriated return home during World War II.

Doyle Watkins was an executive vice president of the Central State Grange Bank in downtown Oklahoma City. A part of his being able to attain that lofty position was from hard work. A large part of his success, however, could be credited to his marriage to Sefton Burton's daughter. Burton was the president of the bank.

Sefton Burton never really cared for the young man despite the latter's hard-earned college education and dedication to his position at the bank—not to mention the marriage to his only daughter. To his dying day, the oldster described his son-in-law as "lean, mean, and as ambitious as a starving coyote." Watkins, with an instinct for survival developed in a boyhood of desperate poverty, was determined to get on the old man's good side.

The son-in-law buttered up the father-in-law every way he could figure out. He rooted for his favorite sports teams; sought unneeded advice and counsel; and registered as a republican and openly espoused the party's causes and endorsed its candidates. When all this didn't seem enough, he went a step further and enlisted in the National Guard.

Since Burton had spent many years as a National Guard officer, it seemed natural that if Watkins also joined up, then he would be able to score a plus in that big pile of minuses where his father-in-law was concerned.

Doyle Watkins participated in the Guard with the same drive and toadyism he demonstrated in the bank job. He served as an enlisted man until his first encampment in the summer of 1928. During those two weeks spent at Fort Sill he was subjected to the military form of class distinction. The officers were quartered and dined in finer surroundings than the common soldiers. This reminded Watkins too much of always being the poor boy during his youth. Upon the unit's return home, he applied for the army's Series Ten correspondence course. When he successfully completed it he received a commission as second lieutenant. This, like his promotions at the bank, was not done without Sefton Burton's applying a bit of his influence in the proceedings.

When World War II broke out Watkins was called to active duty with the Forty-Fifth Infantry Division. Although not a footslogger by any stretch of the imagination (he served as a lieutenant colonel in the G3 Plans and Operations Section of the division staff), Watkins did not appreciate the inconvenience of being pulled in from civilian life. He already hated the Tuesday night drills. Suddenly finding himself a full-time soldier was the last thing he'd had ever wished for himself. Watkins held each individual Japanese and German fully responsible and accountable for this terrible inconvenience. And he was not a man who believed or practiced forgiveness.

Despite this lack of martial fervor, Watkins did possess a large amount of masculine pride in the martial side of his life. After the war he always wore miniatures of his campaign ribbons on his tuxedo on formal occasions, and insisted on being addressed as "colonel" even at the bank and in private life.

The war ended early for Lieutenant Colonel Watkins due to a severe attack of asthma brought on by the chilly Italian winter. Found to be unfit for further service, he was shipped back to the States to be processed out of the army via a medical discharge.

He spent his last days in uniform on a train trip

home from New York City to Oklahoma City. He spent most of the time in the club car enjoying his new freedom with liberal doses of liquor while regaling his fellow passengers with tales of his war service. Normally a social drinker, he lost control of himself and arrived at the family home so drunk he had to be helped from the taxi up to his front door.

The sight of a wife whom he hadn't seen in nearly three years, combined with a bellyful of liquor, brought uncontrollable passions to the surface. His spouse, Laura, always docile and unargumentative, submitted to his lovemaking without reminding him of their usual method of condoms for birth control. It was on that very night that Sybil was conceived.

Sybil's brother Sefton had been born in 1930, a sister Amanda Lou in 1933 and the other sister, Henrietta, in 1936. Henrietta was supposed to have been the last, but Sybil Mae made her surprise appearance in 1943. Her unplanned arrival into the Watkins family made her seven years younger than her nearest sibling.

Despite Sybil's rather disconcerting entrance into the family, her father quickly adapted her into the scheme of things to make sure she shared equally in all opportunities and conditions of life available to her older brother and sisters. After a pampered babyhood and toddlerhood, she, like the other children, was enrolled in the prestigious Kennedy Day Academy, an exclusive private school located in the Oklahoma City suburb of Westborough.

During the formative early years at Kennedy, Sybil showed great promise in both academic and social areas. The little girl was precocious and pretty. She could charm most adults to distraction, and she loved schoolwork, considering it fun, interesting, and easy. The various tasks set out for the lower grades were easily mastered by the little girl. She demonstrated a capacity for hard work and concentration far beyond her tender years. This serious side, undoubtedly inherited from the humorless, hardworking father, was to be a dominant part of her personality.

During the middle of her third grade year, the parents were summoned to visit the school by its founder and director. This woman, an intellectually motivated educator with a tremendous personal drive, named Edwina Kennedy, loved educating young people. She took a sincere interest in them, displaying a caring concern for her students.

When Sybil's parents arrived for the meeting with Miss Kennedy, they were immediately ushered into her office. The school's director greeted them enthusiastically. "I'm so glad you could come by. We have reached a point in Sybil Mae's school career where a more important decision must be made."

"Has she done something wrong?" Watkins inquired sullenly.

"Oh, not at all. On the contrary. Your daughter is one of our prize pupils. In fact, I may safely say that there has never been another student of her equal in the twenty-seven years I have operated Kennedy Day Academy, colonel."

Watkins relaxed a bit. "Sybil Mae is pretty smart, is she?"

"Exceedingly so," Miss Kennedy remarked. "In fact, her intellectual ability is so remarkable that I feel she is wasting time staying with her contemporaries in the third grade. We could skip Sybil Mae to the fifth or even sixth. Though I believe it would be best to try her—"

"I don't want the girl skipped anywhere," Watkins said. "Let's leave her where she is."

"My goodness, why?"

"Because, Miss Kennedy, that is exactly where she belongs," Watkins said in the manner of a pronouncement.

Laura Watkins remained silent, almost as if she were an outsider simply observing the proceedings. She listened to the conversation, showing no more than a casual interest.

"I certainly respect your wishes, colonel," Miss Kennedy said. "But I must tell you that I've personally examined Sybil Mae and have administered various tests to her. The little girl's abilities in mathematics, reading skills, verbal and written communications, and—well, just about every subject, give me the opinion that we most assuredly have a young person with an extremely high IQ on our hands."

Watkins stood up and motioned his wife to do the same. "Leave her where she is."

Miss Kennedy looked at him incredulously. "But Colonel Watkins. Even the music teacher has said she displays an extraordinary amount of talent."

"Sybil Mae is a little girl," Watkins said. "A mighty smart and clever little girl, but a little girl just the same. Taking her away from friends her age and putting her into the sort of situation you suggest might help her out as a student. But she won't be a student forever. Someday she'll be a grown woman with a husband and kids, deeply involved in a life as a wife and mother. Any kind of program of advanced or accelerated classes would cause her confusion and frustration eventually as an adult. She wouldn't be able to function properly like a normal woman should."

"But Colonel Watkins," Miss Kennedy said, her disappointment visible, "surely you wouldn't limit a girl to an area below her intellectual capabilities even if she weren't going to pursue a career or profession. There are many rewards to be had from —"

"I appreciate what you are saying, Miss Kennedy," Watkins interrupted. "But, believe me, I know what's best for Sybil Mae."

Miss Kennedy turned an imploring eye toward the mother. "Mrs. Watkins. What—" She could tell from the woman's expression that further entreaties were useless. She lapsed into a sad silence.

"Thank you so much for your concern and interest," Watkins said ushering his wife toward the door. He opened it and allowed Mrs. Watkins to precede him. Before leaving, he turned. "I know what is needed to give my little daughter the happiness she should have out of life, Miss Kennedy. Really I do. Have a nice day, hear?"

He quietly closed the office door.

Sybil stood under the shower spigot and let the hot water flush the perspiration and stickiness from her body. She could hear Connie singing a cheerful song in Spanish over in the next stall. She listened for a while, enjoying her friend's melodic voice. When Connie stopped, Sybil called over to her, "What's the name of that song?"

"Marieta," Connie answered over the sound of the

running water. "My grandmother taught it to me. It's about a girl being warned not to be a flirt because men aren't to be trusted."

"Very apropos," Sybil joked. "Take heed, young lady."

"Okay, *muchacha,*" Connie said with a laugh. "Though it's tempting to play the *femme fatale* because of all the eligible men around here."

"Going to take advantage of your womanly charms, hey?" Sybil remarked.

"Seguro que si, you betcha!"

Connie was extremely attractive. Short and pretty, she was olive-skinned with shiny black hair which she kept much longer than the regulations permitted. Her physical attributes could best be described as well endowed. Connie had large breasts and wide hips which caused her to poke fun at herself as being "bred to breed."

"Just think," Sybil said taking her razor from the shelf inside the stall, "this may be the only time in our lives when we'll be in a situation where the males outnumber us."

"Not only are they males," Connie said, "they're eager, attentive ones."

Sybil carefully and methodically shaved her legs. If it hadn't been for going to the base swimming pool or occasional trips to the beaches in the south, she wouldn't have bothered. The only clothing she seemed to wear were fatigues or khaki shirts and slacks. Finishing up, Sybil treated herself to another soaking, then turned off the water and stepped out to dry herself.

Connie was nearly dressed. Her fatigues lay in a pile

by her boots. Her fresh Class A uniform consisted of comfortable gabardine pants and shirt sporting an open collar. She pulled on the upper garment and buttoned it. "What took you so long?"

Sybil sighed. "Don't you ever have to shave your legs?"

"I'm not a hairy *gringa,*" Connie said. "A couple of times a month keeps me smooth as a melon."

The two friends finished dressing before speaking further.

"Are you ever embarrassed about all this?" Connie asked, indicating their surroundings with a toss of her head.

"What do you mean?"

"I mean about being officers and having better facilities and living conditions than the enlisted men and women."

Sybil felt cool and refreshed. "I hadn't given it much thought. Why?"

"Oh, I don't know," Connie remarked thoughtfully. "My brothers were in the service, y'know. Esteban, the oldest, was in the marines. He was in Korea and got wounded. The guy went through a lot. But he was an enlisted man and never had things as nice as I do."

"You're a nurse," Sybil said. "Officers are given the better areas to stay, that's all."

"We're not real officers, Sybil," Connie said with a laugh. "I mean we're not leaders, for crying out loud. My brother Carlos was a paratrooper. He was a sergeant and had some other guys directly under his command. Even the baby Jorge is in the Eighty-second Airborne Division now. He wrote and told me he was a fire team leader and in charge of four other soldiers.

Who do we command?"

Sybil laughed. "Ernie."

"Oh, brother!"

"Anyway, it sounds like your family produces gung-ho guys," Sybil said.

"That's the way it is in a Chicano *barrio,*" Connie explained. "All the guys go for the macho stuff."

"John Wayne types, hey?"

"We call him *Juan* Wayne," Connie said with a giggle. "Anyhow I feel self-conscious about this better treatment."

"You're confusing me," Sybil said smoothing down her own cool gabardine Class A's. "I can't quite follow the drift of your conversation."

"I guess I'm just embarrassed about being better off than other people around me," Connie said. "I've always been like everybody else or maybe a little worse off."

"Were you poor?" Sybil asked. She and Connie had been friends for a little less than three months. None of their conversations had covered their families' financial conditions.

"No. My father was a labor contractor for a couple of farm co-ops in southern Arizona. He got Mexican workers for them through the Bracero program. Papa made pretty good money—well, not *real* good. But we always had plenty to eat and a roof over our heads. Our family was just like the other families in the neighborhood." She hesitated. "I suppose that I feel awkward about living in officer country because it's a new situation for me."

Sybil shrugged. "I've never given it much thought."

"Your family's pretty well off, aren't they?" Connie

asked. "You never said one way or the other. I just assumed so from things you've told me."

"We're not rich, maybe, but upper middle class," Sybil allowed.

Connie laughed. "I guess we Montaldos are either lower middle class or upper lower class."

"You're a nurse," Sybil reminded her. "You've been trained and educated in a profession that requires a lot of skill and knowledge. You have a college degree. That's why the army made you an officer."

"Okay, *amigita.* But it's still hard for me to be part of the upper crust. I'm just a Chicana out of Tucson. I suppose that's all I'll ever be deep inside."

"You're a trained professional." Sybil slipped into her low-quarter shoes. "God! These are so much more comfortable than those damned boots."

"Sure are," Connie agreed. "What time are we supposed to meet Ernie?"

"Not for an hour."

The two picked up their soiled fatigues and ditty bags of soap and cosmetics. "I'm going to drop by the ward," Sybil said as they walked toward the door.

"Going to check on that Pullini guy?" Connie asked.

"Yeah. I haven't had time to talk with him today. We were out by those God-awful chopper pads all day. Then by the time we got back I was too busy dispensing medications."

Connie took her arm. "It's good for a nurse to care and be concerned, Sybil—up to a point."

"Weren't we just discussing how professional we are?" Sybil asked.

"Right.Give me your things. I'll wait for you in the

billets."

"Thanks." Sybil handed her bundle over, then hurried out of the latrine. She crossed the compound to the convalescent ward.

The patient she was concerned about was an infantryman from New Jersey named Mike Pullini. A private first class, Pullini had stepped on a land mine a few weeks previously. The maiming wound he had suffered necessitated the amputation of both legs just below the knees. He had proven to be a quiet, morose patient who was obviously going through a bad emotional time without being particularly revealing about it.

Sybil, as a nurse, had a sincere concern for the people placed under her care. But this went far beyond seeing after their physical needs. Sybil wanted to do more than minister to Mike Pullini's stumps; she wanted to give him that extra bit of help he obviously needed.

The one most important bit of psychology that a nurse must practice with an amputee was to be as candid and open about his condition as possible. His affliction was a permanent and irrevocable. He would have to live with it for the rest of his life. Sympathy, while a part of the treatment, would not really help all that much.

Mike Pullini was in the worst possible situation. His injury was traumatic and unexpected. Most civilian amputees face the surgical mutilation because of circulation and other vascular problems. They are prepared for a process that, though very unpleasant, is an alternative to death. After the operation they are helped along in programs which include rehabilitated amputees in many instances. These people show them their lives can still be pleasant and useful despite the loss of a limb.

All Pfc. Mike Pullini knew was that he was walking through a rice paddy when there was a roar and a bright flash. The next thing he was aware of was regaining consciousness in a hospital bed with his lower legs missing. He'd gone, in one instant, from a robust young male to a hospital patient who could not even walk to the bathroom. He had to endure the indignity of a bedpan, and when he did venture from the ward, it was always in a wheel chair. That situation would be the same until he went back Stateside and received his prosthesis. But that wouldn't be for a while yet.

He also suffered badly from the "phantom limb" syndrome in which he felt pain in the missing legs. No matter how hard he tried to convince himself they were gone—severed—nerves cut off from the brain—he could still feel acute pain in those feet that were no longer a part of him.

Sybil walked into the ward. The duty nurse, a captain named Penny Darwin, who slept in the room next to hers and Connie's in the billets, waved at her from the small glassed-in enclosure that formed the ward office.

"Hi, Sybil."

"Hi, Penny." She stepped inside the partition. "I came to see Mike Pullini. How's he doing?"

"The same," the other nurse replied. "Quiet and withdrawn. Whatever thoughts he's having, he's keeping to himself."

"Yeah." Sybil stepped back into the ward and walked down the aisle between the beds. This was a particularly quiet time for the patients. Evening chow was due, and the men waited for their food in silent expectation. Most nodded or spoke a low murmured greeting to Sybil as she passed by them.

Mike Pullini was the last in his row. He lay, as always, on his back with his face to the wall. Sybil smiled as she walked up. "Hi, Mike."

He turned to look at her, his face expressionless. "Hello, ma'am." Mike was twenty years old, extremely muscular with dark Latin good looks accented by bright green eyes. Sybil knew he must be a real lady's man. She was glad he at least had that going for him.

"I didn't get much of a chance to talk with you today," Sybil said. "I was on the reception detail."

Mike continued to look at her in silence.

"It was really hot out there."

Not a word.

Sybil noticed a couple of letters on his bedside stand. "Hear from home?"

"Yes, ma'am."

"Who from? Your mother? Girlfriend maybe?"

"Yes, ma'am."

"I think you were scheduled for physical therapy today. How did it go?"

"Okay."

"Frank Garvin's quite a guy, isn't he?"

"Sure."

"All the patients he works with like him," Sybil said. She suddenly felt very awkward. Most of the time she visited with Mike while on duty. Being here on her own time made her feel somewhat of an interloper. "Well—I came back to the ward for my watch," she lied. "Left it here when I went out on that—that reception detail.

Since I was here I just thought I'd—well, we didn't have a chance to talk today." She looked at him for a moment, a half smile formed on her lips. "Any trouble with the phantom limb syndrome?"

"No change," Mike said.

"It'll go away. Always does." She looked at her watch. "Well, Connie—Lieutenant Montaldo—and Ernie Kaznowski are waiting for me." Sybil stepped back from the bed. "Anything I can get you while I'm out?"

"How about a couple of feet?"

Sybil shook her head. "Sorry. See you tomorrow, Mike."

He turned his face back to the wall.

Chapter Three

Connie Montaldo was sitting on her bunk reading when Sybil went to the nurses' billets to find her. Their room, though small, was arranged in an efficient, military manner—as dictated by the Triple-Nickel's *Standard Operating Procedure.* This publication, mimeographed and held together by metal clasps, dictated practically every aspect of their lifestyle, from the schedule of daily events to the proper disposal of trash.

The two bunks were set by the walls opposite each other. Between them was a desk and chair; at the foot of each bed, standing solemn and soldierly, were double wall-lockers which held the two young women's belongings. Connie had gotten a small throw-rug from her mother. Gaudy and very Mexican in design, it sat on the floor between the bunks. It was removed first thing each morning, and hidden away to avoid Maj. Mother Moorehead's daily inspections.

The young Mexican-American put her magazine down and gave her friend a searching look. "So how'd the conversation with Pullini go?"

Sybil sighed and sat down in the room's only chair. "I can't seem to snap the guy out of his doldrums."

"Christ, Sybil. He's lost the lower parts of both legs. You can't expect him to be a bundle of laughs."

"Of course not," Sybil said. "But his depression is the worst I've ever seen among amputees. There have been a couple that lost their legs almost up to the hips, and their reaction to the dilemma was much better than Mike's. Everybody learns to accept the condition sooner or later. Mike Pullini's dark mood is the most intense I've ever observed."

Connie nodded. "Yeah. Come to think of it, his funk is more than a little unusual. Maybe he's a psychological cripple to begin with, huh?"

"No, I don't think so," Sybil replied thoughtfully. "There's a pretty tough guy there, no doubt. It makes me think there's more to it than the situation shows. I wonder what could be causing that extra bit of gloom."

"He'll be heading home soon anyway. They'll have to deal with it in a Stateside hospital," Connie said getting up.

"I don't like the idea of doing nothing simply because he'll be leaving us," Sybil said. "That's not good nursing, Connie."

"I guess not." Connie got her cap. "We'd better head for the gate. Ernie'll be waiting for us. I don't want the little guy to be upset."

"After talking with Mike, I'm certainly not in the mood to put up with any caustic comments from

Ernie. What I really need is pleasant conversation and diversion," Sybil said following the other nurse out the door.

Ernie Kaznowski stood talking with the air force guard manning the sentry box at the entrance to Long Binh. He waved at the two young women as they approached. "Where you been?"

"I had to go to the ward for something," Sybil said. "Connie waited for me."

Ernie shook his head in a knowing way. "You talked with Pullini, right?"

Sybil felt a little sting of anger. "Sure! Anything wrong with that? The guy is a patient, isn't he?"

"There ain't nothin' you can do to help him, Sybil," Ernie said. "The guy's all tore up about his feet. They'll probably have to put him in for some psychiatric treatment."

"Well, let's not speak about it anymore, okay?" Connie requested. "Baking in the sun all day has put me in no mood to talk shop."

"Right," Ernie agreed.

After displaying their passes to the guard, the three walked through the gate and stepped into the city of Saigon.

"Let's go see Noi, okay?" Sybil requested.

"I want a cold beer," Ernie said.

"We can take a couple of minutes for a short visit," Connie insisted.

The trio of friends walked down the line of peddlers' stalls that bordered the street leading from Long Binh's gate. These enterprising merchants operated out of small booths, selling everything from cheap souvenirs to *canh*—a vegetable soup with meat or fish added. A lot of American servicemen liked to have a hot bowl on the way to an evening's drinking session. They believed the thick liquid coated their stomachs with something that was supposed to impede the absorption of alcohol. Hours later, drunk and reeling on their way back to report in to their units, they would stop for another bowl with the idea that it might sober them up a bit.

One of the booths, where American cigarettes were sold, was operated by an extremely attractive young woman named Nguyen Noi. Sybil and Connie had met her not long after they arrived in Vietnam. Curious about the wares being offered in the area, they had been on a combination exploration and shopping trip when they'd stopped at her booth. An amicable exchange of words had ensued that proved to be the opening of a casual friendship between the two nurses and the Vietnamese woman.

Noi, with the pretty petiteness of the women of her race, had extremely long, black hair. Her mouth, small and always smiling, had a subtle sensuousness about it, as did her dark, almond-shaped eyes. She was always demurely dressed in a long native dress called an *ao dais* that bespoke of her personal modesty. It had a high, standing collar and a long skirt that reached the ankles. Split up the sides, a pair of long pants was worn beneath it.

She was never without her infant daughter named Sai. The youngster, only nine months old, stayed with her mother during the hours she operated the booth.

Sybil smiled a greeting at their friend. "Hello, Noi. How are you today?" She spoke plainly and a bit loudly in an unconscious effort to help the Vietnamese woman understand.

"I am fine," Noi replied smiling. "And how are you, please?" She spoke a deliberate, heavily accented brand of English.

"Just great," Sybil replied.

"Hello, Noi," Connie said.

"Hello to you, Connie."

Ernie gave her a little wave. *"Chao ong,"* he said in Vietnamese.

Noi giggled behind her hands. "No. You say to me, *'Chao ba.'* "

"Really?" Ernie asked. "I learned that from a Vietnamese guy workin' in the PX. He said *chao ong* meant hello or goodby."

"Yes. Yes," Noi agreed. "But *chao ong* is when you speak with mans. When you speak to married womans like me you say, *'Chao ba.'* "

Ernie grinned. "Okay, Noi. *Chao ba* then. How's that?"

"Very fine. Yes."

"How would you speak to us?" Sybil asked. "Connie and I aren't married."

"Okay," Noi said. "I say to you, *'Chao co.'* "

"Very complicated," Ernie complained.

"Oh, no. Very easy. Really," Noi explained. "You always use word *chao* to say hello or goodby. When you talk to mans you put *ong,* with married womans you put *ba,* with not married womans you put *co*. Okay?"

"Okay," Ernie said. "How about a pack o' them Winstons."

"Yes," Sybil said. "I'll take a pack, too."

"Include me," Connie said.

Noi put three packs of cigarettes out for them and

took the piasters they used to pay for the purchase.

Connie leaned over and patted the little girl on the cheeks. "Oh, Noi, I just have to hold her, okay?"

"Okay." Noi picked up the child and handed her to Connie. "I think you be good mother someday. Yes."

"Yeah," Connie agreed. "That's the Mexican in me." She kissed the baby and cooed at her. *"Ay, que muchacha linda!"*

"Now you no talk English, Connie," Noi said. She smiled at Sai's happy reaction to the attention she was getting.

"Nope, that's Spanish. Everytime I'm around a child I naturally fall into it," Connie said. "I suppose that's what comes from being raised in the language."

"She also speaks it when she's real angry," Sybil remarked grinning.

"Or happy about something," Ernie added.

"Or sad, too," Sybil said.

"All right! All right!" Connie said good naturedly. "Hey, kids, we'd better get going." She kissed little Sai again before handing her back.

"You go to Lucky's?" Noi asked. "Drink beer, huh?"

"Yeah, honey, we're going to relax a bit," Connie said.

"Okay. Have good time."

"You bet," Sybil said. "Goodby."

"Goodby," Noi said waving. She turned to her baby. "You say, 'Goodby,' okay?" The child gurgled happily as her mother held her wrist and waved her hand at the departing Americans.

"Chao ong," Ernie said walking away with the girls.

Noi laughed. "No, no. You fo'get. *Chao ba* for me."

"Chao whatever," Ernie called back.

The activities grew noisier and more crowded as they walked down the street. Local entrepreneurs hawked wares and services to them as the nurses and the young medic shouldered through them and the servicemen milling about the boisterous area.

Ernie turned to the girls as they strolled through the throngs. "How come you're all-a-time buyin' cigarettes from Noi? You two don't even smoke."

"Just helping out," Sybil answered. "She's supporting that little girl and herself."

"Didn't you hear what she just said? She's married," Ernie said. "Her old man prob'ly takes ever' *dong* she brings home."

"I don't care," Sybil said. "I'm still going to buy cigarettes from her."

"Me too," Connie added.

Ernie shook his head. "She's a good looker. I'll bet she could make damn good money downtown."

Both Sybil and Connie stopped. Sybil glared at him. "And just what do you mean by that?"

Ernie, who had gone on a few more steps, turned and faced them. "She'd pull in plenty of piasters working as a B-girl. Or in Juicy Lucy's."

"Listen, wise guy," Connie said testily. "For your information not every woman in the world wants to be a goddamned whore! You got that?"

"Hey!" Ernie said with an apologetic shrug. "I didn't mean nothin'. I just said—"

"Shut up, Ernie!" Sybil snapped.

He turned around and angrily preceded them down the street. "Jesus Christ! A guy makes a simple statement and right away ever'body crawls all over him."

"You need to have a few of those ideas of yours

changed around, young man," Connie said.

"Aw! I'm goin' on down to Lucky's," he called back. "I'll see you when you get there. You two walk too damn slow." He treated them to one more indignant frown before stepping up his pace and outdistancing them.

Sybil looked pensive. "Say, you don't suppose we have a tendency to nag Ernie, so you?"

Connie nodded. "Sure. He's a nice guy and we like him a lot. I suppose that's why we want to change some of his socially obnoxious habits."

"You think we should lighten up on him?"

Connie laughed. "No way!"

The Triple-Nickel's unofficial hangout was a bar called Lucky's. Located a few blocks from the 555th's gate, it was run by a Chinese refugee named Lucky Hwan. He chose the name as a commemoration to his life—he thought he was lucky to be alive.

Lucky had been a rice merchant in China prior to the Communist takeover in 1948. When Chiang Kai-shek's troops fled the mainland for Taiwan, Lucky knew he, too, would have to go. The new Red government took a very dim view of enterprising capitalists, and Lucky would have met the fate of many of his less fortunate colleagues if he'd stayed. These former businessmen and landlords were humiliated at public trials before being taken to open fields and executed by firing squads before jeering crowds.

Lucky, after a desperate flight, ended up in French Indo-China. Alone, without funds or friends, he got a menial job of driving a pedicab. These vehicles were no more than bicycles mounted on the front of two-passenger carts. Lucky, his former respectable place in life gone, endured the insults and embarrassment of pedaling passengers around Hanoi. They were mostly drunken French soldiers who would swill cheap cognac and holler at him in a mixture of their own language and Vietnamese. "*Vite, garcon! Mau len!*" they yelled while he strained away trying to follow their orders and move along faster.

Lucky was an enterprising chap, however, and within a couple of years he owned his own fleet of pedicabs, and was able to sit back and sip *cha*—the green tea of the Orient—while lesser mortals worked for him.

But his fate was again unkind. In 1954, after the disaster at the Battle of Dien Bien Phu, Communist North Vietnam was created. The French withdrew from that part of Indo-China and the Reds moved in. Once again Lucky was on the run.

This time he ended up in Saigon. But at least he had a few hundred thousand piasters with him. This enabled Lucky to work out an arrangement with local Chinese loansharks in order to finance his latest enterprise—the bar. He paid plenty in interest, not to mention bribes and kickbacks to the authorities, but he prospered.

The saloon was rustic but pleasant. A long bar dominated one entire side of the building. Three bartenders worked behind it making sure the customers sitting there were given their full attention and spent the scantest time possible with empty glasses.

Cheap, scarred wooden tables and chairs were scattered throughout the rest of the room with a large opening left in the center for dancing. There was a bandstand just off that place on which a jukebox had been placed. The 78-rpm records in it were a wild mixture of old Asian pops, some ancient American country and western standards and a surprising number of swing band songs by such greats as Glenn Miller, Benny Goodman, Tex Beneke, and others. Curiously, there was also a German recording of "Lili Marlene." Lucky Hwan had picked it up from a former bar where French Foreign Legionnaires had once hung out. Because they were mostly Germans, this had probably been one of their favorites.

The people of the Triple-Nickel were good cash customers. They liked this bar and used it as a place to ignore rank and let their hair down. Since most of them were not career military people, they liked the opportunity offered to forget the army for a while. Here they were on a first name basis, except for the doctors. Although they didn't insist on it, even the youngest and most liberal physicians were addressed by their professional title.

Lucky, who always maintained his post at the head of the bar by the door, knew most of his customers by name and much about their personal lives. The difficult years had reduced the middle-aged Chinese gentleman to a wizened thinness. But his eyes, peering through the thick lenses of his glasses, were sincere in their friendliness, and he genuinely liked his clientele. Thus, when Ernie Kaznowski sauntered in, the Chinese bar owner hollered out to him, "Hello, Ernie. Where Sybil and Connie?"

"They're comin'," Ernie grumbled still angry with the young women. "How about a cold one, Lucky? It's been a hell of a day."

"Okay, Ernie," Lucky said cheerfully. He snapped

his fingers at the nearest barkeep. "One beer for Ernie." At that moment Sybil and Connie walked in. "Make it three," he said changing the order. "Hello, ladies. Welcome! Welcome!"

"Thanks, Lucky," Connie said. She poked Ernie in the ribs. "Calmed down yet?"

"I ain't mad at nobody," he said. "Why don't you go over and sit down. I'll bring the beers."

Sybil slipped some money on the bar. "I'll buy the first round." She took Connie's arm. "Let's get a table."

There were a few other Triple-Nickel people seated at the bar and at some of the tables. It was early yet, and the real crowd had yet to show up.

A minute later, Ernie joined them. He set the beer down and settled himself in a chair. "Anything else you want to chew my ass out about? If so, let's do it now so we can relax and take it easy the rest of the evening."

"Don't be such a baby," Sybil said. She picked up a bottle and took a drink. "Wonderful!"

Connie agreed. "If it wasn't for Lucky's I'd have gone crazy months ago."

"Want to go to the movies tomorrow?" Ernie asked. "They're showin' a new one called *Alfie*."

"Oh, hell!" Sybil said. "That means tonight's the last chance to see *Torn Curtain*."

"Hey, that was a good flick," Ernie said. "I seen it the other night."

"I've got too much on my mind I guess," Sybil said. "And I'm a real Alfred Hitchcock fan."

"We could still see it," Connie said. "Want to go?"

Sybil shook her head. "I'm too comfortable now.

I'll see it in the far distant future when I get back to the real world."

Ernie chuckled. "You can see it on the late, late show on TV."

Sybil glanced up when the door opened and an officer walked in. "Oh! It's Frank Gavin. I want to talk to him." She waved across the room and motioned him to join them.

A few minutes later Gavin, with beer in hand, took the empty chair at the table. "Hello, all," he greeted cheerfully. He winked at Sybil. "Howdy, Okie."

"Howdy, Okie," she repeated back at him.

"How's the ol' physical therapy department?" Connie asked.

"We're just a-therapying away."

Capt. Frank Gavin, like Sybil, was from Oklahoma. He had blond hair and a perpetual suntanned handsomeness that made him very popular among the feminine side of the Triple-Nickel's staff. If it hadn't been for the accent, he could have passed for a surfing native of southern California. Short, compact, and extremely muscular, he had attended Oklahoma University on a wrestling scholarship. His interest in physical therapy had evolved from sustaining an injury during his last year of competition. After graduation, he had stayed on to earn a master's degree in the profession.

"I want to ask you about Mike Pullini," Sybil said.

Frank shook his head. "A sad case."

"I don't know what to make of the guy," Sybil said. "Depression is a normal thing in a case like his. But he's taking it to unheard of depths. I don't want to sound cold, but sometimes I think he's carrying his personal disappointments and unhappiness too far."

"I think the term *frustrated* describes your feelings better," Connie told her.

"Yeah," Ernie echoed.

"I just wish I knew what the crux of his problems are," Sybil said.

Frank took a sip of beer. "I know exactly what's at the core of his unhappiness, Okie."

Sybil looked at him intently. "What, for God's sake?"

"This may be a little hard for you to understand, so I'll explain it as fully as I can," Frank said. "Mike Pullini is a weightlifter. That's his favorite sport and he was quite good at it. Mike even went to the Nationals the year before he went into the army."

Sybil was still puzzled. "So? We've seen other athletes suffer wounds that ended their playing days. They were bitter as hell, too, but they showed a better attitude than Mike Pullini."

"You have to understand weightlifting," Frank said. "It's a real popular sport in other parts of the world—particularly Europe. The guys that are good at it there get write-ups in the papers and magazines just like our best football and baseball players do. But it's not that big a deal in America. Our lifters only get rare publicity, and that causes those guys to be a close-knit group. They receive their real recognition from each other and a couple of publications."

"Come to think of it," Ernie said, "I don't think I could name one American weightlifter."

"Right," Frank said. "The sport demands extreme sacrifice in keeping in shape and maintaining the high peak of performance required for competition. So, it's really a subculture. Those iron pumpers are elitist and snobbish. Some that I've personally known actually take a great deal of pride in their isolation. Now, because of the loss of his legs, Mike Pullini can no longer be a part of those traditions or that exclusive brotherhood."

Sybil comprehended fully then. She nodded thoughtfully. "Now I see why his injury is so emotionally destructive."

"I worked with him the best I could," Frank went on "There's no way to reach the guy. The term 'he's out of it' can be taken quite literally in his case."

"Can't anything be done for him?" Ernie asked.

"Nothing I can think of," Frank said.

Sybil fell into a quiet mood, sipping occasionally from her bottle as she absentmindedly twisted it between her hands. After a few minutes of the unhappy silence, Connie could stand it no longer. "Hey, come on, you guys. Let's liven things up around here, eh? This is supposed to be an evening out on the town!"

"Sure," Ernie said. "Let's have another round, okay?"

Connie grinned. "You guys want to know a secret?"

"Sure," Frank said. "Tell us."

They all leaned forward.

Connie's smile widened. "You know what my fondest dream is?"

Ernie smirked. "Goin' to bed with—"

"Watch it, brother!" Connie snapped.

"Sorry."

Connie gave him another disapproving look, then turned back to the others. "My fondest dream is luring Maj. Mother Moorehead in here and getting her plastered out of her mind."

Ernie laughed out loud. "Wow! I could just see her staggering around the room, her blouse unbuttoned down to her belly button while she jumps up on the table and does a strip-tease."

Connie's eyes opened wide. "Gee, fellah! You've got one hell of an imagination. Dull, little me would be happy just to see her throw up on the floor."

"Are you crazy?" Ernie asked. "That's nothin'. If you're gonna get her shitfaced, at least do it in a way that's gonna be worth rememberin' and talkin' about later."

Suddenly Sybil laughed. The tensions of the day, the worries about Mike Pullini and the awful realization she was in the middle of a war, suddenly melted away. She was with good friends, enjoying a few hours of leisure. Sybil was determined, almost desperately, to have a good time.

Somebody went over to the jukebox and dropped a coin in it. The old machine clunked and within moments a scratchy rendition of "Elmer's Tune" filled the bar.

Frank took Sybil's hand. "Hey, Okie. Want to dance?"

"You bet!"

The two stood up and went out on the floor to join the other couples forming up there.

It was past midnight when they left Lucky's. The three friends weren't drunk, just a bit high, as they sauntered back toward the gate. Frank Gavin, the perpetual athlete, didn't believe in abusing his body too much. He had left a couple of hours before.

Nguyen Noi's little cigarette booth was still open. Sybil waved to the Vietnamese woman. "Hello!"

Noi, as usual, displayed a happy smile. "Hello!"

Sybil looked at Connie and Ernie. "Want to stop and visit a while?"

"Not me," Connie said. "I'm too tired."

"I'm going to check out a latrine crap shoot over in the ambulance platoon," Ernie said.

"I think I'll stay a while," Sybil said. "See you two tomorrow." She walked up to the booth. "How was business today, Noi?"

"Very good," Noi answered.

"You'd better let me have a pack of those—those Lucky Strikes," Sybil said.

Noi gave her the cigarettes. "You like all cigarette, no? You all-a-time buy different."

Sybil didn't want her to know she made her purchases out of charity. "I just can't make up my mind what I like best." She peered into the booth and saw little Sai asleep. "The noise around here doesn't seem to bother her."

"Oh, no. Sai good baby. Don't cry much," Noi said.

Sybil spoke with some hesitation. "Well, I see. Does—your husband work around close here?"

"Husband dead," Noi said. "He was soldier and got killed. I alone now."

"I'm sorry to hear that," Sybil said sincerely.

"Yes. He have a friend in army who get his brother to give me license for this cigarette business," Noi explained. "That how I make my money."

"I see."

"I don't got a man," Noi continued. "I a good

woman. I Catholic. My baby, too."

Sybil lowered her voice. "Noi—if you ever need some help, you will tell me, won't you?"

"Help?"

"You know. A little money or something. Maybe clothes for the baby or toys or something."

"Thank you, Sybil. I okay. Got little place, some money. We eat good."

"I'm glad to hear that." Sybil checked her watch. "It's late and I'm on duty in the morning. I'd better go."

"Good night," Noi said.

"See you later," Sybil said walking off.

She walked up to the gate and smiled at the young air policemen there who snapped a fancy salute at her. She glanced over at the hospital area as she strolled toward the billets. The wounded soldiers brought in that day would be resting now. Some still under the effects of the anesthesia from the operations performed to relieve and heal their maimed bodies.

There would be others, too, like Mike Pullini, whose wounds were the kind that neither scalpel nor medicines could cure.

Chapter Four

Sybil moved quietly in the dark room to avoid waking Connie. She took the cigarettes she'd just bought and set them on the desk. She planned to give them to a patient on the ward who smoked Lucky Strikes.

The light from the fire lamp outside the billets shone on the pack of smokes. The round, red logo suddenly reminded Sybil of an old school chum. She smiled to herself and whispered the name out loud, "Joanie Livingston. I hadn't thought of her in months and months."

Sybil Mae Watkins's progression through the Kennedy Day Academy was marked by scholastic honors, a steadily growing maturation and thc formation of her friendship with Joanie Livingston. This particular girl, like a few other people Sybil was destined to meet, would have a strong influence on her life. Joanie was enrolled in

Kennedy during their sophomore year.

Sybil first met Joanie during a trip to the girls' small rest room in the corner of the school's second floor. Situated out of the way in an area occupied by the high school department's science classroom, it was little used. The only reason that Sybil happened to have gone there was because she was working on a chemistry project during her lunch hour. Having to answer nature's call, Sybil left her experiment and went into the rest room.

Her first indication she was not alone there was the sight of smoke curling above one of the toilet stalls. This was immediately followed by a quick flushing of the commode. The door opened and Joanie gingerly stuck her head out. When she saw Sybil she sighed, then frowned. "Oh! It's only you. And I flushed my last cigarette away. Goddamnit!"

"Sorry," Sybil said. She was as shocked by the profanity as by the girl's smoking.

"You don't have a fag on you, do you?" Joanie asked hopefully. "Preferably a Lucky Strike."

"I don't smoke."

"Oh! Damn! I knew I should have picked up a few more out of Mom's purse this morning." Joanie came out. "What are you doing here if you don't smoke? I only come in here during lunch hour to sneak a cigarette."

"I'm working on a project in the lab," Sybil explained. "Excuse me, please." She went into an adjacent toilet.

"You're Sybil Mae Watkins, aren't you?"

"Yes."

"I'm Joanie Livingston. I don't think we've had a chance to meet yet. Although in a way I guess we did when Miss Kennedy brought me in and introduced me to the sophomore class."

Sybil was perturbed by having the sound of her urinating heard by somebody else. But it didn't seem to bother Joanie any. When she came out, the girl was still there.

Joanie, also fifteen, was a bit shorter and heavier than Sybil. She had the same coloring, brown hair and blue eyes, and her facial features could best be described as cute. But there was a certain look in her eye—Sybil couldn't see it—but it was apparent to members of the male sex. It was a gleam that Joanie was to have all her life. The look was invitational; a come-hither, be-welcomed kind of expression meant only for boys and men.

"How long have you been going to school here?" Joanie asked.

"Since kindergarten," Sybil answered washing her hands. "Where did you go before coming to Kennedy?"

"We lived in Dallas the *very* last place," Joanie said. "It seems we used to move every three or four months. My daddy is an independent oil speculator. He finally hit it big when he got in on an investment in a wheat field that had about a jillion cubic feet of natural gas under it."

"Wow!" Sybil said.

"Daddy's been in that cutthroat business of free-lance oil operations all his life," Joanie said. She laughed. "This time the deal involved a deceived farmer, a half-dozen swindled investors, and two cheated partners."

Sybil smiled weakly. "I hope none of them are real upset with your daddy."

"Are you kidding? Any of 'em would gladly shoot him dead as a side of beef at a Texas barbecue. That's why we moved to Oklahoma." Joanie searched frantically through her purse. Then sighed angrily. "That's it for sure. I'm out of cigarettes."

Sybil spoke in the hesitating way she always did when correcting or contradicting someone else. "You know—it's against the rules to smoke—here in school, that is."

"Of course it is, honey," Joanie said laughing. "Why do you think I'm sneaking around about it?"

"You shouldn't do it," Sybil insisted rather weakly.

"Sure," Joanie said good-naturedly.

"Well, I'd better get back to my project."

"Say, Sybil Mae. You wouldn't mind if I watched you until lunch was over, would you? I don't know any of the other kids and I feel real dumb just sitting around in the cafeteria all by myself."

"I don't mind."

Sybil walked out the door with the other girl following closely. They went down the hall and turned into the science lab. Sybil went to her work bench. "I'm doing an extra experiment. Miss Stensland gave me special permission."

"What are you trying to do?" Joanie asked with a grin. "Come up with a secret formula to blow up the world?"

Sybil laughed. "No. It's just an advanced project at college level that involves the reaction of hydrogen and oxygen when subjected to—"

"Yeah," Joanie interjected looking with complete disinterest at Sybil's notes and the apparatus she was employing. "Many cute boys in school here? I haven't had much of a chance to check 'em out."

"Sure, there's lots," Sybil said.

"You going steady with anybody?"

Sybil's own interest in her work began to fade. "Not a *steady* steady. But there's a boy I go to lots of dances and movies with."

"Yeah?" Joanie said displaying genuine curiosity. "Who?"

"Teddy Davenport," Sybil answered. She felt a little thrill about speaking of him in this light. She had kept her crush a very personal secret. "His folks and mine are real good friends. I've known him all my life."

"Teddy—Davenport—" Joanie mused about the name. "Now which boy is he?"

"Well—" Sybil smiled. "He's real cute. Curly blond hair and he's kind of tall."

"Yeah! He sits up toward the front of the class, right?"

"That's him," Sybil answered. Although the students went to different rooms for each class, it was Miss Kennedy's rule that the seating arrangements stay the same.

"Say, Sybil Mae! He *is* cute!"

"Did you date any boys in Dallas or those other places you lived?"

"Date, honey? Before we moved to Oklahoma, I was going steady with two at once," Joanie announced with pride.

"Two? Wasn't that kind of hard to do?" Sybil asked.

"One was in my school and the other went to the University of Texas."

Sybil's mouth opened wide in astonishment. "You went steady with a *college* man?"

"Sure did, honey. And it was easy. While Billy Joe was out of town, I'd go with Danny. As soon as ol' Billy Joe came home for the holidays or something, I'd make excuses to Danny and go out with Billy Joe."

"My stars!"

"Worked great." Joanie winked. "I had a lot of fun, too."

"I'll bet!"

"Now tell me about you and Teddy Davenport."

Sybil smiled shyly. "There isn't much to talk about. We go out together and see each other lots. Since last year we've been going to the country club dances."

"Ever kiss?"

Sybil smiled. "Once."

"Oh, Sybil Mae! Tell me about it!" Joanie implored jumping up on a nearby stool.

"It was on a Sunday afternoon last summer," Sybil said. "Our families go to the same church." She changed the subject. "Which church do you go to?"

"We don't go, honey," Joanie said. "Now tell me about that kiss, huh?"

"Okay. Well, like I said, it was on a Sunday afternoon after church. My parents had decided we'd all have dinner together over at our house. While the grown-ups were inside visiting, Teddy and I went out to the backyard. It was kind of hot and the shade was real pleasant under the cottonwoods. My daddy's going to have them cut down on account of the mess they make. That stuff gets all over—"

"To hell with the cottonwoods!" Joanie snorted. "Get back to you and Teddy."

"We were just walking around back there until we got to the gazebo. We went inside and sat down. We were talking about school and stuff. Then, all of a sudden, Teddy kissed me."

"Where?"

"There in the gazebo."

"No, no! I mean where? On the mouth?"

"No. On the cheek." She pointed to the right side of her face. "Right there."

Joanie smirked. "I guess that's better than nothing.

Then what happened?"

"I asked him why he'd done it and he said because he wanted to," Sybil went on.

"Then what?"

"After awhile we went back up to the house for dinner," Sybil answered.

"Didn't he try to kiss you again?"

"No."

"Didn't he even try to touch your boobs?"

"*No!*" Sybil treated Joanie to an exhibit of her most shocked expression. Then she relaxed. "You don't let boys touch you—there."

Joanie laughed. "Honey, Billy Joe has practically crawled right inside my brassiere."

"He didn't!" Sybil's eyes went unconsciously to Joanie's bosom. The girl, without a doubt, could boast of having the largest brassiere size in school—and that would include the ladies on the faculty, too.

"Sybil Mae, if you don't let 'em, they'll just go off and find some other girl who will."

Sybil glanced up at the wall clock. "I think we'd better leave now. Fourth period will be starting in about five minutes."

"Sure, honey, let's go," Joanie said jumping down from the stool. She took Sybil's arm. "But from now on I want you to stick close to me. I'm putting myself in charge of your *real* education from now on."

The chief of nurses, 555th Field Hospital, was Maj. Tacita Moorehead.

Called Mother Moorehead by other members of the Triple-Nickel, the major had been in the army for over seventeen years. Her first tour of foreign duty had been a difficult one. Assigned to a MASH (Mobile Army Surgical Hospital) in Korea during the winter of 1951, she had served under adverse conditions. The Chinese Communist forces had come in to back up their North Korean allies, and many times Moorehead had done her stint in the operating tent with enemy units steadily closing in. She also had known the terrible inconvenience and danger of quickly packing up to either move forward to areas the MASH unit was needed, or to evacuate rearward in order to avoid being overrun.

The major was a tall, thin woman in her late thirties. She never wore makeup and kept her hair tied back in a severe bun. There was a cold glint in her eyes and she could display her displeasure with a slight rising of the brows. This look, above all, was dreaded by the younger nurses. It conveyed the major's ire in a subtle way that was worse than a shrill bawling out. Humorless and uncompromising, Moorehead, a native Vermonter, was the classic New England old maid.

The major ran a tight ship where her nurses were concerned. Her headquarters was located in the senior nurses' billets (referred to as Menopause Manor by the younger ladies), and it was from this minor Mount Olympia that she not only issued her orders and directives but held the staff meetings in which she emphasized her wants and requirements.

The only ally and confidant she seemed to have was the martinet Sgt. Maj. Al Rafferty. As the 555th's senior noncommissioned officer, Rafferty was able to expound his own influence in the application of discipline in the unit. Happily for him and Moorehead, they both agreed as to the amount of severity and uncompromising dedication to army regulations that was necessary for the efficiency of their outfit. The Triple-Nickel's commanding officer preferred to stay out of their way.

Second Lts. Sybil Watkins and Connie Montaldo attended a staff meeting conducted by Mother Moorehead on the morning after their sojurn to Lucky's Bar.

Though not actually hung over, the beer they had consumed that previous night did not set well with the exposure to the overwhelming heat they'd endured the day before out at the helicopter landing pads. Headachey and tired, they felt drowzy and fatigued in a sort of nauseous way when Mother Moorehead opened the session.

"Good morning, ladies." The words, like the pursed lips from which they were issued, were terse and crisp. "We have several announcements this morning before you are released to relieve the night crews." She glared at Connie. "Are you listening, Montaldo?"

"Yes, ma'am."

"The first item I wish to cover involves military courtesy and discipline," Mother stated. "While it is true we are not a combat infantry or armored unit, the Five fifty-fifth Field Hospital is still a military organization and an important part of the United States Army's efforts in Southeast Asia. Therefore, discipline is just as important here as in the line outfits. Certain persons of commissioned rank have been seen consorting with enlisted personnel not only in a social way in town, but also on post and during duty hours." She glared at Sybil and Connie. "That will stop."

Connie held up her hand. "What do you mean *consorting,* ma'am? Does that mean talking or being friendly? If so, it would be impossible to work on a ward with an enlisted man or woman without exchanging friendly words. Besides, when you get to know a person and they're nice, it's rather difficult not to develop a certain amount of affection."

"Friendly, but respectful, conversation between officers and enlisted personnel is a common and accepted part of military life, Montaldo," Mother said primly. "That, however, precludes being personal friends." She turned to the other nurses. "Keep your distance, ladies."

"But, ma'am," Connie said.

Mother's eyebrows arched. "That will be all, Montaldo. I believe I have expressed myself in a way that a person of your intelligence and training can understand," Mother said. "Remember. You are an educated person and a commissioned officer."

Connie was in no mood to give up. "Folks here in the Triple-Nickel—"

"I do not condone the use of the slangy expression *Triple-Nickel,"* Mother Moorehead said in a cold, flat tone. "We are members of the Five fifty-fifth Field Hospital which is a subordinate unit of the Forty-fourth Medical Brigade."

"Yes, I understand. What I was going to say was—"

"Never mind!" Moorehead's eyebrows arched some more, and her eyes switched from Connie to bore into Sybil. "My remarks to Lieutenant Montaldo include you."

"Yes, ma'am," Sybil said.

"You're talking about Specialist Kaznowski, aren't you?" Connie insisted.

Sybil grabbed her friend's arm. "Shhh!"

Connie stood up. "Aren't you, major?"

Mother Moorehead stared daggers over her podium. "Very well, if it's necessary to spell everything out completely."

"Do it for me, please, ma'am," Connie said.

Sybil grimaced. She whispered, "Oh, Connie!"

"You and Lieutenant Watkins have been entirely too chummy with Kaznowski. It is not militarily nor socially correct for you to maintain that much of a degree of friendship with someone who is a subordinate. He is an *enlisted man,* and a rather slovenly one with a bad attitude."

Connie's temper snapped. "I have four brothers who either are or were enlisted men."

"Then, my dear Lieutenant Montaldo, you outrank them, don't you?"

"Major Moorehead!" Connie exclaimed in exasperation.

"Sit down!"

"Yes, ma'am." Connie, seething, took her seat.

"The next and last announcement involves early mess call for the night shift," Mother Moorehead said. "It has been noted that persons not required for such duty have been showing up to eat at those same hours. This must cease. The mess sergeant is given a certain number of meals to prepare in the afternoon. When you present yourself to eat, you simply take food away from others who have no other time to dine. Control your appetites, young ladies, and wait your proper turn to seek nourishment."

Sybil held up her hand. "Major Moorehead, what about the food brought into the wards for bed patients? Somebody is either pilfering it or there are inadequate requests going in. A lot of times there isn't enough and some of the boys have to share."

"Submit appropriate remarks in your daily report,

lieutenant," Mother Moorehead said. "That should be made a part of your regular ward paperwork."

"I've done exactly that without any positive results," Sybil said. "Couldn't we just tell somebody and have it looked after?"

The major ignored her question. "That is all, ladies. Remember the little lecture I've just given on military courtesy—and practice it. Dismissed."

Connie leaped up from her chair and started for the front where Mother Moorehead was, but Sybil grabbed her by the wrist and hustled her out the back of the Quonset hut.

Connie was a bit angry with Sybil. "I just wanted to talk to her."

"You've done that before," Sybil reminded her. "And got yourself into a load of trouble."

Connie relented. "*Ay, que la chingada*! Let's go to work."

They walked through the other buildings to the convalescent ward. The night nurse, Penny Darwin, was waiting impatiently for them. "Did Mother hold another meeting?" she asked.

"Yeah," Sybil answered. "At least this wasn't one of her marathons. Anything to pass on?"

"Nope," Penny said gathering up her things. "Breakfast has already been served the bed patients, and the ambulatory guys are at the mess hall. I've also passed out the morning medications. Rounds will be at one thousand hours—" She stopped speaking and thought a moment. "Let's see if that's all. It should be, since there's been no difficulties or emergencies to speak of. Except for something you might be interested in, Sybil."

"What's that?"

"Pullini didn't eat his breakfast."

"He's done that before," Connie interjected.

"He didn't eat supper either," Penny added.

"God! You don't think he's going to starve himself, do you?"

"If he's turning suicidal, that's about the only method he has to accomplish it," Connie said.

Penny picked up her purse and slid the strap over her shoulder. "We'll have to keep him under observation. There's no doubt he's sunk a bit deeper. Perhaps he'll pull out of it when he gets hungry enough."

Connie looked concerned. "I'm not so sure of that, you know?"

"Yeah," Sybil said. "This could be serious. If he doesn't eat, both his energy and recuperative powers will diminish."

"Keep a close eye on him then," the nurse said. "I made an entry of it in the ward log, so everyone will know about it."

"I'll tell the doctor about it when he comes in," Sybil said.

"Don't forget."

"Okay. Thanks, Penny," Sybil said.

"So long, ladies. See you tonight. Or, if more wounded come in like yesterday, I'll be helloing you this afternoon."

Sybil sat down at the desk. "I guess there's not much that can be done for Pullini."

"Probably not," Connie agreed.

"That weightlifting thing must be real important to him."

"Yeah. One of my brothers did that."

"Good Lord! How many brothers do you have?"

"Just the four," Connie said. "Anyway, Ramon lifts weights, but not like Pullini. He's a powerlifter, not a weightlifter."

"What's the difference?" Sybil asked.

"I'm not sure," Connie said. "They all use barbells but pick them up differently. In fact, there was one lift Ramon did where he lay down on a bench and pushed the thing up. I remember watching him working out on the patio."

"What do you mean he lay down on a bench?"

"Exactly that. He'd lie down on this bench on his back and pull the weight off a rack. Then he'd do his thing. He even called it a bench press."

"Didn't he stand up?"

"No! Don't you understand? He was on his back."

"Yeah! I understand. He didn't use his legs."

"You've got a gleam in your eyes, Sybil!"

Their conversation was interrupted when Ernie Kaznowski strolled onto the ward. "Mornin' girls. I seen your meeting through the window. What'd Mother have to say?"

"She said we should stay away from you," Connie said. "And she's right."

Ernie grinned. "Now you know she didn't mean that. Mother Moorehead knows how lost you two would be without me." He held out his hands which held several packets of Kool-Aid. "Look what I brung you."

"I thought you used it all up yesterday," Sybil said.

"Nope. I got another package from my ma. So I thought I'd share it with you. Soon as I get a chance I'll scare up some sugar over at the mess hall. Then we can keep some mixed up and in the medicine fridge, huh?"

"Good idea," Sybil said pushing him toward the patients. "But in the meantime, you get the morning routine going. I'll be back before rounds."

"Hey!" Ernie protested. "Where are you off to?"

"I've got to see Frank Gavin," she answered. Then, without another word, she hurried off the ward.

Gavin, as head of the physical therapy ward of the Triple-Nickel, worked in his own little world. His area looked like a gym—which it was, up to a point—with weights, exercise apparatus, and special setups for severely injured men to employ in special programs designed to help them regain the use of their damaged limbs.

Sybil found Frank and a couple of the medics assigned to him preparing to receive the day's patients. He was surprised to see her. "Hey, Okie," he called out. "What brings you here?"

Sybil walked into the room and glanced around. "You have barbells here, right?"

Frank nodded. "Sure. Also dumbbells, pulleys, leg machines, etcetera, etcetera. Why?"

"There's something I want to find out," Sybil explained. "Can you do bench presses here?"

"Sure," Frank said. He turned and motioned to one of the medics. "Hey, Taylor. Do a bench press for the lady."

"Okay, sir," the soldier responded cheerfully. He walked over to a low bench. There was a rack attached to it that held a barbell. The bar, six feet long, looked ominous as it sat there with the heavy iron discs mounted on each end of it. "How much weight?" Taylor asked.

"Don't set any world records," Frank said. "Just give us a demonstration."

Taylor lay down on the bench and reached up, grabbing the barbell. He pulled it from the rack, then lowered it to his chest and pushed it back up to arm's length. Then he replaced it and sat up. "How was that?"

"Great," Frank said. He turned to Sybil. "Now you've seen a bench press. Why the interest?"

"I just heard about that particular exercise from Connie," Sybil explained. "She said one of her brothers did that as a weightlifter. But he wasn't the same kind of lifter as Mike Pullini."

"Right," Frank explained. "Her brother was probably a *power*lifter. That sport uses the bench press, deadlift, and squat. Pullini's sport is *Olympic* weightlifting. That particular event consists of the press, snatch, and clean-and-jerk."

Sybil smiled. "I haven't the slightest idea what you're talking about. But I do have one burning question. Could Mike Pullini perform a bench press?"

"Sure. But I've had him working his legs," Frank said. "We've got to strengthen them for his prostheses."

"You think you could interest him in bench pressing?"

Frank shrugged. "I doubt it."

"What about a contest?"

"We have contests around here all the time. Usually it's in the evenings when the work is done," Frank said. "They're impromptu and informal. I get in on them now and then, too."

"How about including Mike Pullini?" Sybil asked.

Frank shook his head. "He hasn't shown much interest, Okie."

"What if you held a real, bonafide contest? Maybe with a prize or something?"

Frank turned thoughtful. "That never occurred to me. Special Services sponsors all sorts of sports—softball, volleyball, touch football, and so on. they give out plaques and cups to the winners. I know the NCO in charge over there. I'm sure he'd authorize their sponsorship. All it would take would be a letter of request from our CO." Suddenly he laughed out loud. "Oh, boy, am I dumb! I see what you're after, Okie. A setup like that might shake Pullini out of his crappy mood."

"Right!" Sybil acknowledged with a wide, delighted grin.

"I'll get right on it," Frank said. "Keep in touch."

Sybil, happily smiling in this new mood, returned to the ward.

Ernie, who had just finished the regular pulse and temperature taking routine, was turning in the patient records so Connie could prepare them for the doctor's rounds. They looked up as Sybil walked back on the ward. Ernie couldn't help but notice her expression. "What's got you lookin' like the cat that just swallowed the mouse?"

"Oh, I'm up to some devilishness with Frank Gavin – and that's *canary,* not mouse," Sybil answered. She glanced down the beds. "How's Mike Pullini?"

"The same," Connie said. "I didn't talk with the guy or anything."

"Then I think I'll go have a chat with him," Sybil said. She left the ward office and went down the row of beds. She found Mike in his usual position, lying on his back with his face turned to the wall. Sybil made her voice cheerful. "You ought to know this side of the building real well by now."

Mike turned and faced her. He was customarily docile, without displaying any overt bad temper or sadness.

Sybil noted his large upper arms. When he moved them, the muscles rippled under the taut skin. "I was just down in physical therapy."

Mike made no comment.

"Your name popped up in the conversation, and Captain Gavin told me you were a weightlifter."

"Yeah."

"Must be quite a sport trying to push those heavy barbells up over your head, huh?"

There was a change in his expression. Not so much a facial reflex, but a barely perceptible flicker of his eyes. It expressed his depression more forcibly than if he'd sobbed aloud.

Sybil wisely decided to change the subject quickly. "I hear you weren't hungry this morning."

He shrugged.

"And I also heard you didn't eat supper last night."

"No appetite," Mike said.

"That's not good, Mike," Sybil said. "You need protein, and lots of it during your healing process. Your strength will wane badly if you eat poorly."

He had reassumed his rather blank, uncaring gaze.

"Do me a favor and have some lunch. Okay?"

He nodded affirmatively.

Sybil lowered her voice. "This situation could get real serious for you, Mike. The doctor's going to take a very dim view of your eating habits."

Mike shrugged.

"You don't want intravenous feeding do you?" Sybil asked.

"*Forced* feeding, you mean?"

"I'm afraid so," Sybil said. She immediately tried to lighten the mood. "We can't have you starve on us, can we? I mean, think of all the paperwork we'd have to turn in. And that could mean the psycho ward for observation. Believe me, it's really unpleasant over there on the Funny Farm. I worked a couple of shifts on that ward when I first came here."

Silence.

Sybil wanted more than anything to mention the upcoming bench press contest, but something deep inside her stayed that desire. Somewhere along the line of her nursing training and experience, she had developed a deep cognizance of patients' feelings. At that moment, hee instinct told her to back off and let the young man alone. Sometimes solitude was the best medicine.

Sybil managed a smile. "I have to get back to the ward office and get ready for rounds. When you talk to the doctor, tell him your appetite is back, okay?"

Mike nodded. "Sure." He shifted his gaze back to the wall.

Connie was openly curious about whatever it was that Sybil and Frank Gavin had cooked up. She wasted no time in cornering her friend. "Clue me in," she demanded.

"We're going to have a weightlifting contest," Sybil explained in a soft voice. "But let's keep quiet about it, okay? This definitely isn't the time to spring it on Mike."

"He can't lift weights!" Connie exclaimed.

"You want to bet?"

Connie narrowed her eyes and gave her friend a close scrutiny. "You're being very, very sneaky."

Sybil put her arm around Connie's shoulder. "*You* gave me the idea."

"Me? How?"

"When you told me about your brother, the powerlifter." Sybil smiled. "Frank tells me Mike can bench press—if he wants to."

Connie nodded. "That's the crux, *amigita*—if he wants to. I really think that guy is beyond your help."

Ernie, his work done, was loafing in the corner of the office with a comic book. "Connie's right."

Sybil became angry. "What do you two know?"

"I'm a nurse, Sybil," Connie said. "And there's one thing I can certainly recognize about Mike Pullini. You're aware of it too, but you won't admit it."

"What's that?" Sybil demanded.

Connie slowly shook her head. "Sybil—the guy is beyond your help."

Chapter Five

Mike Pullini watched Sybil at her work. When he spoke, his voice was low with a ring of bitterness in it. "How can you stand to look at 'em?"

"What? The stumps?" Sybil asked. She knew he hated the word, but there was no other way to refer to the ends of his limbs. There were no feet there anymore. To pretend the situation was something else would have been much more cruel than sincere candorness.

Sybil expertly bandaged the ends of his legs. "I've seen worse than this, believe me. I've even witnessed amputations being performed."

"Mine was done by the Viet Cong," Mike said. "No charge."

"The initial damage was done by them," Sybil said. "One of our surgeons performed the final work. And he did a good job. You're having absolutely no problems in your recovery process. Although your attitude could use some changing."

Mike sighed. "Why do we have to do this? And why so many times during the day?"

"This bandaging is necessary, Mike," Sybil said as she continued to apply the wrappings, "because it shapes the stumps and prepares them for the prosthesis. If we didn't do it, they'd be flabby and unfittable. It also prevents edema."

"What's that?"

"A collection of fluids in the tissues. That would cause swelling," Sybil explained. She wound the bandages in oblique turns. She could recite, in cold-blooded terms, the procedure she followed so carefully.

Take care that the mass of the gastrocnemius and soleus muscles are not pulled toward the medial aspect of the tibia. Also do not compress the popliteal area. If the wrapping will reach the thigh, the knee must be in extension with the patella uncovered.

Mike was silent for a couple of more minutes before he spoke again. "God! I hate this!"

"How much can you bench press?"

He raised his head at the unexpected question. "What?"

"I asked how much can you bench press?"

"Not very damned much right now. What do you know about bench pressing?"

"The things I know might surprise you." Sybil had been doing some very fast but thorough homework. "Lieutenant Montaldo has a brother who's a power-lifter. He's done two seventy-five. That was an Arizona state record for lightweights in 1965."

"What brought all this on?" Mike asked.

Sybil sensed his talkativeness. Many times, even the most morose patient will fall into a period of loquacity. If Mike was about to cut loose verbally, Sybil wanted to take advantage of it. "Remember when I mentioned Frank Gavin told me you were a weightlifter. Well, it came up in conversation with Connie. That made her remember that her brother was a powerlifter and she told me how much he could bench press. So, naturally, I was curious about what you'd done."

"I'm heavier than Lieutenant Montaldo's brother," Mike said. "When I was competing, I was a heavyweight. I only benched as an assistance exercise because it wasn't a regular Olympic lift. But I think maybe I maxed out about three hundred pounds one time."

"All right!" Sybil said. She'd finished her work and pulled the sheet up over him. "You ought to represent the ward in the contest."

"What contest?"

"They're having a meet in the therapy gym in a few weeks," Sybil said. "They're going to find out who the best bench presser in the hospital is. It'll be between the medics and convalescents. They're even going to use the same weight categories as in regular competition. Special Services is awarding a loving cup to the winners."

"Sounds exciting," Mike said insincerely.

"Are you interested?"

"No."

Sybil forced a laugh. "It's either you or skinny, little Ernie."

He shrugged his indifference. "I wish him luck."

"Ernie only weighs about a hundred and twenty-five pounds," Sybil said.

"Featherweight," Mike said.

"I beg your pardon?"

"Kaznowski's a featherweight. That's the category he'll be lifting in," Mike said. "I wish him luck."

Sybil smiled. "He'll need it. Too bad you're not in the mood to get into some sort of athletic competition. Especially when it involves barbells."

"I'm not in shape anyhow," Mike said.

"It would certainly give you something to do if you went into training."

Mike emphasized his complete lack of enthusiasm by going back to staring at his wall.

Sybil gathered up the old bandages. "See you later." She dropped the soiled bandages off in the laundry cart by the latrine, then went inside the ward office where Ernie had turned from his comic book to making a diagram on a piece of paper. He was working so hard on his project that he didn't notice Sybil's entrance.

"Where's Connie and what are you doing?" Sybil asked.

"She told me to tell you she's goin' over to the PX. And I'm making a sweat-sheet," Ernic said. He worked the pencil laboriously as he began writing numbers within a bunch of squares he'd just drawn with the help of a ruler.

"What's a sweat-sheet?" Sybil, with real paperwork to do, pulled out the daily patients' log from the desk drawer.

"It's to mark off the number o' days I got left 'til I go back to the world," Ernie said.

"Good Lord, Ernie!" Sybil exclaimed with a laugh. "You just got here. You have ten months or so to go."

"It sounds too long like that," Ernie said. He displayed his handiwork. "See? I got three hundred and seven days. Tomorrow I'll 'x' out the top square, and it'll show three hundred and six days."

"What a waste of effort," Sybil said.

"It's good for my morale," Ernie insisted.

The sound of the ward door opening interrupted them. At first Sybil thought it must be Connie returning, but the scuffle of feet gave evidence of several people. She looked up in time to see Maj. Mother Moorehead, Sergeant Major Rafferty, and Col. Phineas Sedgewick appear at the office door.

Ernie leaped to his feet shouting, "Tin-*HUT!*"

"Don't get up," Colonel Sedgewick said. "We're just dropping by for an informal look-see." He smiled at Sybil as he glanced at her name tag. "How are you today, Lieutenant Watkins?"

"Fine, thank you, sir," Sybil replied.

Sedgewick was a quiet man who rarely sallied forth from his office. He was short and bald with a round, ruddy face that seemed to bear a perpetual expression of acute embarrassment. His countenance could be described as almost cherubic except for the heavy beard that appeared dark and shadowy on his jowls. He shaved twice daily, but displayed a permanent five o'clock shadow despite his best efforts.

Col. Sedgewick's idea of being a commanding officer was threefold: Delegate all the authority possible; keep the paperwork caught up; and lastly, maintain a low profile.

For those reasons, Sybil was rather surprised to see

him. "What can I do for you, sir? Is there anything you're particularly interested in?"

"No, nothing specific." He seemed awkward. "Everything going smoothly here, nurse?"

"Yes, sir."

Mother Moorehead checked her duty roster. "Lieutenant Montaldo is also assigned here." Her eyebrows arched in irritation. "Where is she?"

"At the PX, ma'am," Sybil answered.

Moorehead pursed her lips. "Afternoon medications dispensed?"

"Yes, ma'am."

"Pulse and temperatures taken and recorded?"

"Yes, ma'am."

"Patients' Log up to date and ready to turn in?"

"I'm attending to that now," Sybil said.

"It's due to be picked up by the message center runner in less than an hour," Mother said. "Why are you still working on it?"

"I had to bandage an amputee's stump and—"

"—And Montaldo wasn't here to begin the paperwork. Correct?"

"Well—"

"*Correct?*"

"Yes, ma'am," Sybil conceded. "But there's plenty of time."

Mother Moorehead took a deep breath. "I have told you over and over and over, Lieutenant Watkins. Complete all your tasks first, then relax."

"Yes, ma'am."

While Mother continued to speak to Sybil—and the colonel waited patiently—Sergeant Major Rafferty stepped past them and approached Ernie. The NCO was a tall man, and soldierly as an oiled bayonet. Square-jawed and keen-eyed with wide, straight shoulders, his appearance was always immaculate. Rafferty's uniform was forever starched and pressed with creases that would cut through cosmoline. His attire—whether fatigues or class A's—looked as if their wearer was about to be presented to the Joint Chiefs of Staff.

Ernie Kaznowski, on the other hand, could be put into the fancy uniform of a British grenadier guard and within a minute take on the appearance of a man who'd been sleeping in the gutter for a week.

Rafferty, standing in front of the small soldier, glared down at him from the dual advantages of his height and rank. "Your left pocket is unbuttoned, Kaznowski."

"Yes, sergeant major."

"What did you shine those boots with? A Hershey bar?"

Ernie started to look down.

"Keep your eyes to the front!"

"Yes, sergeant major."

"Your sleeve insignia has loose threads around it, Kaznowski. In short, you are filthy, unsanitary, and unfit for decent human companionship." He looked at the table where Ernie had been seated. He picked up the paper there. "What's this?"

Ernie swallowed hard. "My sweat-sheet, sergeant major."

"Kaznowski, you've got nothing better to do than sit around here playing with a sweat-sheet?"

"No—er, yes, sergeant major."

Rafferty, his indignation evident mostly through his

blazing eyes, took a small notebook from his trouser pocket. After writing Ernie's name on the top page, he replaced the pad. The sergeant major stared down into Ernie's frowning face. "It pains me to see idle young hands, Kaznowski. I'll find something for you to do after duty hours. Report to the CQ for extra duty at eighteen hundred."

"Yes, sergeant major."

Meanwhile, Mother Moorehead flipped through the patient's records. "What about this amputee?"

"That would be Pullini, ma'am," Sybil said. "You have a question?"

"It's been noted here that he's refused food."

"Only two meals," Sybil explained. "He's rather down in the dumps."

"Which one is he?" Mother asked peering out into the ward.

"He's in the last bed in this row."

"Mmmm." Mother was thoughtful. She turned to Colonel Sedgewick. "It might be a good idea to put him into the psychiatric ward."

"Perhaps," the colonel sort of agreed.

"Oh, major, that won't be necessary!" Sybil exclaimed. "He simply wasn't hungry for supper and breakfast."

"*Two* meals in a row?" Mother asked.

"He's eating now," Sybil said. "I just finished bandaging his stump, as I mentioned, and we had a rather nice chat."

Mother turned to Colonel Sedgewick. "What do you think, sir?"

"Well—when a patient doesn't eat or is acting erratic, it disturbs the other boys."

"If he's carted off to psychiatric it will delay his transfer home while he's under observation there," Sybil protested. "I think it's of utmost importance that his convalescence and recovery be hurried along without any undue delays."

"On the other hand, if he's chatting away," the colonel mused.

Mother turned a sharp eye to Sybil. "I'll be taking a personal interest in him, lieutenant. As, evidently, *you* are."

"Yes, ma'am."

The colonel rubbed his hands together. "Well! Shall we continue our little trip through the hospital?" Without another word he turned and walked away.

Mother Moorehead again snapped her gaze at Sybil. "And keep that enlisted man occupied!" Then she hurried after the commanding officer.

Rafferty took only enough time to say to Ernie, "Remember, eighteen hundred hours," before he, too, rushed off the ward.

Ernie stood silently for several seconds. He finally spoke. "Oh, fuck it!" Then he flinched against the expected slap to his shoulder from Sybil.

"Relax," Sybil said. "He deserves it this time."

A couple of minutes later Connie Montaldo walked into the office. "Hi, guys. How's it going?" she greeted cheerfully.

"Just great," Sybil scowled.

"I just saw the Gruesome Twosome—Mother Moorehead and Sergeant Major Rafferty—going across to the orthopedic ward with Colonel Sedgewick. Were they just here?" Connie asked.

"In all their charming glory," Sybil remarked.

Ernie sighed. "Christ! Three hundred and seven days to go!"

The day shift was finally coming to an end.

Connie, pleading an absolute crisis if she didn't get the post cleaners, had taken off early—again. Ernie, disgruntled about having to report to the charge of quarters after chow, was also gone. Presumably to drown his sorrows in a PX milkshake with a cheeseburger chaser.

Sybil, alone, waited for Capt. Penny Darwin, the night nurse, to show up and relieve her. She sat at the desk peering absentmindedly out the glass of the enclosure that made up the ward office.

"Excuse me, lieutenant."

Sybil, startled, turned and caught her breath. A Special Forces officer—with the insignia of captain pinned to his green beret—stood in the door. She cleared her throat. "Uh—yes, may I help you."

The man was a shade over six feet tall. Well-muscled but slim, he had black hair and green eyes, and was, without a doubt, the handsomest man that Sybil had ever seen in her entire life. He smiled, which immediately took away the seriousness of his appearance. "Is there a Sergeant Nicholson on this ward?"

"Sergeant Nicholson?"

"Yes. A Special Forces trooper. Knee wound. They told me in orthopedics that he'd been sent to convalescence."

Sybil started to look through the ward records, then stopped. "Oh, of course. He just arrived yesterday. Right down there in the middle of the far row."

The officer smiled. "Thanks. How's he doing?"

Sybil pulled the man's medical records and glanced at them. "Seems to be recovering nicely."

"That's good," the captain said.

"Maybe not," Sybil said. "He evidently wasn't hurt enough to return to the world."

"He doesn't want to go," the captain said. "Nicholson is real hard-core." He took off his beret and walked onto the ward.

Sybil watched the officer, feeling lust—primitive, undeniable lust. She hadn't experienced such longings in months. The man moved with a fluid grace, his slim hips sensuous in his tight-fitting fatigue uniform as he strode silently on the rubber soles of his jungle boots. This was the warrior incarnate, Sybil decided. He must be what the centurions of Rome looked like. She could imagine him in a plumed helmet with a shining breastplate of armor, his muscular calves showing above the high-top sandals.

The Green Beret was not a peaceful man, yet his soldierliness didn't give an aura of violence, only of a certain self-assuredness that somehow comforted the feminine side of her own makeup.

"Sybil."

Her mind dwelled completely on this stranger.

"Sybil!"

Sybil couldn't take her eyes off him.

"*Sybil*!"

She turned at the sound of her name. "What?"

Penny Darwin stood in the ward door. "What's the matter? You going deaf?" Penny walked in the office and put her things on the desk. She took a casual look out on the ward, then spotted the captain talking to one of the patients. She gasped and grabbed Sybil's arm. "Who is that?"

"I don't know," Sybil answered. "He's visiting that sergeant that came in yesterday."

"What a hunk!" Penny exclaimed.

Sybil said nothing.

"That is the best-looking man I've ever seen," Penny said. She looked down at Sybil still sitting in her chair. "You leaving or staying?"

"Staying."

Penny laughed. "Can't say that I blame you."

After a few minutes passed, the officer left his friend and walked back to the office. "Hi. Could either of you tell me a good place to get some chow? I just got in earlier this morning. Besides seeing Nicholson, the only other thing I've managed to do is get debriefed."

"There's the mess hall," Penny said with a silly smile.

"I've been eating C-rations for quite a while," he answered. "The thought of GI food—even class A-rations—is far from appealing. I'm really in the mood for some greasy hamburgers and french fries."

Sybil stood up. "There's a snack bar at the PX." Suddenly she added. "I'm on my way over there myself."

"Oh? Well, would you join me for some good ol' American food?"

"Yes!" Sybil calmed down. "I mean—yes, I would be glad to. I hate to see a stranger just wandering around alone."

"Good." He held out his hand. "Brian Mallory."

"Sybil Watkins." She could feel the warm strength

even in his gentle handshake. Sybil could also feel a delicious, itching horniness like she hadn't experienced in months.

"Can we go now, Sybil, or will you still be on duty for a while longer?"

"We can go now—Brian."

They stepped outside the ward into the steamy afternoon heat. Sybil gasped a bit, but noticed Mallory didn't seem to mind the discomfort. She smiled at him. "You mentioned you'd just gotten in. Where were you stationed?"

"I was out on an operation," Mallory said. "The same one Nicholson was hit on."

"It wasn't the First Cavalry, was it? The reason I'm asking is that a bunch of their wounded were flown in here the other day."

Mallory shook his head. "No. We work in our own small detachments."

"Your sergeant is the first Green Beret customer we've had," Sybil said. "I got a letter back home from my parents, and they mentioned that your outfit is getting to be quite the heroes with the public."

"We probably won't stay that way," Mallory said.

"For heaven's sake, why not?"

He returned the salute of a couple of enlisted men who passed them. "I've read the history of the French involvement here. This is going to be one war that's going to try the American public's patience. Unless we pull out all stops and really charge ahead."

"Isn't that what we're doing?" Sybil asked.

"Not yet, because it isn't necessary," he answered. "But it's going to be. The Communists want this part of the world. It's too important to them to let us keep it. They'll go the whole nine yards to get it. The question is—are we willing to match their efforts?"

"You could be right," Sybil said. She pointed. "The PX is on the other side of this building."

The Post Exchange was a large, rambling edifice of one story. Several air conditioners mounted on the roofs hummed in an uncoordinated chorus of vibrating sounds. The place looked a bit dilapidated despite what was obviously a fresh coat of paint. A stenciled sign, mounted next to the entrance, informed customers that the hours of operation were from 1200 to 2000 hours—noon to 8 P.M.

They went inside, immediately feeling the coolness. There were a lot of GIs obviously loafing and enjoying the pleasanter temperature. Most stood at a large magazine and book rack, idly thumbing through girlie publications. These men, termed casuals, would soon be sent out as replacements in units committed to operations in the field. Some would be back sooner than scheduled—either as wounded on stretchers, or corpses in bodybags.

"The snack bar is in a separate room down there," Sybil said.

"Lead on," Mallory said, allowing her to go ahead of him.

Sybil passed a counter where potato chips, candy bars, and other snack items were sold. She caught sight of Ernie Kaznowski down at the far end. She only had time to note what he was buying: packets of Kool-Aid.

"See somebody you know?" Mallory said.

"Yeah. A friend," Sybil said, wondering why he would be purchasing something his mother sent to him on a regular basis. She laughed a little. "He must really be crazy about Kool-Aid."

"Pardon me?"

Sybil laughed again. "A private joke."

Brian Mallory opened the door for her. The snack bar was operated cafeteria style. They went to the head of the line and each took a tray. When they got to the drink section, the little Vietnamese man working there, a white paper hat perched precariously on his head, greeted them with a bored expression. "Yes, please?"

"I'll have an iced tea," Sybil said.

"Make mine a chocolate milkshake," Mallory ordered. Then he added, "A *thick* chocolate milkshake."

"All the same," the Vietnamese said. He slid a premixed shake toward the captain.

Mallory's green eyes narrowed, and his voice lowered to an ominous tone. "*Cai do khong du.*" He pushed the drink back.

The PX waiter started to say something but, after looking into Mallory's face, he hesitated for only a moment. "Okay, *Dai-Uy.* I fix you up." He got an empty cup and liberally filled it with ice cream, chocolate syrup, and milk. After running it on the mixer he handed the cold drink over to the American Green Beret.

Mallory nodded without smiling. "*Cam on ong.*"

The Vietnamese smiled uneasily. "*Khong co gi.*"

Sybil has sensed a mood of animosity during the exchange. "What was that all about?" she asked as they moved down the line.

"I wanted a thicker shake than he offered me at first," Mallory said.

"I suppose I should learn some Vietnamese," Sybil said. "I've become friendly with a local young woman who had a peddler's stall outside the gate. I really like her, and her baby. But we speak in English."

"I had a crash course in Vietnamese back at Bragg," Mallory explained. "And I've been working pretty close with ARVN units, so I've managed to pick up quite a bit."

They reached the grill and she ordered a hamburger. The woman cooking there smiled up at the tall officer. "Yes, captain?"

"Three cheeseburgers and a double order of french fries," Mallory ordered.

"Wow!" Sybil said laughing. "You must be hungry."

Mallory grinned. "That's all I've been thinking of digging into for the past three months."

"Lord, you were out there a long time."

"I sure was."

"All that time without one thought of filet mignon with a baked potato and apple pie-a-la-mode for dessert?" Sybil asked.

"Nope. Nor pheasant under glass, Lobster Newburg or angel food cake," Mallory said. "Just cheeseburgers, fries, and a big, thick chocolate shake."

After the cardboard plates holding their food were passed across the counter, they moved down to the cash register. A young Vietnamese woman, ignoring the keys of the machine for an abacus sitting beside her, quickly added up the sum.

"It's on me," Mallory said, paying for the check with MPCs. This scrip—military payment certificates—was the currency in which American military personnel were paid in Vietnam. The paper money was printed in the same denominations as U.S. dollars. They could be turned in for piasters at official exchange points.

"There's a table over in the corner," Sybil said.

"Okay. You're on the point."

"What is that?"

"The first man in a column or patrol is called the point man. Or 'being on the point.' He leads the way."

"Oooh!" Sybil groaned and shuddered. "Sounds dangerous."

"When you get back to your ward ask Sergeant Nicholson," Mallory said. "That's how he got wounded." He set his tray on the table and walked around it to hold Sybil's chair for her.

"Thank you," she said sitting down and thinking how very much she would like to go to bed with him if the right circumstances ever presented themselves.

Mallory joined her, taking a large bite out of one of the cheeseburgers.

"How is it?" Sybil asked.

He chewed and swallowed before answering with a satisfied smile. "Delicious."

Sybil gave both her lone hamburger and the deep green of his eyes a few moments of attention before speaking again. "I forgot to ask you the one question that is always first among us expatriates."

Mallory laughed. "I know. You want to know where I'm from."

"Right."

"Long Beach, California. What about you?"

"Oklahoma City," Sybil answered with a quick glance up into his face. She figured Penny was right. This, indeed, was the handsomest man she'd ever seen.

"Been in-country long?"

"About six months," Mallory answered. "I'm not a career officer. I volunteered for a tour of duty through the reserves."

"Oh, you're a reservist?"

"Yeah," Mallory said. "I pulled a three-year hitch about ten years ago in the Eighty-second Airborne as an enlisted man. When I got out I went home and did the college bit, but joined a local Special Forces reserve unit over in San Pedro because it was airborne. I ended up getting a commission, and about nine months ago I got the urge to see a little more of the army. So here I am, not particularly bright, perhaps, but honest and dedicated."

Sybil smiled at his humor as she sipped her iced tea. "This is interesting. Since you're not a professional soldier, may I ask your usual occupation?"

"I was in advertising," Mallory said. "After this tour is up, I'll go back to it. And believe me, I'll never stray away again."

"The advantage of being a nurse is that I can do it on the outside as well as in the army," Sybil said. She figured he would be very dashing and masculine in an open-neck sport shirt and slacks. "I won't stick with the military, but I know I'll be wearing a white, starched dress in some hospital."

"That's a good deal. I can't very well apply my military skills in civilian life," Mallory said. "Unless I become a hit man for the Mafia or something."

Sybil finished her hamburger, dabbing at her mouth with a paper napkin. "You know. Something just dawned on me. You don't even have to be in the military, do you?"

"Nope. I've already done my bit from 1955 to 1958," Mallory said. "And something just dawned on me, too."

"What's that?" By then she had decided she would rather see him in a tennis outfit. All white, to contrast with his black hair.

"We haven't been referring to each other by our names—Sybil."

"Is that right—Brian?"

"Tell me, Sybil," he said with a smile. "Are you stationed here permanently? Or are you just TDY?"

"I'm assigned here to the Triple-Nickel Field Hospital on a permanent basis," Sybil told him. "In other words, this is my home."

He finished his own meal. "Sybil, I'm up the road at the SF camp, but only for a little while until my team goes back out on operations."

She smiled at him, feeling very bold. "Then you're not familiar with the local area. What you need is a competent guide."

"Right, Sybil. Since you've shown me a good place to snack, maybe you can let me know of a good bar. Now that my cheeseburger addiction is satiated for the moment, I would like to turn my attention to beer—cold beer. Some night life wouldn't be unappreciated either."

A quick sensation of thrilling anticipation shot through her body. "There's a bar called Lucky's just out of the gate by our headquarters hut," Sybil said. "Everyone in my outfit goes there for their recreation. We all know the owner real well—and vice versa—and there's dancing to go along with that cold beer."

"Sounds great. Are you going to be there tonight?"

Sybil, who had planned on not going to Lucky's with Connie and Ernie that night, quickly changed her mind. "Sure!"

"Can you save me a place at the bar, or will there be some strapping guy that'll pound me silly if I try to sit next to you?" Brian asked.

Sybil laughed out loud with thoughts of little Ernie. "No, Brian. Please feel free to join my friends and me at our own table. We had already planned an evening at Lucky's tonight. There'll be my best friend Connie Montaldo—also a nurse—and our ward medic. He's a young guy named Ernie Kaznowski. Our interest in him is definitely not romantic, as you will soon perceive when you meet him."

"I'll be there at—" he checked his watch. "—twenty hundred hours as they say in the army."

"We may be a bit late," Sybil said. "Ernie has fallen afoul of the unit sergeant major. He's been ordered to report to the CQ for extra detail. That generally entails a couple of hours, so we'll be leaving at eight p.m." She paused. "On second thought, *I* don't have to wait for him."

"Okay," Brian said. "Think we should take off now?"

"Yes. I have to change," Sybil said. "That'll take me a while."

"And I have to officially check in for billets at our cantonment area."

The thought suddenly dawned on her. "Say! That's a pretty hush-hush operation over there, isn't it?"

"Not the whole place," Brian said. "But there's always a few of us Sneaky Petes working on some projects."

The two stood up, and Sybil led them toward the exit. "I don't suppose you're allowed to talk much about what you do."

"That's right," Brian said.

They left the PX together and paused for a goodbye back at the ward. Brian, who had driven a jeep over from the Green Beret's camp, got into his vehicle. He gave her a little wave. "I'll see you at Lucky's later." Then he drove off.

Sybil watched him leave, then turned and hurried over to the nurses' billets.

Connie was gathering up her shower things when Sybil came into their room. The Chicana gave her an inquiring look. "Hey, where've you been? I waited at the mess hall for you."

"I hope you're still planning on going to Lucky's tonight."

Connie shrugged. "Sure. Why wouldn't I? Ernie's run-in with the sergeant major won't keep us back that long. Have you changed your mind about going with us?"

"I sure have." Sybil picked up her ditty bag and change of uniforms. "Why don't we go over there early and wait for him?"

"What's the rush?" Connie asked.

Sybil started to answer her when the loudspeaker in the compound burst into life. "Incoming wounded! Incoming wounded! Special Emergency Team report to the chopper pads!"

"Who's on detail?" Sybil asked. "If my memory doesn't fail me—" She let the words falter off.

"I'm afraid you're right," Connie said, grabbing her cap and the medical bag from her locker. "It's us."

"Oh, hell! Another fifteen minutes and we'd have been clear." Sybil swore. But she wasted no time in following Connie out the door. The Special Emergency Team duty was rotated among the various wards. They were only called on in special cases, so the duty wasn't considered a particularly big deal. But if only a quarter of an hour had passed, another team would have been on the roster and had the requirement of receiving the injured personnel.

They had only to wait for a few moments before the ambulance, with Ernie and Joe Sampson, charged up to the billets. "All set, ladies?" Joe greeted them.

Ernie leaped out of the vehicle and rushed around to the back to open the doors. He piled in after the two nurses. "Let 'er rip, Joe."

"What's the skinny on this?" Sybil asked.

"Shouldn't take long," Ernie said. "Commo told me it was only one guy they were bringing in. A noncombat burn injury. They say he was gassin' up a deuce-and-half with a lit cigarette in his mouth."

Sybil's initial anger and disappointment faded away with thoughts of the patient. A young soldier, scared and hurt, was depending on her and the others for aid and comfort, while she had been upset about the possibility of being late for a date.

Joe stopped the ambulance at the helicopter pad. The team left the vehicle to wait at the edge of the concrete. Ernie pointed in the distance. "Here he comes. Right on time."

Sybil and Connie waited as the aircraft made its approach. It landed, and the two medics rushed to it for the litter. Ernie and Joe worked fast, bringing the stretcher back. Both looked upset.

Sybil could see why. The patient was horribly burned. She wasted no time. "Give him ten milligrams of morphine," Sybil instructed Connie.

"I'm way ahead of you," Connie said preparing the shot. "This is the most active way to reach burn pain."

"I'm glad you learned that lesson," Sybil said making a quick visual examination. The skin was destroyed over half the young soldier's body. Deeply charred, Sybil knew the patient would face innumerable skin grafts over a long period of years.

"Load him into the ambulance and head for the emergency hut," Sybil said. "We don't have a lot of time."

The team operated efficiently without wasteful movement. Within five minutes the patient had been carried into the Quonset and set on a gurney. Sybil went straight to work. "Ernie, make sure the burn team has been notified."

"Right," he said. He went into the next room to make the call.

Sybil checked the genitalia. They were badly burned. "The urethra is probably going to close off," she said to Connie. "We'll use a Foley catheter."

"I'll take care of it," Connie said.

Ernie came back. "The notification's been made." He looked down at the patient. "At least it didn't get his face. So we don't have to worry about his breathing."

"Yeah," Joe Sampson agreed. "And he don't have to worry about endin' up lookin' like a Frankenstein. Whew! But what a smell! Is he expectant?"

"He's damn well not going to be!" Sybil said with determination. "Give me the large scissors."

"Right," Connie said. She handed Sybil the instrument.

Sybil carefully snipped away the clothing, peeling them away. At the same time, large patches of burned flesh came with them.

The patient came to a dulled consciousness. He watched her with shock-dulled eyes. Sybil gave him a reassuring smile.

"We've got to find out how deep this got you," she said in a routine way. She took a pin from the medical kit and poked him with it in several places. "Feel that?"

"No—no—I'm all burnt up."

"What about my fingers? Can you feel them?"

"No—no—"

Sybil knew the burn was deep. She reached down on his thigh and pulled at the hairs there. They came out easily—another indication for damage to an extreme depth. Still she maintained her calm exterior. "Okay, soldier. We're going to clean you up a bit now."

"God! It hurt awful when the fire started," the soldier said, unaware he was slipping deeper into the effects of morphine. "I'm hurt bad, ain't I?"

"Don't you worry," Sybil said continuing to work. "We have folks here that are real good at this sort of thing. They're on their way here now." Using a sterile saline and phisohex, Sybil gently sponged away the dirt and bits of clothing burned into the skin. Connie helped her with the process. They took their time, working slowly and carefully. The morphine had taken effect, and the patient rested easier.

"Me and Ernie might as well cut out," Joe said. "I'll turn the ambulance in."

"Yeah," Ernie said. "And I still got that extra duty to do for Sergeant Major Rafferty."

"Fine," Sybil said not looking up. "We'll see you later."

"We're going to Lucky's, right?" Ernie said. "You gonna meet me at the gate like always?"

"No," Sybil said softly mopping at the massive burn. "We'll see you there."

"Okay."

Ernie and Joe left the two nurses. As they walked through the door, the burn surgical team arrived. The doctor in charge had yet to scrub. "They got me over at the officers club," he said. "How's it look?"

"Third degree over fifty percent," Sybil announced. "The genitalia are affected."

"I'm glad to see you didn't waste any time with the catheter," the doctor said.

"We gave him ten milligrams of morphine," Connie said.

The other burn specialists, ready to begin work, took over from the two nurses. Sybil and Connie stepped back and watched for a couple of minutes. Then they stepped outside into the humid air.

"That poor guy," Connie said.

"Yeah," Sybil agreed. "His troubles are just beginning."

They walked slowly back to the billets, their spirits improving as they drew closer. Connie looked closer at her. "We still didn't quite settle why we're not going to meet Ernie at the gate."

The thought of Captain Brian Mallory brought Sybil's spirits back up. She smiled at her friend. "I'm in a hurry, that's all." She opened the door of the billets and allowed Connie to precede her.

"So what's the big rush all about?" Connie asked, leading them down the hall and into their quarters.

Sybil winked at her. "Never you mind. We'll just go over by ourselves and wait for Ernie."

"I guess we could," Connie conceded. "But, again, I ask—why?"

Without pausing to give an answer, Sybil grabbed her ditty bag and rushed from their room for the showers.

"Hey! Hold it!" Connie called. "You better explain what's going on. There's definitely something afoot." By the time she got outside, Sybil was already out of sight. "Sybil Watkins, I have some questions I want to ask you!"

Chapter Six

Sybil quickly shucked her clothes and got into the shower. She had some deep feminine feelings that teased her emotions with a pleasing excitement. Sybil felt she was about to become involved in a romance. At least she had to admit to herself that she certainly hoped so.

It had been a long time.

By the time Kennedy Day Academy's Class of 1961 had reached their senior year, Sybil Mae Watkins and Theodore Davenport, Jr. were an item.

Teddy was considered the cutest boy in school by the girls. Very tall, with blond curly hair, blue eyes, and a sort of Nordic clean-cut look about him, he would have fit in fine on any ski slope from Aspen to Saint Moritz. Although he was far from the best athlete in school, he managed to do well enough in the intramural program to be noticed. Miss Kennedy did not permit the academy to participate in athletic competition against other schools. She considered physical activity barbaric, but did grudgingly admit there was some advantage to it where young, active people were concerned. However, it did take Mr. Johnson, the mathematics teacher who doubled as physical education instructor, several years to convince her that including touch football for the boys would be a good idea.

Teddy's real accomplishments were academic, however. A brilliant student, like Sybil, he shared the exclusive company of being on the school's elite honor roll. It was because of these high scholastic achievements that he and Sybil earned that made their parents approve wholeheartedly of the two going together. Each was thought to be a good influence on the other.

Teddy's father operated a Buick agency in Oklahoma City. Ted Davenport had met Doyle Watkins through his dealings with the Central State Grange Bank. The financial institution, as its name implied, had first been formed to do the majority of its business with farmers. But as the years rolled by—and conditions changed with the city's growth—the bank's dealings became more urban.

Davenport had come from old money in Louisiana. His was the type of family that fascinated Watkins. While the latter, a poor farm boy out of Kiowa County, had waited tables, fired furnaces, and swept and mopped to finance his austere, no frills college education; the former had attended Louisiana State University, generally goofing off while belonging to a fraternity, going to illicit night spots that were so important to a prosperous young college man during Prohibition, and patronizing several of Louisiana's plushest bordellos.

Davenport's ambition to succeed was fired up after completing his education. This was not so much because of a sudden devotion to the work ethic. The young man liked money, and once away from the apocryphal world of books and academia, he set out to add even more riches to his generous allowance and future inheritance.

He was a wild and woolly young man, taking chances and losing more than he made without his enthusiasm waning one iota. His luck, however, finally got so bad that if he entered any more ventures that failed, he would be wiped out with only his future inheritance to wait for. Thus, he'd gone to the bank to secure a loan for a sure fire business venture—a Buick dealership.

Doyle Watkins was the loan officer who approved the transaction. That preliminary meeting led to other dealings. These eventually evolved into social occasions until the Watkins family and the Davenport family became close friends.

Thus, Sybil had known Teddy all her life. Born at about the same time—though Teddy was seven months older—they grew up practically as brother and sister. Any siblinglike feelings on Teddy's part had disappeared by puberty, and he had demonstrated this shrinkage of platonic affection and growth of passion that afternoon in the gazebo.

Sybil's own feelings were romantic too, however, and combined with the things she was learning from Joanie Livingston, she began to do more than just respond to Teddy's clumsy attempts at kissing and hugging. Sybil started going to great lengths to see that the proper circumstances were created to facilitate Teddy's growing advances.

Sybil's relationship with her parents was not very close. The father was aloof, distant, and not particularly interested in any of his daughters. His occasional entrances into her life, other than at meals, were to dispense parental justice. respond to a request, or grant permission regarding some activity or other. To Sybil he was the perfect male authority figure: unblemished, autocratic, and infallible. Something she could never hope to live up to.

Her mother, on the other hand, was easily manipulated—if not outright fooled—and was a mortal with most definite feet of clay. The woman could make no decisions, handle no crisis, nor perform any function in life other than eat, sleep, dress, and accompany the father to parties and other events.

When Sybil really needed advice or someone to talk to in the feminine sense, there was Joanie Livingston. Joanie, since arriving in Oklahoma City a couple of years previously, had gone through several boyfriends and was currently dating a dropout from Oklahoma A&M whose family ran an auto supply business. It was under Joanie's tutelage that Sybil launched her campaign to develop the romance between herself and Teddy.

Whenever possible, Sybil arranged her time so she was available when her parents were gone from the house. She would coyly let Teddy know, for example, that on a certain Saturday afternoon her parents would be at the country club for a luncheon and she would be home alone studying.

These sessions were rather innocent during the latter part of their sophomore year, but by the first semester of their junior year, the first serious petting began.

Sybil had given a Halloween party in the basement rec room on a Friday night. There had been the usual games and dancing at the affair which was closely chaperoned by Mrs. Watkins and her best friend, Mrs. Davenport. There was dancing, a few parlor games with prizes, and a rather elaborate snack bar. All the guests were students at Kennedy and had known each other for most of their young lives.

The festivities were supposed to have come to an end by 11 P.M., but one of those heavy rainstorms so prevalent in the prairie country had swept into the area. The water had come down in sheets, making some streets impassable and causing long delays in the guests' ability to leave. Even those who had their own transportation were unable to get out through the deep water that had collected at the bottom of the Watkins's driveway. Most parents, who had planned to drive over to pick up their offspring after the party, were as unable to reach the house as the others were to leave.

It was almost one o' clock before the last young guest finally rushed out the door in the rain to jump into her parents' automobile. By then Sybil and her mother were too tired to do any straightening up. This entailed a minor disaster, in that the Watkins's maid had come down with an early case of the flu. That meant the house had to be either cleaned up by Sybil and her mother or stay messed up all weekend.

Teddy's mother, ever the volunteer, spoke up. "Don't worry, Laura," she told Mrs. Watkins, "I'll come by tomorrow and give you both a hand with this."

"Oh, thank you so much, Opal." Then she suddenly remembered something and put both hands to her face in a demonstration of minor consternation. "But tomorrow's the bridge club at Julie Christine's!"

Teddy, with a sly wink at Sybil, turned an innocent and unselfish expression toward his mother. "I could come over and help Sybil Mae clean up. You could drop me off on the way."

Sybil had smiled inwardly. "Sure. Don't worry, Mama."

Laura Watkins smiled. "Yes! That way I could ride over with you, Opal, and you can pick up Teddy when you bring me back."

Thus, the stage was set.

Mrs. Davenport showed up the next morning with Teddy in tow. After some preliminary instructions on what was expected of them, the two young people were left alone as their mothers made a hasty exit for their card game.

The cleaning up was done in a sloppy frenzy. A large, plastic trash can was placed in the middle of the floor and all paper plates, cups, and napkins were scooped up and dumped in. Teddy, with the anticipated smooch session so tantalizingly close, was in a big hurry to get the decorations down. He tore over half the paper jack-o-lanterns, skeletons, and other Halloween paraphernalia as he ripped them from the walls, ceiling, and light fixtures. He grew so impatient that he even took the good ones and threw them away, too.

Finally, with the furniture pushed back, the only thing left was the sweeping. Teddy, the pushbroom flying, sent up clouds of dust as the accumulated dirt was assembled into piles to be quickly picked up in the dustpan. The remainder was swept out into the laundry room. After throwing the cleaning apparatus into the closet, Teddy took Sybil's hand and led her to the sofa.

Teddy slipped his arms around Sybil and kissed her gently on the mouth. She, as usual, didn't actually participate much more than to pucker her lips and let him do what he wanted.

She jumped back when his tongue darted into her mouth.

"What'd you do?" she asked.

"It's called frenching," he said. "You like it?"

"No!" She stared at him. "Where'd you learn about that?"

"Oh, around," he said mysteriously. He pulled her toward him, but she resisted. Teddy frowned. "What's the matter?"

"You're not going to do it again, are you?"

"No."

"Okay, then."

They continued their innocent kissing for a while, until Teddy once again brought his tongue into the game. Sybil tried to pull back, but he was ready for her. He had already placed his hand on the back of her head, and she had to clench her teeth.

Sybil was angry. "Don't do that, Teddy!"

"Oh, why not? Everybody does."

"Oh, yeah? How do you know?"

"The other guys talk about frenching all the time," he said.

Sybil's eyes opened wide. "Teddy Davenport! You don't talk about us smooching to other boys, do you?"

He laughed. "Sure. You don't want 'em to think we're a couple of creeps, do you?"

"I don't like you talking about us," she insisted.

"Looky here, Sybil Mae. You talk about us to your girl friends. I'll bet you tell Joanie plenty."

"She's my best friend."

"If she's your best friend how come she wasn't at the party last night?" he demanded.

"Because her boyfriend is older and doesn't want to hang out with a bunch of us high school kids," Sybil said. "And that's the truth."

"Yeah," Teddy conceded a bit. "Maybe. Anyhow, everybody frenches, so I don't see why you won't."

"It feels icky!"

"Jeez, Sybil Mae! You haven't even really done it before. Give it a chance."

She sat in silence.

Teddy, despite his inexperience with women, recognized this was the kind of wordlessness that was supposed to mean she was thinking about it. He nuzzled her neck a little, then worked his mouth around until once more he had made contact with hers.

This time she didn't resist as his tongue probed the inside of her mouth. He stopped for a moment. "You're supposed to do it, too."

Sybil responded, and it wasn't long until they had got the hang of it. The two youngsters tenderly put the tips of their tongues together. She felt an excitement growing deep in her stomach and a growing wetness between her legs. The moisture in her panties had been uncomfortable before, but this time it had a different kind of feeling for her. Finally she was moaning and pushing up against him.

Teddy's hand went to her breasts, molding and massaging them through the cloth of her blouse. Sybil had allowed him this privilege on an extremely limited basis for the previous three months. As soon as she figured he had done it enough, she would push him away. Sybil wanted him to stop at that moment—yet she didn't, and within another two minutes they were both breathing rapidly, their hands wandering over each other.

Suddenly Sybil jumped up and stepped back.

Teddy frowned. "What's the matter?"

"Nothing."

Sybil could see the hardness in his trousers. She had felt it against her various times before while they were dancing or kissing standing up, but she'd never seen it to the extent that the crotch of his pants positively bulged.

"C'mon and sit down, Sybil Mae!" Teddy pleaded.

She held up a hand in a restraining motion. "I think we better take it easy, Teddy,"

He got up and roughly grabbed her, pressing his mouth against hers. Sybil struggled with him and finally broke loose.

Teddy had a strange look in his eye. "We're just going good."

She laughed weakly. "Too good."

He sighed. "What's the matter?"

"Nothing."

"Then let's make out some more, okay? You're not

afraid, are you?"

"No."

"These feelings are good," Teddy said, approaching her again and taking her in his arms. She resisted for only a minute, before allowing herself to be led back to the sofa.

Before the afternoon was out, Teddy had slipped his hand into her brassiere. Sybil enjoyed the feel of his hand gently molding the soft flesh of her breasts. The hardening of the nipples caused subtle ripplings of pleasure to course through her. After a while she allowed him to go even further in this game. Not only did she let Teddy unbutton her blouse, she loosened the brassiere to ease his efforts.

They took a short break for lunch, then went back to their game until the sound of the Davenports' Buick could be heard coming up the drive and stopping in front of the house.

The two youngsters jumped up and began to straighten themselves up. Teddy had to help her replace the brassiere, but his fumbling, frantic fingers made the job tougher.

"Oh, Teddy! Let me do it," she finally said in an exasperated tone.

When she was again properly dressed, they took another look around the rec room, putting a few things they'd missed before back in order.

The basement door opened and the two ladies stepped in. "My!" Mrs. Watkins said. "Are you just finishing?"

"We took our time," Sybil said.

Opal Davenport motioned to her son. "Let's go, Teddy. Your daddy's waiting for us down at the agency.

He'll be cross as a bear if we're late."

"Okay." Teddy turned, his face out of view of their mothers, and winked at Sybil. "See you later."

"Okay."

Mrs. Watkins let them go in front of her, then turned and gave Sybil a close scrutiny. If she suspected anything had been going on she kept it to herself.

Sybil followed the other three up the basement stairs. The new sensations she had experienced required some intense discussion. She knew it would be useless to try to converse about the various issues bothering her with her mother. Tomorrow, after church, she would get away and go visit Joanie.

It was two o'clock that next day before Sybil was finally able to tear herself away from the family's Sunday routine and get over to Joanie's house. She had called her friend to see if she'd be home and dropped some heavy hints about what she wanted to talk about.

Joanie wasted no time when Sybil showed up at her front door. She took the other girl's arm and hurried her up the stairs to her room. She didn't wait for Sybil to take her coat off before she began grilling. "Okay. What happened that's got you in such a dither?"

Sybil was a bit nervous. She took off her coat and laid it across the bench in front of Joanie's dresser. The room was a perfect reflection of Joanie's personality: The bed was unmade; there were ashtrays filled with butts scattered around among romance and movie magazines; and various items of clothing were either lying on the floor or carelessly slung across the furniture or even the top of the bathroom door.

Sybil sat down on the bed. "Your folks aren't

around where they can hear, are they?"

"Daddy's out somewhere and Mom's half snookered in her little sitting room," Joanie assured her. "Now shoot!" She sat down beside Sybil.

"Well – Teddy and I were cleaning up yesterday from the party Friday night," Sybil said. "Gee, I wished you'd been there, Joanie. We had a lot of fun."

"Yeah, me too, honey," Joanie said. "But Ralph doesn't want to hang around with a bunch of high schoolers. So go on."

"We were alone because our moms went over to a bridge party," Sybil continued. "We finished cleaning up and then sat down on the sofa."

"Yeah, yeah," Joanie said. "And you started making out, right? Okay. So then what happened?"

"Teddy was kissing me and he stuck his tongue in my mouth."

Joanie smiled delighted. "He frenched you, huh?"

"Yeah, he said everybody does it."

"He's right about that," Joanie said and winked.

"We kept doing it and I got a real funny feeling," Sybil said. "He was playing with my boobs, too. It was real good and exciting, but it scared me, too."

Joanie laughed. "Sybil Mae, you were getting hot."

"Hot?"

"Got wet too, right? Down there."

"Yeah," Sybil admitted.

"Listen," Joanie said going over to her dresser for a cigarette. "You and I've talked before, but we haven't really *talked,* you know what I mean?"

"Yeah. Not really down deep."

Joanie lit up. "I'm going to bare my soul to you, Sybil Mae, and you'll have to do the same."

"Sure, Joanie. I want to. I really do."

"But we both have to make a pact of secrecy, okay? If special friends like us tell each other things, we must promise to never, never tell anyone else."

Sybil felt good at this growing intimacy and friendship between them. "Oh, yes, Joanie!"

"Okay," Joanie took a drag off her cigarette. "To start off let me tell you this." She walked back and sat down on the bed with Sybil. "I'm not a virgin."

Sybil put her hand to her mouth. "Oh, Joanie! You've never said a thing. Who did you do it with, Ralph?"

Joanie burst out laughing. It took several minutes to bring herself under control. "Yes—with Ralph and Billy Joe and Danny back in Dallas, and some boys whose names I don't even remember."

"Joanie!" Sybil was horribly, wonderfully shocked. This was something unheard of for her. Girls who "went all the way" were the ones who attended public schools. Their fathers were mechanics, plumbers, and things like that; their mothers worked; and the girls themself were rather shallow, dull-witted creatures who didn't study or do their homework. They stayed out late and hung around drive-ins all the time.

Joanie was from Kennedy Day Academy. True, her scholastic standing wasn't too high, but it wasn't because she couldn't do better. Her high intelligence was as obvious as her lack of interest in schoolwork. To think of Joanie as not being a virgin boggled Sybil's mind.

"Aren't you scared of getting pregnant?"

"Hey, that's what I want to talk to you about," Joanie said. "I was lucky. The guys I did it with were in the know. They used rubbers. You know what they are?"

"Sure," Sybil said. "They're bands they put around their things to keep the stuff from coming out."

Joanie laughed. "No, silly! They're like sheaths that fit over their penises. They come into them instead of you."

"What do you mean they come?"

"Okay, Sybil, brace yourself," Joanie said snuffing her cigarette out. "I'm going to enlighten you. You know when you were talking about the stuff coming out of their things? Well, honey, that's coming."

Sybil was up in Joanie's bedroom until five o'clock. She would have stayed longer, but her mother called on the phone wanting her to come home to supper. In the meantime, however, Joanie had managed to administer a complete course in sexology, biology, birth control, lovemaking, and other related matters that a sexually active teenaged girl should know. Actually the session was a rehash and an emphasizing of things Sybil already knew, but the refresher course was useful just the same. At the end of the afternoon Sybil was well prepared to deal with what she would face as her relationship with Teddy deepened in intensity.

But Sybil remained true to traditions and most of the time, she was determined not to lose her virginity. Whether she married Teddy or another boy, she would meet her womanly obligation of presenting herself pure and undefiled to her future husband.

Meanwhile, she and Teddy continued their romance.

Their necking always included heavy petting after that. Whether it was at her house, where the opportunities were few but quite satisfactory when available, the drive-in movies, or parked in the dark in one of the local lovers' lanes, the sessions left them both groaning, passionately unfulfilled, and physically tortured.

The first time Sybil gave Teddy sexual satisfaction was late one evening in front of her house. They had been to Kennedy Academy's spring dance—the school's version of a prom—and after a few hours of ballroom dancing, sipping punch, and munching on cookies, Teddy had driven her home.

It was dark under the cottonwoods that bordered the Watkins's curving drive. There were no lights in front of the house, giving the two youngsters the happy knowledge that her parents were up in their own room at the back of the residence.

They had been groping at each other for almost twenty minutes, when Teddy emitted a pleasure-pain moan. "God, Sybil Mae! I can't stand it!"

Sybil, relishing the wonderful sensations coursing through her, had an instinctive awareness of his expressed frustration. "What's the matter, Teddy?"

"Oh—Sybil Mae—" Suddenly he took her hand and put it down on the erection that strained against his suit pants.

She instinctively pulled it away. "Teddy!"

But he was insistent, forcing her back to it. "Leave your hand there."

"No, Teddy!" she said trying to remove it.

"It's the same as when I touch your boobs," he said.

"No it isn't." But she was becoming fascinated with the feel of the gently pulsating organ that responded to the slight pressure she put on it.

Teddy pulled away from her, fumbling with his

pants. Suddenly he sighed. "Ahhh." He took her hand again and moved it toward his lap.

This time she felt flesh—warm, firm flesh. She grasped it, confused yet fascinated. "Teddy? You want me to hold it?"

"Move your hand up and down."

Sybil made an awkward attempt.

"No. Tighten up a little and do it like this." He showed her what he wanted.

"Okay, Teddy." She knew a little something about what she was doing from what Joanie had told her, but she still didn't fully comprehend the action.

"Sybil Mae!" Teddy exclaimed. He leaned back with his eyes closed. Suddenly his breathing increased. "Oh—oh, do it faster—faster. Sybil Mae!"

She felt a throbbing, then a softening of the shaft as a warm, thick liquid flowed over her hand. Although this was new to the act, she knew to stop when the flesh in her fist had turned flaccid and much smaller.

"Oh, Sybil Mae," Teddy said. "Oh, Sybil Mae. It was so good when *you* did it."

A shock of jealous anger shot through her. "What do you mean—when *I* did it. Have you done this with any other girl?"

Teddy laughed. "No. I do it myself. There's some Kleenex in the glove compartment."

"You do this to yourself?"

"Yeah. While I'm thinking of you. Hey, get those tissues, okay?"

Sybil hit the button making the door pop open. She could see her hand in the faint light of the small bulb. The stuff on it was white. "Yuk!" she said.

Teddy cleaned himself off and rearranged his trousers. He was much calmer. "That was great."

Sybil, her own passions now waned, sensed the evening had drawn to a close. "I'd better go in."

"Okay." He got out of the car and walked around to open the door for her.

Sybil got out feeling as if, somehow, he was finished with her for a while. It was as if she'd served some temporary purpose, and had been dismissed. "I'll see you tomorrow," Sybil said as they walked to the door.

"Okay," Teddy said. He kissed her goodnight, then turned and hurried back to his car.

Sybil opened the front door and went into the house.

Teddy took her to the movies the next night. The previous evening's activities were repeated. After that it became a regular thing for them.

Teddy stopped being so crude about it after a while. He went from shoving her hand down on himself, to asking for it: "Sybil Mae, use your hand, okay?"

That became their byword for sexual play. They would smooch and make out until he could stand it no longer, then those words, frantic and urgent, would be whispered in her ear:

"Oh, Sybil Mae! Use your hand!"

They did it on every date. Teddy now always parked in the rear row of the drive-in theaters, or away from other cars during visits to the lovers' lanes. He continually saw to it that each time they were together, the entire evening evolved around eventually getting Sybil to "use her hand." One time she even did it for him in a movie house balcony with his overcoat over his lap.

Sybil began to develop a disturbing feeling that somehow she was being used. As usual, when things developed to the point that she felt uneasy or troubled, she turned to Joanie Livingston.

Teddy came down with a cold and missed a couple of days of school. The two girls took advantage of the situation to get together at Joanie's house after classes. Teddy usually drove Sybil home, but, because of his illness that particular day, she had driven her own car. She followed Joanie's MG over to the Livingston residence.

They enjoyed an after-school snack of Cokes and potato chips in the kitchen. The Livingston maid, a rotund black woman who had her own room complete with TV and telephone, ran the house to suit herself. The only time she couldn't have her way and exercise her personal preferences and plans was at meals and the frequent parties the family had. She knew Sybil well and approved of her. There was no doubt that Joanie was a wild girl and destined for trouble unless something headed her off.

After the snack, the two girls retreated upstairs and closed Joanie's bedroom door. Sybil wasted no time in telling Joanie about "using her hand."

Joanie laughed. "So you're jacking him off now, huh?"

"So that's what it's called?" Sybil asked.

"Yeah. That, and jerking off or a hand job," Joanie said. "All the boys do it to themselves, too."

"Yeah. Teddy said he did. And I guess before you started going all the way, you did it for boyfriends, too," Sybil said.

"Yes, honey, and still do during my periods," Joanie said. "When the boys want it, they want it, no matter how."

"I'm getting tired of doing it," Sybil said. "It seems every date we go on is planned around me using—that is, jacking off Teddy."

Joanie nodded her understanding. "I know how you feel. But, face it, girl. We're sex machines. That's what we're put in the world for. When we get married, our husbands will be crawling on and off us every night. The only break we'll get is when we're pregnant or sick."

"Big deal! So, during those times, instead of intercourse, we'll be jacking them off," Sybil said.

"Speaking of intercourse—" Joanie let the question hang.

"I'm still a virgin," Sybil said answering the unspoken inquiry.

"I guess Teddy considers a hand job enough," Joanie surmised. "Or he doesn't know any better."

"That's it." Sybil sat down by the dresser. "I don't exactly *dis*like it, understand? But it's so often. You know, I did it to him in the gazebo one afternoon."

Joanie laughed. "Like I said, honey, that's our function in life. It's either go along with it, or live without men. What's it going to be?"

"I'll have to think about that a while," Sybil said.

Joanie sat down beside her. "Now *I* have something to tell *you!*"

Sybil was instantly curious. "What?"

"I comed."

Sybil frowned in puzzlement. "What do you mean? Like a man? We can't do that—can we?"

"It's an orgasm. I thought you knew about them."

Sybil shook her head. "No."

"Sybil Mae, you can't limit your reading to the list

from Kennedy," Joanie said. "You're going to have to branch out if you want to really learn about lovemaking. You know the school's attitude about sex education."

"I've been relying on you," Sybil said with a laugh. "Now tell me about your—your *orgasm*."

"Well, I was out with Ralph and we were at this party. One of his friends has a cabin south of the city between Moore and Norman. It's a really neat place. A big living room, with a kitchen and four bedrooms. His buddy's folks entertain there a lot, I guess. Anyhow, the guy got their permission to throw his own party. There was a lot of drinking and stuff. We were dancing, and Ralph was really getting loaded."

"Ooh!" Sybil exclaimed. "Real grown-up stuff, huh?"

"Oh, hell, I go to those kinds of parties all the time," Joanie said. "Anyhow, Ralph and I went into one of the rooms. He locked the door and we got with it. I'd been drinking too. Anyhow—" She giggled. "Ralph was so potted he couldn't come. He just kept pumping away. Generally, he slips it in and *pop!*"

"I wish Teddy could finish that quick," Sybil said. "Sometimes I get real tired."

"You'll change your mind on that when you two start going all the way," Joanie informed her. "Anyhow, like I said, Ralph is generally pretty quick. Every time I get hotter'n a pistol, he does his thing. Then it takes me a while to simmer down and get back to normal. But this time it was different."

Sybil smiled in anticipation. "Tell me how!"

"It was like I kept getting hotter and hotter. I was so damned hot, Sybil Mae, that I thought I was going to die. Then all of a sudden my bottom started jerking in delicious spasms. Oh, God! It felt so wonderful!"

Sybil's eyes opened wide. "Sounds fantastic."

"It was! Then all that hot just drained out of me. I was satisfied, Sybil Mae, *satisfied*."

"That must be the ultimate for a woman."

"It is, believe me." Then Joanie's expression faded. "But it hasn't happened since."

Sybil giggled. "I guess you're going to have to get Ralph drunk every time you do it, huh?"

"Yeah."

They sat in silence for several minutes before Sybil spoke. "Well, I'm glad to hear my problem with having to use my hand on Teddy is normal. I was afraid I was really into something that was going to turn out to be real weird."

Joanie placed an arm around Sybil's shoulder. "Like I said, honey, we women are just sex machines."

And, on that sad note, the two girls spent another hour together, bemoaning the cruelty that nature had foisted upon their gender. Then they went downstairs for a solemn goodbye, and Sybil drove home.

Sybil's romance with Teddy continued on through the school year to graduation. He still planned their dates and, as always, the activities included his being masturbated. The one big change in their relationship came after graduation: They became officially engaged.

This was not from any particularly overt action on their own parts. It came out of a decision by both fathers. Each pictured the forming of a dynasty through the marriage. Doyle Watkins and Ted Davenport had killed many a late evening sipping bourbon and discussing the establishment of a regime that would someday dominate the political and commercial worlds of Oklahoma, then spread out to the nation—and, perhaps, the world.

Their grandsons, great-grandsons, and great-great-grandsons, inheriting the superior genes of the Davenport-Watkins clans, would prove their biological superiority through massive achievements that would rival the Kennedys of Massachusetts, the Rockefellers of New York, and even the Churchills of Great Britain.

Doyle's only son, Sefton, had proved a bit of a disappointment. At age thirty-one he was a rather low-ranking corporate lawyer in an oil firm in Tulsa. The Watkins's two daughters were fast turning into frumpy housewives—Amanda Lou right there in Oklahoma City and Henrietta up in Wichita, Kansas. Part of Watkins's dream during those dreary years of working his way through Oklahoma University and, later, the Central State Grange Bank had been the establishment of a powerful family with vast holdings, unlimited power, and enough influence to be able to be crooked down to the soles of their boots without having to experience any realistic fear of the law.

The two fathers' plan was that Teddy would go for a law degree. Upon his graduation in six years, the two young people would be married. Then Teddy, while he and Sybil were breeding and producing the expected superior stock, would use his brilliance and unfailing intuitiveness to establish himself in law and business under the fathers' tutelage and direction. Later—after spending the ensuing years making the right connections—they would all get into politics as king makers, or if their luck ran a bit worse than expected, Teddy could be set up as an office holder. Surely, by then, their cartel would have enough money to finance some election campaigning.

Nobody discussed Sybil much during this time. It was assumed, without actually saying so, that in the meantime she would bide her time, attending parties and other social events befitting a proper young woman of her social station. When the time was right, she and Teddy would be mated and bred.

Both families were excited about the entire affair. Their joyful anticipation lasted through the summer and into early September of that year in 1961 when Teddy was supposed to enroll in Oklahoma University.

Then the entire plan collapsed when Ted Davenport, Sr. had a fatal heart attack.

This was bad enough. What made it worse was that it happened in the apartment of his paramour. A minor scandal burst forth in the local papers. Opal Davenport shrieked in rage and wept in grief and the juicy details proved to be enough for two weeks of publicity.

Then the real bad news was found out.

Posthumous examinations of Ted's papers and financial records showed he'd spent his entire life living on the edge of monetary disaster and collapse. He died so deeply in debt that he had nothing to leave his widow and son except the family home, a small annuity and an insurance policy that provided just enough money to get Teddy through one year of school.

After seeing to Ted Davenport's burial, his best friend, Doyle Watkins, had one more item to attend to: breaking up Sybil and Teddy as soon as possible.

Without much money, the young man's attraction as a son-in-law had faded into zilch.

Although a cold, impersonal man at best, Watkins wanted to use a little finesse. After several days of deep thinking on the subject, he summoned the young couple before him and spoke kindly to them in this first part of his scheme.

"Teddy is going to have a real tough time getting through law school now," he said. "It'll require a lot of hard work on his part, and it'll be an uphill battle." He beamed at the boy. "But you can do it, Teddy. *I* worked my way through college, and I was a better man for it, believe me."

"Thank you," Teddy said. He was disappointed. He had rather hoped that Watkins would advance him the money for his education.

Watkins, who knew the best thing he could do in these preliminary maneuverings was to separate the couple, then gave his fond attention to his daughter. "And you, Sybil Mae, now have extra responsibilities placed on your shoulders. You'll have to lend a hand to the young man. That means you'll be forced to help out financially. And to be able to do this, you'll require further education of your own."

Sybil smiled. "Yes, Daddy." The thought of going on to college thrilled her.

"So I've decided you'll attend nursing school."

"Nursing school?" she exclaimed.

"Yes, indeed," Watkins said. "There's a good one at the Presbyterian Hospital up in Wichita. You can live with your sister Henrietta while attending classes." All this information had been borne out the night before on a phone call to Kansas.

"Daddy, becoming an RN is the same as getting a degree," Sybil argued. "Why can't I study something I want to? Anyhow, I'd rather go to O.U. with Teddy. I'll be too far away from him way up in Wichita."

"We must be practical in times like these, my dear," Watkins said. He figured she would grow sick enough of that type of training to be ready to return home and get back into the social swirl after about a year. By then he would have completed phase two of the operation, and have Teddy Davenport completely out of the way. At that time Sybil would be ready to meet some *real* eligible bachelors. "As a nurse, you'll be able to get employment when necessary and help out over the humps you two young folks face." He reached out and patted her shoulder. "Be a good little woman, honey."

Sybil grimaced. Evidently, she thought, we women aren't only sex machines and baby factories, we're supposed to be providers, too, if the circumstances warrant.

Chapter Seven

Lucky's was noisy and crowded. Sybil and Connie sat together at a corner table enjoying their first beers in silence. Connie, who had been enduring a mysterious evasiveness to her inquiries regarding Sybil's hurry to get to the bar, eyed her companion in a pensive gaze.

"Now that we've rushed over here, are you happy?" Connie asked.

"Sure."

Connie frowned in puzzlement. "You seem to be anticipating something."

"We're waiting for Ernie, aren't we?"

"There's no real reason why we couldn't have relaxed in the billets for a while, then meet him at the gate as usual," Connie remarked. "Besides, I hardly think his arrival will cause even the slightest ripple of excitement."

"Don't you ever get tired of the same old routine? We always meet him at the gate. So this time we're altering our evening's customary preliminaries. Anything wrong with that?"

Connie made no reply.

Sybil treated herself to another drink of her beer. "Speaking of Ernie, didn't he say he'd recently received a package from home? One with Kool-Aid in it?"

Connie nodded. "Yeah. What about it?"

"I just saw him buying some more over at the PX this afternoon."

"Maybe he gave so much to us he ran out," Connie suggested.

"How much of that stuff could the little guy be drinking?" Sybil asked. "We haven't even touched what he left on the ward."

"Oh, who cares?"

Sybil took a sip of beer. "You certainly seem tense."

"I'm not tense," Connie said. "I always act this way when I'm dying of curiosity."

"About what?"

"About your mood for one thing. And about the way you've been acting ever since you showed up at the billets," Connie said. "I also want to know the real reason we came straight over here without Ernie. You're driving me—" She suddenly stopped talking. Her eyes widened and she leaned close to Sybil. "You've met a guy, haven't you?"

Sybil laughed. "Yeah."

"Aha! And he's going to be here tonight."

"Right."

Connie fell into an extremely poor imitation of Ed Sullivan. "And tonight, ladeez and gennelmen, right here on ar stage—live and in person—we're gonna present the mystery man in Sybil Watkins's life."

Sybil giggled again. "Wait'll you meet him."

The jukebox started up once more. The dancers who left their tables and went out on the floor now blocked Sybil's view of the door.

Connie spoke over the sound of "Tuxedo Junction." "Did you fall in love today?"

"I don't know," Sybil said.

"Ay Dios mio! This sounds serious."

"There's always the possibility."

"And this all happened today?" Connie exclaimed. "I can't wait to meet this guy."

Lucky Hwan suddenly appeared from the crowd and stepped up to the table. "Hey, Sybil, this fellah say he look for you."

Sybil raised her eyes and saw Brian Mallory standing behind the bar owner. He was dressed in comfortable civilian clothing: a loose, short-sleeve sport shirt, slacks, and a pair of black loafers. He looked trendy and casual in an Ivy League kind of way.

"Hi, Sybil," Brian said. "You sure get good service here. I asked this gentleman if you were in, and he escorted me right to the table."

"Sit down," Sybil said. "Brian, this is Connie Montaldo."

Brian smiled. "Hi, Connie."

Connie's mouth was open, and she only nodded.

"Everybody want drinks?" Lucky asked them.

"Sure," Brian said. "Whatever these ladies are drinking and a San Miguel for me."

"Okay. I get one of the girls," Lucky said. He looked around until he spotted one of his waitresses. He snapped his fingers at her.

The woman, a middle-aged Vietnamese, came up to the table and took their orders.

Brian watched her walk away. "I noticed the women working here are a bit past the prime of their lives."

"Yeah," Sybil said. "Lucky's a legit bar, so younger ones can earn more money as B-girls in other places."

"Oh, good," Brian said with a laugh. "I was afraid you had lured me into a den of iniquity."

"We're just plain nice folks here," Connie remarked.

"Do you remember the new patient, Nicholson?" Sybil asked her.

"Huh?"

"Listen to me."

Connie reluctantly turned her attention from Brian to Sybil. "What'd you say?"

"Our patient Sergeant Nicholson is in Brian's outfit," Connie said.

"Well, we'll keep a real close eye on him then," Connie said. "Don't worry about a thing."

Sybil nudged him, getting a slight thrill from the touch. "How do you rate civvies?"

"We've got the okay to keep a low profile," Brian said. "Which is kind of stupid. I drove over here in a jeep."

"Brian's in Special Forces," Sybil said to Connie. "The Green Berets."

"Oh, top secret stuff, huh?"

Brian only smiled. The music in the jukebox gave out about the same time Lucky had wandered around to their table again. The waitress also showed up, balancing the order on her tray. Lucky watched her as she set the fresh bottles down in front of them. "Where Ernie?"

"In trouble," Sybil said.

"Ah! Sahgint Major Rafferty get on his case, hey?"

"He'll be in soon, I'm sure," Connie said.

"Okay," Lucky said. "I send him over. See you later." He meandered away to visit other customers.

The jukebox jumped back to life. This time with a rendition of Cole Porter's "I've Got You Under My Skin."

"The music here isn't exactly the latest, is it?" Brian said laughing.

"Lucky's taste runs from the ancient to the ridiculous," Sybil said.

"It's a nice song anyway," Brian said. "Care to dance?"

"Love to," Sybil said.

They threaded their way through the tables to the dance floor. Brian took her lightly in his arms and glided out into the crowd. The other members of the Triple-Nickel stared at the stranger in the civilian clothing. The women's looks, however, were more than inquisitive. Even the shyest and quickest of the glances betrayed strong hints of feminine curiosity mixed strongly with admiration. Sybil knew that comments and gossip were welling up in the crowd as everyone took note of the stranger dancing with one of their nurses.

Brian, however, didn't seem to notice them even though his eyes met theirs from time to time. He turned most of his attention to Sybil. "This is fun."

"Mmm," she agreed with a smile.

"I'm almost starting to feel human again," Brian said. "First the cheeseburgers, and now dancing with an American girl. Maybe life is worth living after all."

"No doubt," Sybil said.

She moved in closer to him and was happy to feel that his arm tightened around her. She felt a subtle joy at his touch that reached down into her suppressed sexual desires and tickled them in a gentle, teasing way.

The music ended.

When they returned to the table, Ernie was sitting there. Sybil quickly introduced Brian. Ernie, as usual, didn't care a thing about rank, but something about the captain stirred the martial side of his personality to the point that he addressed him as "cap'n."

Sybil took the chair that Brian held for her. She looked at Ernie. "Are you squared away with the sergeant major now?"

"Yeah," Ernie said. He winked at Brian. "Got a little extra duty, cap'n."

"It was unfair," Sybil said. "The CO, chief of nurses, and that awful Rafferty stormed onto the ward. The sergeant major acted like he was on a parade ground."

Ernie smirked. "I had a button undid."

Brian nodded sympathetically. "Sounds like he runs your outfit by the book."

"Yeah," Connie said. "He came to us from an infantry unit. You'd think a few months in the Triple-Nickel would soothe him some, and change his attitude."

"Aw," Ernie said. "Goes to prove you can't give an old dog new bones."

Sybil laughed. "*Teach* an old dog new *tricks*."

Connie looked at Brian. "This guy tears up cliches like you wouldn't believe."

Ernie grinned. "You oughta hear my nursery

rhymes."

"No!" Sybil exclaimed. "I hate them."

"Are these special ones or something?" Brian asked.

"They're the real things when he starts out," Sybil said. "Then he twists them to fit his own weird tastes in what he thinks little kids should hear."

"C'mon, let me tell some, Sybil," Ernie begged. Without waiting for her response, he recited, "Humpty-Dumpty sat on a wall; Humpty-Dumpty had a great fall. All the king's horses and all the king's men eat shit."

It didn't elicit any hearty laughs, but Ernie wasn't discouraged.

"Okay. How about this? Little Miss Muffet sat on her tuffet, eating her curds and whey. Along came a spider and sat down beside her, and scared the shit out of her."

Brian and Connie both laughed.

Sybil frowned. "I can't stand them! And they don't even rhyme."

"Another one," Ernie announced. "There was a little girl who had a little curl right in the middle of her forehead. When she was good, she was very, very good. But when she was bad, she was a regular little bitch."

The response was even better than the previous one. Sybil groaned. "You're going to encourage him."

"Mistress Mary, quite contrary, how does your garden grow? With cockleshells and blueberry bells, and little sonofabitches all in a row."

Sybil glowered at him. "Er-nee!"

"Okay, I saved my piece of resistance for the last," Ernie said. "There was an old woman who lived in a shoe, who had so many children her cunt fell off."

Connie reached over and slapped him hard on the shoulder with her open hand.

Brian, however, burst into laughter.

Sybil nudged Brian. "You're only adding to his personal delusion that he's funny and charming." Then she glared at Ernie. "Now don't tell any more, hear?"

Ernie chuckled. "Whatever you say, ma'am." He was too pleased about Brian's reaction to be upset with having to stop. The Green Beret captain was the sort that lesser men would hero-worship. He displayed qualities of leadership, but he also had an open friendliness that elicited trust and manly affection.

"Are you stationed here permanently?" Connie asked Brian.

"In a way," Brian explained. "We operate out of the Special Forces' camp up the road. We're gone a lot."

"But you'll be back here between trips, right?" Connie inquired.

"Right."

Connie smiled. "That's good."

"The last time he was out, it was for three months," Sybil said.

"Wow!"

The music started up again. Brian looked at Connie. "Dance?"

"Sure."

Sybil felt a deep, angry stab of jealousy as she watched the two go out on the floor. Ernie scooted his chair closer to hers. "Hey, what's the cap'n to you, huh?"

"I just met him. You know that guy Nicholson?"

"The knee wound in bed seven?"

"Yeah," Sybil said. "He's in Brian's outfit. He dropped in to check on him, and we went over to the PX snack bar afterward. I told him about Lucky's and invited him to join us tonight."

Ernie grinned. "He's a nice guy. An officer, but definitely not chickenshit."

Sybil nodded her agreement. She made seemingly casual glances around the room, but no matter where she looked, her eyes always came back to Brian and Connie out on the dance floor.

Ernie winked. "Is he what women consider good-lookin'?"

"I suppose."

"Boy, I'll bet he don't have to pay for it," Ernie said in sincere admiration.

Sybil angrily snapped her eyes his way. "Christ, Ernie! Sometimes you're so fucking gross!"

His mouth opened and he gleefully pointed a finger at her. "You said the word this time, Sybil Watkins!"

"Shut up, Ernie."

"Yes, ma'am."

They lapsed into a period of no talking as the music played on. A few minutes later it ended, and Brian brought Connie back to the table. He held her chair for her, then sat down himself. Brian checked the bottles around the table. "Ready for another round?"

He had no sooner spoken than the waitress made an appearance. "Four beer?"

"Sure thing," Brian said.

"So you're between trips out to the fighting, huh?" Connie asked.

"Yeah," Brian answered. "Poor old Nicholson got hit a few days before we were due to be exfiltrated."

"You combat guys are somethin' else," Ernie said in admiration. "Specially you Sneaky Petes. How long you back here for?"

Brian shrugged. "I don't know for sure. At least a month, I'm pretty sure."

The waitress reappeared, all smiles, and served their beer. She turned to leave and bumped into Joe Sampson, the black medical corpsman who had been with the reception team.

"Pardon me," Joe said. He took an instant to give Brian a quizzical glance, then looked down at Connie with an apologetic grin. "Guess what?"

Connie gritted her teeth. "Tell me."

"You're supposed to report to the ward for duty 'til midnight," he said. Then he quickly added, "Mother Moorehead's orders. She sent me herself."

"My God!" Sybil exclaimed. "What's that old bitch do? Wander around the hospital twenty-four hours a day?"

"I guess so," Joe said. "I was on duty with Cap'n Darwin and she come by the ward. She went over and talked wit' that Pullini dude, then come up to the ward office and poked around awhile. All of a sudden she says to me, 'Go fetch Lieutenant Montaldo and tell her she's on duty 'til midnight.' "

"What's going on?" Brian asked.

Sybil laid a hand on his arm. "Mother Moorehead is the chief of nurses. She was on the ward this afternoon and found out Connie had gone to the PX. She's probably been seething about it all day."

"I stalled around," Joe said. "But they wasn't nothin' I could do. It'll be my ass if I don't bring you back, lieutenant."

Connie sighed. "Okay." She stood up.

"How you doing, Joe?" Ernie said. "Want a drink o' my beer?"

"Hey, no thanks, Ernie," Joe said gratefully. "If I go back to that ward with it on my breath, ol' Mother Moorehead'll hang me out to dry."

Connie nodded to her companions. "See you later. Nice meeting you, Brian." She took Joe's arm and pushed him ahead of her. "Let's go, soldier. Duty calls."

Sybil was so angry she couldn't speak for a few minutes.

Brian took a drink of his beer. "I take it that your OIC is on the chickenshit side."

"That's putting it mildly," Sybil said. "The old bitch is married to that hospital—and the army."

"Want I should seduce her and bring her under my manly influence?" Ernie asked with a grin.

"Stop making stupid jokes, Ernie!"

"Jesus!" He looked at Brian. "I get in trouble with them two broads—ladies, *ladies!* I said, 'ladies'—ever' time I open my mouth."

"I hope our evening isn't ruined," Brian said.

"Of course it isn't," Sybil said. "It's just a shame, that's all."

"Then I take it you'd be in the mood for another dance," Brian said.

"Sure."

"Great. Let's go stick some money in the jukebox and get this joint jumping," he said.

Ernie tipped his bottle back and drained it. "Hey, I'll see you two later. I'm goin' out and look for some action."

Sybil's eyes narrowed in suspicion. "You're not going to that Juicy Lucy's, are you?"

"Naw."

"What's Juicy Lucy's?" Brian asked.

"A local whorehouse," Ernie said getting to his feet. "Sybil and Connie are bound and determined that I ain't gonna have any fun while I'm here in 'Nam. They'll allow me a little beer, but in the meantime I'm supposed to give up smokin' and women."

"You'll get one of those hard-to-cure strains of gonorrhea," Sybil warned him.

"Nice meetin' you, cap'n," Ernie said. "See you on the ward in the mornin', Sybil." He grinned and walked away toward the exit.

"Let's put on some music," Brian suggested.

"Good idea," Sybil responded. The beers she'd consumed and Brian's presence had made her feel horny.

Brian took her hand, and the two walked up to the jukebox. They read the selections together, and he laughed out loud. "Gee, I don't believe this. Look what we've got here. 'Pennies from Heaven,' 'I've Got My Love to Keep Me Warm,' 'Deep in the Heart of Texas'—can you believe it?"

Sybil joined his laughter. "I told you so. Let's pick something slow and dreamy, okay?"

"Sure, let's see—" His eyes scanned the list. "Ah, here we go. What about 'Sentimental Journey'?"

"Sounds good to me," Sybil said.

Brian checked the coin slot. "What does this thing take?"

"Can you believe it? American nickels."

He fished around in his pockets. "Uh-oh! All I've got are MPCs."

"Here, let me." Sybil, who always brought some each time she came to Lucky's, reached into her pants' pocket. She slipped a coin in and hit the selector button.

The machine groaned and clicked, its mechanism swinging the record onto the turntable. The needle arm dropped and the slow, languid notes of the tune issued forth from the speakers.

Brian took Sybil in his arms and spun slowly out onto the floor in time with the music. He held her tighter than the previous dance, and Sybil pressed in close to him. She wished she'd been wearing a dress—a sexy, low-cut civilian one—to really catch his attention.

Sybil felt a wonderful contentment in his arms. The melody, despite coming from an old phonograph record, was tranquil and romantic. Sybil, who had kept a close rein on her emotions for most of the previous year, sensed a loss of control as a combination of the beer, the music, and the man lulled her sentiments.

By the time the music had ended, their dancing posture had evolved into a tight embrace in which each held the other in both arms. They broke apart reluctantly and walked slowly back to their table. This time Brian had his arm around her waist.

"They're corny, but I love those old songs," Sybil said.

"Me too," Brian agreed.

Lucky made another appearance. "Hey. Where Connie? Where Ernie?"

Sybil smiled contentedly. "They had to leave."

"Oh! Too bad! Too bad!" Lucky said. "But you stay, right?"

"Right. Don't worry, Lucky."

"Okay, evr'thing fine then," the bar owner said wandering off once again.

"Lucky is like an old mother hen. You've probably noticed that he hovers around each table in turn, making sure everything is okay. Lucky's always been that way," Sybil explained. "If you're in his place, he considers everything you say or do his business."

"He runs a nice bar, though," Brian remarked.

"I agree."

"I just realized something," Brian said. "It's been almost two years since I've done any dancing." He winked at her. "It showed too, I'll bet."

"No, you did just fine." Sybil said.

They finished their beers in time for the waitress to come by and take their orders for refills. They didn't say much during the time it took her to return with fresh bottles.

"Say, I don't want to take you away from your friends," Brian said. "But I was wondering if you'd have dinner with me tomorrow night at the officers' club."

"Sure," Sybil said inwardly ecstatic. "I come off duty at seventeen hundred."

"Okay. I'll come by your quarters and pick you up at six," Brian said.

"Do you know where the nurses' billets are in the Triple-Nickel's compound?" Sybil asked.

Brian grinned. "Yeah. I checked into that before I drove through the gate after we left the PX."

"Good," Sybil said.

Brian glanced at the jukebox. "Looks like somebody else is going to play some music. Shall we dance again?"

Sybil accepted wordlessly and stood up. Within a minute they were again lost in the folds of a love song.

God, I like this man, she thought, and not as a friend either. This is romantic affection—wonderfully painful, deep man-woman affection. And there's not a blessed thing I can do to stop it.

The music, slow and sentimental, swirled around the couple, separating them from the rest of the world as they sank into deep feelings that neither realized at the time were so mutual.

It was the worst time of the day on the ward.

Doctors' rounds were over, the medication and shots given out per individual instructions for each patient. Now it was the time to change dressings and bandages.

Sybil Watkins, however, was too deep into her own reveries to let the unpleasantness of the moment penetrate them. She hummed as she inspected Mike Pullini's stumps. "You're doing just fine. Some heavy sweating, though."

"I've always been that way," Mike said. "Even a light workout in the gym used to leave me wringing wet."

"An application of talcum powder should keep you comfortable," she said. She applied the substance and began the bandaging procedure.

Mike looked at her. "You seem to be in a good mood."

Sybil smiled. "You're right about that."

"I'm glad somebody around here is." He watched

her work for a few minutes. Then he noted the ward door open. "Here comes Captain Gavin."

Sybil had spoken with Frank Gavin again regarding getting Mike interested in the bench pressing contest. They had decided that Frank should bring the matter up and discuss it with their patient. They figured a man-to-man dialogue might bring more positive results.

Ernie was with Frank when he approached the bed. Frank smiled a greeting at Sybil. "How's it going?"

"Just fine," Sybil answered as Ernie slipped up beside her to watch the work. Sybil glanced up at the physical therapist. She feigned not knowing the reason for his visit. "What can I do for you?"

"I've come to see Mike," Frank said.

Mike nodded. "How you doing, captain?"

"Great. Listen, big guy, there's something I want to talk over with you."

"Shoot," Mike said.

"We're having a bench press contest in the therapy room in a couple of weeks," Frank said.

"Yeah, I know. Lieutenant Watkins already told me about it."

"Okay. So when do you want to go into training for it?" Frank said adopting an affirmative attitude.

"I'm not up to it," Mike said.

Frank acted surprised. "Really? Jesus, Mike, I figured an old lifter like you would be chomping at the bit to get some iron up over his head."

Mike shook his head. "I just couldn't get with it."

Ernie chimed in. "Hey, if you don't do it, I gotta."

"What do you mean you *gotta?*" Mike asked a little irritated. "There's nothing in the ARs say you have to lift weights."

"I know the army doesn't make me," Ernie said. "But I want the ward represented." He had been well rehearsed.

Mike gave him a close scrutiny, then spoke as diplomatically as he could. "I think it'd be better if that black guy Sampson represented the ward."

"He don't want to," Ernie said. "Like you say. The ARs can't force a guy into it."

"Then it looks like you're the man of the hour," Mike said.

Frank crossed his arms and looked down at Mike. "C'mon, Mike, you know this guy doesn't have a chance."

Mike shrugged. "Then why's he doing it?"

"Because," Ernie said with a frown, "*I* got balls!"

Mike's face reddened with anger. "And you're saying I don't?"

"If the shoe hurts, take it off," Ernie said.

"What?" Mike asked, puzzled.

Sybil spoke up. "He means, if the shoe fits, wear it."

"Yeah!" Ernie said.

"Don't talk to me about balls," Mike snapped. "I'm a goddamned paratrooper. I belonged to a fighting outfit, not some rear echelon hospital unit."

"I may be a rear echelon, straightleg, skinny-ass twerp," Ernie said in a superior tone, "but I'm gonna pump iron, buddy boy!" He treated Mike to a sincere look of disdain, then turned his attention to Sybil. "By the way, my ma sent some more Kool-Aid. If you and Connie want some, just let me know."

Sybil was puzzled. She'd seen him buy the packets of the drink mix the day before. She started to say something to him, but he'd already left the bed pushing an imaginary barbell in the air.

"Well, Mike?" Frank said. "Are you going to let him go one better than you?"

Mike scowled. "Knock this shit off already."

Frank gave Sybil a long, meaningful look that expressed his frustration.

The explosion, sounding like multiple thunderclaps, swept over the ward, rattling windows and knocking things off bedstands with its concussion.

Frank made a quick grab for Mike Pullini, pulling the patient from the bed and into his arms in one quick movement. He set him on the floor and then leaped back up. "You ambulatory guys!" he yelled. "Grab the bed patients and get 'em to the deck quick!"

Most of the men who were able were already on the floor as the echoes of the terrific blast faded away into the tropical sky. Being combat veterans with recent exposure to enemy fire, they had instinctively gone down when the explosion first went off. Now they wasted no time in grabbing their helpless buddies and getting them down to a safe area under the beds.

It was uncomfortable for most of the bed patients. Not only was the concrete floor hard, but many of them wore large, bulky casts that precluded them from getting into physically bearable positions.

The ward was absolutely silent for a few moments.

"What the hell was that?" somebody asked.

"Christ!" another muttered. "I already been hit once. Wouldn't you know Charlie'd mortar me to death after I'd gone through an operation and ever'thing."

"That wasn't no incoming round," a patient remarked.

"Naw," a third agreed. "Sounded like C Four to me." He referred to Combination Four plastic explosive.

"I think you're right," Frank Gavin said. He reached across to where Sybil lay on the floor. "Let's wait this out for a bit to make sure there won't be more."

Sybil swallowed hard. "Good idea." She crawled out into the aisle between the beds and called out. "Connie?"

"Yeah?" Her voice was loud even from the other end of the ward down at the office.

"Everything okay up there?"

"Just some stuff scattered around," Connie hollered back.

Finally Frank got to his feet and edged up to a window. After looking out, he turned back into the ward. "There's a lot of smoke just outside the gate."

At that moment the ward door was flung open and a medical sergeant leaned inside. "Who's in charge here?"

Sybil, dusting herself off, waved at him. "I am."

"A bomb went off in the peddlers' stalls on the other side of the fence. How about sending a couple of people over there? I'm gonna round up some more help."

"Right," Sybil said. "Connie, stay here." She grabbed Ernie and headed for the exit. Frank Gavin began helping the bed patients back onto their beds.

Sybil grabbed the emergency medical kit out of the ward office. She ran out of the building with Ernie right behind her.

By the time the two arrived on the scene, it was chaos. Several badly mangled bodies lay sprawled among the wreckage while American medical personnel frantically searched among the shattered stalls for injured survivors.

"Oh, my God!" Sybil cried out suddenly remembering. "Noi!"

She and Ernie, leaping over debris and dead people, shouldered their way through the rescuers until they reached the site of Noi's stall.

Noi, with Sai's blood seeping into her dress, stood with the child in her arms. She was in shock, crying out to anyone who would listen, "My baby! *Curu toi voi!* My baby!"

Sybil rushed to her Vietnamese friend and gently took Sai into her own arms. A quick glance showed the infant had massive, serious injuries. "Come with me, Noi. To the hospital."

Moi seemed to come out of her frantic stupor a bit. "Yes Sybil! Yes! You *y-ta,* you nurse. You help my baby. Oh, Sybil, she all I got."

Without speaking a word, Sybil, still carrying the child, rushed back toward the gate as Noi, hanging onto Ernie's arm, followed.

An air force jeep, the motor turning over in neutral, was parked at the gate. The driver, a young airman, stood looking on at the scene. Without hesitating, Sybil leaped into his vehicle. She indicated the direction in which the surgical huts of the Triple-Nickel were located. "That way!"

"Yes, ma'am!" He leaped into the driver's seat, slammed the jeep into gear, and sped off.

Noi, with Ernie, watched them streak away. "Sai!

Sai!"

Ernie tugged her along. "We're going over there, Noi. Sybil don't want to waste no time."

The air force driver slammed to a stop in front of the hut. Sybil leaped from the vehicle and charged into the operating room. A surgical team, already assembled, was preparing for casualties. Sybil laid the baby on the operating table.

"Okay, clear out," the senior surgeon said to her. He and his people moved quickly into action.

Sybil went back outside. The air force vehicle was gone, but she could see Colonel Sedgewick and Major Moorehead checking the area's preparedness. The chief nurse, with the colonel beside her, noted the blood on Sybil's uniform.

"Did you just bring in a casualty?"

"Yes, ma'am," Sybil said. "A baby."

"Get back to your ward now, lieutenant," Mother Moorehead said. "We want everybody at their stations in case they're needed."

"Right. The child's mother is coming now." She pointed across the open area where Ernie and Noi hurried toward them.

"We'll have to make arrangements to get the patient out to a civilian hospital as soon as it's feasible," Mother said.

"These are personal friends of mine, major," Sybil said. "Couldn't we keep her here?"

"Of course not!" Mother snapped. "Regulations don't permit the prolonged treatment of civilian casualties. Only in the case of emergencies."

Sybil wasn't about to give up. She turned to the colonel. "We have an empty room in the nurses' billets, sir. The child could be cared for on our own time."

Mother's eyebrows arched. "Even though we are all standing here in informal conversation, you are going outside of channels, Watkins."

"Oh, hell, never mind," Colonel Sedegwick said. "Check in with me on it later, lieutenant. We've got too much to worry about now."

"Get back to your ward," Mother said with a scowl before she and the colonel hurried off.

Ernie and Noi arrived. Sybil took the woman in her arms. "Sai is being looked after in there, Noi," Sybil said indicating the hut.

"She no dead, Sybil?" Noi asked hopefully, her eyes brimming with tears. The Vietnamese woman trembled noticeably.

"I don't know her condition," Sybil said. "I'll have Ernie stay here with you, Noi. I must return to my duties. Do you understand?"

"Yes—yes!" She burst out into tears and grabbed Sybil, clinging tightly to her. "Oh, I don't want Sai to die!"

"They'll do their best, Noi," Sybil said. She looked at Ernie. "Be as much help as you can. I have to get back to the ward." She gently released herself from Noi's embrace. "And keep me informed."

"Right, Sybil," Ernie said. He now noted the amount of blood on both Noi's dress and Sybil's uniform. He swallowed hard. "Damn!"

Chapter Eight

Sybil, following Mother Moorehead's orders, went directly back to her ward after turning Sai into the surgical team. But, impatient to follow the case, she sent a note to Penny Darwin, begging the night nurse to relieve her as early as possible.

Penny, after hearing the full circumstances of the situation, readily agreed and got out of her bed early in the afternoon to take over Sybil's shift.

Sybil was so grateful she hugged her friend. "God, Penny, you don't know what this means to me."

"I was more than happy to help out," Penny replied. Then she winked. "Besides, I'm going to let Connie do most of the work anyway."

Connie, looking up from the ever-demanding patients' log, laughed. "Then it'll be just like when Sybil's here."

"Wise guy!" Sybil said over her shoulder as she left. She went directly to the operating hut. The surgeon and his crew were still hard at work on the baby when she got there. One of the medics informed her that Ernie and the infant's mother had gone down to the Triple-Nickel's dayroom to await word on the operation.

Sybil found them there. Ernie, bent over the pool table about to make a shot, looked up at her entrance. "Hi, Sybil. We still ain't heard nothin'."

Noi, her arms nervously crossed, turned from the window that she'd been standing near. "You no hear nothing too, Sybil?"

"No, Noi," Sybil said. "I've come to stay with you until we know for sure how the baby is."

"Oh, Sybil. Thank you. I glad you here."

Ernie went back to his listless game while the two women went to a nearby sofa to settle in and endure the awful hours and anticipation. Noi wept quietly into a handkerchief that Ernie had lent her.

It was late afternoon when a medic, still wearing his green OR uniform, stuck his head in the door. "Doctor'll talk to you now." Then he rushed off.

The three found the surgeon, a captain named Ryder, enjoying a cigarette and coffee outside the hut. His first words brought some hope. "She's alive."

But Sybil, being a nurse, knew that wasn't the news they wanted to hear. The statement only commented on her present, and possibly, temporary state. "What's her condition, doctor?"

"Critical," Ryder answered taking a drag off his cigarette. "The little girl was torn up pretty bad. We must have spent an hour alone digging splinters out of her."

"Oh, Lord," Sybil moaned.

"Was she inside a frame house or something?"

"A wooden peddler's stall," Sybil explained. "The thing was disintegrated by the blast."

The doctor took another sip of coffee. "Jesus! Anyhow, they're bringing an ambulance around to take her to whatever civilian facility is available."

"No!" Sybil exclaimed. Then she calmed down. "I have permission to monitor her recovery in the nurses' billets."

"The billets? That's no ICU, for God's sake!"

"It's a better Intensive Care Unit than any of the local hospitals," Sybil countered. "Unless you'll authorize her admittance into our own ICU."

"You know I can't do that, nurse. We've already extended our facilities far beyond what is normal for emergency treatment. And that includes several pints of blood."

"Then we must take the best alternative," Sybil said. She desperately decided to stretch the truth. "Colonel Sedgewick told me it would be okay."

"Really?" Ryder was skeptical. "Hell, nurse, you don't have the proper equipment over there."

Sybil felt she'd gone far enough, but she was still desperate. "He didn't say anything about it, but I imagine he meant for us to take what we need."

"The old boy must really be getting generous," Ryder said. He hesitated before he spoke again. "This is really irregular, but if the colonel told you it was authorized, I guess I won't try to stop you. Or check up on you either. But let me warn you, nurse. It's your ass in the sling, not mine, if the shit hits the fan over this."

"Sure, I understand," Sybil said.

"We've got some apparatus you can use—catheter, intravenous bottles, and so on."

"What about medications?" Sybil asked. "And the intravenous equipment is useless unless we have the proper solutions. She's going to go into shock without—"

The doctor interrupted. "What I don't know, I don't give a damn about." He pointed to Ernie. "Kaznowski's the biggest thief and scrounger in the Triple-Nickel. I'll tell my head ICU nurse to look the other way for about fifteen minutes."

"Thank you, doctor!"

"But you'd better watch out for Moorehead," Ryder warned. "I don't care what Colonel Sedgewick told you. She'll fight anything that's not in the books. And you can expect trouble on this one." He finished his coffee and dropped the cigarette to the ground, crushing it out with his foot. "She'll have your pretty little ass in a sling, believe me."

"I'm ready for that," Sybil said. "There's one more thing."

"What's that?"

"It's obvious we'll need a doctor—"

"Hold it! If the colonel okayed this, then *he'll* get you a physician. I'm not going that far out on a limb." To emphasize his refusal, Ryder turned and went directly back into the hut.

Sybil intercepted the ambulance crew, and they took their pathetic little burden to the billets. There was an empty room with two beds. Noi could sleep in the one that Sai didn't occupy. While Ernie made his run on the ICU supply room, Sybil, now with Connie helping out, prepared their impromptu recovery unit.

She looked down at Sai still sleeping under the anesthesia. The baby was wrapped in bandages, her little fists clinched tight as she breathed in shallow gasps.

Noi, her face streaked with tears, looked up into Sybil's face. "Please—please, Sybil. She not die, okay? I alone without my baby. I no got nobody."

Sybil put her arms around the smaller woman and pulled her close. "We'll do our best. That's all we can do." She led Noi to the other bed and sat her down. "I have to get Sai settled in."

Two hours later, with antibiotics dripping into her little body along with a epinephrine solution to fight shock, and the catheter in place, little Sai began the most critical stage of her recovery—fighting to stay alive.

Several other nurses, either coming or going off shift, stopped and looked in the room out of curiosity. "What's going on in here?" one asked. "The ICU suddenly too crowded?"

"We have a civilian patient," Sybil explained. "The little baby. She was hurt in the explosion this morning. I've got permission to treat her here."

The women quietly went to the bed. "Poor little thing," one said.

"We need help," Sybil said. Then she sighed. "I might as well tell you—I haven't gotten this cleared yet."

A young nurse smiled. "Does that mean it might upset Mother Moorehead?"

"I'm afraid so," Sybil admitted.

"Then you can count on me!"

The other nurses also volunteered their time to help out. Each was introduced to Noi and the Vietnamese mother was shown where their rooms were in case they were needed. As it was, there would be hourly visits on a twenty-four hour basis by a nurse. Sai was in good, caring hands.

Then Maj. Tacita Moorehead made an appearance. She had decided to conduct one of her surprise visits to the nurses' quarters. As usual, she went from room to room opening the doors and peering in to make sure her charges were up to no shenanigans. When she opened the door to the empty room—which she knew was not assigned as quarters—she gave the scene inside one brief, incredulous stare.

Sybil and Connie, both checking the baby's condition, looked up simultaneously.

Connie swore in Spanish under her breath, and whispered. "I'll finish up. You'd better talk to her."

Mother's eyebrows arched. "What's going on here?"

Sybil, who had just checked Sai's vital signs, walked to the door and tried to usher Moorehead out. But Mother wasn't moving. Sybil, her voice in a whisper to keep from alarming Noi, spoke urgently. "This is the patient I spoke to you about earlier."

"You were most certainly not given permission to treat her here," Mother hissed. "And where did you get that equipment and medicine?"

"From the ICU supply room," Sybil said. "And my request was not refused by Colonel Sedgewick."

"He most certainly did not approve it, and he won't! This is unauthorized and illegal!" Mother snapped in indignation. "Those drugs and that apparatus have been stolen—*stolen!*"

Sybil finally maneuvered her out of the room into the corridor. "The patient is in critical condition and can't be moved now. Let's take the mother into consideration too, shall we?"

"Don't give me instructions, lieutenant!"

"We're nurses, for God's sake! We're supposed to take care of people first, and worry about the rules and regulations second," Sybil argued.

"*I* am responsible for what goes on in the nursing unit," Mother said. She tapped the gold maple leafs of her rank pinned to her collar. "As the chief of nurses I would be held accountable for this illegal activity."

"Let's talk to Colonel Sedgewick," Sybil requested.

"We most assuredly will," Mother said. She nodded her head toward the exit. "We'll walk over to his office this very minute."

Sybil pulled her hat from her back pocket and called through the door. "I'll be back, Connie."

Following Major Moorehead across the compound to the 555th Field Hospital Headquarters was like marching in a parade. Sybil, seething with anger and a growing feeling of frustration, couldn't keep up with the woman's long strides without breaking into a little trot now and then.

When they entered the building, they did so with a flourish. Sergeant Major Rafferty looked up from the work on his desk. He smiled at Mother. "Yes, ma'am, major. What can wc do for you?"

"I must see Colonel Sedgewick immediately."

"Yes, ma'am." Rafferty got up and went to a door behind him. He rapped gently and stepped in. In a moment he reappeared. "The colonel will see you."

Mother charged into the office and saluted. "Colonel Sedgewick, this nurse is treating an unauthorized patient in the nurses' billets."

"Beg pardon?" Sedgewick seemed confused, his chubby face screwed into a quizzical expression.

"You're going to have to run that by me again."

Sybil quickly spoke up. "Remember this morning, just after the explosion, and I met you and—"

"*At ease!*" Moorehead commanded, ordering Sybil into silence. "Lieutenant Watkins is referring to that Vietnamese baby she brought into the area after the explosion this morning."

"Ah, yes," Sedgewick said. "I presume our surgical crew operated on the child."

"Correct. Now the infant is classified as critical," Moorehead went on. "At least that's what Watkins says. But it is unauthorized for the patient to be receiving care here, much less in the nurses' billets."

Sedgewick stood up and walked to the coat rack in the corner. He took his hat. "Let's go see the child."

Moorehead and Sybil, with both Sedgewick and Sergeant Major Rafferty, returned to the billets. The Triple-Nickel's senior noncommissioned officer, after eavesdropping on the conversation, decided he should include himself in the situation.

When they entered the room, Connie stepped back. Noi, sitting on her bed across from the baby, looked at the newcomers in confusion.

The colonel wasted no time in examining the child. He finished and looked at Sybil. "Who was the surgeon?"

"Doctor Ryder."

"Wait here." He disappeared out the door.

Mother watched him go. She glared at Sybil, then shifted her eyes to Connie. "Ah, Montaldo. I'm not surprised to see you involved in this."

Connie smiled in defiant delight. "Always glad to lend a hand, ma'am."

"Please," Noi said in her small voice. "What ever'-body do, please?"

Sybil walked over and gently patted her arm. "Everything is fine, Noi. Don't worry."

The sergeant major sighed. "Well, I suppose I'd better arrange to get an ambulance out of the motor pool to transport this kid the hell out of here."

"You stay where you are!" Sybil said through clenched teeth, whirling to confront him.

Rafferty's eyes opened wide in indignation. "Just a minute!"

"You wait just a minute," Sybil said. "I outrank you, buster, and I don't give a good goddamn what you think is proper or improper."

"Watch it, Watkins," Mother said almost snarling. But she motioned to Rafferty. "Wait until the colonel comes back. He'll set things right."

"Yes, ma'am." The sergeant major glared at Sybil. "You're *not* in my chain-of-command. I don't care what your rank is."

Noi began to sob again.

The room was engulfed in an uneasy silence for a full ten minutes. Finally Sedgewick returned and stepped into the group of sullen people. "Okay. I got the full story now." He looked at Mother Moorehead. "You're right. This is improper as hell, major."

Moorehead almost smirked. "Of course it is!'

"But the child stays," Sedgewick quickly added.

Mother frowned in bewilderment. "Now, colonel. This situation could have far consequences."

"And I have assigned myself as the doctor of record," Sedgewick said. He turned to Sybil. "I presume you've made nursing arrangements for the child?"

"Oh, my God, yes!" Sybil replied happily. "There will always be somebody in attendance."

"Fine." He looked at Rafferty. "Get back to the office for my instruments. They're in the closet behind my desk." Next he turned his attention to Connie. "Go see there's no ladies in the latrine," he said. "Even if I am a doctor, they might not understand I need to wash my hands prior to examining my patient here." He grinned. "I'll have to knock the dust off my medical knowledge and perk it up a bit, but I'm looking forward to it." He noticed Noi. "Is that the mother?"

Noi answered for herself. "Yes. You the doctah?"

"Sure am, ma'am," Sedgewick said. He walked over and bent down to speak to her. His voice was low and gentle. "Your baby has been seriously injured, my dear. Do you understand?"

Noi started weeping again. "Oh—yes—yes—"

Sedgewick tenderly laid his pudgy hand on her shoulder. "But I'll do my very best for her."

"Thank you," Noi sobbed.

"Now, if you're going to sleep in this room, I'll have a few things you can do to help out, okay?"

Noi, now feeling much better, nodded enthusiastically. "Yes, Doctah."

Connie returned. "The latrine is clear, sir."

"Good. Now my first order is that everybody, with the exception of the mother and—" he glanced at Connie's name tag— "Lieutenant Montaldo clear out of here."

Sybil was so happy she could have wept.

Captain Brian Mallory was wearing a class A uniform when he dropped by the billets to pick up Sybil for their date. He looked quite dashing to her. He wore a green beret, a khaki outfit with a short-sleeved, open collar shirt, and spit-shined jump boots. His campaign ribbons and silver parachutist badge were pinned above his shirt pocket.

Sybil, dressed in a uniform blouse and skirt, felt a bit more feminine than she had at Lucky's. When she stepped outside the door with him, she stopped and stared at his mode of transportation. It was a 1959 Chevrolet Impala. "Now where in the world did you get that?" she demanded with a laugh.

"It belongs to one of the ARVN officers assigned to us," Brian explained, referring to a lieutenant in the army of the Republic of Vietnam. He opened the door for her. "His family is unbelievably corrupt. He tells me they've got no less than a half dozen American cars."

He went around and got in the driver's side, settling down behind the wheel. It took several tries to get the engine started. Even then, it didn't run very smoothly. "Unfortunately, the Vietnamese aren't great believers in practicing preventive maintenance on their cars. This thing really needs a tune-up."

"As long as it runs," Sybil said.

"That explosion this morning must have really shook up the old Triple-Nickel," he said backing the car up. He slipped it into drive and headed out the parking lot. "It was mighty close to you."

"Sure was," Sybil said. "It turned out to be a terrorist bomb set off right in the middle of the shopping bazaar. I just can't figure out what anyone would think they could prove by such barbarity."

Brian ruefully shook his head. "They could prove a hell of a lot."

"Really? Like what?"

"Like, for example, the government can't protect those people from the Viet Cong," Brian said. "It proves Charlie can move around pretty much as he pleases, and do exactly as he wants. He is also making an example out of people who deal with the Americans. Whatever Charlie doesn't like, Charlie blows up. At least here in the heavily populated areas."

Sybil shuddered. "God awful, that's what it is."

"What's that General Sherman said?"

"*War is Hell,*" Sybil intoned. "But that is a great big understatement."

"I agree."

"Do you remember my Vietnamese friend I told you about?"

"The woman who sells cigarettes?"

"Right," Sybil said. "Well, her little daughter was seriously wounded in that blast. She's just an infant. A defenseless, innocent baby."

"If she's badly hurt, she'll die anyway. The hospitals around here aren't all that great," Brian said.

"She's being treated in the Triple-Nickel," Sybil said happily.

"How in the world did that come about?"

"I took the bull by the horns," Sybil said. "I simply had the child placed in a room in the nurses' billets. Then, with a little thieving by Ernie, and a big surprise in Colonel Sedgewick himself participating in the effort, things turned out quite well."

"Good for you," Brian said.

"But I'm not congratulating myself yet," Sybil said

warily. "Mother Moorehead and Sergeant Major Rafferty will be doing their best to queer the operation."

"People like that live by a basic philosophy," Brian mused. "They believe in always saying 'no' unless there's a hell of a good reason to say 'yes.' "

"When Colonel Sedgewick put himself on the case I wanted to positively crow," Sybil said laughing. "You should have seen their expressions. They looked like they'd just been hit in the face with a wet towel."

Brian turned off the road and into the drive leading up to Long Binh's officers' club. He parked the Chevy between a couple of jeeps. He looked around the immediate area. "Looks like we're the only civilian vehicle in the whole place."

"Gee, I hope nobody steals it," Sybil said.

"Don't worry," Brian remarked. "Remember I said the guy that owns it has five more."

Sybil felt deliriously happy in being with Brian as they walked up the steps to the wide entrance. A Vietnamese doorman held the large portal open for them. He smiled and affected a French-style salute.

The foyer was carpeted with potted plants arranged around the plush furniture. A bulletin board, with official mimeographed notices tacked to it, ruined the decor somewhat, but it was still an attractive place.

"I take it you've been here before," Brian said.

"Only a couple of times," Sybil said. "I prefer Lucky's and the folks from the Triple-Nickel. Sometimes these other people around here are too military for my taste."

"Shall we have a drink before dinner?"

"Great idea," Sybil responded.

They went into the bar. While not exactly up to the

standards of Stateside officers' clubs at the large posts, this one could hold its own pretty well. The furnishings were nice, even if the building itself lacked something in sumptuousness.

They sat at the bar. The bartender, a Filipino like many club employees serving American armed forces in Southeast Asia, slid a paper napkin in front of each of them. "Yes?" he asked pleasantly.

"A Dewar's and soda with a twist," Sybil said ordering her favorite drink.

"Bourbon and water," Brian requested.

A couple of minutes later they took their first sips. Brian smiled. "Mine's great. And yours?"

"It'll more than do," Sybil said. "Are you married?"

"Whoa!" he said laughing. "You just shoot questions right at a guy, don't you?"

"Well?"

"Divorced," Brian said.

"I don't know much about you," Sybil said.

"Well, let me say on my word as an officer and a gentleman to an officer and a lady, that I'm an eligible bachelor," Brian said.

"Good," Sybil said. "I never, never date married men. Especially when their wives are thousands of miles away."

"And you?"

"I'm an eligible old maid," Sybil said. "Now tell me your life story."

"The whole thing?" he asked chuckling.

"Leave out any murders or extended periods of horse thievery, but tell me everything else."

"Okay." He took another sip of his drink. "I was born and raised in Long Beach, California. As a matter of fact, I've never lived anywhere else except the army."

Brian, in a rare, talkative mood, began relating his personal history by first mentioning his father.

"My dad was an Alabama farm boy named Donny Joe Mallory," he said.

Sybil interrupted laughing. "*Donny Joe?*"

Puzzled, Brian smiled. "Yeah. What's funny?"

"The double name," Sybil said. "It's so southern. I have to confess to you, that back home I'm called Sybil Mae. Sorry about that. Now go on."

"Well, there was a depression on, so Dad joined the navy and ended up aboard a ship that had Long Beach as a home port. He was a radioman. Part of his job was to keep the equipment stock in the communications room—or whatever they call them on a ship—and he got this stuff through a navy contract with a local supplier."

"Yes?" Sybil took a drink.

"That supplier was my grandfather and my mom worked in the store. So, as the story goes, they fell in love, married and when Dad left the navy he went into the family business. Which he inherited when my grandfather died."

"Very interesting."

"And they moved into a house on Coronado, just off Seventh—know where that is?"

Sybil laughed. "Let's see—between Sixth and Eighth, right?"

"Sure you haven't been to Long Beach?" he asked with a wide grin. "Anyhow, that became the family home where they still live."

"Now inject yourself into this story," Sybil said.

"Whatever you say, ma'am."

Brian was born in 1936. He had a normal southern California boyhood with the usual oceanside and sunny weather activities. But growing up in Long Beach during World War II exposed him to so much navy he grew sick and tired of it. After graduating from Wilson High School's class of 1954, he enlisted in the army. During basic training at Fort Ord, he met several other young men who had volunteered for the paratroops. Being young and inclined toward the adventurous side of life, he went along with them.

Brian served three years in the crack Eighty-second Airborne Division. He was discharged with the rank of sergeant and returned home to California. There was a detachment of the Seventeenth Special Forces Group out at nearby Fort MacArthur. Since it was a Green Beret paratroop unit, he joined up to satisfy the still very much alive adventurous side of his nature on a part-time basis.

In the meantime, he attended Long Beach State University and earned a bachelor's in commercial art. After graduating he got a job in a Los Angeles advertising agency. He did well in the agency, rising to become an account executive in a relatively short amount of time.

"And that's where I met my wife."

"Tell me about her," Sybil asked.

"Her name was Jill Paterno," Brian said. "A photographer's model. Very blond, leggy—what is called full-figured—and all the rest of the equipment of her trade."

"Sounds like she was beautiful."

"I suppose," Brian conceded. "At any rate, she seemed ideal for an up and coming advertising executive in metropolitan Los Angeles. And I suppose she was. She continually nagged and pushed me to expand my horizons. I ended up taking a big chance and opening my own agency."

"Sounds great!"

"It was," Brian said. "And I made good money, too. The only trouble was it wasn't coming in as fast as Jill could spend it."

Within a couple of years, they were deeply in debt, fighting continuously and absolutely miserable. Jill was as shallow as she was flashy. The situation deteriorated to the point that he moved out of their apartment and went back home to his parents' house on Coronado.

"I figured we'd probably stay separated for a while until we could work things out," Brian said. "But I had divorce papers served on me."

"Not expected at all?" Sybil asked.

"I had no idea that was what she wanted," Brian said. "It was a bit devastating. Anyhow, a quick consultation with a lawyer convinced me that I would either spend the rest of my life giving Jill about half of everything I made, or I could get it over in one swell swoop."

"Which did you go for?"

"The latter," Brian said in a flat tone.

He signed his business over lock, stock, and barrel. Then went down to his army reserve unit and put in papers requesting active duty. Brian wanted to get the hell away from things and sort them out before planning the rest of his life. He had been in the exact same position he was in at high school graduation. By the time of his divorce he was a first lieutenant and didn't have long to wait for the arrival of orders putting him on active duty.

After assignment to the Seventh Special Forces Group at Fort Bragg, North Carolina, he participated in several training exercises. Then he received orders—along with a promotion to captain—to go to Vietnam. Once there, he was committed to a couple of dangerous operations that penetrated deep into enemy territory. These sorties into hell were relieved with short periods of rest. During those times, after his nerves calmed some and when the next mission was scheduled, he was ready to go.

Now Brian set his empty glass down and looked at Sybil. "So. Here I am."

"Most interesting," Sybil said, finishing her own drink. "And I presume you'll be returning to civilian life when your tour of duty is completed."

"Absolutely correct," Brian said. "I heard from my parents that my agency fell apart under Jill's direction. It no longer exists. But at least I'm free and clear to start something else when I get back."

"Sounds like this brief sojurn back into military life was a real breather for you," Sybil mused.

"Yeah. It's straightening up my head." He grinned in his boyish manner. "And scaring the hell out of me at the same time." He checked his watch. "Good time to eat. Shall we?"

"Fine."

They went into the main dining room and were shown to a table. The place was about three-quarters full. There were several ARVN (Army of the Republic of Vietnam) officers there with beautiful women of their own country.

Sybil leaned across the table. "Have you ever noticed that these ARVNs all have such attractive wives?"

"They have wives—yes—but not necessarily with them," Brian said. "The upper-class Vietnamese generally have marriages of convenience. These jokers are probably with their mistresses."

Sybil laughed. "How wicked!"

They were interrupted by the waiter. He took their orders for two more drinks and left dinner menus. The bill of fare was surprisingly good.

"Can you believe it?" Sybil asked. "Just like a fancy restaurant back home."

"Yeah," Brian said. "Now where are the steaks?"

"Sure you don't want cheeseburgers?"

"Not this trip," Brian said. "A New York cut with a baked potato and salad will be fine for me."

"I'll try the sea bass," Sybil said. "Growing up in Oklahoma didn't offer me many opportunities for fresh sea food."

"We take it for granted in Long Beach," Brian said.

The waiter returned with their drinks. "Are you ready to order?"

"Yes," Sybil said.

When they were alone again, Brian raised his glass. "Here's to us."

"To us," Sybil said touching her glass to his. She looked into his eyes and felt a thrill at what she perceived there. Deep, deep in her heart, Sybil knew a relationship was developing.

"Now it's your turn to spin your life story," Brian urged her.

"It's not very interesting," Sybil said. "I'm just a bachelor girl in the Army Nurse Corps from a most unremarkable background."

"Oh, I doubt if it's that drab," Brian said smiling.

"And I want to hear it."

Sybil barely took ten minutes to tell of her parents, Oklahoma City, nursing school, and finally of going into the army. She talked about her friendship with Connie Montaldo and Ernie Kaznowski, relating various episodes of the trio's relationship. When Sybil had finished, she shrugged. "And that's it. The stirring saga of Sybil Mae Watkins."

"I admire the camaraderie between yourself and Connie and Ernie," Brian said.

"I'm terribly fond of both of them," Sybil said in a sincere tone. "They mean everything to me over here. I only hope that somehow we can continue being together after we return to the world."

"Maybe you could all get jobs in the same hospital," Brian suggested.

Sybil didn't seem sure. "Oooh, perhaps," she mused. "But it seems like an unreal idea."

"Probably is," Brian said. "Wartime friendships have a bad habit of waning when things change back to normal."

"I suppose that would be the same for wartime romances, too."

Brian shook his head. "I don't know about that. There are plenty of war brides, you know."

Sybil brightened. "Yeah! I suppose there are."

Their food was served on heavy china plates. The waiter, solicitous and careful, made sure everything was completely to their liking before he withdrew.

Sybil and Brian consumed the meal with little conversation. They didn't become talkative again until dessert was eaten, and the after-dinner cups of coffee were set before them.

"How was the sea bass?"

"Great. And your steak?"

"Just the way I like it," Brian said.

"You're not real particular about your food, are you?" Sybil inquired.

"Not lately. After spending weeks and weeks consuming C-rations, it's hard to get real excited about rations," Brian said. "I think my taste buds have atrophied."

"Except for cheeseburgers and french fries, right?"

"Right!" he agreed laughing. "I don't know why, but everytime I'm in the field, I keep hungering for the stuff. Maybe I have a lot of happy memories tied up in that kind of food. You know what I mean? Friday and Saturday nights at the drive-in restaurants after a date."

"All psychological," Sybil said.

"I noticed there was some activity in the ballroom when we first arrived," Brian said. "Pardon the cliche, but shall we trip the light fantastic again?"

"Sure."

When they finished their coffee, they left the dining room and walked across the club to the ballroom. A sign outside informed them that a USO dance band from the States was being featured.

"We'll have more modern music tonight evidently," Brian said. At that moment the band struck up "Come Rain or Come Shine." He glanced over at the band and saw the sign advertising Joe Nolan's Band of Nostalgia. He laughed out loud. "Oh, no!"

"Looks like we're doomed to ancient music," Sybil said giggling.

The place was pretty crowded and they had to squeeze themselves onto the dance floor. Sybil, once more in Brian's arms, felt the same romantic contentment she had experienced at Lucky's the previous night.

They got a table after that first dance, and spent the rest of the evening in quiet talk, dancing and enjoying occasional drinks. Sybil knew he liked her. It was an intuition all women had when they receive a special kind of attention or smile from a male companion. Often it was a signal for them to slow down or back off if the situation appeared to be going farther than they could handle. But, as in this case, it could cause ripples of excitement to travel through the female soul.

Sybil and Brian got a bit high—actually pleasantly sloshed—and their time spent swaying to the music was punctuated by tight embraces.

Brian finally kissed her.

It was around midnight. Sybil responded tenderly, pressing her own mouth against his. Afterward they looked wordlessly into each other's eyes for several long moments.

"I want you," Brian said.

Sybil smiled, her happiness more intoxicating than the drinks she had consumed. "And I want you."

"Shall we go to the Empress Hotel?" Brian asked.

"Yes."

The hotel, located on the same road as Lucky's, was a rambling affair that had grown out of the increase of population in the area. Rustic, but comfortable, the owner was an ARVN general who detailed his own soldiers as guards around the place to ensure his clients' safety. Actually, it was the least he could do for the Americans who stayed there. It was U.S. tax dollars that had provided the building materials for the establishment.

Brian took Sybil's hand and together they walked back through the foyer and out to the car. Once inside, he kissed her again. Their passion was more evident now as they held each other tightly. She parted her lips, and Brian gently probed her mouth with his tongue.

Sybil felt lust—naked, driving, undeniable lust. The romantic dinner, old music—everything—had made her so horny she felt positively ferocious. She hadn't been with a man in almost a year, and the absence of any real meaningful feelings for anyone had left her in an emotional void that Brian Mallory was fast filling.

It took only five minutes to reach the hotel, and another ten to check in and go up to the room. Sybil stepped across the threshold. Brian followed, switching on the lights, then closing the door.

She turned and faced Brian. Again, there was a long kiss. Then Sybil gently broke it off. "I have to put in my diaphragm."

"Okay," he said with a smile.

"I know the pill is better, but—" she looked at him meaningfully— "I haven't had a reason to be on it lately."

When she went into the bathroom, he turned down the sheets and undressed. After turning out the lights, he slipped between the covers and waited.

Sybil came out of the bathroom, still in her uniform but with all her undies removed.

"Leave the light on in there," Brian said.

"Okay." A dull glow from the open door barely lit the room. She joined him in bed. "You're naked." She said it as a statement of fact.

"And you're not," he replied.

Wordlessly, she unbuttoned the blouse and dropped it to the floor. The metal military insignia pinned on it clinked in the dark. Then she slid out of her skirt.

Brian reached out and gently folded her into his arms. He kissed her passionately but with a great caring. She responded by letting herself go. Moans of pleasure hummed through her lips as Brian continued kissing.

"Brian," she said softly, taking pleasure in saying his name. "Brian."

His hands slid down to cup her breasts, gently feeling the unfamiliar flesh that was being offered to him. From there he stroked the outside of her thigh, then slid up across the more sensitive inner part.

Sybil's own hands roamed at will across his body, feeling the thick mat of hair on his chest that continued across his belly to the rigid flesh that responded to her fingertips.

She wordlessly obeyed the pressure of his touch, rolling over on her back and allowing him to join her—then enter.

The ecstasy grew, seeming to gain altitude, as their two bodies joined and pressed together. Their breathing, like their psyches, blended in rhythm and substance all the way to the highest plateau. Then it cascaded down for Brian to the final shuddering moments of orgasmic pleasure.

Sybil felt his throbbing inside her, then sighed as her own built-up passion began its gradual descent.

Chapter Nine

Brian walked Sybil up to the door of the billets. The sun was only a dull red glow on the horizon as they paused, their arms around each other, to stand silently for several moments under the dim bulb of the exterior light.

Finally Sybil spoke. "I'd better go in. I have to check on little Sai."

"Okay." He kissed her. "It was wonderful, Sybil."

"Yes, Brian."

He slowly released her. "Be sure and call to let me know when you'll be free again."

She patted her shoulder bag. "I've got the number right here."

"Good night. Or rather, good day."

"Make it good night. Sounds more romantic." She watched him go back to the car. Brian opened the door and gave her a little wave before getting in. As soon as he started the engine, she turned and started to go inside the building. But an unusual sight caught her eye.

Two soldiers were struggling along with a third, trying to get their companion across the compound. Sybil watched them for several minutes before she realized they were dressed in class A uniforms. Undoubtedly, they were just coming back from town.

At first she thought the soldier being helped was drunk, but there was something strange about him. She walked toward the trio, then noticed the man in the middle was bleeding badly. She rushed to them, pointing toward the emergency Quonset. "That way."

"Yes'm," one said drunkenly.

Sybil would have preferred a stretcher, but he had been brought this far, and it appeared that taking any amount of time would prove fatal. She led them into the room.

A duty medic, asleep with his head on a desk, stirred when they entered. "What's going on?"

"We'll find out in a minute," Sybil said. She turned to one of the men, a sergeant, and looked at him. "Well?"

"We was comin' back from—from—"

"I don't give a damn about that," Sybil snapped. "How was this man injured?"

"He was shot—by a Charlie—in an alley—or something," the sergeant mumbled. "Pr'ty bad when the bastards shoot at ya while ya're in town on pass." Then he staggered over to the wall and vomited on the floor.

Sybil snapped her fingers at the medic. "Get the duty doctor. What are you waiting for?"

The first thing Sybil did was elevate the man's feet. He was in shock, and the walking around his drunken buddies had forced on him hadn't helped out that condition nor his heavy bleeding.

She cut the injured man's shirt from his body. A cursory examination showed her a gunshot wound in the area of the heart. She hadn't time for proper measurements, but she noted shallow breathing and a weak, erratic pulse.

The doctor, yawning and lethargic, arrived. It was Captain Ryder. "Well, Lieutenant Watkins, we meet again," he said in sleepy pleasantness. "What have we got here?" He took a look, then instantly leaped to full wakefulness.

"GSW in the heart," Sybil said. "Heavy hemorrhaging in the wound."

"Give him fifty milligrams of Tetracaine and begin the epinephrine solution."

"But, doctor, we haven't scrubbed," Sybil protested.

"He'll bleed to death before infection gets him, Watkins," Ryder said. "We're going to open him up." He glanced at the drunks. "Get the hell out of here!"

They mumbled something, then staggered out the door.

Sybil was uneasy. "My OR experience—"

"—will be just fine," Ryder said. He momentarily turned his attention to the medic. "Follow the emergency procedure and alert the OR chief surgeon."

"Yes, sir!"

Sybil wasted no time in retrieving a tray of prepared surgical instruments from a nearby cabinet. She waited for further instructions.

"Let's get to work," Ryder said picking up a scalpel. "I'll need you on the retractors to hold the ribs apart."

"Yes, doctor," Sybil said.

Within moments, wearing masks and gloves, the

two bent over the patient, peering into his chest cavity. Sybil noticed the beating heart as she aided the doctor in tying off the severed arteries.

"There's the bullet," Ryder said, indicating a dull piece of metal under the heart. "Bounced off a rib—see the nicked one? If it hadn't been for that, he'd been torn up a lot worse. Well, the slug is going to work deeper into the heart muscle unless it comes out now." The doctor picked up a pair of forceps off the tray. "Now here's what I want you to do, Watkins—and be careful. Slip your hand under the heart there and gently, gently, gently lift it. I'll slide the forceps in and grasp the slug. Ready?"

Sybil gulped. "Yes, sir."

"We don't want to jostle, do we?"

"No, sir."

Sybil slid her hand into position, feeling the warm, pulsating organ. She applied easy upward pressure, watching as the forceps slipped in.

Ryder gently locked them onto the slug and slowly eased back. Then he removed them. "*Voila!*" he announced. "From my forensic experience, I'd say this was a .45 Colt."

Sybil slowly let the heart go. "Hemorrhaging again, sir."

"Right."

They bent to the task of tending the bleeding. There was more clamping and tying off until the regular surgical team arrived to take over.

Sybil stepped away from the gurney and removed the mask and gloves. "How does he look?"

"Iffy," Ryder said. "Time will tell. Once they've got him inside the OR, they can undo our damage."

"Our damage!" Sybil exclaimed.

"Just joking, Watkins, honest," Ryder said. He winked at her. "You did a great job. See you later."

He strolled away like they had just finished playing a game of croquet.

Sybil went back outside and walked back across the compound to the billets. She decided to check on Noi and the baby before going to her room.

When she walked through the door, Noi, lying on the bed, opened her eyes and sat up. "Yes? Yes, please?"

"It's me," Sybil said. She tiptoed over to the bed and peered at the baby.

Noi looked at her from across the room. "You have blood on you, Sybil. What wrong?"

"We just took care of an emergency," Sybil answered. "Has there been anybody in here lately?"

"Connie was here awhile ago. She tell me everything same."

"Sai seems to be sleeping soundly," Sybil said.

"She wake up and cry a little," Noi informed her. She slid off the bed and walked over to stand beside her American friend. "Three hour ago, maybe."

"Mmmm," Sybil acknowledged thoughtfully.

"Oh, Sybil, she hurt so bad!" Noi said, her anguish evident in her voice.

"Yes," Sybil told her. "We can only do our best and hope."

"I pray for her," Noi said.

"Me too."

"You Catholic, Sybil?"

"No," Sybil answered. "My family is Protestant."

"But Christian, no?"

"Christian, yes."

"All the same good," Noi said in her strange English.

Sybil patted her kindly on the shoulder. "I'll be back later. Get some sleep."

"Yes. Thank you, Sybil."

Sybil went back outside to the hall and walked down to her own room. Connie was asleep, her breathing regular and deep.

Sybil quietly opened her locker and began to change into a duty uniform. She was concerned about Sai. Not only personally, but with a nurse's interest. Sybil recognized she had a rather acute vocational problem. She never seemed able to be coldly clinical or to be the detached professional.

She slipped into the fatigue trousers, then went over to the sink to tend to rearranging her makeup for the coming day. There was no sense in going back to sleep, although she would have liked to take a nap. The delicious dozing in Brian's arms had been too short, though quite sweet.

Sybil looked at her face in the mirror.

And to think, she thought, I almost didn't become a nurse.

It is said that rebellion begins with but a single word: NO.

It was that way for Sybil Mae Watkins. The first year of nursing school at Wichita's Presbyterian Hospital brought about several big changes in her life and, more importantly, in her personality.

The first big thing she discovered was that she liked nursing. Evidently there had been something deep inside her that found a great deal of satisfaction in helping others. The more she delved into the profession, the more convinced she became that she'd finally found her niche in life.

That one profound discovery affected her in several ways. It made her past lifestyle seem as useless and trivial as her mother's. After comparing the worth and necessity of nurses with women who were mere ornaments and party givers for their husbands, Sybil would never be content with an ineffectual, valueless existence.

The gradual but difficult acquisition of skills nurtured her self-image and self-worth. Not only was a nurse able to care for others, Sybil quickly realized, but she could most assuredly care for herself, too.

That meant outside male authority figures, such as school principals, boyfriends, and fathers, had less influence on her. And why not? They had a lot less to offer. What was the sense in being servile to them, if they became unnecessary? When that knowledge finally sank in, Sybil began saying, "No!"

Feelings, deep and suppressed, surfaced even during the first weeks of nursing school. She began to question old values and standards that she'd been raised to automatically accept or take for granted. This caused an underlying resentment that piqued her conscious mind from the depths of her subliminal self. Surprisingly, the anger wasn't all directed toward her father; it seemed that half of that irritated resentment was for Teddy Davenport, too.

She often mused that it was too bad she had lost her virginity to Teddy before she'd turned him out of her life.

He had been up to Wichita from Norman during the Thanksgiving vacation. Her sister Henrietta, and brother-in-law Herbert Langely, had invited the young man to spend the holiday with Sybil and them in their home. There was an extra guest room he could use.

When Teddy first arrived, Bert and Henrietta were out attending a luncheon which had been planned for some air force general who was in charge of military contracts involving the aircraft company where Bert was employed.

Sybil, who stayed at home to greet Teddy, had let him in the house and had shown him to his room. Sure enough, he wasn't there five minutes before he had her jerking him off. He evidently had been saving it all up with a great deal of anticipation. Sybil couldn't remember such an intense erection or such a copious ejaculation in all the times she'd serviced him.

This was still pretty early in her first year, and her normal submissiveness was still strong despite the separation from her father. Her anger, at that particular time, was deeply suppressed and even denied by her conscious mind.

Her life with her sister and brother-in-law had been a near extension of how she lived at home. This situation was probably the catalyst for the behavior she was about to display toward Teddy. Bert and Henrietta, while having no children of their own, had definite ideas as to how a single young woman, living under their roof, should conduct herself. They weren't a bit bashful about enforcing their set of rules either. But Sybil did notice that Henrietta displayed an extraordinary fondness for drinking.

When the two returned from their social engagement, they visited with Sybil and Teddy for the remainder of the afternoon. It was obvious from their attitude that they expected no hanky-panky from the young people. Finally, after a light supper, Sybil and Teddy made their excuses to go to the movies. When the young couple went out to the car, Sybil noticed the auto's exterior was badly faded, and the seat covers inside were becoming frayed.

Teddy still had the same Buick he'd gotten from his dad a few months before the fatal heart attack. It was relatively new but deteriorating fast. Teddy wasn't used to having to take care of his cars. He'd always gotten one every year. He couldn't seem to get it through his head that he wouldn't be receiving any more free replacements.

Teddy started the engine. "I guess we'll have to look around for a private place."

Sybil looked over at him. "I thought we were going to the movies."

"That's what I said to Bert and Henrietta," Teddy said with a leer. "You know what I need."

Sybil was angry. "I just took care of you a couple of hours ago."

Teddy crudely grabbed her hand and clamped it down in his lap. "Does that feel like I'm taken care of?"

Sybil, seething inside, pulled her hand away. She stared straight out of the windshield. "I want to go to the movies, Teddy. There's a good one at the Orpheum, brand new, called *West Side Story.*"

"I don't know where that theater is anyhow," Teddy said. "You can see it later."

He drove around for almost an hour looking for a

through street out of the city before he finally blundered onto one that led them to open country. He eventually turned off a dirt side road and parked. Teddy slid over to her, taking her in his arms and kissing her quickly and sloppily on the lips.

Sybil could tell he didn't give a damn about her feelings or reactions. He was only doing what it took to get himself worked up.

"Sybil, undo your bra, okay?"

"No. It's cold."

"C'mon," he begged. His hand slid up her thigh to her panties. He fingered the hem for awhile, then slid underneath, pulling hard at her pubic hairs.

"Take 'em off," he urged her.

Sybil complied, as always, but she nourished an angry dissatisfaction that seemed to ebb and flow in a disturbing way.

He inserted his finger, wiggling it, then finally pushed her back, lifting her skirt and coat.

"Teddy!" Even though her head was down on the seat, Sybil could see him fumbling with his zipper and belt. "What are you doing?"

"This is the time, Sybil," he announced. Teddy jammed his straining erection against her with his hips undulating. Finally he penetrated slightly. "Oh, Sybil!"

"Ouch!"

He pushed harder, then entered her dry, tight vagina. The action gave her a sharp pain. Sybil could feel him sliding in and out, irritating her sensitive inner tissues. Suddenly he pulled it out and she felt the warm liquid splash on her stomach.

"I didn't want to make you pregnant," he said magnanimously. Again he fumbled with his clothing. Then he withdrew to his side of the car.

Only then did Sybil notice the ridiculous position she was in. Her skirt and coat were pulled back and bunched around her waist. One foot was up on the dashboard while the other hung over the back seat. And there was a gob of spermatic fluid sitting on her stomach. Then the thought struck her: She had been deflowered.

What a disappointment! A real disillusionment! She felt pure, unadulterated dissatisfaction and disgruntlement. There had been his hot, selfish assault, a stab of pain, then that stuff of his squirted all over her tummy.

"The Kleenex is in the glove compartment as usual," Teddy said.

Sybil got a handful of tissues and mopped her stomach. While she replaced her panties and smoothed her skirt down, she saw his stupid, smug expression.

"Take me back to the house, Teddy!"

"We have lots of time," he said languidly.

"Take me back *now!*"

"Hey, what's the matter with you? That was great, wasn't it?"

Sybil's face expressed her fury in no uncertain terms. "I said for you to take me back to the house!"

He balked at the ire directed at him. "Sure, sure. If that's what you want." He started the car. "You didn't answer me, though. How'd you like it?"

Sybil declined an answer. She remained silent all the way home. When Teddy pulled to the curb, she jumped from the car and stormed into the house with him on her heels.

Henrietta, holding a drink in her hand as always, looked puzzled at their entrance. Bert, just settling down in his recliner with the *Wichita Beacon,* displayed his own look of alarm. "Something wrong?"

"Teddy is leaving," Sybil announced.

Teddy smiled weakly. "Wait a minute, Sybil Mae."

"Get your stuff and get out of here!" she shouted at him.

"Sybil Mae!" Teddy exclaimed in surprised anger. "It cost me a lot of money to drive up here. I won't be able to see you again until this spring."

Sybil, her lips compressed in rage, spoke in a near growl. "Go away! And I don't want to see you this spring—or ever!"

Bert, a bit unsure of himself but feeling this was the time for him to display himself as the lord and master of his home, struggled to his feet. "You'd better do as she says," he announced. "This can be straightened out later."

Henrietta's voice was a bit slurred. "What the hell happened between you two?"

Sybil, her face a mask of angry frustration, glared at Teddy with such intense dislike that he said nothing else.

Henrietta, sipping her drink and displaying a silly grin, looked at Sybil. Bert, still standing in pudgy confusion, said nothing.

Within ten minutes, Teddy had reappeared with his bags in hand. He looked at Sybil with a superior, condescending expression on his face. "Now, Sybil Mae," he said in a placating tone. "Let's just calm down—"

"Get the hell out of here!"

Teddy went to the door and opened it. He paused to

make his exit more dramatic. "I won't stand to be treated like this, Sybil Mae. Either you calm down or we're through. And I mean it!"

"Go away. Go far, far away," Sybil said in an irritated undertone.

"All right. That's it then!" Teddy went through the door, displaying more of his disdain by leaving it open.

Sybil walked over and kicked it shut.

Henrietta giggled. "What's the matter? Didn't you like the movie?"

Wordlessly, Sybil went upstairs to her room.

That was the first of three acts of defiance Sybil was to perform before her nursing school days were over.

The second involved Bert and Henrietta.

Bert, himself, was harmless enough. A hard charger, he was in a well-paid management position at one of Wichita's numerous defense plants. Completely wrapped up in his work, he spent long hours away from home, and there were monthly business trips, too. Most consisted of a week or so.

Henrietta, bored to tears and fading fast at age twenty-five, had been married to Bert for seven years. She spent most of her days in an alcoholic haze. With her hair in curlers, wearing a flannel housecoat, she wandered her home with drink in hand. The three television sets, one each in the living room, the basement game room, and the bedroom, were always on. Henrietta went unsteadily from one to the other most of the day, taking a break only to mix a fresh drink or collapse into a nap on the sofa.

It would have been obvious, even to the most casual observer, that the two young women were sisters. They looked alike in facial features and coloring, but the resemblance faded on closer examination. Henrietta's face was puffy with circles under her eyes. Growing thick around the middle, she was putting on weight in a slow but undeniably steady manner. Five years previously, when she first started fighting her boredom with the bottle, she had been a quiet, rather pleasant drunk. But now, as the need for alcohol began to become a physical dependency and mental crutch, a new side of her personality emerged.

Henrietta had the capability of being nasty.

The first run-in between the sisters occurred in the early part of the spring semester of Sybil's first year. Sybil returned home from school late one afternoon to find Henrietta, drunk as a street slattern, leaning unsteadily on the wall outside her bedroom. She held a glass containing her favorite drink—a strong vodka martini.

Sybil, curious about the interest in her room, gave her older sister a quizzical look. "Hi, Henrietta. What's going on?"

"Looka that room!"

Sybil peered in. She'd been late that morning and had hurried off without making her bed. Aside from that, the place didn't look bad. "Something the matter?"

"The goddamn room's a mess!" Henrietta exclaimed in her slurred voice. Then she staggered inside, expressing the enormity of the crime with a wide gesture of her arms. "It's a goddamn, rotten mess!"

Sybil was a bit alarmed about the erratic behavior. "Now, Henrietta," she said soothingly. "It's not that bad."

"*You little bitch!*" Henrietta shrieked, whirling around drunkenly to face her. She stood wavering, with unfocused glazed eyes, in silence for another minute or so. "The goddamn room's a mess."

Then she brushed past Sybil and left her alone.

Henrietta was not at supper that night. She was passed out on her bed, lost in the deep swirling fog produced by the drinks she'd consumed that day. The next morning, a bit worse for wear, she seemed her old self at breakfast.

Sybil gave her a stern look. "I made my bed this morning."

Henrietta smiled in curiosity. "Really? Are you expecting a gold star or something?"

"Well, you were so upset that I didn't make it yesterday, I wanted to make sure you knew everything was tidy and straightened up today."

"Sybil Mae! What in the world are you talking about?"

"And I don't appreciate being referred to as a bitch," Sybil added tartly.

Henrietta could not recall one word about the yelling and raging of the day before. It was a situation that was to become the norm around the house.

Henrietta, drunk and enraged, would scream and curse at Sybil over trivial matters—either real or imagined—but the next day would not only not recall the incidences but deny they had taken place.

Sybil bore up under the difficult situation as best she could, but things came to a head late one evening. Bert, as usual, was out of town, and Sybil was up in her room preparing for a difficult anatomy test scheduled for the next day. Her concentration was abruptly broken by Henrietta's entrance into her room.

Sybil turned from her work and looked at the intoxicated woman swaying in the doorway. "Yes, Henrietta?" She made no effort to hide her exasperation.

"Y'better leave 'im 'lone, you little slut!"

"What in the world are you talking about now?"

Henrietta, reeling badly, stumbled forward a few steps. "I'm not fooled a bit. You're throwing yourself at Bert, arncha? Huh? Gonna take my man, little sis'er? Huh? Izzat what you want? Huh? You wan' my man, huh? Huh?"

"Oh, my God, Henrietta!" Sybil cried. "Are you out of your mind?"

"I'll pack your li'l ass back to Okl'oma City, tha's what I'll do," Henrietta threatened.

That was too much.

Sybil wasted no time in making the proper arrangements. Without even bothering to contact her father, she moved into the student nurse dormitory at the hospital. He would find out about it when her school costs went up.

The third and final step in Sybil's rebellion occurred at home between the first and second year of school. With Teddy completely out of the picture now, Doyle Watkins had achieved his goal in that situation. He made an announcement to his daughter on a warm summer afternoon. Sybil was sitting in the gazebo reviewing a few books she would be studying during the next semester.

"There you are," Watkins said. "I've been looking all over for you, Sybil Mae."

"What do you want, Daddy?"

"Nothing real important. I just wanted to let you know you won't have to go back to that nursing school next year," he told her. "Good news, hey?"

Sybil, her mouth wide open, dropped her book, "That's *awful* news, Daddy! Why aren't I going back?"

Doyle, angrily puzzled, frowned at her. "Because there's no reason for you to. Are you crazy or something? You didn't want to go there in the first place."

"But I want to go back now, Daddy," Sybil said. "I want to be a nurse. I truly do."

"That's silly," Watkins said. "Nursing's a fine profession for some women, but you're not one of them."

Sybil stood up defiantly. "I'm first in my class, Daddy."

"Oh, darling, you're always first in your class," Watkins said with a laugh. "Ever since your kindergarten days at Kennedy. But nursing isn't for girls like you. You'll be settled back into your old life real quick. And you'll like it, too." He gave her a rare show of affection – a fatherly pat on the shoulder. "And you'll meet a fine young man, too. That means enjoying parties and dances again."

"I'll *hate* it!" Sybil exclaimed. "I don't want to be an empty-headed ornament on some bozo's arm! I'm going back to nursing school."

"You are not!"

"I am too!"

"Well, little lady, I'm not going to pay a dime towards it," Doyle announced. "And that puts an end to any further argument." He gave her a final look that registered both surprise and anger, then walked rapidly away from the gazebo.

Sybil, dejected, slowly sank back to the bench. There was no way she could finance her way through Wichita Presbyterian. The demands of the curriculum were such that it required full-time devotion to studies. It would be impossible to hold a job somewhere and maintain the high degree of scholarship required.

Sybil sighed—then suddenly brightened as a very important fact dawned on her. Not only could a nurse take care of herself, but so could a *student* nurse under certain circumstances.

Smiling happily, Sybil hurried into the house and up to her room to write a meaningful letter.

It was addressed to the school's scholarship committee. Her grades qualified her for several of the school's financial aid programs. By getting on one, she would have enough money to get her through the rest of the course. It was the greatest triumph she had enjoyed in her life up to date. Better than honor roles, straight A's or anything else.

And she'd met the qualifications on her own.

But, in the end, Sybil never did have to use the money from the school. When Doyle Watkins saw how determined his youngest daughter was to become a nurse, he gave in and paid her way. He tried to save face by insisting she live with Bert and Henrietta, but Sybil was adamant. She would attend school and live in the dormitory.

Watkins gave in, but he wasn't happy. He lamented his disgruntlement over a late supper with his wife Laura on the night Sybil went back to Wichita. "You know," he mused, "somebody or something up there is sure changing that little girl around."

Sybil finished the first two years of her course, then moved into the advanced phase. This meant she served as an apprentice of sorts under the supervision of working nurses in the regular part of the hospital, while attending classes between work stints. It was terribly demanding. Sybil had little spare time after shifts on various wards and class time which required studying hard for assignments and tests.

It was unpleasant on various occasions, too. The emergency room, with its victims of auto accidents, sudden illness, and crime showed her the seamier sides of life. When this was interspersed with working on cadavers during labs, Sybil knew if she could stick that out, she really had what it took.

But she wasn't prepared to meet the emotional side of nursing, and this, above all, brought about her first moment of truth in the nursing profession.

The patient's name was Nellie Simpson.

Nellie was a seventy-five-year-old woman going through the terrible process of slowly dying from breast cancer. The woman had never known that the lumps in her breasts had any special meaning. They'd been there for years, not causing any pain, so she never concerned herself. It was only when they became sore, that she finally availed herself of medical care. But, by then, it was too late.

Nellie was all alone in the world, with no visitors or letters, as she lay on those stark white sheets growing weaker day by day.

Sybil always found time to drop by Nellie's bed for a little chat. The strength of the small woman amazed her, and one day she commented on it. Nellie smiled, her wrinkled face still displaying character despite the debilitating sickness that was taking her life. "We got to be strong whar I come from, Sybil Mae. If'n yew ain't, yew don't live long to begin with."

"You wouldn't mind telling me about yourself, would you, Nellie? We've spent a lot of time visiting, but I hardly know a thing about you, other than what's on your hospital records," Sybil said. "But you don't have to tell me if you don't want to. I know it's probably none of my business."

"Now don't yew talk like that, Sybil Mae. Yo're a kindly young woman," Nellie said, laying a thin hand on the young nurse's arm. "I don't mind a bit."

"I'd like to know about the place you're from, and what family you had."

"Ain't much to talk about, child," Nellie said. "And it starts such a long time ago."

"I want you to tell me about it," Sybil begged.

"Wal, sure, if'n yo're inter'sted," Nellie said smiling weakly.

She had come up from Wichita from Arkansas with her husband at the outset of World War II. Monroe Simpson had spent his life trying to beat a living out of the hard, rocky ground of a hillside farm in the Ozarks. Nellie, as undereducated and unread as her husband, brought five children into the world. All had been born in their primitive cabin, watched over by a mountain midwife. One died in childbirth, two didn't make it past their third year, but two of the boys did survive the unsanitary conditions and malnourishment to make it to adulthood.

It seemed the Simpsons, like all their neighbors, were doomed to spend their days in the awful poverty they endured, bearing the perpetual hard times in that mean, confining environment.

Then a wandering cousin made a rare visit home. He didn't talk about the grand, mind-boggling sights of the great cities that he'd seen, nor of their museums or libraries. He told the people of the things they could relate to. About folks stacked one on top of the other in rundown tenement neighborhoods, of tough cops, and crummy bosses who treated a man like hell while overworking and underpaying him. But he also told of a developing situation where even people from rural Arkansas could finally find the good life. The big war was on, and there was plenty of work. The closest place to them was up in Wichita, Kansas where Boeing Aircraft, among others, had a big plant.

Sybil nodded. "So that's how you came here?"

"Oh, yes. We wasn't young, yew unnerstand, Sybil Mae. Monroe was 'bout fifty or so, and he din't know a blessed thang other'n farmin'. But, Lord help us, he found work as a janitor at Boeing."

"Was that better than the farm in Arkansas?" Sybil asked.

Nellie laughed weakly. "Child, we thought we'd died and went to heaven!"

"The job worked out real well for your husband, did it?"

"Sure," Nellie said. "We lived over to Plainview and had a li'l ol' house the guv'ment give us to live in. War'nt big, but it was sure fixed up nice. Roof din't leak and they was this li'l ol' stove in it that kept it so nice and warm of a cold winter's day."

"Then you made it through the war years okay then?" Sybil asked.

"Yeah, we did," Nellie said. " 'Cept that our oldest boy Richard got killed a-fightin' the Japs. He'd been in the navy fer quite a few y'ars, and had him a wife out to San Diego. But we never heard from her or nothin'. I prob'ly got grandkids somewhar's out west."

Sybil admired the strength the woman showed.

"What about the other child, Nellie? You said two grew up."

The old woman's face clouded over. "That'd be R.J. He's in the penitentiary, Sybil, in Illinois this time. I prayed fer the boy, but it didn't do no good. He was in trouble even back in Arkansas. He got hisself a streak o' mean that just won't leave him be. I reckon he's known more jail than freedom."

"That's too bad," Sybil said.

"Nothin's perfect, child, least of all life. I lost Monroe two y'ars after the war come to a end," Nellie said.

"I'm sorry about that," Sybil said.

"I couldn't take keer of myse'f," Nellie said with a shamed smile. "I went on the county. They put me in a hotel down on East Douglas near the railroad depot."

"That must have been awful!"

"Oh, 't'warn't too bad. Yew take what it gives you and trust in the Lord."

Then Nellie had wanted to hear all about Sybil and her own family. Sybil kept the story short, not only because her rather pampered life seemed insipid and shamefully soft in comparison to Nellie's but also because the old woman had grown tired and needed to sleep.

Sybil left her and went out in the hall. The supervisor of nurses called her over to the nurses' station. The woman was a heavy, cheerful sort, named Miss Barker. But that day her expression was serious.

"You've become quiet fond of Nellie, haven't you?"

Sybil nodded with a sad smile. "I truly am."

"I want to give you a bit of advice, Sybil Mae," Miss Barker said. "Not an order, understand, just a friendly hint from an older nurse to a young one."

"I would appreciate that, Miss Barker."

"I think you should avoid Nellie."

Sybil shook her head. "Oh, I couldn't!"

"I'll even see to a transfer for you," the supervisor said.

"But why, Miss Barker?"

"Sybil Mae," the supervisor said with a kindly tone. "You're about to head for your first heartbreaker."

"What do you mean, ma'am?"

"That's my term for a situation that involves a terminal patient that one grows very fond of," the supervisor said. "Nellie is dying."

"I know," Sybil said.

"You're going to lose her."

Sybil felt a catch in her throat. "Yes—yes—"

"It's going to be a terrible time for you."

Sybil, who had pushed the thought back so far in her mind that she angrily denied its existence to herself, nodded. "I'll be ready. Please don't transfer me, Miss Barker."

"Whatever you want, dear. I hope you'll be emotionally ready for it. But it'll be no comfort to you when you fully realize it's not going to be the first time."

That was Sybil's premier lesson that candor, while painful, is always the best tactic in the nursing profession.

There were to be other conversations and visits with Nellie Simpson. Later, remembering them, Sybil considered them one of the most important phases of her education—as valuable as any textbook or lecture. After a privileged childhood, with the best things that money could buy taken for granted, this exposure to soul-grinding poverty and terrible circumstances in which to live—and die, provided an opening for Sybil's intellect to grow.

Nellie was an ignorant woman, no doubt, but somehow the holes in her meager knowledge had been filled with a simple dignity and acceptance of the way things were. This gave stark evidence that people like the Simpsons would always be around, because it was their simplicity and rawness that gave them the greatest of all animal traits: survivability.

Dignity, the type that could never be beaten down, also played a large part in their makeup.

Nellie, dying with tubes shoved into her wasted body from every conceivable angle, hung on to it. Her eyes were steady and proud, with a trusting in her Maker that impressed even a casual churchgoer like Sybil. The religion was like Nellie's life—fundamental and basic—with an unquestioning but rock-strong acceptance of the message in the scriptures that gave courage and strength in the worst of circumstances.

Nellie Simpson was dying. She knew she was dying, but the frail, little old woman hadn't the slightest fear about it.

There were evenings when Sybil would do something she'd never before done in all her life. She would neglect her studies. This time was spent at Nellie's bedside, holding her hand, listening to her, talking to her, and loving her so much it seemed Sybil's heart was going to break. This was the first truly unselfish person the little rich girl had ever met.

Nellie died on a bleak February winter's day.

The funeral cost was born by the county, and Nellie was put to rest in a little cemetery on the edge of Wichita. The only people present was a preacher—who made extra money doing that sad duty—and Sybil, who had brought a single rose along. Nellie had once remarked that roses were her favorite flowers.

The ceremony was brief, with a cold wind whipping around the tombstones and whistling through the stark, leafless limbs of the few dormant trees scattered throughout the graveyard.

After the minister left, Sybil stood with one hand lightly holding the flower and the other shoved deep into her overcoat, looking down at the cheap coffin. She had felt deep grief, but it gradually disappeared as an aura of contentment swept over. Sybil was happy Nellie's suffering was over, and she truly hoped that the woman's religious beliefs would turn out to be true. Somehow, she found comfort in thinking that Nellie Simpson was in that heaven she'd spoken of so many times. "A-singin' with the angels and a-gloryin' in the presence of the Lord."

Sybil was also happy that she'd known Nellie Simpson, and felt her own life fuller because of it.

It was that moment, too, that she fully realized her decision to become a nurse had been the right one for her.

"Excuse us, Miss."

Sybil turned to see a couple of gravediggers standing rather impatiently with their shovels.

"We gotta fill it in now."

"All right," Sybil said. She looked back at the grave, then dropped the rose in. Then she turned and walked away—back to nursing.

Chapter Ten

Sybil finished brushing her hair, then caught the reflected sight of Connie in the mirror. The Chicana had evidently just awakened and was watching her with sleepy disinterest.

Sybil turned and smiled. "It's not time to get up yet. But too late for me to get into bed."

Connie yawned, then checked the alarm clock on the desk that sat between their beds. "Just getting in?"

"Guilty as charged!'

"Well—as the boys say—did you get lucky?"

Sybil walked to the chair by the desk and sat down. "I never kiss and tell."

Connie sat up, coming awake. "Well you just better this time! I'm going to die if I'm not kept up to date on this romance."

"Okay," Sybil said smiling. "But let's wait until there's a chance for a nice long talk."

Connie was reluctant but agreed. "I'll give in this

time." She turned serious. "Have you checked on Sai yet?"

"Just a few minutes ago," Sybil answered. "She's resting comfortably."

"*Pobrecita!* Poor little thing," Connie said. "Never did anything wrong to a soul, and look how she's suffering. She'll be badly scarred on her torso, you know."

"Yes. Plastic surgery is out of the question."

"Is it? Having her recover in our billets was out of the question, too," Connie reminded her.

"Let's take one thing at a time," Sybil insisted. "When the time is right, we'll circumvent Mother Moorehead's authority on that issue. Right now, all I want to have to worry about is her survival."

"Colonel Sedgewick came in and checked on her last night," Connie said. "He's quite a guy."

"It's strange how he's our commanding officer, but we don't even know him."

"That's the way he is," Connie said. "Withdrawn and introverted. I tried to get him into a conversation but I didn't have much luck. He's a nice old guy, but will only go so far with small talk, then he cuts it off."

"What's that old saying? Familarity breeds contempt. Maybe he's a strong believer in that."

"They say it's lonely at the top," Connie said. "I think the good colonel prefers it that way. Though I must admit he's certainly been warm and caring around that baby."

"Noi seems to be taking it pretty hard," Sybil remarked. "When I walked in there she jumped straight up out of that bed like a shot."

"Can't blame her, Sybil. That baby girl is all she has

in the world. I'm afraid Noi will be utterly destroyed if the child dies," Connie said.

"I'm afraid you're right," Sybil agreed.

Connie threw the sheet back and sat up, swinging her feet over the side of the bed and setting them down on the floor. She wore a shorty nightgown that came down to mid-thigh. She wiggled her limbs. "You think I have pretty legs?"

"Sure. You worried about them getting fat?"

"Constantly," Connie said. She glanced carefully at Sybil with an appraising look. "You have nice pins." Connie laughed. "Even if they are real hairy."

"Hey!"

"Just joking," Connie said. "I might as well get up."

"Have any of the nurses besides yourself checked on our patient?" Sybil asked.

"Lord, yes! Noi and Sai have become unofficially adopted by the nursing staff," Connie said. "It's great the way somebody is always stopping by and checking things out."

"Let's hope they don't become too helpful and disturb the baby," Sybil said. "Or neglect their duties and get more of Mother Moorehead's most unwelcome attention."

Connie smirked. "She got put down in a most emphatic manner, Sybil. Which means you're on her *mierda* list."

"You made the meaning of that word clear enough so that no translation will be necessary," Sybil said with a laugh.

"What really matters is the baby," Connie said.

"Speaking of babies—that Ernie is really on my mind."

"For heaven's sake, why?"

"The Kool-Aid."

Connie shrugged. "What does that have to do with anything? So he gives us the stuff his mom sends him. That's no big deal."

"But why was he buying it at the PX too?" Sybil asked. "It doesn't make sense."

Connie went to her locker and got her toilet articles. "Maybe he's just crazy about the stuff."

"Not that much, he isn't," Sybil insisted. "The trouble with this damned army is that you can become real close friends with somebody, yet only have superficial knowledge of their background. I'd like to find out more about him."

"Go look at his Two-oh-one File," Connie suggested.

"What's that?"

Connie laughed. "It's easy to tell you haven't had a mess of brothers in the service. That's the folder that has his records in it. Everything's there—military career, civilian background, education, and so on. You name it, it's there. You have one, too. It's that cardboard contraption they send around with you wherever you go."

Sybil felt a little embarrassed. "I've been in the army almost a year, and I still have lots to learn. Where do I find this file?"

"In the sergeant major's office," Connie said.

"Fat chance that big goon is going to let me look at somebody's private records," Sybil said.

"Rafferty won't be there yet. Tell the CQ you have to check on something or other," Connie said.

"Like what?"

"Use your head. Sometimes you're too open and honest for your own good," Connie complained good-naturedly. "Tell the guy a bunch of medics are going to be picked for something or other like some special classes, and you want to check their qualifications."

Sybil, smiling happily, grabbed her hat. "Yeah!"

"Look at the DA Form-Twenty first," Connie advised her. "It's a thick, yellow sheet of cardboard that has a lot of stuff on it. It might save you from having to dig further."

"Thank you. I'll see you on the ward," Sybil said going out the door. She walked down the hall in time to see another nurse tiptoe out of the improvised ICU. "How's the baby?" she asked even though it had only been a short time since she'd seen it.

"Sleeping fitfully," the nurse said. "Weak pulse and running a temperature. But what else can you expect?"

"Not much I guess," Sybil said.

She hurried from the billets across the compound to the headquarters Quonset. The unit was quiet at that particular time of day, but like any military organization, there was always somebody performing some sort of duty.

A bored sentry, slowly walking back and forth at his post, took dull notice of her, then turned back to the monotonous plodding as he waited for the hour of his relief to come.

Sybil went into the hut. The charge-of-quarters, wearing a brassard with the letters CQ around one brawny arm, was pouring himself a cup of coffee. The CQ's job was passed around among the noncommissioned officers on a regular basis. The task required them to stay in the headquarters Quonset to take messages, check the area during the night, and, in general, be in charge after the normal duty hours.

"Good morning," Sybil said.

"Oh, hi, lieutenant. How ya doin'?" The man, a sergeant in one of the medical platoons, seemed glad to have some company after the long night. "Whattaya need?"

"I need to look at the—the Two hundred File folders," Sybil said. She couldn't remember exactly what Connie had said.

"The what?"

"The enlisted men's files."

"Oh! The Two-oh-one Files," the sergeant said grinning. "Sure. They're right over there in the big gray filing cabinet."

Sybil walked over and pulled the drawer marked A–K. "There's some special school coming up and we want to pick somebody who's qualified," she explained. She turned to say more, but the man had walked out of the room. Glad to be alone, she pulled Ernie's file out and opened it.

The yellow Form Twenty, the squares and lines filled in by various clerks who had handled it during the young man's time in the army, told of the training he had received, the places he was stationed, and other data. Sybil checked the next-of-kin box. Her eyes opened wide. She put the form aside and thumbed through the other papers clamped together on the thick folder until she reached the Statement of Personal History File.

Sybil read every bit of information there. It was neatly typed, with certain boxes bearing Ernie's stilted handwriting where he had been required to personally verify the data there by initialing it.

"Oh, Ernie!" she sighed softly after finishing.

She put the papers back into the folder, then replaced it in the proper order between the Two-oh-one Files of Johnson, Arnold T. and Kendell, Roger G.

When she closed the cabinet drawer, the charge-of-quarters had returned to the room. His voice was cheerful. "Find what you were lookin' for, lieutenant?"

"Definitely nothing I like, sergeant," Sybil said. "Thanks."

"You can get more stuff up at brigade in personnel," he informed her. "I got a buddy that works up there if you need any help."

"Thanks," Sybil said solemnly. "I'll keep that in mind."

She decided against breakfast, instead going straight to the ward. Penny Darwin, surprised to see her, inquired after Noi and Sai.

"Still critical," Sybil said. She took a seat. "Go ahead and leave if you want, Penny. I'm in the mood to start early today."

"Hey, thanks!"

"That's okay. I owe you, anyway," Sybil said.

"I'm still appreciative," Penny said. She checked her watch. "Sampson will be here any minute to wake up the ward. The chow wagon will be around in a half-hour."

"Right. See you later, Penny."

Sybil watched the other nurse leave, then looked out at the men sleeping on the ward. Ernie reentered her thoughts, and she felt a momentary sadness combined with curiosity.

"Hey, Lieutenant Watkins!" It was Joe Sampson. The black medic gave her a friendly grin. "What're you doin' here so early?"

"I'm just too restless to sleep," Sybil replied.

"That's what I call a good attitude," Sampson said cheerfully. "Well, it's time to get this show on the road." He walked onto the ward and began to wake up the men.

The ambulatory patients slowly eased their way out of bed. Their wounds and injuries, which had stiffened during the night, prevented graceful movement. They shuffled slowly and painfully toward the ward latrine, their ditty bags shoved under their arms. Some showed a dull surprise at seeing Sybil at that hour, giving her nods or little waves of greeting.

"Snap it up, ambulatories," Joe said. He turned toward the others. "Bedpans," he called out. "Get your bedpans! Red-hot bedpans!"

The men confined to the beds, most no longer embarrassed about the clumsy method of handling nature's call, either asked for one of the devices or indicated they had a full one to turn in.

Mike Pullini, in the back, made an impatient gesture. "Better hurry, Joe. I gotta piss so bad my back teeth are floating."

"Tie a knot in it 'til I get there," Joe said hurrying up. Then he laughed. "Though I don't think you white boys got enough to do that."

There were catcalls and jeers as black and white patients responded in kind to the good-natured jibe.

Sybil heard it and her mind turned to the way in which the young males of the species acted. So macho at times, even when badly hurt; and their humor, ninety percent of which had some sexual connotation or other, bolstered them through times of trouble, pain, and fearful uncertainty. Yet, on other occasions, they were so vulnerable and easily hurt. Then there was the one strange little guy that salved his emotions with Kool-Aid of all things.

Within a half-hour, the men were shaved and washed up as best as could be accomplished amidst the bandages, splints, and plasters of casts. They seemed to be in relatively good moods, the banter between them light and cheery. The chow wagon, actually a mobile steam cabinet, was pushed in, laden with prepared breakfasts.

This was the signal for catcalls and hoots that were directed at the Vietnamese man who had brought their food. He was used to it, though, and took it all with smiles and his own wisecracks delivered in broken English. The ambulatory patients, those with two good hands, fetched trays for their fellows who couldn't fend for themselves. After the most disabled were cared for, the others settled in for their breakfasts.

The morning's menu consisted of milk, orange juice, coffee, scrambled eggs, sausage, and toast. Even though Sybil hadn't eaten since dinner with Brian the night before, the smell of the hot food couldn't stimulate her appetite.

A half-hour after the food had been consumed, the trays removed, and the morning cleaning routine completed, Connie arrived on the ward at the same time Joe Sampson took off for other duties.

"Hey, I was waiting for you in the mess hall," she said to Sybil.

"I wasn't hungry this morning," Sybil said. "So I

came over early and relieved Penny."

"I'll bet she was glad of that," Connie said. She looked around the ward. "Where's that dopey Ernie?"

"He's not dopey!" Sybil snapped.

Connie looked at her, a puzzled frown dancing across her features. *"Oye!* What's this? I'd say you got out of bed on the wrong side this morning, but you didn't sleep in it. At least not your own."

"Oh, Lord, Connie. I'm sorry," Sybil said.

"Nothing wrong in the romance department, I hope. Maybe we should have that talk now."

"No. Everything's just fine there," Sybil acknowledged.

"Glad to hear that," Connie said. "Now the next thing I want to talk about is why you're so down in the dumps."

"Is it obvious?"

"It sure is," Connie insisted.

"Well, I went over—"

"Mornin'." Ernie slumped into the office.

"Hi, Ernie," Connie said. "Listen up. Our best friend here is in a bad mood. She's about to enlighten us as to why."

"Never mind," Sybil said.

"Come on, Sybil," Connie urged her.

"Never mind!"

"Jeez! Okay," Connie said. "Maybe we better get to work." She nudged Ernie. "Watch out, kid, or you'll end up getting your head snapped off."

"Yeah," Ernie said in a detached way.

"Ay Dios de mi vida!" Connie exclaimed. "You too? And what's your problem?"

"Nothin'." Ernie got up. "I better take the temps

and pulses." He got the record cart and wheeled it out of the office.

Connie raised her hands in exasperation and dropped them to her sides. "Boy, are you two going to be fun today!"

Sybil wordlessly turned to the daily paperwork.

Connie, a naturally peppy and happy person, endured her friends' sullen moods until after doctor's rounds. During the quiet period between that event and the serving of the noon meal, she called them into the ward office. When they had both complied with her request, she closed the door and turned to face them.

"You two are driving me *loca*—crazy—you know? Now we're practically the Three Musketeers even if we haven't known each other very long. And I want to be put wise—wait! Let me put it another way—I *demand* to be put wise about what the hell's troubling everybody." She pointed at Ernie. "You first."

"There ain't nothin' wrong," he mumbled.

"Ernest Kaznowski!" Connie yelled.

He stuck his hands in his pockets and stared out over the ward.

"I'm going to ask you one more time," Connie said with a strong determined tone in her voice. "What the hell is bugging you?"

"I got the clap."

"You little idiot!" Connie exclaimed. "What symptoms do you have?"

"I'm runnin' and it burns when I piss," Ernie announced artlessly and directly.

"For God's sake, Ernie!" Sybil hissed. She went to the phone and picked it up, waiting for the switchboard operator to answer. When he did, she spoke tersely. "VD clinic."

"What're you gonna do?" Ernie asked sullenly.

"I'm in pretty good with the head nurse there," Sybil said. "We'll get you the royal treatment—fast." She started to say more, but the voice on the other end indicated she'd gotten the correct party. After speaking for a couple of minutes she hung up. "She'll be waiting to look after you. Ask for Lieutenant Belknap."

"Awright," Ernie said. He walked up to the door and turned to face Connie. "Can I go out now?"

"Yes, you little idiot from Juicy Lucy's," Connie said. She watched him leave with a shaking head. Her gaze, the Latin eyes flashing, turned to Sybil. "Now let's find out what's driving *you* around the bend."

"I looked up Ernie's Two-oh-one File," Sybil said.

"And?"

"He's a foundling."

"Say that one more time."

"He's an orphan, Connie. He has no family."

"How can that be?" Connie asked. "His mother sends him packages with Kool-Aid and other goodies all the time."

"It's true. Every piece of paper that lists next-of-kin shows that Ernie has none," Sybil said. "He was raised in foster homes in Chicago. A quick check of home addresses listed in his file indicates dozens of them, Connie, dozens! I couldn't even count them all."

"Ay, Chihuahua!" Connie said. "Come to think of it, I've never seen any of those so-called packages from home."

"Me neither," Sybil said.

"You mean he's been buying that Kool-Aid at the

PX, then coming in here with it and telling us that his mother sent it to him, huh?"

"It seems that way," Sybil said.

"Maybe he has a sister or an aunt or something?"

"Connie, I'm telling you the little guy has no next-of-kin. Nobody—zilch—he's without family."

Connie sat down. "But why Kool-Aid? Why not cookies or cakes or something like that?"

"Too hard to fake?" Sybil suggested.

"Maybe. But if all he shows are packets of Kool-Aid, then why not fruitcakes or packages of other goodies, like candy? What in the hell is so fascinating to the guy about Kool-Aid?"

"I intend to find out," Sybil announced.

Connie frowned uncertainly. "Maybe you shouldn't, Sybil."

"Of course I am. We're all close, aren't we? I most certainly am going to get him to tell us why he's deceived us about something like that all this time."

"We've only known each other three months," Connie cautioned her. "And putting the situation into the concept of being a deception might be going too far. Anyhow, maybe he'll tell us after awhile."

Sybil was adamant. "I'm not going to wait."

"There could be some terrible, dark secret we'd be prying into *amigita,*" Connie cautioned her.

"As soon as he gets back from the VD clinic, I—that is, *we*—are going to talk to him about it and get down to the bottom of the situation."

Connie was thoughtful. "That might not be for a couple of hours. You can change your mind between then and now."

"No way," Sybil said.

"You might with me nagging you."

Sybil checked her watch. "Almost time for the noon chow wagon."

The ward's midday eating routine took almost three-quarters of an hour. It was a repeat of breakfast, except the menu had been changed. Sybil tended to her duties with impatient glances at the ward door waiting for Ernie to return. She had just finished bandaging Mike Pullini when he reappeared.

Connie, adjusting an abductor pillow on a hip wound in the next bed, looked up at his entrance. "He's back."

Ernie spotted them and waved. He hurried down to the two nurses, a happy grin dancing across his young face. "Guess what?"

"Mmmph!" Connie smirked. "You're dying of a terminal venereal illness, right!"

"Wrong! I got strain," Ernie said proudly. "That comes from bein' too sexually active in a short period of time. So there!"

Mike Pullini showed a little interest. "What happened to you?"

"I thought I'd caught the clap, man. I had all the symptoms and ever'thing," Ernie explained.

Mike smiled. "I wish that was my problem."

"Don't worry, pal," Ernie said with a wink. "It will be real soon."

"You're depraved," Sybil said gathering up the soiled bandages she had just replaced.

Ernie ignored her. "Hey, Mike, while I'm here I got a question about bench pressin', okay?"

"Oh, hell. All right."

"I ain't makin' hardly any progress or nothin',

y'know? What's wrong? I been workin' out on the schedule I was gave."

"What kind of a workout are you doing?" Mike asked.

"All kinds of presses," Ernie said. "Lemme think – I do inclines, military presses, dumbbell bench press – "

Connie burst out laughing. "That's you all over. A dumbbell doing bench presses."

Ernie frowned. "Hey! This is serious. Okay?" He turned to Mike. "So?"

"You're skinny," Mike said. "And probably weak in the tricep muscles. Do dips on the parallel bars. Captain Gavin can show you how. That'd strengthen up the muscles in the back of your arms."

"The triceps, I know what they are," Ernie said. "You don't have to say in the back o' the arm. I'm a medic, y'know."

Sybil nudged him. "Well, medic, get down to the ward office. Connie and I want to talk to you."

Ernie walked with her up to the front. "Hey, lay off, okay? I tole you I got strain. If you don't believe me just ask your friend Belknap. She'll back me up."

"That's not what we want to talk to you about," Sybil said. She glanced back to make sure Connie was following.

When the three arrived at the office, Sybil stood aside while her friends entered. Then she followed them in and shut the door. Ernie grinned at her. "We've been doing that a lot today."

"Wc have something to discuss," Connie said.

"Oh, Jeez!" Ernie exclaimed in exasperation. "Is this the *You Shouldn't Go to Juicy Lucy's Lecture Number Six?"*

"No," Sybil said. "We want to talk about Kool-Aid."

"Kool-Aid?" Ernie asked. "Have you drunk up what I gave you already? Well, don't sweat the small stuff. My ma'll send some more in a coupla days."

"Where are you getting that Kool-Aid, Ernie?" Sybil asked.

"You know. My ma sends it to me."

"You buy it at the PX."

"I do not!"

Connie appeared a bit nervous. She crossed her arms and leaned against the closed door, idly tapping one foot on the floor while she watched the proceedings with controlled anxiety.

Sybil sat down on the edge of the desk. "I saw you, Ernie. Just the other day when I went over there with Brian."

"I might've been buyin' somethin', but it wasn't Kool-Aid," Ernie said defensively. "You crazy or somethin', Sybil? What're you doin', lookin' over my shoulder?"

Sybil reached down and pulled open the desk drawer exposing several packages of the drink mix. "That stuff came from the PX."

"My mother sent it!"

"Your mother's whereabouts are unknown," Sybil said. "Or she is deceased."

"What?" Ernie asked angrily. "Are you crazy? That's a hell of a thing to say about a guy's ma!"

Connie felt terrible misgivings, but she wanted to back up Sybil. "Tell us about it, Ernie."

He became stupidly evasive. "About what?"

"About yourself," Connie said.

"I'm Ernie Kaznowski and I'm a specialist fourth grade in the U.S. Army," Ernie said. He affected a grin. "And I'm real good lookin'. Anything else you want to know?"

"Yes," Sybil said. "We want to know about your mother."

"What about her?" Ernie asked.

"Yes, Ernie," Connie said softly. "What about her?"

Ernie started to speak again, a defiant grin on his lips, but suddenly his mouth quivered. He abruptly turned away and walked to the window to stare out at the compound outside.

All three friends were silent for several very long moments.

Finally Ernie turned and pulled his wallet from his back pocket. He fumbled through it, then produced a small piece of notebook paper encased in plastic. He handed it to Sybil.

"What's this?" she asked.

"Read it."

Sybil looked down at it. There was a single sentence written there in faded pencil. The handwriting was a bit awkward, but was obviously that of a young woman or teen-age girl. It read: *His name is Ernest Thomas Kaznowski.*

"I don't understand."

"When the cops noticed me layin' on the bench in that Chicago police station, this was pinned on the blanket that was wrapped around me," Ernie said. "It was put in my file. I stole it from the folder in the Children's Home office." He smiled weakly. "I even had it laminated, see?"

"Oh, Ernie. Your mother wrote this."

"Prob'ly. It's all I got of her." He pulled the office's one chair out and sat down on it. "What wised you up?"

"Ernie, I wasn't really prying, only curious," Sybil said. "I peeked at your Two-oh-one File. Are you angry with me?"

"And me?" Connie interjected.

Ernie shrugged and grinned weakly. "Naw. You two was always too smart for me."

"Tell us about it, Ernie," Sybil begged him. "Why the Kool-Aid and all that? You could've just talked about a nonexistent family."

"It's dumb," Ernie said. "Hell, *I'm* dumb."

"Oh, no, Ernie!" Connie exclaimed. "You're not dumb. And you know that Sybil and I are very, very fond of you."

He swallowed. "Yeah. I know, I—I like you girls, too. I like you a whole lot." He smiled wistfully. "Y'know, I never said that to nobody—that I liked 'em."

"Tell us about the Kool-Aid," Sybil repeated. "There's something very deep there."

"Aw! It's easy enough to explain," Ernie said. "I was in this foster home one summer, see? I guess I was about ten or eleven. There was some kids that lived next door. They were around my age. I tried to be friends with 'em."

"Were they snobbish?" Sybil asked.

"Naw. But their ma sure was. She knew I was put there by the welfare people, and she didn't want her little darlin's havin' anything to do with a kid like me. The old broad figgered I was illegitimate or somethin'—which I prob'ly am."

"Ernie," Connie said softly.

"Well, who knows? They never did find no record o' my birth or nothin'," he said. "They think I was maybe borned outta Chicago or even the state and brung in by my mother." He laughed. "I don't even know my real birthday, y'know? They kinda figgered out my age from examinin' me, and made one up for the records."

"Go on, Ernie," Sybil said not wanting him to wander.

"Anyhow, it was summer like I said. And hotter'n hell, too. There was this big ol' oak tree in the yard where I was stayin'. I used to climb up in it and watch them next-door kids play. They couldn't see me on account o' the leaves."

Connie walked over and stood beside him. "It must have been real sad for you not being able to go over there and play."

Ernie laughed. "Hell, bein' sad wasn't nothin' special. And, like I was sayin', I'd watch them kid play. When it got real hot in the afternoons their ma'd call 'em to the door and pour 'em cold drinks."

Sybil's eyes widened. "Kool-Aid."

"Yeah," Ernie said. "Kool-Aid. I used to think how nice it'd be to have a ma who'd give you Kool-Aid on a hot day. Fact is, I used to think about that a lot."

"That's understandable, Ernie," Sybil said. She noticed that he suddenly looked so very much like a small boy. There was a poignancy in his expression.

"I think I worry more'n the average guy about getting killed over here," Ernie said. "There'd be nobody to bury me, y'know. I guess they'd stick me in the ground somewhere or criminate me."

"Cremate," Sybil corrected with tears in her eyes.

"And, Jesus! If I lost my legs like Pullini, I'd go back to nobody, y'know? I'd be stuck all alone in a VA hospital. Without visitors, without anybody at all."

Both nurses now understood fully why Ernie fantasized about a mother who would send him Kool-Aid while he was stationed in steamy Vietnam.

"I guess I got a real thing on about that stupid brand o' drink," Ernie said.

"Mother's love is Kool-Aid, right?" Connie asked.

"I suppose," Ernie said. His eyes turned a bit misty as he looked at them. "Maybe all love is Kool-Aid."

Then the fully realization of what he'd been doing dawned on Sybil in one instant. "Oh, Ernie!" she exclaimed. "You gave us Kool-Aid."

"Yeah."

Connie grabbed Ernie and pulled him to his feet. Then she hugged him tightly. "And when you thought we were hot and thirsty, you—" Tears streamed from her eyes, and she sobbed. "Ernie—baby brother—Ernie—"

He resisted the show of affection for an instant, then put his arms around her. After a moment he freed himself, walking over to Sybil. He hugged her, too.

Sybil's eyes were also full of tears. "You're not alone in the world anymore, Ernie."

Ernie abruptly dropped his arms and went to the door. He opened it, looking back in the office. "Time for the afternoon pulses and temps to be took." But before leaving, he turned. "So! Now you two know what I think about ya."

Then he left them.

Chapter Eleven

The loudspeaker blared in its metallic incessancy. "Incoming wounded! Incoming wounded! All reception personnel report to the landing pads! Incoming wounded!"

Sybil and Connie, who had just reached the nurses' billets, didn't bother to go inside. They waited by the door. Within a few short moments, Ernie Kaznowski and Joe Sampson arrived with the ambulance.

The team sped to the landing areas at the same time a swarm of helicopters could be seen coming in over the horizon. "Just in time," Ernie said.

"Be sure an' keep track of them stretchers we take off," Joe said.

Sybil was curious. "What's that all about?"

"The supply folks are upset because there's a shortage of litters," Ernie explained. "They ain't gettin' back as many as we're takin' off. And, naturally, they're blamin' the Triple-Nickel for the disgracefully."

"Discrepancy," Sybil said.

"Okay," Ernie said. "So we gotta turn in a count on each delivery o' wounded guys."

"What a crock!" Sybil said.

"Yeah!" Connie agreed. "As if we don't have enough to do."

They were interrupted by the arrival of a jeep. The driver, a sergeant, yelled out, "Hey! They sent me to grab two nurses for the emergency hut. How about it?"

"Okay, big boy," Connie said. She grabbed Sybil's arm. "Let's go, *amigita.*"

Ernie waved to them. "Me and Joe'll move over to another pad and help out."

The sergeant said nothing during the ride across the bumpy field. When they arrived at the Quonset, he nodded a goodby. As soon as the two nurses climbed from his vehicle, he took off again on some other errand.

Captain Ryder greeted Sybil and Connie when they arrived. "You the two extras?"

"That's us, sir," Sybil answered. "How're you doing?"

"Pretty good—right now," Ryder said. "But get ready to go to work. There's lots of wounded coming in."

Sybil and Connie barely had time to change into surgical suits when the first ambulances arrived. The wounded were laid out on gurneys, and the emergency crew swung into action.

The moans and cries of the injured soldiers intermingled with the shouts and instructions of the medical personnel. Sybil and Connie, working with Ryder, moved into the bedlam of activities.

The first patient had a poncho over him. Pale, with clammy skin, he kept asking what time it was. Sybil pulled the poncho back and, despite her experience, blanched. The man's right leg was upside down beneath the jagged stump of his thigh.

"I know it got blowed off," he said in a southern accent, "but I just couldn't stand the thought o' leavin' it out there. So I tole the medic to put it on the stretcher with me." He hesitated. "What'll happen to it?"

Sybil picked up the limb and set it on the floor by the wall. "It'll be buried."

Both Sybil and Connie started to snip away at his clothing until Ryder yelled over at them. "Hey, one nurse per customer."

"Right," Connie said. "I'll move on," she said to Sybil.

"Okay," Sybil replied as she continued the task of stripping the soldier down for surgery.

"What time is?" he asked. "What time is it?"

"I don't have my watch," Sybil remarked throwing the remnants of his filthy uniform over to the floor. "What difference does it make?"

"I want to know how long I been without my leg," he said. "I'm gonna keep track. My daddy said if I was to get hurt, I shouldn't forget nothin' about it. I got to keep ever'thing straight for my disability pension. My daddy hurt his back in the service and didn't get a thing for it."

Sybil shook her head in amazement. "Didn't they give you any morphine? You're babbling like you're on a high of some kind."

"Hell, lady, I was weaned on Kentucky moonshine," he said. His speech suddenly grew hesitant. "It'll take—more'n—more'n—"

Sybil look closely at the man. "Let's get an IV over here! This one's going into shock." There was no response. "I said give me some goddamned epinephrine!"

A medic appeared with the proper equipment and hooked it up.

"My daddy said—" The soldier's eyes shut. "My daddy—"

The man was wheeled away, and Sybil's next patient, a lieutenant, was sitting on the gurney holding his hand. She took the injured member and began to unwrap the heavy bandages around it.

"My grenade went off before I could throw it," he said. "Real stupid thing to do." He shook his head in dismay. "A real bad example for the men, you know."

When Sybil cleared the field dressings away, all she could see was a shapeless mass of bloody, seared flesh with bone splinters protruding through it.

"Serves me right," he said looking at the mangled mess at the end of his arm. "It truly serves me right."

"Lie down," Sybil said. "We've got to get you out of those clothes."

"Yes, of course," he said in a soft voice. "I'm really very sorry to be such a bother. It was my fault, you see." He followed her instructions and carefully reclined.

Sybil cut his boot laces and pulled them off. "We'll have you fixed up real quick, lieutenant." She looked at him. His eyes were open and vacant. Sybil quickly grabbed the wrist of his good arm, but could find no pulse. "Oh, my God!"

Ryder, working on the next gurney, turned. "What's the matter?"

"He's—well, he's dead," Sybil said. "Grenade fragmentation wound in the hand."

"He was holding it when it went off?" Ryder asked.

"Yes. That's what he said."

Ryder roughly jerked open the man's fatigue jacket. The t-shirt he wore was soaked with blood. The doctor pointed at it. "Some of the fragments hit his body. Nobody noticed it. Some could've worked into his heart or caused heavy bleeding. Who knows?"

"I should have known," Sybil said feeling sick.

Connie, with her own patient, glanced in Sybil's direction. "What's the matter, *amigita?*"

"It was my fault this man died," Sybil said.

"The hell it was," Ryder said. "Even the medic in the field didn't realize the extent of his injuries. If, by chance, his shirt was torn more, or he wasn't wearing one, we would've known."

Sybil shuddered. "It was still my fault."

"Shut up and get to work," Ryder said. "I don't want any dramatics around here until the work is done."

"Yes, sir," Sybil said.

The afternoon turned into a long one of preparing the bloodied wounded for surgery. Most of the wounds were shrapnel. The hunks of metal propelled by explosives turned healthy, fit young men into sliced pieces of meat that needed to be put back together. It required more cutting, this time with sharp instruments wielded by the skilled hands of combat surgeons. Then this further mutilation was sutured closed while the IVs dripped their solutions into the punished bodies.

Sybil finished her last patient while Connie and Ryder labored over another. She went over to help but found she was simply getting in the way.

"We're finished up here," Ryder told her. "Take off, if you want."

Connie nodded. "I'll be over to the billets shortly."

"Okay," Sybil said. "I think I'll check on Noi and Sai."

"I'll meet you there," Connie said.

Sybil changed back into her fatigues, dropping the blood-soaked surgery suit into a hamper by the door. She stepped outside and paused to breathe in the cleaner air. At least she could smell no blood anymore or hear the sounds of the wounded.

A moment later she snapped out of it and walked back to the billets. She stopped at Noi's room and rapped gently on the door. When she stepped inside, Sybil was surprised to see Colonel Sedgewick bending over little Sai. Noi, fidgeting nervously, stood behind him. She rushed to Sybil and took her hand.

"Sai bad sick!"

"We'll see," Sybil said calmly. She walked over to join the doctor.

Sedgewick checked the rectal thermometer. "Temperature is up to a hundred and one," he announced.

"What is this please?" Noi asked frantically.

Sedgewick set the instrument down and gently took her arm, leading her over to the bed. "Nothing to worry about, my dear. Just a normal reaction and part of the healing process. You get some rest now."

Noi was hesitant. She looked at Sybil. The nurse smiled reassuringly. "Do what Doctor Sedgewick says." That was the first time she had addressed him other than colonel.

Sedgewick gathered up his things and headed for the door, motioning for Sybil to follow. Outside, alone, he spoke to her in a low whisper. "The child is not improving."

"How much could we expect from such a short time?" Sybil asked.

"More than this," Sedgewick said. "I had hoped for changes that aren't occurring."

"Is she in acute danger?"

"Not *acute,* perhaps, but her condition is remaining critical." He shook his head. "Perhaps even deteriorating a bit."

They were interrupted by Connie's arrival. The Chicana sensed something wrong. "Have we reached a crisis?"

"Oh, no," Sedgewick assured her. "At least not yet. Who's the next nurse on duty?"

"That's me, sir," Connie said.

"Fine. Let's go back inside. I have some additional instructions," Sedgewick said. He went to the door and opened it for her.

"I'll stay with Connie," Sybil said.

"No, it'll only worry the mother," Sedgewick told her. "And there's really no need for it. As I said, I don't expect a crisis. Even if it occurs, it won't be right away. If you have plans for this evening, feel free to proceed."

"All right," Sybil said. "I do have something to do. I'll check in early in the morning."

"Fine," Sedgewick said. He and Connie went back inside the billets.

Sybil left the building and walked through the compound with worried thoughts about Sai. She didn't feel much better when she arrived at the communications hut. A young commo man was on duty there. She rummaged through her pocket and produced Brian Mallory's phone number. "Can you reach this for me?"

"Sure, Lieutenant," he answered cheerfully. "Grab the phone over there and I'll crank up the ol' switchboard."

Sybil's call went through three separate telephone junctions before it was finally completed. The voice that answered was faint and tinny. "Three-Shop, Dixon."

"I would like to speak to Captain Mallory, please," Sybil said wondering what a Three-Shop was.

"I can't read you, say again."

"I want to speak to Captain Mallory!"

"Mallory? Roger. Wait."

"No! Not Roger Mallory. Brian Mallory," Sybil said quickly. But there was no one there.

"Mallory," came Brian's voice barely recognizable.

"Brian? Sybil. How are you?"

"Oh, hi."

"Can we meet tonight? I'm free."

"Great!" Even the bad connection couldn't hide the enthusiasm in his voice. "How's seven o'clock?"

"All right. I can hardly hear you."

"It won't get any better," Brian said. "See you at seven."

"Okay. Bye."

"Out."

Sybil handed the field telephone back to the message center orderly. "Is this the best we've got?"

"Afraid so, ma'am," he answered. "Charlie cuts the wires and steals 'em as fast as we put 'em up."

"I can understand them wanting to sabotage our communications," Sybil said. "But why the theft of lines?"

"Charlie uses the wire for electrical explosive charges," the soldier explained.

"Lord! In essence we're supplying them, aren't we?"

"Sure are. Out in the field I understand they even take the dead radio batteries our guys throw away. There's enough juice in 'em for Charlie to detonate somethin' at least once with."

"We're so wasteful," Sybil said.

"We're so rich," the man said.

"I guess you're right about that." She started to leave but turned back to the soldier. "The man on the other end of the line said he couldn't 'read' me. What in the world did he mean?"

"Just another word for 'hear' in army commo jargon," the switchboard operator explained. "For example, telling somebody you read 'em 'five by five' means 'loud and clear.' "

"God! I'll never learn all this stuff," Sybil said with a laugh. "Well, thank you for putting the call through."

"Anytime, Lieutenant."

Sybil stepped outside the hut onto the boardwalk that led to other structures in the Triple-Nickel's compound. That had been a recent addition made necessary by the coming monsoon season. Sybil looked around the garrison area and sighed. Except for

Brian—and her friendship with Connie and Ernie—this whole Vietnam episode was growing intolerable.

This was definitely not the way she had pictured her life in the army to be.

Sybil's decision to become a military nurse happened in her fourth and final year at Wichita Presbyterian.

The graduating students had been called to a special assembly in the auditorium so that a member of the Army Nurse Corps could address them and make a pitch for recruitment. The talk given the class was centered around the growing conflict in Southeast Asia, where mounting casualty lists were causing an extraordinary need for medical personnel.

Sybil was far enough into nursing at that time not to have any schoolgirl illusions about what the job would entail. There were no mental images of wiping the fevered brow of a handsome, wounded soldier boy dancing through her head.

She knew what blood was. Injuries, maimings, and even death were no strangers to her. But there was still a sense of romantic adventure involved in her decision to volunteer for the service. Raised in the type of home provided by Doyle Watkins, she had a deeply patriotic love of country. Communism, with its totalitarian system and smothering of civil liberties and capitalist enterprise, was certainly a menace to freedom-loving peoples everywhere, Sybil thought, and it was not unpleasant to realize she could be of some comfort and succor to the young men who were wounded while fighting that evil.

There was another consideration, too. Going into the army, even if she didn't go overseas, would most certainly mean a quick, faraway destination to go to right after graduation. Sybil recognized a very deep, very vital need to put some distance between herself and her family. Even if only for a couple of years.

When the army nurse, citing the latest fighting in Vietnam, asked for volunteers, Sybil did not hesitate to raise her hand. She and a few others stayed behind after the talk for further questions and to fill out the applications to enter the service. Full physicals and complete background checks were required, but there was plenty of time to complete those tasks before graduation.

The potential servicewomen took their physical and mental exams locally at McConnell Air Force Base located just south of Wichita. Despite the fact they took care of this at the first opportunity, it was a scant week before the passing out ceremony at the school that Sybil received an official letter informing her that she had been accepted into the Army Nurse Corps. That should have served as an indication to her how the army functioned. Her papers came in a large packet which included, besides further instructions, a set of mimeographed orders telling her where to report.

Sybil only had time for a couple of weeks at home before she had to leave for the medical training center at Fort Sam Houston, Texas. A quick check of a map showed her she would soon be domiciled just outside San Antonio.

"Colonel" Doyle Watkins, a bit surprised and nonplussed about her entrance into the service, still could not hide his pride in his youngest daughter's decision.

He was so moved, in fact, that rather than speak to her at the dinner table or in the living room, he invited her into his den.

Sybil hadn't been in the room more than half a dozen times in her entire life. It seemed like hallowed ground, a sort of Mount Olympus where mere mortals—or, as in this case, *mere* daughters—did not tread. It had always been a somber place to her. Dark furniture, heavily upholstered in leather, was arranged in a geometrical layout that gave the place a rather well-ordered look. The walls were paneled in a deep brown mahogany, and the heavy curtains were always drawn tight across the windows. A single, small lamp glowed on the desk that matched the paneling. Her father seemed foreboding, sitting there in the semidarkness. The dull glow on his face made him appear older and sterner to Sybil than at any other time in her life.

"So, Sybil Mae, you'll be in the army awhile."

"Yes, Daddy." She stood there because he had not invited her to sit down. Why, oh why, she thought, did she feel like a child again?

"Well, there's no doubt your country can use you," Watkins said. "President Johnson is building up our forces over there in Indo-China."

"I don't know if I'll even be going there, Daddy," Sybil said. "I might even be stationed at Fort Sill when I'm finished with my training down there in Texas. That's less than a hundred and fifty miles away. Wouldn't that be funny?"

"Oh, I don't know about that," Watkins said. "I was sent there for a little while during the Big War." He pulled a cigar from the humidor beside the lamp. "Anyway, I had a reason to call you in for this little talk."

"Yes, Daddy?"

"Even though you're going off to the armed forces, you're still one of the Watkins's girls, and we'll expect you to keep in close touch," he said.

"Of course, Daddy. I'll write home regularly. I always did in nursing school, didn't I?"

"Yes—yes, but this will be different," her father continued. "You'll have decisions to make."

Sybil was puzzled. "Like what?"

"Well, hell, I don't know for sure," he said. "I haven't been in the Army for over twenty years. I suppose you'll have a chance to volunteer for something or other. But I don't want you doing it without consulting me first."

"But why?"

"Why? Why? Because you're a young woman, that's why," Watkins said. "You don't have a husband to give you the guidance you need. And, until you do, that's my job. Women need men to look after them. Or other men will cause them hurt and grief. That's the way things are, and that's what a family's all about, young lady."

Anger bubbled in her interior, but she smiled grimly and said, "Yes, Daddy." But she knew at that moment, contacting him for any sort of advice would be the last thing she would think of doing.

"That's what brought about civilization as we know it," Watkins expounded. "My God, if it wasn't for men wanting to protect their women, there wouldn't even be law and order. It's the basic tenet—the cornerstone—of everything we hold sacred."

Sybil felt her father was going to open up to her on an intellectual level. "What about religion, Daddy?

Doesn't it have a lot to do with how we live?"

"Up to a point," Watkins said. "Still, if men didn't worry about their women – their *personal* women – even religion wouldn't be much more than ceremonial functions for hunters praying for luck or good weather maybe." He waved his hand in a dismissing gesture. "Anyway, that's a bit deep for the feminine mind. It's something women have never fully realized." He sighed to emphasize the load he carried as a male. "And they never will – the little darlings."

Sybil was silently furious.

"Life is complicated enough for a man," Watkins said. "For a woman – particularly a young, vulnerable one – it is absolutely hazardous."

"I'll remember that."

"Good. I'm proud of you, Sybil Mae. You'll do a fine job, I'm sure. And your country needs you."

"Yes, Daddy."

He looked at her in silence for a couple of minutes, then made a waving gesture with his cigar. "That's all."

Sybil turned and walked out of the den feeling not like an adult woman with highly developed professional skills but as if she were a ten-year-old in a frilly pinafore.

"God!" she exclaimed to herself, "I almost curtsied!"

"Oh, wait," Watkins said just as she reached the door. "There is one more thing I almost forgot."

"Yes, Daddy?"

"Your allowance," he said magnanimously. "We can't have you eking by on a lieutenant's pay, can we? I thought – "

"No, thank you, Daddy," Sybil said. "I don't want

an allowance—or anything from home."

There was a slight tone of surprised anger in his voice. "Really? Why in the world not?"

"Because, Daddy, I don't need it," Sybil stated.

"But—"

"I'm certain I can get along fine on what the army pays me," she added, not wanted to appear outwardly belligerent or rebellious.

"Well," he said with an all-knowing smile, "if you need any money, you know where to get it."

"No, thank you, Daddy. And I mean that."

She walked out of the room feeling a bit better.

In the ensuing months she would think about that conversation and be glad she had turned down the extra money. Somehow it was a gesture of freedom that gave her a final cut from whatever bonds held her close to the family home.

She had hoped the two weeks she had available before reporting in for duty would give her a chance for several long visits with Joanie Livingston. But she found that her old school chum had moved to San Francisco to live with a cousin. Sybil smiled at the news. She could just imagine the lifestyle that Joanie would follow out on the West Coast.

Sybil spent the remainder of her time in self-imposed seclusion, reading in her room and coming down only for meals or an occasional walk around the neighborhood. After a few days she was really chomping at the bit, wanting to begin her new life in the worst way.

Fort Sam Houston, Texas proved a most interesting experience. The move into the army entailed learning about military discipline, courtesy, and the service's peculiar medical procedures. The new nurses were billeted in pleasant quarters. The regimen was rather easy, and there was plenty of free time—with lots of men available, though that didn't particularly mean much to Sybil.

The work at the hospital did get a bit demanding sometimes, but it was most interesting and valuable to a young nurse. The one thing she couldn't quite get used to was the fact that in an army hospital, the patients cleaned up their wards by themselves. There was no janitorial service—except for the officers.

Despite all the new things she had to learn, Sybil still felt a sense of relief and freedom. After sending Teddy packing over three years previously, she had turned all her energies to studying. For the remaining semesters of school she purposely avoided dating, though there were a few times when she went out with a fellow student's brother or obliged a friend who was in a situation where an extra male had made an appearance. These were all innocent dates, and she never went out twice with the same man.

Sybil was completely turned off to sex and romance, and she wasn't worried a bit about the situation. Her rare thoughts on the subject brought forth the comforting opinion that when the time was right, the man was right and she was right—she would fall in love, marry, have kids, and live happily ever after—or whatever.

In the meantime, Sybil was bound and determined that she'd lose no sleep over her lack of interest in that particular department.

She had been in the army less than a month when she met Stan Logan.

He was a lieutenant in the signal corps assigned to a communications outfit at Fort Sam Houston. A bit stocky, he had thinning blond hair which looked even more sparse because of the GI haircut he wore. Stan had blue eyes, a thin nose, and a sensuous mouth. Not strikingly handsome, he was acceptable looking in a rather pleasing manner. Soft voiced and unobtrusive, he seemed like the typical "nice guy."

She met Stan while having a drink at the officers' club with another new nurse. Stan had come in with a friend who knew the other woman. It had all begun casually with enjoyable conversation at the bar, then a move into the ballroom for dancing. It was Friday night, and a local swing band out of San Antonio had been booked for the weekend.

That first evening was a short one, ending at eleven. The two officers gave Sybil and her friend a ride back to their quarters. The goodnights were friendly and noncommittal among everyone. All in all, it had been a very nice evening for Sybil after the years of keeping her young nose to the academic and medical grindstone of nursing school.

She didn't hear from Stan until a week later. Sybil received a call early on a Wednesday evening. She was in her room reading when the young WAC, who acted as a dormitory clerk of sorts, knocked on her door announcing a telephone call. Sybil, thinking it might be her father, went downstairs with minor feelings of misgivings.

Stan's voice was a welcome surprise. "Hello," he said. "This is Stan Logan. I met you the other night in the officers' club with Frank. Remember?"

"I sure do," Sybil answered in a pleasant tone.

He was almost apologetic. "I hope I'm not disturbing you," he said.

"Oh, no, of course not," Sybil replied.

"I was wondering if you'd care to see the local sights with me Saturday," Stan said. "Since you're new I thought you'd like to have a look around. Unless you've already done the tourist bit since coming here."

Sybil was happy with the invitation. "I haven't even been into San Antonio once. Can you believe that?"

"Well! I'm just in time. Suppose I pick you up around ten in the morning, then we can drive in. Look around, have lunch, look around some more, have dinner, then take in a movie."

"Sure," Sybil said, "I'd love to."

"Fine," Stan said. "Since we'll want to be comfortable during the day and dress informally, we can drive back to the post and change, then go back into town. It's not that far."

"Sounds fine," Sybil remarked agreeably.

"Or—" He hesitated. "Don't take this the wrong way, okay?" He laughed a little. "I keep an apartment in town. If you want, we can drop off your evening clothes there, then pick 'em up after sightseeing. I'm completely trustworthy, believe me."

Sybil laughed with him. "Okay. I'll bring along something appropriate for dinner."

"Great! See you Saturday at ten."

Sybil hung up, sincerely looking forward to the date.

That Saturday, Stan showed up a few minutes early. He was dressed casually in a Hawaiian-style sport shirt, tan slacks, and loafers. Sybil noticed his ears tended to stick out a bit, but he was nice-looking just the same. He took her clothesbag and carried it for her on their way out to the car.

The day was a whirlwind of seeing the sights. They made the obligatory visit to the Alamo, ate lunch at one of San Antonio's best Mexican restaurants, took a boat ride at Olmos Basin Park, went to the zoo, then finished up the day with a leisurely stroll through the McNay Art Institute.

Stan was true to his word. He took her to his apartment and behaved as a perfect gentleman. After she had changed into a dinner dress, he emphasized his good intentions by taking her casual clothes out to the car and putting them in the trunk, indicating he was making no excuses to return to the apartment after the evening's activities.

They drove to an excellent and quite expensive restaurant before seeing the new movie *Doctor Zhivago*. Afterward, they went straight back to Fort Sam Houston.

On the way out to the post, Sybil had to admit she enjoyed his company a great deal. She felt talkative. "That's a very nice apartment."

"Oh, you like it? Thanks. But I can't take any credit for decorating it," Stan said. "It's furnished."

"It looks expensive, if you don't mind me saying so."

"I have money on the outside," Stan remarked. "It gives me a bit more independence than the average junior officer."

"Very nice arrangement," Sybil acknowledged, thinking of the money she'd turned down from her father.

The goodnights, as before, were friendly and left

her wanting to see him again.

They went out three more times before finally going to bed together.

It was no great romance, as Sybil was to admit to herself later on, but it had been an absolute necessity for her to get into that relationship. After Teddy and his constant need for masturbation—not to mention his clumsy tearing away of her virginity—she needed to have some sort of experience with a man. Even if it wasn't going to be a permanent one.

Stan, of course, wasn't the first completely naked man in Sybil's life, but he was the first male to ever see her nude. She felt a bit self-conscious the first time. She hadn't given the disrobing bit much thought, but Stan did it with such casualness that she shucked her clothes quickly despite a nervousness about it.

Stan, stripped for lovemaking, wasn't a bit bowlegged and, like many balding men, had heavy body hair. It curled up on his shoulders and spread down like a thinly knit blond sweater. While it didn't turn her off, she didn't find it particularly attractive.

She unconsciously compared his penis with Teddy's. Stan's organ was only the second erect one she had seen—not counting sleeping patients and a lecherous old man who had raised his hospital gown at her and another student nurse one time—and seemed pretty much the same except for being much shorter, though larger around.

His lovemaking was adequate, with a considerate amount of foreplay always in the offing. Sybil was frankly surprised she could feel lust for a man she only liked a bit, but she had to admit she found sex wonderful and exciting.

The only demand that Stan made was that she get a diaphragm. He really didn't like using condoms, he explained, then added the old line about its being similar to taking a shower with a raincoat on. Sybil complied, not so much to please him, but because she considered it a good idea herself. She was fitted at a local doctor's office in town that another nurse had recommended to her.

The affair with Stan lasted for almost three months. After she completed the army nurse course, she went on status as a casual waiting assignment. It was in that phase of her military career that Stan broke off the relationship.

He was very nice about it.

They were in bed on a Sunday morning. They had the newspaper spread out between them while sipping fresh, hot coffee. Stan finished his and set the cup down. "Well, this is it for a while."

"This is what?" Sybil asked looking over at him.

"We won't be able to see each other for about three weeks," Stan said. "I'm off to home on leave for twenty-one days starting tomorrow."

Sybil felt no regret. "I'll be gone somewhere by the time you come back. They say our orders are due any day."

"Then things are coming to a close on a permanent basis." Stan hesitated, then added, "It's best anyway. I'm getting married when I get home."

"Really?" Sybil remarked. She suddenly realized that he had absolutely no intention of looking her up again after coming back from furlough anyhow. Sybil couldn't believe she was so *blasé* about the thing. "I didn't even know you were engaged."

"I have been for two years." Stan explained. "I had to wait for Ruth to graduate from college. It was something we promised her folks." He paused, as if anticipating some sort of an unpleasant reaction from her. When it didn't come, he continued on in his good mood. "I met her in college back in Ohio."

"Well, congratulations."

"Thank you."

That was the last they mentioned of it for the rest of the day. They went out for brunch and came back to the apartment. After making love in the late afternoon, Stan drove her back to Fort Sam Houston.

Their goodby was as uneventful and emotionally low-keyed as their meeting.

"It was nice, Sybil. It surely was."

She smiled and pecked him on the cheek. "Good luck always, Stan. Goodby."

"Goodby."

That night, lying awake in her bed, Sybil was a bit restless and edgy until a big truth dawned on her: She had been using Stan. And there had been a bit of meanness in her about it, too, she had to admit to herself. Each time he ejaculated, she felt as if she had emasculated him as his penis softened. She wondered if the attitude was from a deep-seated desire to get back at Teddy—or maybe even her father.

She shrugged it off. When they parted, the need for this striking out had immediately faded. No doubt, Sybil had gotten a whole lot out of her system from sleeping with Stan. She felt like a new woman, cleansed and renewed.

The realization made her smile, then she turned over and drifted off into a deep sleep.

She returned to her old routine but didn't have any real time to really sink back into it. Orders sending her to South Vietnam arrived. Within twenty-four hours of receiving them, she had taken a bus to San Antonio International Airport with authorization for commercial air travel to McCord Air Force Base, Washington, where she would board a Military Air Transport Service C-44 for the long trip to Southeast Asia.

Sybil had one fellow passenger—another nurse. She had noticed the Mexican-American girl during various activities but had never been paired up with her or even worked on the same shifts at the hospital. Their seats were together and the stranger did not hesitate to introduce herself with a friendly smile. "Hi! I'm Connie Montaldo."

"Sybil Watkins," she had said.

"I think I've seen you around the detachment from time to time," the other young woman said.

"Yes," Sybil acknowledged. "I guess we never received the same duty assignments. I'm happy to finally learn your name, Connie."

The other young woman laughed. "Actually, I'm Maria Consuelo Montaldo, but I go by Connie."

Sybil smiled at the display of frank friendship Connie was showing.

"All the women in my family have the same first name," Connie said. "Maria." She paused and frowned. "Am I babbling? If I am, I'm terribly sorry. It's a bad habit."

"Of course you're not babbling," Sybil said. "That sounds very interesting about the name Maria."

"Ah, yes! We're Mexicans—as you've probably noticed, eh? Well, I have two sisters Maria Teresa and

Maria Josefina. My mother is Maria Guadalupe. So, naturally, we go by our middle names. We younger ones Anglicize ours, thus my sisters are Terry and Josie, and I'm Connie."

"My situation is almost the opposite," Sybil said. "Back home I'm called Sybil Mae, but I've dropped the middle one."

"Where's back home?"

"Oklahoma City. And you?" Sybil inquired.

"Tucson," Connie answered. "Say, am I right in presuming you're on your way to Vietnam via McCord, too?"

"Yes," Sybil answered with a smile. She liked the girl immediately. It was one of those rare occurrences between human beings when a sincere rapport and affection is immediately established. Sybil rightly sensed the feelings were mutual.

The hours of travel pulled them closer, and the two found themselves telling each other of several of the most personal aspects of their lives. Connie heard about Teddy and Stan, while Sybil was informed of no less than three affairs.

Connie had attended nursing school in Phoenix on a scholarship. Like Sybil, she was an excellent scholar and totally dedicated to her new career.

"Look," Connie told her during a particularly long leg of the voyage, "if you get tired of my Spanglish, let me know. I really shouldn't do it so much, but it's gotten to be such a habit."

Sybil was curious. "What in the world is Spanglish?"

Connie laughed. "That's the way we talk in the border country, Sybil. A non-language consisting of a combination of English and Spanish. It stretches from Texas, across New Mexico and California."

"Sounds interesting," Sybil said. "Give me an example."

"Well, say, for example, you want to tell somebody to shut the goddamn door," Connie explained with a grin. "Instead of saying that, you'd come up with *'Cierra la* goddamn *puerta.'* "

"I presume that *puerta* is door," Sybil surmised.

"Right, and you didn't say that too bad," Connie said. "Something else in Spanglish are just words like *bebito,* which means 'little baby.' They took the English word baby, changed it to a Spanish spelling and made it a diminutive by adding the suffix *ito* onto it."

"I understand," Sybil said. She thought for a moment. "What if I wanted to say 'little nurse'? Would it be *nursito?*"

"Yes, in the masculine, but *nursita* in the feminine," Connie said. "All Spanish nouns, even inanimate objects, are either masculine or feminine. The letter 'o' makes it a boy, the letter 'a' makes it a girl."

"Gets complicated," Sybil said.

"Forget it and indulge me," Connie requested with a grin. "I'll be constantly throwing Spanish words into my conversations. Sometimes I can express myself better with a word in that language." She laughed out loud. "Even though it doesn't help my listener one whit. I'll probably refer to you as my *amigita.*"

"Wait a minute, I figured that out!" Sybil exclaimed. "*Amigo* is Spanish for friend—everybody knows that. You change the 'o' to an 'a' to make it feminine, then go further by making it 'ita.' " She thought for a moment. "That translates as small, feminine friend."

Connie laughed. "Never, never make literal translations, *amigita,* they rarely work."

Sybil joined in the laughter. "That's something I'll have to remember."

Their friendship grew more solid as the long trip continued. When they arrived in South Vietnam they landed at Tan Son Nhut Air Base. From there they were bussed to the Forty-fourth Medical Brigade at Long Binh.

At that point the army was most efficient. Orders were awaiting them in the brigade personnel office. Both young women were delighted to find out they'd been assigned to the same outfit: The 555th Field Hospital.

Upon arrival at their new home they were amused, frightened, and delighted.

They were amused when they learned the 555th was called the Triple-Nickel by the people assigned to it.

They were frightened by their first encounter with the chief of nurses, Maj. Tacita Moorehead, who gave them the most unpleasant greeting possible. Evidently, they surmised, the major felt they were going to be doing a lot of things wrong, so she had begun the bawlings out ahead of schedule.

They were delighted on their first duty day when they received their permanent duty assignments to the Convalescent Ward. Their new orderly, a charming little guy named Ernie Kaznowski, displayed an unabashed friendliness and careless disregard for army regulations that endeared him to them immediately. A three-way friendship—platonic, deep, and sincere—fast developed among the intrepid trio.

That had been three months ago, and the relationship had prospered and grown more beautiful.

Sybil lay in Brian's arms. The light from the hotel room's bath spread faint and yellow across the bed. She felt dreamy and peaceful after the wonderful sex they had just had. She sighed audibly, then lifted her head and kissed his cheek.

"I thought you might have dozed off," Brian said.

"No," Sybil said softly. "I was just slowly easing myself back to normal."

"I tried to hurry that along," Brian said. "But I guess it didn't quite work out." His voice had a tone of regret in it. "I held back as long as I could."

She raised up again, curious. "What are you talking about?"

"I wanted to keep going long enough for you to reach an orgasm."

"Oh, that! I've never had one," Sybil said.

"Really?"

That was something Stan Logan had discussed with her, too. She started to make a remark about it, but somehow didn't want to even mention the other man while she was with Brian. "Maybe I'm just one of those women that can't reach that great release," Sybil remarked. "I don't care. Sex with you is still wonderful. I can enjoy it without an orgasm, really."

"We've got something to work on then," Brian said.

"What's a Three-Shop?"

He burst out laughing. "You've got a strange habit of suddenly injecting completely unrelated subjects into conversations."

She smiled, "I know. When thoughts occur to me, I just blurt them out." She poked his shoulder. "What's a Three-Shop?"

"Where did you hear that?"

"When I called you this afternoon, the guy who answered the phone said it."

"Oh, I see," Brian said. "A Three-Shop is the S-Three office. In other words, the operations and training section of the staff. S-One, the One-Shop, is administration. S-Two is intelligence and S-Four, that is, the Four-Shop is supply."

"I should pay more attention to those things," Sybil said.

Brian chuckled. "You'd find the army a less confusing place, believe me."

She laughed. "There's a lot I have to get used to. When I called and asked if you were in, the guy that answered said, 'Roger.' At first I thought he meant that as your name, then I realized that he was saying, 'Yes.' "

"Yeah, it's what they call voice procedure," Brian said. "Just like 'wilco.' "

"Now I'm not sure of that one," Sybil said. "Let me think a minute—wilco—wilco—wilco—"

"How many guesses do you want?" Brian asked.

"Don't be a wise guy!"

"I'll give you a hint—it's a contraction of two words."

"Wilco—wilco—" Sybil mused. Then she said, "Oh, go ahead and tell me."

"Wilco means 'will comply.' "

"Oh, how clever!" Sybil exclaimed in a little girl's voice. "Poor little ol' me just can't keep up with you big soldier boys and the way you talk."

"I'll 'roger' that," he said.

She scowled good-naturedly. "Just for that, I may not let you take me to the party."

"What party?"

"At Lucky's tomorrow night. They're throwing a shindig for Colonel Sedgewick, our commander. It's his birthday."

"Hey, sounds like fun."

"It'll be something different," Sybil acknowledged. "Even Major Moorehead is going to be there."

"That's somebody I'd truly like to meet."

"Well, it's not for sure you're going yet."

"Oh, yeah? And why not?"

"Because you haven't even asked me."

Brian gently took her in his arms and pulled her close to him. Their noses were almost touching. "Will you go to the party as my date?" he asked.

Sybil laughed in delight. "Roger Wilco!"

Chapter Twelve

Sybil, freshly showered, entered the room. She nodded a greeting to Connie who was pressing a uniform. "I just stopped by to check on Sai. She's still running a high temperature."

"I don't like the looks of things, *amigita,*" Connie said. "Who's with her?"

"Penny," Sybil answered going to her locker. "She said Colonel Sedgewick had just been in for a look-see. He didn't say much, but it was obvious he wasn't happy with the situation."

Connie ironed her uniform shirt with occasional glances at Sybil peering into the mirror hanging in her wall locker door. "I lit a candle at the chapel this morning. I hadn't done anything like that in a long time."

"I never had much enthusiasm for religion," Sybil mused running a brush through her hair. "I think whatever awe or respect I had for it has been turned off by the people involved in churches and such."

"I'm the same way," Connie admitted. "But let me tell you something. I'm going to confession so I can take communion, then I'm going say some prayers for little Sai." She sighed. "I haven't gone through that routine in ages. But I guess it shows there's a spark of Catholecism in me. Particularly when I practice the sacraments in order to pray for something that really means a lot to me."

"You have to do all that to pray?"

"No, but I really want to be in good shape with the Lord when I'm this sincere and worried," Connie said.

"I prayed, too," Sybil said. "Not a real heart-rendering plea to the Almighty, or anything like that. But I asked Him to help Sai."

"Good for you!" Connie's face broke into a smile. "I feel better now. What about you?"

"Yeah. Me too," Sybil said. Then she added, "I suppose."

It was crowded in their small room. The ironing board took up most of the space between the two beds. That meant Sybil had to turn sideways when she decided to get the cosmetic kit on the desk.

Connie grinned at her as she scooted down the cramped area. "Good thing we're friends."

"I read you five-by-five," Sybil said.

"Hey! Where'd you pick that up?"

"From the kid in the communications shack," Sybil explained. "I guess with all those brothers you had in the service, you already knew that stuff."

"Yeah," Connie said.

"What about the staff sections?" Sybil asked. "Do you know about them?"

Connie shook her head. "All I can remember about

that is that each one is an 'S' with a number, but I can't recall which is which."

Sybil slid back to her mirror. "Well, just in case you should have to know, the S-One is administration, S-Two intelligence, S-Three operations, and S-Four is supply."

"All right! All right!" Connie acknowledged with a laugh.

Sybil put on her lipstick, pausing between words during the application. "Or you—can call—the—the—One-Shop—Two-Shop—and so on," She turned to her. "Anything else you want to know about the army?"

"Yeah!" Connie exclaimed in feigned irritation. "How do you transfer away from a know-it-all roomie?"

"You can't," Sybil said. "According to army regulations, you are stuck with me throughout your military career."

"Really?"

"Oh, yes, indeed. And you have to support me for the first six months I'm out of the service."

"Oh, yeah? Well, we'll see about that, *amigita.*" Connie put the shirt on a hanger and picked up a pair of trousers off her bunk. "We'll be going over to the birthday party at Lucky's together, hey?"

"Right. Brian's out on a short FTX," Sybil explained. She turned to Connie. "Do you know that—"

"Field Training Exercise," Connie announced grandly, laying out the apparel to be ironed.

"Ooooh! You're so damned smart!"

"You betcha, kid."

Sybil's expression sobered. "I hope that isn't a bad sign. Being out in the field could mean they're preparing for another operation."

"Did he say anything about it?" Connie asked.

"No," Sybil answered. "He's not allowed to discuss hardly a thing that he's involved in."

"That's the way it is with those Green Berets," Connie said.

"Damn, Connie! I don't want him going back to that awful war," Sybil said.

"Are you in love?" Connie asked in candor.

Sybil sighed. "I don't know—I really don't. The only thing I'm aware of is that Brian is on my mind every waking hour."

"And you probably dream of him at night."

Sybil smiled. "I sure try to!"

"I think you're in love," Connie said. "Have you two talked about any commitment or future plans?"

"No," Sybil replied. She stared dreamily into her locker. "But I've fantasized certain things. Like becoming engaged, life together after the army, all that sort of stuff."

"Well, if he's doing the same thing, you're certainly edging toward some sort of arrangement together," Connie surmised.

Sybil came out of her reverie. "Yeah, I suppose."

"Y'know," Connie remarked. "There used to be this strange sort of thought that kept running through my little Chicana head about you."

"What's that?"

"I often wondered about you and Frank Gavin," Connie mused. "Whether there could be anything between you two."

Sybil shrugged. "I like Frank, but I never had any particular romantic notions about him."

"He's real good-looking," Connie said. "And I figured since he's from Oklahoma like you, there might be some sort of attraction or at least a minor man-woman rapport there."

Sybil shook her head. "No. He's a real nice guy to me. But that's all."

"It's probably just as well. You'd be in a real pickle if you were going with Frank and fell for Brian, wouldn't you?"

"I'll say!" Sybil glanced impatiently at Connie working. "Well, let's go, troop! Finish ironing those duds and get into 'em."

"Yes, ma'am, lieutenant," Connie said smirking. "This is going to be like the good ol' days—us going over to Lucky's together. Are we going to meet Ernie at the gate?"

"Not this time," Sybil said. "He's going to work as a waiter at the party."

Connie put the fresh ironed uniform on the bed and began dismantling the ironing board. "I didn't think he was the kind to volunteer for that sort of work."

"He didn't. Mother Moorehead and Sergeant Major Rafferty planned the party and even set up a roster of waiters since Lucky didn't have enough girls working there to tend to such a large affair."

"Ay, Chihuahua!" Connie exclaimed. "I'll bet the little guy is steamed about that."

"Steamed? Did you say steamed?" Sybil asked. "That's such a weak adjective in this sense, my dear. He's *furious!*"

"I can imagine," Connie agreed. "Well, let me get dressed and put my face on. Then we'll get over there. This is going to be a very interesting party!"

"My! You're such the champion of the understatement this evening," Sybil remarked, laughing.

Lucky Hwan was a nervous wreck. Ever since he'd gotten the request to close his bar for a private party honoring the Triple-Nickel's commander's birthday, he'd been working himself into a state of pure panic. There would be no low-ranking persons attending the affair. All would either be officers or senior sergeants. This caused his Chinese soul to boil with anxiety and a desire to make everything perfect.

He had even yelled at his waitresses on a couple of occasions. This upset the women, causing them to perform their tasks in a sullen efficiency.

At that particular moment, his two bartenders were tacking a huge paper sign across the back wall. Lucky, who couldn't read or write English, had gone to a Vietnamese signpainter to have it done. The man, whose grasp of English was much less than his knowledge of French, had taken a dictionary of the two languages and formed a literal translation which he had rendered to the paper.

The banner bore huge red letters that spelled out:

HAPPY BIRTHDAY TO MISTER THE COLONEL SEDGEWICK

The entire bar was decorated with faded, second-hand bunting that the Vietnamese had also furnished. Although red-white-and-blue, the stuff was actually from France. It had last been used for a Bastille Day celebration some fifteen years previously by a French army unit.

Lucky had also completely rearranged his place. Several tables had been pushed together and set up by one wall to accommodate the highest-ranking guests at the party. The other seating arrangements were organized so that the others attending the celebration would be able to look easily at the honored colonel and the various speakers who would be giving him their best wishes on the occasion.

All the food, drinks, and other refreshments had already been paid for. Lucky's supply of dinnerware was severely limited—all he had were cocktail glasses and beer mugs—so that he had to make arrangements with a restaurant supplier to rent plates, silverware, and extra glasses.

Between that expense and dealing with a caterer, quite a bit of Lucky's profit for the event had been drastically cut. In fact, in comparison with a regular business night, he was losing money. But he didn't care. He was deeply touched that his establishment had been chosen to honor such a high-ranking officer, and he was most gracious about the cut into his income.

Lucky would probably not have been so pleased had he known that he was the second choice. All the officers' clubs at Long Binh had been previously booked, and were unable to accommodate the planned festivities.

After another feverish check and lecture to his bartenders, waitresses, and the three soldiers detailed to help with the serving, Lucky stood by the door to await the arrival of the crowd. Although it was a good hour before the festivities were scheduled to begin, he wanted to be ready.

The first person to turn up was Sergeant Major Rafferty. Although not a regular patron of the bar – he preferred to do his imbibing among his cronies at the noncommissioned officers' club – he had visited Lucky's on enough occasions to be recognized by the harried owner.

"Ah! Sergeant major!" Lucky exclaimed with a bow. "So nice to see you. Please to come in."

Rafferty was dressed in a gabardine uniform complete with tunic. The huge gold chevrons, rockers and star insignia of his rank, coupled with the six slanted hash marks denoting over eighteen years of service, almost covered the sleeves.

He took several steps into the bar and gave it a sweeping scrutiny. His critical eye caught the sight of two tables slightly out of alignment. He pointed to the offending furniture. "That's a goddamned disgrace!" he snapped. "Straighten 'em up!"

"Oh, yes. Right now!" Lucky exclaimed. He scurried over and motioned to one of his bartenders. He gave him curt instructions. Within moments the task was taken care of, and Lucky hurried back to Rafferty.

The sergeant major noted a couple of other things that either needed lining up, straightening, or looked sloppy to him. His eyes scanned the banner offering best wishes to "Mister the Colonel." He pointed to it. "This side of that sign is lower than the other." The words painted on it failed to register with him. They had nothing to do with "dressing right" or "covering down," so the language error was not perceivable. As soon as that discrepancy was straightened up, he was satisfied. "Where's the waiters we furnished?"

"In back room," Lucky said. He pointed. "Go through door at other side of bar."

Rafferty paraded across the expanse of the room and hit the doorknob. The flimsy portal flew open with a crash, startling the three soldiers seated at the table behind it. The sergeant major glared. "What's this shit?"

The three, including Ernie Kaznowski, had automatically leaped to their feet. Ernie frowned in puzzlement. "What's what shit, sergeant major?"

"The place out there looks like the aftermath of a Mongolian cluster fuck, and you three jerk-offs are sitting in here on your dead asses."

The other two gladly let Ernie continue as their spokesman. He swallowed, then spoke. "We're on a chow break. The party's gonna start in about a half hour or so."

Rafferty glanced down at the table and noted the hamburgers and french fried potatoes the trio was consuming. "Where did that come from?" he asked, pointing at the food.

"From the PX snackbar," Ernie answered.

"And how did it get over here?"

"We chipped in and Trent went over and got it," Ernie said.

"Who put you on this detail?" Rafferty demanded.

"You and Moth—Major Moorehead," Ernie answered.

"Then who takes you off?"

"You and the major."

"Young soldier," Rafferty said in angry undertones. "I don't recall either one of us giving permission to leave the work area to fetch chow."

"We thought—"

"The goddamned army don't pay you to think!" Rafferty snarled. He pointed at the beer bottles among the food. "And you're drinking on duty, too."

Ernie's temper snapped. "Goddamnit! I got stuck on this fuckin' shit detail to be a goddamned waiter on my own time. And if Lucky gives me a beer I'm gonna drink it!"

Rafferty seemed to calm down, but the coldness in his eyes had not receded. "A smart guy, aren't you, Kaznowski?"

Ernie wisely shut up.

"I'll be dealing with you later on this," Rafferty said. He pointed to the other soldiers. "And that includes you. Now shitcan that chow and get your asses back out there. And I want to see three happy little faces while you're serving the food and drinks."

Rafferty gave them another warning glance, then turned and went back outside. He motioned to Lucky to come up to him.

Lucky trotted over. "Yes?"

Rafferty jerked his thumb toward the door. "If those three yardbirds give you any shit tonight, you let me know, hear?"

Lucky laughed. "Oh, they nice boys! Work good."

"And don't give 'em any more beer."

Lucky was surprised at the other's attitude. But he knew Rafferty was a powerful man in the Triple-Nickel. "Yes, sergeant major. Whatever you say." He watched Rafferty go over to the big table to make another check on things. The Chinese bar owner spoke to himself in English under his breath. "What a prick!"

A quick glance of his watch showed that the guests were due to arrive at any time. He went over to the door and waited. After fidgeting for fifteen minutes, he was relieved that the first people had finally arrived.

These were three sergeants, already slightly drunk, who greeted him in a bit less than boisterous manner. Lucky exchanged quick salutations, then directed them toward the tables. Name plates already were there, so all they had to do was search for their proper places.

They had no sooner sat down than more people arrived. They all noticed the sign and pointed to it with delighted laughter. Lucky beamed. He figured their remarks were compliments about his thoughtfulness in having it done.

Lucky's mood brightened somewhat with the entrance of more people. All were cheerful and friendly, making him feel better after Rafferty's ominous intrusion.

When Sybil Watkins and Connie Montaldo walked in, Lucky was his old self again. "Hello, ladies. Welcome to big party. Oh, you look very nice!"

"Thank you," Sybil said. They usually wore fatigues during visits to the bar, but this time, due to the festivities, they had dressed in gabardine Class A's complete with skirts and high heels.

"Yeah, thanks, Lucky," Connie said. She looked around. "The place looks real nice."

"Oh! Thank you very much." Lucky was genuinely pleased with the compliment.

"Who did the sign?" Sybil asked pointing to it.

"Vietnamese friend who can write in French and English do it," Lucky replied. "You like?"

"It's very attractive," Sybil said. "I'll bet Mister the Colonel Sedgewick can't wait to see it." She glanced at the tables. "Oh, there are name plates."

"Yes. You find yours and sit down," Lucky said. "Pretty smart, hey?"

"Uh, yeah," Sybil said doubtfully. "Tell me, are Connie and I together?"

"I don't know," Lucky said. "I can't read English. The sergeant major put them all where he want them."

Connie hissed under her breath. "That dirty rat! He'd keep us apart on purpose."

"To hell with him," Sybil said defiantly. "Come on!"

She went out to the tables and searched around until she found her name, Connie's, and Brian's. She exchanged them with others so they would be at the same table.

Rafferty, over by the big table, spoke up. "I've already arranged the seating."

Sybil smiled. "This will be more convenient. Trust me, sergeant."

"The correct manner to address a sergeant major is by his complete rank," Rafferty said. "Not just 'sergeant.' "

"Right."

"I think you should clear any changes in the seating with Major Moorehead," he suggested.

"Good idea," Sybil said taking a seat.

"Right after the party," Connie echoed joining her.

Rafferty walked over to them, a strange smile on his lips. He looked down at the two nurses. His voice was only a whisper so he wouldn't be overheard. "That little Polack buddy of yours is really on my shit list now. And you two are gonna get it from Major Moorehead. You know that?"

Connie, also whispering, said, "Yeah. We know it. You want to know something? We don't much care, Rafferty."

"My rank—"

"Stick it in your ear, Rafferty," Connie said. "Now go away, or I'll drop you for ten."

Rafferty was so angry his face purpled. He started to reply, but only gasped. Then he walked back to the big shots' table.

"What's that mean?" Sybil asked. "Dropping him for ten?"

"That means making him get ten push-ups," Connie said.

Sybil giggled. "Could we make him do that?"

Connie was hesitant. "I suppose if the regulations were interpreted very strictly, but it wouldn't be a good idea. Sergeant majors are powerful entities in the army. In fact, my brother told me I'd be better giving a captain a hard time than a senior NCO."

"I'd like to do that once," Sybil said smirking. "Just tell him to do ten push-ups and watch that arrogant jerk have to do 'em."

Connie cautioned her with a wagging finger, "That, *amigita,* is definitely not a good idea."

"You're probably right," Sybil agreed. She glanced around. "Oh, there's Ernie." She waved. "He's coming over."

Ernie, wearing a starched white waiter's jacket borrowed from one of the Long Binh clubs, walked up to their table. "So how's it going?"

"Great," Connie answered. "You look real spiffy, kid."

"Thanks." He bent down and whispered to them. "I'm gonna see that Connie gets what she most wants tonight."

"You've gotten me a date with Ricardo Montalban?"

"Better than that," Ernie said.

"There's nothing better than that," Connie protested. "But tell us what you're up to."

"Remember you said you wanted to see Mother Moorehead get looped in here? Well, kiddo, tonight's the night," Ernie said grinning.

Sybil poked him in the ribs. "She doesn't drink, Ernie."

"I know," he said. "In fact, I was to see that her glass is kept filled with her favorite drink—Seven-Up."

"Are you going to spike it?"

"Is a dope Catholic?"

"Is the *Pope* Catholic," Connie interjected.

"Whatever. Yeah, I'm gonna doctor her drinks with vodka."

"God!" Sybil exclaimed. "It'll taste awful."

"I can handle it," Ernie said. "Whoops! I'd better move on. The sergeant major is lookin' this way."

"Good luck," Sybil called after him. She watched Ernie go back across the room and join the other waiters. She turned to Connie. "Think he can do it?"

"No, *amigita,*" Connie replied. "And I'll bet he gets into a lot of trouble before this night's over."

Sybil started to speak but saw Brian come through the door. She stood up and waved. Her heart seemed to beat faster as he gestured back. His masculine good looks with the black hair and green eyes gave her a little thrill.

Brian, who was wearing a Class A uniform for the occasion, joined them. He seemed fatigued despite being obviously freshly showered and shaved.

Sybil frowned in concern. "How're you feeling?"

"Tired," Brian admitted. "I haven't had any sleep for the past forty-eight hours. That FTX was a ballbuster."

"I'm not surprised," Connie commented. "You boys in the Green Berets play rough."

Sybil smiled and put an arm around his shoulder, whispering in his ear, "Not *all* the time!"

"We've a bit of suspense tonight," Connie said to Brian. "Ernie says he's going to get Mother Moorehead sloshed."

"With vodka and Seven-Up of all things," Sybil said.

"How in the world is he going to pull that off?" Brian asked.

"We'll just have to wait and see," Sybil said.

The bar was filled to capacity by then. Every table was occupied, and the staff—including Ernie Kaznowski and his two buddies—kept the glasses filled and drinks served. Sergeant Major Rafferty, seated with a few of the officers at the main table, kept checking his watch. Finally he got up and went to the front door. He looked out in the street a few times before turning to face the crowd.

"Tinch—HUT!" he bawled.

Everyone stood up and assumed the position of attention. All eyes were straight ahead, the shoulders back and thumbs properly along the seams of skirts or trousers.

Rafferty, after a critical glance at the crowd, opened the door. He stepped back and saluted.

Colonel Sedgewick and Major Moorehead entered together. Sedgewick nodded and spoke greetings to people he recognized as the two went up to the table, respectfully followed by Sergeant Major Rafferty. Mother Moorehead's face, on the other hand, bore such a grim expression, she would have fit in well at a funeral or even an execution.

When they reached their seats, a smiling Sedgewick nodded to the crowd. "Please take your seats."

As everyone sat down, Ernie appeared behind the couple. He set a drink down in front of the Colonel. "An old-fashioned," he announced.

"Ah!" the colonel said. "My favorite drink."

"Yes, sir. Ever'thing's checked out ahead o' time," Ernie said. He set a drink in front of Mother Moorehead. "And a Seven-Up for the major." He smiled at the two. "I been assigned as your waiter for this evenin', so if you need anything just let me know."

"Fine, thank you," Sedgewick said.

"Kraznowski!" Mother exclaimed setting her glass down.

"Yes, ma'am?"

"This tastes awful!"

Ernie affected a casual grin. "Oh, yeah. The stuff Lucky gets is from a local bottlin' comp'ny. I think it must be the water. You'll get used to it."

Mother took another sip. "I'll try."

Ernie leaned closer to her. "It'd be nice if you didn't act like the stuff was lousy, major. Lucky's real sensitive."

She took another drink, winced and set the glass on the table.

Sergeant Major Rafferty, occupying a place a couple of places down, rapped on his empty beer bottle with a fork. "Krasnowski! You make sure there's a bottle o' beer in front o' me all night, got it?"

"Right, sergeant major."

The festivities began with a short speech from the Triple-Nickel's second-in-command. The officer, a thin, nervous lieutenant colonel named Nappy, wished

Sedgewick a happy birthday and hoped his next one would be back home with his family.

The next speaker was Major Moorehead who gave the commander greetings from the nursing staff. Sergeant Major Rafferty was the third, and windiest, of the orators. He not only offered a birthday salutation on behalf of the enlisted men, but also launched into a talk about the sacred mission the 555th Field Hospital was performing in the great crusade of ridding Southeast Asia of the communist threat.

Then it was time for the toasts—and Ernie Kaznowski hovered behind Major Moorehead, making sure her glass of specially treated Seven-Up was kept full.

They toasted the president, the Joint Chiefs of Staff, the Republic of South Vietnam (there were several ARVN officers present), the American flag, the United States Army and anything else members of the crowd could come up with.

When the last toast was drunk, Mother signaled to Ernie and held out her glass for a refill. "You're right," she told him. "You do get used to this stuff."

Ernie smiled. "Yes, ma'am!" He poured her another drink. "I gotta help serve the food now," he said. "You want I should leave this bottle with you? It's nice and cold."

"That would be a good idea," Mother said. Then she actually smiled at him.

Ernie, his head shaking in wonder, went to the backroom to aid in passing the dinner out.

When he got to his friends' table, he winked at them as he set the plates out in front of them. "Operation Get-Mother is in full swing," he said.

"She's really drinking that awful stuff?" Sybil asked.

"Drinkin' it? Hell, she's askin' for more now," Ernie said with a giggle. He winked at Brian. "How you doin', cap'n?"

"Good," Brian answered. "If you pull this off I'll get you a commission in Special Forces."

"Better get them gold bars ready then," Ernie said. "I'll see you guys later." He hurried away to complete the task of serving the food.

Everyone found the dinner excellent. Lucky, circulating around while keeping an eye on things, was pleased to receive several compliments. The only thing wrong was that the salad was a bit wilted because the ice used to keep it cool had melted fast. But the main course of Szechwan duck, rice, and flaky French rolls had been prepared to perfection.

"Poor Brian," Sybil said. "Fresh out of the field and no cheeseburgers or fries."

Brian grinned. "I'll rough it with this."

"I heard about your uncontrollable lust for junk food," Connie said. "You'd be an easy man to cook for."

Sybil laughed. "You wouldn't have to cook. Just run down to the local hamburger stand and get a bunch of greasy food to go."

"It'd be heaven," Brian said.

"Speaking of the field," Sybil said, "when do you have to go out again?"

"I don't know," Brian said. He reached over and took her hand, gently squeezing it. "But I have this weekend free. What about you?"

"It could be arranged," Sybil said. "Have anything particular in mind?"

"How about Saigon?"

"The whole weekend?" Sybil asked. She raised her free hand to his face and gently stroked it.

"Sure. What do you think?"

Sybil was thrilled. "You know what I think."

Brian started to speak, but a sudden, quick explosion of shrill feminine laughter sounded over the festivities.

"Ay Dios!" Connie exclaimed. "That was Mother Moorehead."

The three glanced up at the big table and saw Ernie, grinning wickedly, pouring the chief nurse another drink. Mother was displaying a silly expression while holding a wavering glass under the spout of the bottle.

"My God!" Sybil said under her breath. "I think he's going to pull it off."

"Surely she can taste the vodka in that stuff!" Connie exclaimed.

"Not necessarily," Brian interjected. "Ever drink screwdrivers or any other vodka mix? After a while it's impossible to detect the liquor."

They watched for a few more seconds until the major went back to eating her meal.

"Well," Brian said. "What time can you get away?"

"I come off duty at five-thirty Friday afternoon," Sybil said looking dreamily into his eyes.

"Great! Let's leave at six."

"Wait a minute! I'm a woman, I can't just get ready and rush off in half a hour. Pick me up at seven, okay?"

"It's a date," Brian said.

The meal was finished within a half-hour. Ernie and his buddies reappeared. This time their job was to clear off the dishes. As he stacked the plates from his friends' table, he winked at them. "Whattaya think?"

"I think you're getting the job done," Sybil said.

"Keep it up, Ernie," Connie said. "You're the man of the hour."

"Yeah. I'll get back there as soon as we get this stuff put away." Within twenty minutes the tables were cleared except for the celebrants' drinks.

"Oh, look!" Connie said. "They're bringing in the birthday cake."

Two of Lucky's bartenders carried the huge pastry up to Sedgewick's table and set it down in front of him. Lieutenant Colonel Nappy stood up. "Okay, ladies and gentlemen, it's time to cut the cake. I have to apologize for the lack of proper dinnerware, but there just wasn't enough for the main course and the cake, too. We've got paper plates and plastic forks up here. So if you'll form a line, you'll each be served. But first let's sing our best wishes to Colonel Sedgewick on this happy occasion."

Everyone, holding their glasses, stood up.

"Happy birthday to you—Happy birthday to you—Happy birthday, dear Colonel Sedgewick—Happy birthday to you!"

One feminine voice, loud and shrill, dominated the singing. It was Mother Moorehead, waving her hands in time to the tune, enjoying herself to the hilt.

The partygoers lined up and were served one by one. Mother Moorehead, drinking regularly from her glass, hummed to herself. Finally, she nudged Sedgewick in the side. "You better hurry up. At the rate you're cutting that thing, it's gonna get stale."

Sedgewick gave her a funny look but smiled. "Right, Major Moorehead."

Mother struggled unsteadily to her feet and lurched

over to Sergeant Major Rafferty. She leaned across him, her face almost touching his. "How ya doin', han-'some?"

Rafferty, his eyes opened wide, swallowed. "How's that, ma'am?"

Mother put an arm around his shoulder. "You're a helluva man, Raff'ty. I'll tell you what. Together, you'n me, we'll shape this outfit up, right?"

Rafferty smiled weakly. "Yes, major. We'll do that for sure."

"Damn right!" Mother exclaimed.

Sybil, standing with Connie and Brian just in front of the pair, stared incredulously at the sight of the intoxicated chief of nurses. The woman strongly reminded Sybil of her sister Henrietta back in Wichita.

Mother patted Rafferty on the shoulder, then staggered back to Colonel Sedgewick and pushed her face into his.

"Now if Sar'nt Maj'r Raff'ty was cuttin' the cake it'd all be served out," Mother said with a noticeable slur in her voice. She put an arm around his shoulder. "Can I tell you sumthin'?" She giggled. "No! No! I don' wanna tell you sumthin', I wanna ask you sumthin', okay?"

Sedgewick, trying to cut and serve, was slightly distracted by her. "Uh, sure, major. What's on your mind?"

"Why don't you run 'is outfit like you got balls?"

The colonel had just started to serve Sybil, but he stopped and looked at the woman hanging on him. "What did you say?"

"You ac' like a fuggin' pussy, Seg-wick," Mother said.

Sedgewick's eyes widened. "Damn! You're drunk out of your mind!"

"Hell I am!" Mother pushed him, then she stepped up on her chair. Her voice had a sirenlike quality. "Lissen up, ever'body!"

The people in the room, expressions of shock, surprise, and humor dancing across their faces, looked up at Major Moorehead standing unsteadily on the chair, gazing down on them in an unfocused glare.

She was silent for several seconds, then slowly raised her glass. She started to speak, but only opened her mouth and continued to stare. Her eyes were glassy and blank. Finally, still standing straight with her glass raised high over her head, she slowly leaned forward—farther, farther, and farther until she crashed face down into the remnants of the birthday cake.

The table, a flimsy affair at best, burst under the impact and collapsed on the floor.

Lucky, on the other side of the room, turned to his chief bartender, his face screwed into a quizzical frown. "American birthday very strange, hey?"

Chapter Thirteen

Saigon was one of the most exotic cities in the world. Although more than fifty miles inland, a navigable river that bore the city's name flowed through it, permitting ocean-going vessels to tie up at its docks. Thus it offered the color and excitement of a port metropolis, with foreign ships and strange cargos, while the docks teemed with seamen, stevedores, and other waterfront characters.

The water traffic was also made up of smaller boats, fishing craft and junks that clogged the waterway. Another mode of transport, similarly varied, was also quite evident on the city's streets in the form of pedicabs, automobiles, bicycles, motor scooters, and other types of land vehicles. This traffic was a virtual bedlam, with sweating policemen in white uniforms trying to maintain some sort of order in the chaos.

But, off the main boulevards, quieter places awaited the visitor. There was a modern cafe area offering the best in Oriental and French cuisine. The more cultured of the population could enjoy the theaters and cinemas, as well as several museums that boasted extensive exhibits from Indo-China's past civilizations.

Duong Tu Do was the main street. At the end was the post office and cathedral. Not far from that stood Independence Palace which served as the executive mansion of the Republic of South Vietnam.

The Cholon district of the city was the Chinese area, and being the most colorful area in the midst of even all this exoticism, offered its own varied attractions which ranged from those that appealed to the visitors' highest intellectual tastes, down to the very sinful, which tickled the most base of sensual instincts.

But none of this meant much to Sybil Watkins and Brian Mallory as they drove into the city in the borrowed Chevrolet. Their destination was L'Imperatrice d'Orient Hotel. The couple's plans were vague and uncertain after registering. The only thing that concerned them was that they were going to be together for an entire weekend without interruptions.

The hotel was Saigon's finest. Laid out in rambling colonial style of white masonry and delicately carved gingerbread decor and ornate iron work, it boasted numerous gardens and patios that caught the rare cool breezes of tropical evenings and wafted them toward the screened windows and doors of the rooms. The fifty-year-old design, now no longer necessary with the advent of modern air conditioning, had been done in order to catch the most breezes and block out the sun during the hottest part of the day. Despite being functional, it also pleased the eye of the most discerning European visitor.

Brian wheeled the car up to the entrance and brought it to a rather noisy halt. The brakes and shocks, long overdue for replacement and adjustment, squeaked out their protest as their worn parts rubbed against each other.

A doorman, wearing a fancy braided uniform despite the heat, saluted deftly, barely touching his fingertips to the bright red *kepi* he wore. He opened the door for Sybil, then looked over the top of the vehicle at Brian. "Shall I have it parked, *monsieur,* and see that any luggage you may have is taken care of?" Although Chinese in appearance, he spoke with a marked French accent.

"Yes, please," Brian responded. "We won't be taking it out until Sunday evening."

"*Mai oui, monsieur.*" The man snapped his fingers and a bellboy and chauffeur appeared.

Brian opened the trunk and allowed the bellboy to take the one large valise and two small bags there. As soon as the luggage was unloaded, the chauffeur put the car in gear and drove off. Sybil studied the three-storied building as they walked under the long awning to the entrance. "Quite a place! So beautiful, with a menacing air about it that is absolutely fascinating."

"Makes you think of spies and intrigue involving beautiful and mysterious women, doesn't it?" he remarked.

Sybil laughed. "Brian, you're a bit of an adventuring romantic at heart, aren't you?"

"Of course," he said. "And I fully expect to see Sydney Greenstreet and Peter Lorre, looking quite sinister and threatening, sitting in the lobby when we go in."

But, besides some rather innocuous appearing civilians, there were only some American army men and several naval officers of undetermined nationality who seemed to be waiting for rides, appointments, or something. They sat in small groups, scattered throughout the many sofas and chairs, talking softly among themselves. Sybil noticed the approving glances they gave her as she and Brian walked across to the large, mahogany desk.

The clerk, a small Vietnamese with a closely clipped moustache, greeted them politely. "*Bonsoir, monsieur, madame.*"

Brian nodded. "Good evening. We have reservations for two rooms. Mallory and Watkins."

The man checked his card file. "Ah, *oui. Monsieur le Capitaine* Mallory, *et Mademoiselle la Lieutenante* Watkins. You are in room two-oh-three, *monsieur.* The lady in two-oh-nine."

"Couldn't you get two closer?" Brian asked disappointed. "I even requested that the rooms be adjoining."

"*Pardonez-moi, monsieur,*" the clerk shrugged apologetically in a typically Gallic manner. "These are the closest available. I am sorry."

Brian sighed. "Very well then."

After they signed the register, they were led to the elevator. The creaky conveyance let them off at the second floor. Brian tipped Sybil's bellboy, and the youth led her a short distance down the hall.

The room, because the inner door inside the screened one had been left open, was as warm as the outside air. As soon as the bellboy put her two bags down, he went to the window and shut it. Then he turned on the air conditioning. He marched to the door with great dignity and faced her. "Does the *mademoiselle* require anything else?"

Sybil, fighting the desire to laugh at his pomposity,

shook her head. She decided to try a bit of schoolgirl French. "*Non, merci.*"

"*Bien, mademoiselle. Bonsoir.*"

He left, shutting the door. Sybil turned and surveyed her room. It was overly decorated, with a large bed, ancient dresser and bedstand, and an out-of-date overstuffed chair situated beside a small table that held a lamp and telephone. The phone intrigued her. It was an ornate, European job in white. There was an old painting on the wall. It showed an Alpine scene with little farms nestled in the valleys below the large snow-peaked mountains. Evidently it had been placed there to ease the homesickness of the tourists in the former days of France's colonial grandeur.

Sybil checked out the bathroom. Like the rest of the place, it was old-fashioned and rather creaky looking despite being obviously looked after and kept clean. The sink was a deep porcelain affair with brass fixtures, and the toilet tank was the overhead type with a chain.

She went back out into the room in time to hear a knock on the door. "Yes?"

"Me." It was Brian.

"*Entrez, monsieur,*" Sybil said.

He came in and shut the door, walking over to her and taking her in his arms. "Ah! You speak zee French, no?" Brian said in an exaggerated Charles Boyer style.

"*Oui, monsieur,*" Sybil replied. She embraced him around the waist. "Courtesy of the Kennedy Academy of Oklahoma City. I studied the language for two years. Would you care to hear a few verbs conjugated?"

"Not really, but I'm impressed!" Brian said with a laugh. "But a knowledge of the language might come in handy around here."

"I'd be better off if I'd studied Spanish," Sybil said. "At least I could practice with Connie."

Brian kissed her tenderly, then gradually pressed his lips tighter against hers. He ended the activity reluctantly. "This is the best way to start a Friday evening," he said.

"Mmm, yes. Do it again," Sybil invited.

He complied and they clung to each other for several long moments before slowly parting. "I still wished we could have gotten adjoining rooms," he said.

"Why not get just one anyway?" Sybil asked.

"Propriety, my dear," Brian said. "This isn't like the hotel in Long Binh. One has to make reservations and register here. What would the army think of one of its nurses openly sharing a room with a man not her husband?"

"I hate that double standard," Sybil complained. "It seems all right for the boys in the outfit to go out and get a woman under any circumstances—even some down-and-out whorehouse like that Juicy Lucy's that Ernie goes to. But if we nurses try to get birth control pills or a diaphragm, we're ostracized and given extra counseling by Mother Moorehead. That's why I've stuck with my original method of birth control."

"It's always been that way, fair or not," Brian said. "In college, the guys could stay out all they wanted, but there was a strict curfew for the girls."

"How would they find out we were registered together anyway?" Sybil asked.

"Are you kidding? The CIA checks on all guests here," Brian said. "I wouldn't doubt that the desk clerk and half the bellboys are on the agency payroll—not to mention a double agent here and there who also works for the Viet Cong."

"Frightening," Sybil remarked. "Still you'd think in modern times like 1966 we wouldn't have to worry about such things as sleeping together," Sybil complained. "But you're right."

"I'm afraid we Americans have brought our moral values here and thrust them into certain situations where they would normally be laughed at."

"I suppose," Sybil surmised.

"It doesn't matter anyway. We'll stay in this one room." Brian walked over and sat in the chair. "There's something I'm dying to know."

"What?"

"In fact," he continued, "I avoided asking about it in the car because I want no distractions when you tell me."

"What in the world are you talking about?" Sybil asked with a smile. She walked over and sat down in his lap.

"What happened to Mother Moorehead?"

Sybil burst out laughing. "It's hilarious, really?"

"So tell me."

"They took her back to the hospital and checked her out. All she got from that fall into the cake was a slightly bruised shoulder," Sybil said. "Of course she was sick as a dog. They say she vomited all through the night, then sort of passed out or slipped into an uneasy sleep."

"Yeah? Go on."

"That's about it," Sybil said. "She's been a recluse all day long."

Brian's smile faded. "That's not good."

"And why not?" Sybil asked.

"I hate to throw a damper on things, but the shit's going to hit the fan over this one," Brian stated solemnly.

"Are you sure?"

"The woman is a teetotaler, right? Well, she was obviously drunk. And if she thought she was drinking nothing but Seven-Up, guess what conclusion she's going to jump to."

Sybil frowned. "Oooh, yeah! That somebody slipped her some booze."

Brian nodded. "And who do you think is going to be the logical suspect?"

"Specialist Fourth Grade Kaznowski," Sybil said. She brightened. "But wouldn't they have already gotten him if they'd wanted to?"

"The thing only happened last night," Brian reminded her. "As soon as that major is back on her feet, she'll be wanting blood."

"Maybe, since she was insubordinate and insulting to Colonel Sedgewick, she'll just let it drop. Or transfer out," Sybil suggested hopefully.

"I can tell you one thing for sure," Brian said. "Colonel Sedgewick, for the sake of discipline, can't ignore the incident. Not since it happened in front of so many witnesses. And if he hangs Moorehead, she'll be damned sure that anybody else she can get her hands on will swing with her."

"That'll be—"

"Ernie," Brian said completing the sentence.

"What can we do?"

"Nothing," Brian said. "That's the way it is in the army. Somebody's going to take some lumps. Just be ready to defend yourself. Like they say—CYA."

"Yeah," Sybil agreed. "Cover your ass."

"I may be judging Ernie rather superficially since I don't know him all that well," Brian said. "But I don't think this will be the first time he's been in trouble."

"You're right about that," Sybil said. "He was already on Rafferty's list before that happened."

"They may even try to tie you and Connie in on it."

"Then we're *all* in trouble."

Brian nodded. "Yes."

Sybil sank into a sullen silence—but only for a moment. "Oh, to hell with it! I'm going to enjoy this weekend."

"Me too," Brian echoed.

"Then kiss me, you savage!" Sybil said with a laugh.

He responded, and they pressed their mouths together for a long time. The kiss ended gradually, with a slow parting of their lips.

"Want to go downstairs to the dining room for dinner?" Brian asked.

"What? Now?"

He gave her a quick kiss on the tip of her nose. "Or have it sent up?"

"Brian! You mean eat here in the room? It would be so romantic." Then she noticed their clothing. "But not in these damned uniforms."

"I've got an idea," he said. "I'll go get my things and move in here. After the waiter brings up the chow, we can change into something more appropriate."

"Chow? *Chow?*" Sybil exclaimed laughing. "You refer to our romantic dinner as chow?"

"Oh, God! I've been in the army too long."

"Well, I guess a *rose is a rose,* right?" Sybil slipped out of his lap. "Go get your stuff. Then you can call room service and order chow."

"Right!"

The hotel's staff proved to be an efficient organization. Within an hour of Brian's call to room service, a waiter appeared at their door. Behind him, carrying a dining table and two chairs, were a couple of busboys. They quickly set up the impromptu dining arrangements. The food, complete with a bottle of champagne chilling in an ice bucket, was set out. After receiving tips from Brian, the team bowed politely and withdrew.

"Quick!" Brian said. "Let's change before the food gets cold."

Laughing, they disrobed and frantically hung up their clothes in the closet. Then, naked except for their bathrobes, they sat down at the table. Brian popped the champagne and poured them each a glass of the bubbly. He raised his. "To us," he said.

Sybil smiled and clinked her glass against his. "To us." She reached out playfully with one bare foot and playfully tickled his toes.

After a sip of the drink, he glanced at the meal. "Let's see how this stuff looks." Brian pulled the coverings off the plates.

The meal's main course was boned hen. It had been stuffed with chestnuts, mushrooms, onions, and meat, then basted with honey during the baking phase. There was the ever-present rice and a side dish of *cha-lua,* a pork dish seasoned with cinnamon and other spices. For dessert there were French pastries.

Sybil smiled at him. "And you would refer to a meal like this as chow?"

"I'm such a peasant," he said pouring them more champagne.

Between the good food and the drinks, Sybil sank into a mellow mood. The conversation was light and pleasant, punctuated with touching each other across the table—and also under as the game of "footsie" continued. They ate slowly, taking an hour to consume the delicious repast.

When they finished, Brian dabbed his mouth with a napkin. "I'll call them to remove this and get another bottle."

"Wonderful idea," Sybil said serenely. "Fantastic idea." She felt a little drunk, but with a nice silky glow. She knew it was going to be a wonderful weekend.

After summoning room service, Brian put the phone back on the hook and gently took her hand, beckoning Sybil to stand up. She did so and was folded into his strong, yet undemanding embrace. She lifted her head and he kissed her with a tender passion.

"I love you, Sybil."

She didn't say anything, only put her head against his shoulder.

"Sybil?"

"That's a bit of a serious thing to say," Sybil remarked in a whisper.

"Hope it didn't spoil the evening," Brian said.

She shook her head. "No."

"I love you."

"Those words should never be spoken unless you mean them."

"I do mean them," Brian said. "I love you."

She reached up and put a finger on his lips. "Don't say it again—not for a while, okay?"

He pulled her closer. "I did ruin things."

"No, no. I just want to think a little," Sybil said. "The champagne is tickling my head, and I guess I wasn't quite ready for that."

Brian started to speak, but was interrupted by the arrival of the waiter and his small crew. They left off a fresh bottle and removed the remnants of dinner. After Brian tipped them for the second time, they graciously withdrew.

Brian again popped the cork. He poured them each a fresh drink and brought Sybil's to her. "Another toast to us?"

"Of course."

"Then—to us."

"To us," she echoed. She took a drink, peering at him over the rim of her glass. "Brian—"

"Yes?"

"I love you," Sybil said.

Brian slipped his free arm around her, drawing her close. "Looks like things are getting serious around here."

"They seem to be," Sybil agreed. She raised herself on her tiptoes and kissed him. "So? What happens now?"

"We figure out where we want to go from here," Brian said.

"Aren't we in a weird situation?" Sybil remarked. "Both involved in a war, far from home and uncertain about when and where we can get together."

"I've only got about four months left on my tour," Brian said.

"I have ten."

"I could extend," he offered.

"No!"

"Why not?"

Sybil set her glass down and put both arms around his waist. "Because that would mean more fighting for you to be exposed to."

"Yeah," Brian said. "Would it be better if I went back

to the Continental U.S.?"

"At least you wouldn't run the risk of getting shot back home," Sybil said. "Since such a thing would put a big damper on our romance, I think we should do what we can to avoid it."

He grinned. "I'll go along with that."

"Which reminds me," Sybil said. "How will I know when you go back to the war? Can you call me and let me know you'll be gone?"

"No," Brian said. "We're not set up for wives—or lovers—so I'm afraid there's not much consideration shown. I suppose you'll find out when you telephone and are told I'm on TDY."

"That's only Temporary Duty. Anytime somebody is sent out from their unit on a temporary basis in normal circumstances, they're classified as TDY."

"You're right," Brian said. "But in the case of Special Forces, the meaning is a bit more ominous."

"TDY," Sybil said thoughtfully. "I hope I never hear those awful letters. T—D—Y—"

"Try to think about something more pleasant," Brian urged her.

"Good idea," Sybil agreed. "Let's consider what will be going on after your tour in Vietnam is over. Where do you think you'd be stationed?"

"Fort Bragg," he answered. "You know the post?"

"No," Sybil answered. "The only place I'm familiar with other than Long Binh, is Fort Sam Houston, Texas."

"Fort Bragg is in North Carolina," Brian said. "That's where the headquarters for Special Forces is located." He thought a moment. "Of course there's always the chance I'd end up in Germany or Panama. We have groups in both those places, too."

"Why not get out of the Green Berets altogether?" Sybil asked. "You're not required to remain in that outfit, are you?"

"No. I could transfer out. But I wouldn't be very happy in a conventional unit. There's enough bullshit in Special Forces. The rest of the army's swarming in it."

"Well, there's no guarantee I'll be sent where you're stationed anyway," Sybil surmised sadly.

"But, without a doubt, I'll go from here straight to Bragg," Brian said. "Once I get there I can make sure I'll stay. That's no problem. I can get a letter of acceptance from some commander and settle in for the duration of my term of service." He was thoughtful. "I suppose I could leave Special Forces and find a place in the Eighty-second Airborne Division. That's my old outfit from my enlisted days. And they're at Fort Bragg, too."

"Is it important to you to be stationed there?"

"Yeah. It's pretty close to Washington and the Pentagon. I could run up there and bug some folks I know to make sure you were sent to Bragg when you came back to the States."

"Could you do that?"

"Sure! A lot of people travel to the big building and stick their noses into things. And you don't have to be part of the brass either," Brian explained. He winked at her. "Some of those female clerks would think it real romantic to get us together."

"Bless their hearts," Sybil said.

Brian put his arms around her and kissed her again. He slid his hands around to the front of her robe and opened it. Then he opened his and pressed his flesh against hers.

Sybil moaned and clung to him.

His lips brushed lightly against hers, then he reached up and slid her robe off, letting it drop to the floor. She did the same to him, feeling his hardness press against her stomach.

"Diaphragm," she said.

"Oh, yeah. You'd better take care of that," Brian said.

"I won't be long." Sybil rushed into the bathroom and prepared herself. She hated this break in the romantic mood of the moment. She decided to go on the pill—even if it did mean a black mark in her efficiency report after she requested them.

When she was ready, Sybil went back into the bedroom. "Sorry about the delay."

"It's all right," Brian said.

Sybil allowed herself to be led over to the bed. She lay down and Brian joined her, continuing the delicious teasing with his lips and tongue as he kissed her neck, then slid down slowly until he mouthed the soft flesh of her breasts.

"Brian!" she said in an urgent whisper. Sybil slid her hand down the front of his body and grasped his manhood, manipulating it in a slow, undulating motion. She could feel him strain against her in his passion, and it pleased her to know her man had grown excited.

Brian gently sucked her nipples, teasing them to an erect firmness. Sybil felt the growing waves of passion lifting her up to the wildly exciting heights that caused involuntary moans to escape through her lips.

Now Brian was lower, kissing her stomach, causing more ripples of excitement to dominate her being. She could feel his tongue as it traveled down to her lower belly, then inside her thighs with its moist gentleness.

"Oh, Brian—oh!"

Sybil looked down and could see his head between her legs, then suddenly a fresh wave of excitement—one she'd never felt before—shot through her. She gasped and instinctively clasped her legs around him as her hands slid to the back of his head. Her fingers were entwined in his hair.

"Oh—sweet—man!"

Her sensations heightened under the pressure of his tongue, adding to the growing excitement. It was as if she didn't know what to do in order to accommodate Brian's efforts. Sybil alternately opened her legs as wide as she could, then closed them on him. She pulled him in tighter, then when the sensitivity seemed unbearable, she forced him slightly away—then repeated the action.

Sybil was no longer aware of her surroundings. The only thing in the whole world were those fantastic sensations she was experiencing. She groaned, gasped and cried out. Her abdominal muscles spasmed as she writhed and undulated her hips in rhythm with Brian's oral lovemaking.

Then it seemed she reached the height of excitement. It continued at a high intensity. If Sybil had any conscious thoughts at all, they were wishes that whatever was happening to her would go on forever.

"Brian! Oh! Oh! Brian! Brian! My love, my sweet man, my Brian!" she cried out.

Suddenly there was no control at all. Her body took over, and Sybil simply went along with whatever it wanted to do. She was aware of a series of wavering convulsions, and it was only pure instinct that let her know she was coming. The relief came in waves and waves of invisible pleasure that finally left her limp, unable to speak.

Brian, knowing she had experienced the orgasm, stopped his efforts and gently eased up to kiss her slightly opened lips.

Finally, after a few deep breaths, she opened her eyes. "Oh, it was wonderful." She looked into his face, feeling very much in love and satisfied. "Brian, Brian," she said softly. "Oh, my darling, it was pure ectasy."

Brian kissed her again. "I love you."

"I love you, too."

Sybil laid her hand on his face and caressed it gently. "You're very handsome."

"And you're very pretty."

She kissed him, then felt him position himself between her legs. He slid into her, his hips moving back and forth as he worked his way into her body. Sybil felt love for the man and wanted him to penetrate deeper, deeper. She embraced him gently kissing his face.

She remained silent until she felt the gentle ejaculations inside her and knew his seed had been expelled.

Brian raised up and looked at her, then again kissed her. Neither spoke as he remained inside, their bodies pressed closely together. Finally he started to withdraw.

"No," Sybil said softly. She wrapped her arms and legs around him. "I don't want you to go."

Brian smiled. "I love you."

"Oh, Brian, I love you, too. I've never felt so—so womanly and satisified as I do right now," Sybil said. She pulled his head down to her shoulder. "I'm so much in love."

"Me too—whoops!" He laughed softly.

She smiled. "You're slipping out."

"Yeah." He pulled himself free, then lay down beside

her.

Then they drifted into the moments of silence that only lovers experience. An unspoken expression of love, satisfaction, and peacefulness.

Sybil and Brian spent the entire weekend in that hotel room. They even had all their meals brought in.

The lovemaking strengthened their emotional bond in a persistent, yet gentle way. As their affection for each other deepened, so did the ease and freedom they felt in reaching out in a spiritual as well as physical way.

With all restraints now removed between them, their sexual activity evolved to mutual oral techniques. She learned to reciprocate by going down on him. At first Sybil was hesitant, but the strong desire to please him overrode her preliminary uncertainties, and she took him into her mouth. After several times, she found she could heighten his passion with gentle teasing motions of her tongue. It pleased her greatly to have him writhe in sensual pleasure as she made love to him.

Her skills for her personal excitement increased, too. Sybil developed a way to maintain her own degree of sexual enjoyment by prolonging the plateau phase of her orgasm. Each time it seemed different, and at one particularly delicious moment, she experienced multiple comings so pleasurable that she almost screamed out.

Between eating and making love, they settled down to a serious discussion on their relationship.

"I want everything—our feelings for each other, this weekend—*everything* to have some serious meaning," Brian told her.

"Oh, me too, Brian," Sybil said. "Lovemaking with a caring commitment like this is a once in a lifetime experience. It has to lead to something fulfilling and permanent."

"I want us to be able to be together when you get back to the States," Brian said. "I've got plenty of leave time coming. And you will, too, when your Vietnam tour is over. I'll be released from active duty about two months after your return."

"What will we do then?"

"Play it by ear," Brian said. "Maybe we should work on getting you stationed at Fort MacArthur. That's in San Pedro, right next to Long Beach." He was thoughtful for a few minutes. "Yeah! That's it."

"Do they have a hospital there?"

"Sure. It's a small post. And I'm sure you'll fall in love with southern California. The lifestyle there is just right for a young woman like you. Then when you're discharged, there'll be no big changes or moves for you."

"Wonderful!"

"While you're completing your service, we'll be in the same city, and I can get back into the advertising game. Either in business for myself or get a position on one of the big Los Angeles agencies," Brian said. "I've got plenty of contacts."

They were sitting on the bed. She reached over and hugged him tightly. "But, oh my God! But we've got to wait ten months. That's almost a year."

"But not that much time apart," Brian said. "We'll have four months together in Vietnam. I still have that long to go here myself. Four from ten leaves six months we won't be together."

Sybil's face suddenly showed concern. "Do you have to go back to the fighting?"

He shrugged. "Well—"

"You do, don't you?"

"Yeah. There's going to be at least one or two more operations," he said.

She suddenly felt anger. "Damn," Sybil said. "Damn! *Damn! DAMN!*"

"Hey, take it easy," he said softly taking her in his arms. "There's nothing to get excited or upset about."

"I've only just found you," Sybil said. "I don't want to hear you've gone TDY."

"Shhh."

"I couldn't stand—" She suddenly began crying with a terrible grief at the thought of losing him.

"Sybil, darling. You're getting emotional over nothing," Brian said trying to soothe her.

But she continued to cry for another ten minutes before finally getting herself under control. She wiped at her eyes with a Kleenex.

"Feel better now?"

She nodded her head. "Yeah. I don't know what made me break down like that. I'm sorry."

"Just relax now."

She laughed a little through the waning tears. "Come to think of it, I *do* know what made me act like that—I'm a woman in love."

"Well, I'm real happy about that," Brian said.

"I promise not to do it again," Sybil said.

"It's all right."

"Brian?"

"Yes, darling."

"Make love to me."

That was late Saturday night. They made love one more time that night, then again early in the morning at dawn. The final physical and emotional joining took place late Sunday afternoon just before they had to check out.

They drove out of Saigon early Sunday evening. Brian traveled up Highway 1 toward Long Binh. Sybil, sitting in the middle of the seat next to him, rested her head on Brian's shoulder. Their journey was slowed when they caught up with a South Vietnamese army convoy heading north.

Sybil could see the young soldiers in the back of the trucks. Their faces had babylike qualities in the glare of the headlights. Each bore a wistful expression, staring forlornly out into the dark countryside.

"Wonder where they're going?" Sybil mused.

"To the war," Brian answered.

"Lord! They're just kids."

Brian nodded. "Yeah. Draftees whose families didn't have enough money to keep them out of the service."

Sybil sat up. "You mean to tell me that the sons of the wealthy Vietnamese don't fight?"

"That's right."

"The more I find out about this war, the worse I feel about it," Sybil said. "American boys are getting hurt and killed over here while the rich just sit back and watch. It's not fair!"

"It's certainly not my idea of the proper way to fight communism in Southeast Asia," Brian said. "But from where I sit, there's not too much I can do about it."

"Couldn't we write a letter of protest to somebody?" Sybil demanded.

"How far through channels do you think it would get?" Brian asked.

"Let's not even talk about it," Sybil said sullenly.

They arrived in Long Binh late, but found their favorite officers' club serving a light supper. After eating, they went into the bar and took a corner table. Brian looked over at her. "Care to dance?"

Sybil slowly shook her head. "No, darling. I just want to sit here and enjoy your company for a couple of more hours before this wonderful weekend is over."

"Yeah," he said softly. "Me too."

They wound down over glasses of Dewar's and soda for Sybil and bourbon for Brian, feeling lethargically happy while whispering their new love to each other.

Chapter Fourteen

The alarm buzzed into Sybil's curtain of sleep. She forced her eyes open and, at the same time, reached over and hit the snooze button. She glanced across the short distance of the room to Connie's bunk.

Connie was looking at her in sleepy indifference.

"Hi," Sybil said.

"Mmmm."

"I'm in love."

The Chicana's brown eyes popped open. "*Que?*"

"I said I'm in love. And so's Brian."

Connie sat up. She grinned and wiped at her face in a sleepy movement. "Okay. Okay. You going to tell me about it?"

"Let's sleep another ten minutes."

"No!" Connie put her feet on the floor and stood up. She walked over to Sybil's bed and shook her. "*Despiertate!* I want to hear all about this."

"Oof! Let me sleep," Sybil begged.

"No." Connie sat down on her bunk and kept shaking until Sybil finally sat up. "Tell me how you trapped that man."

Sybil made a face. "I don't like to think I *trapped* him!"

"I know you did, and you know you did," Connie said. "The important thing is that he doesn't know it, right?"

"I am hereby informing you most emphatically that it was a mutual thing when Brian and I decided we're in love," Sybil saidT the excitement of what she said brought her wide awake. "Oh, Connie, it was wonderful! Wonderful! And we mad a commitment to each other. We've got plans and everything."

"You're getting married?" Connie asked.

"We haven't gone that far, for heaven's sake! But we want to be sure we're both in the same place when I get back to the States," Sybil explained. "Let's go shower. I'll tell you all about it."

Connie sprang to her feet and rushed to the wall locker to get her ditty bag. "Damned right you're going to tell me all about it."

Sybil got out of bed and slipped into her robe and slippers. "This weekend was the most important of my whole life." She got her shower things. Suddenly a feeling of depression swept over her. There's still the war, she thought to herself, that has to be gotten over with before she could truly be happy.

Connie looked closely at her. "Is something the matter?"

Sybil smiled weakly. "No—no, nothing."

"Okay then." Connie opened the door and waited for her. "Don't tell me everything until after we get back to the room, okay? I don't want any distractions."

"Right. I'll keep mum."

Connie clung to her arm as they walked to the latrine. "I didn't mean for you to keep *completely* quiet. Just drop me a few interesting hints from time to time."

Sybil, her high spirits now returned, laughed. "Hey, our friendship doesn't make it mandatory to spell out the most intimate details."

"The hell if it doesn't!" Connie shouted.

Sybil began protesting as they went in for their morning baths.

The Triple-Nickel's officers' mess was in its usual boisterous morning activity. There was a clash of shifts as those eating early, to relieve people already on duty, tried to eat and were due to report to work shortly.

The pair found two empty chairs and quickly grabbed them. The other people at the table, a couple of surgeons, gave the young women no more than a casual glance before going back to their own conversation.

Connie, excited, looked at Sybil. "Is he going to give you a ring?"

"I'm not engaged," Sybil said. She started to say more but was interrupted by the Vietnamese waiter who took their breakfast orders, then hurried through the crowd to get the food.

"We haven't talked much about that," Sybil said. "Our situation is really hectic. There's so much arranging to do in order that we can be together when I go back. He has a marvelous idea."

"Tell me!"

"There's a hospital on a small post near Long Beach," Sybil said. "Brian thinks he can get me stationed there. That way he'll take a thirty-day leave and we can be together for that month. Then all he has to do is go back to get processed out of the army and come right back."

"Fantastic!"

The waiter appeared and set their trays in front of them. After pouring two cups of hot coffee, he scurried away to other tables. Connie started to speak again, but the two doctors got to their feet and exchanged a couple of words before parting company.

"Oh, God!" Sybil suddenly exclaimed. "I forgot all about Sai. How could I?"

"You didn't *completely* forget her, I'm sure," Connie said. "Anyhow, she's still critical, but Colonel Sedgewick is keeping a close eye on her."

Frank Gavin's appearance interrupted them. "Hi, ladies." The head of physical therapy slipped into an empty chair.

"How are you, Okie?" Sybil asked.

"Great. And you?"

"She's going steady," Connie interjected.

"Hey, congratulations," Frank said with a wide grin. "I presume the lucky guy is that Special Forces captain."

"That's him," Sybil said.

"Good news," Frank said. "And I have more wonderful tidings to bestow on you."

"What's that?" Sybil asked.

"Mike Pullini is training for the bench press contest," Frank announced.

"Wonderful!" Sybil exclaimed. "When did that come about?"

"Saturday morning," Frank said. "That was a good idea you had, Okie. He was doing his regular therapy while some of the other guys were working out. Finally, he just couldn't stand it. After he finished his exercises, he had me wheel him over just to watch. After awhile he gave them a bit of constructive criticism and some advice. But before long he was on the bench pumping iron."

"How's he doing?" Connie inquired.

"Great. The guy's a natural athlete and pretty damned strong," Frank said. "Even the weeks of recovering from his wound hadn't sapped his strength too much."

"How's his attitude?" Sybil asked.

"Improving every day," Frank answered. "He's starting to enjoy the camaraderie of the gym now. He jokes and makes wisecracks with the other lifters. He may not be completely recovered, but seems to be well on his way. I hope he stays that way."

"Me too. But I'm so glad to hear he's at least temporarily come out of the blues," Sybil said sincerely. "If he maintains that high, it will mean a fast return to normal life when he gets back to the States."

"The most important thing is keeping his fighting spirit up," Frank said. "This bench pressing thing is putting quite an edge on his natural competitive spirit. Once he's back to being a scrapper, he'll have more than half the battle won."

Connie looked meaningfully at Sybil. "You're a natural-born nurse, *amigita.* It was your concern for a patient that brought him so far along."

"Well, maybe," Sybil said modestly. she finished up her eggs. "We'd better get on the ward."

"See you later," Frank said.

"Right. Come on, Connie."

The two left the mess hall and walked across the compound. Connie playfully nudged Sybil in the side. "I still haven't heard all the juicy details about your weekend."

"I never promised to tell you *all!*" Sybil protested with a laugh.

Their bantering continued until they reached the ward. The two paused at the door. Sybil suddenly turned serious. "I felt a lot of resentment against males in the past," she admitted. "But my relationship with Brian has soothed most of the turmoil in my inner feelings."

Connie, surprised by the remark, agreed nonetheless. "That's a bad habit we women have," Connie said. "We seem to have an unreasonable urge to subjugate ourselves to men." A spark of anger flashed across her face. "And we've got to stop it!"

"Let's talk about it later," Sybil suggested. She opened the door and they went on the ward.

Penny Darwin stood up as they walked into the office. "Hi, you two." She winked at Sybil "How was the weekend?"

"Great."

"Glad you enjoyed yourself," Penny said. "Listen, I have to go over and relieve Norma. She's watching Sai. As soon as I can, I want to hear all about it. Bye."

"Bye."

"Whoops!" Ernie Kaznowski coming through the door almost bumped into Penny on her way out. "Boy! She's in a hurry, ain't she?" He carried a cardboard box with him. "Hi, you two. Anybody want some Kool-Aid? I just got a package from home."

"Ernie!" Sybil said.

He laughed. "Hey! It's the truth. Connie's mom sent me a box of goodies."

Connie laughed. "I wrote her about you. I figured she'd do that."

"Yeah!" Ernie acknowledged happily. He sat the parcel on the desk. "Look. Chocolate chip cookies. Your sister Terry made 'em. They're in a little tin box and everything."

"That's just great, Ernie."

"There was a letter saying they'd be sending me stuff on a reg'lar basis," Ernie said. He looked at Connie. "That's real swell, Connie. Means a lot to me."

"I'm glad it does, Ernie," Connie said.

"Hey, I'm gonna take these cookies out on the ward and share 'em with the guys before I take the temps and pulses, okay?" Without waiting for an answer he left the office.

"When did you write your mom?" Sybil asked.

"The next day after we talked with Ernie," Connie said. "Let me tell you something. That kid's situation is just the type that'll tear at a Mexican mother's heart. You've heard of Jewish mothers? They're nothing—*nada*—in comparison with Chicana mamas. That kid is going to get a package at least twice a month now."

"Did you make sure to tell her to put Kool-Aid in them?"

Connie laughed. "Yeah. No sweat. Between my

mom and sisters, that kid is going to get a bicultural bunch of goodies. All the traditional American stuff along with *chorizo, dulces, panocha, jalapenos—*"

"Hold it!" Sybil said laughing. "I don't know what that stuff is. But I'm sure he'll like it."

"We'll like it, too," Connie said. "We'll make him share the stuff with us."

Ernie came back in the office. He set the remainder of the cookies on the desk so the two nurses could have some. "I'm gonna have to go see the sergeant major today."

"Did he tell you so?" Sybil asked.

"Naw. But all through reveille formation this mornin' he kept givin' me the civil eye."

"*Evil* eye," Sybil corrected.

"Whatever," Ernie said. He pulled the record cart from its place and pushed it toward the door. "Well, to work."

Sybil sat down at the desk and pulled the ever-demanding patients' log out to enter the latest data on it. She had just flipped it open to the current listings when the phone rang. She picked it up. "Convalescent Ward, Lieutenant Watkins speaking—yes—is that right away? Okay—I mean 'roger.' "

Connie looked at her.

"Ernie was right."

"Him? About what?"

"He has to report to the sergeant major immediately."

"Uh-oh!" Connie said.

"And we have to report to Colonel Sedgewick at ten."

"Oh, no!"

"Oh, yes."

"I'll go tell Ernie," Connie said. She tended to the task and returned. "He's on his way."

"Brian warned me about this."

"He figures we're all in deep *mierda?"*

"Yes," Sybil said.

"Well, no time to worry about it now," Connie said. "I've got to get out on the ward and finish taking those temperatures and pulses before doctor's rounds."

"Okay. I'll stay on the log."

The two tended to their tasks and were ready to accompany the doctor when he showed up to examine the patients. Since there had been no serious relapses or emergencies among the wounded soldiers, the activity didn't take much time.

At nine-thirty, Ernie walked into the office. "Hi."

"What happened?" Sybil asked.

"I got nailed for gettin' Mother snockered," Ernie said. "Rafferty was really pissed. For a minute I thought the big sonofabitch was gonna punch me out or somethin'. He chewed my ass, then drug me into the colonel's office. I got a lecture on what a no good rat I was, then offered a court-martial or Article Fifteen."

"I know what a court-martial is," Sybil said. "But what's an Article Fifteen?"

"Unit punishment," Ernie said. "That's what I chose."

"What did they dish out to you?" Connie asked.

"I got busted a rank down to Pfc."

"Oh, Ernie! Did they make a specific charge against you?"

"Yeah. I think they said it was insufficiency."

"In*efficency,"* Connie said.

"No matter. Don't worry about it. I got busted twice from Pfc before I made specialist anyhow."

"It's still a shame," Sybil said.

"Yeah. Well, I was told to remind you that the colonel is waitin'."

"Do you suppose we'll be reduced in rank?" Sybil asked.

"No way, kid," Connie said. "Officers aren't busted like the enlisted men. We'll end up with our butts chewed and bad efficiency reports."

"Doesn't seem fair," Sybil said. She checked her watch. "Let's go over there now. It's close enough to ten."

"Okay," Connie said.

Sybil had never been in trouble before in her life. All through school she was a straight A student on the honor role without a disciplinary mark against her. Somehow the world seemed different with punishment and chastisement hanging over her head. Sybil, true to her nature, suddenly felt guilty.

Connie, on the other hand, was defiant. "We didn't do a goddamn thing!" she said under her breath as they walked along. "That old bitch has been asking for it. She's nothing but a chickenshit, miserable martinet. And that goes for that stupid Rafferty, too."

"Connie, calm down."

"I won't! We do a good job, and so does Ernie," Connie insisted. "If he got Mother drunk it was because she asks to be treated that way."

Sybil stopped and grabbed Connie's arm. "I want you to promise me something."

"What?"

"That you won't get belligerent, okay? Whatever

you do, don't talk back. That's all I ask."

Connie hesitated. "You're such a cold soul at times, *amigita*. Just the opposite of this *Latina*." She was thoughtful. "Okay. I'll cool it. Unless I feel either you, me, or our collective intelligence is insulted."

Their arrival at headquarters was greeted with a wide smile by Sergeant Major Rafferty. He asked them to wait, then went into Sedgewick's office to announce them. He returned and displayed another toothy grin. "The colonel will see you now, ladies."

Connie started to say something, but Sybil grabbed her and hustled her into the office. They both saluted and reported properly, as instructed at Fort Sam Houston, then stood in silence, waiting for whatever the colonel had to say.

Sedgewick, sitting at his desk, surveyed them while tapping his fingertips together. Finally, he asked. "Did you two know that Kaznowski was getting Major Moorehead drunk at the birthday party?"

"Yes, sir," Sybil answered.

"Did you think it might be a good idea to stop him?"

"No, sir," Connie quickly responded.

"This puts me in a hell of a situation," Sedgewick said. "An enlisted man pulling a thing like that on a senior officer, with the knowledge of two subalterns, is something that can't possibly be ignored. And let me add something else. It was a very mean thing to do."

Sybil felt truly ashamed now. She hadn't said anything to Connie or Ernie, but she had felt sorry for Mother Moorehead.

"I realize that Major Moorehead is not a very popular person around the unit," Sedgewick continued. "But she has a job to do—a difficult job that involves supervisory responsibility and the administration of discipline. Have any of you considered that?"

"She is disrespectful to her staff," Connie said.

"How's that?" Sedgewick inquired.

"Her nurses are not a bunch of bonehead children," Connie said. "We're young, yes, but we've proven that we can be dead serious about things, too. I feel safe in saying there's not an incompetent nurse in the Triple-Nickel. But, boy! We're treated like we're each a disaster waiting to happen."

"I see," Sedgewick said. "So, because of that, you considered it okay to intoxicate the woman without her knowledge in the full hope she'd make a fool of herself under the influence of alcohol."

"Yes, sir," Connie said.

"Careful, lieutenant," Sedgewick said coldly. "I should probably ask you if you're aware of your rights under the articles of the Uniform Code of Military Justice."

"That means we're not required to say anything that could be used against us," Connie said.

"Oh, never mind," Sedgewick said. "I'm not going to court-martial you young ladies. Hell! I'm not even going to enter this in your efficiency reports. I just want to counsel you."

"Thank you, colonel," Sybil said sincerely.

"I respect you—all of you nurses—but you two especially. I've seen your genuine concern and compassion and I think it's wonderful," Sedgewick said. "But I want to advise you that doing things to superior officers—even unpopular ones—is not only wrong. It's childish."

Both Sybil and Connie nodded.

"In fact, it was ill-advised as hell," Sedgewick said. "I'm probably going to have to face the wrath of the ARs as it is, myself. That Vietnamese baby is going to be an albatross around all our necks."

"Oh, Christ!" Connie said.

Sybil felt sure of herself. "I don't care. We did the right thing, and nobody can convince me any different."

Sedgewick said, "I won't argue with you." He looked at them again. "There is one more unpleasant subject to cover."

"What's that, sir?" Sybil asked.

"Your conduct toward the sergeant major. It was indefensible," Sedgewick said. "He is an enlisted man. You outrank him, though I'll admit he had a lot of power as a senior sergeant that gives him advantages over junior officers like yourselves."

"Rafferty has always been quick to point out to the nurses that he is not in their chain-of-command, sir," Connie said.

"Well, he most certainly isn't, but he's closer to me than you are in the army's system of things," Sedgewick pointed out. "I'm going to have a few words with him to put things right where you young women are concerned. But I want a mutual understanding and respect between you and him."

"Yes, sir," Sybil said.

"That's all," Sedgewick said. "Remember what we've spoken of here. Let's change our personal attitudes. You're doing good jobs—hell, you're doing great jobs—keep that side of your careers up, and do things the army way."

"We'll do our best," Sybil promised.

"Fine. That's all."

They saluted and went back to the outer office. They wordlessly walked past Rafferty's desk. As they went out the door they could hear Sedgewick's voice call out loudly, "Sergeant major!"

They trudged slowly back to the ward. "I don't know what to think," Sybil said.

"I still think Mother Moorehead asked for it."

"I suppose the key words in the whole discussion was when Colonel Sedgewick told us we should concentrate on doing things the army's way."

"Yeah," Connie agreed.

"I'm going to stop off at the communications hut and call Brian," Sybil said. "I want to let him know what happened about this situation. He was afraid I'd be confined to quarters or something."

"I'll meet you on the ward," Connie said. "Say hello for me."

"Right."

Fresh lines had been installed by the signal unit since Sybil's last call. This time the connection was made without a hitch.

The voice on the other end was loud and clear – five by five, as they said in the army. "Three-Shop, Dixon speakin'."

"I want to speak to Captain Mallory, please," Sybil requested.

"Sorry, ma'am. The cap'n is TDY."

Chapter Fifteen

Sybil walked dully back to the ward. She nodded to Connie, then sat down at the desk to begin work on the patients' log.

"Did you tell Brian you weren't going to the stockade?"

"Mmm," Sybil said nodding. She didn't want to talk about the situation at that particular moment. She made a mistake in the log and tore out the paper, tossing it into the wastebasket.

Connie, arranging the medications on the dispensing cart, smiled at her. "None of us are perfect, my dear."

Sybil made no response. But she did repeat the error. "Damn it," she said under her breath.

Connie chuckled. "If at first you don't succeed—"

Sybil glanced up at her without smiling, then turned back once again to her chore. She made the same mistake for the third time. "Oh, shit! Shit!"

Finally Connie was fed up after watching her have to fill out the same form three times in a row. "Hey! What's the matter with you, *amigita?*"

"Nothing's the matter!" Sybil snapped. "You just pay attention to your own business."

"Sorry."

Sybil sat quietly for several seconds. "Oh, Connie!"

"I say again – what's the matter?"

"Brian is gone," she answered.

"You mean to combat?" Connie softened her voice. "Are you sure?"

"Yeah. TDY. They said he's TDY," Sybil said. "In their jargon that means he's back in the war."

"I guess you don't know where, huh?"

Sybil shook her head. "No. And I won't hear from him until he gets back."

"I'm sure that'll be real soon, *amigita*."

"He was out three months last time," Sybil said. She laughed bitterly. "At least I know he won't be gone more than four. That's all he has left on his tour."

Connie gazed closely at Sybil for several long moments. "Go back to the billets. I'll finish up the paperwork. Lie down and rest. I'll come get you and we'll go to the mess hall together."

Sybil was grateful. "Thanks a lot. I appreciate it, Connie, I truly do."

"Sure. I'll pick up some scotch at the package store and we'll have a few drinks and talk the evening away. How's that sound?"

"Sounds fine," Sybil responded.

"Right. See you later."

Sybil walked off the ward feeling worse than she'd felt in a long, long time.

* * *

It was still dark the next morning when Sybil woke up. She checked the luminous hands on the alarm clock and noted that it was four o'clock.

The soft sound of Connie's deep breathing filled the room. Sybil slipped from under the covers and plugged in the hot plate on the desk. After putting a pot on the burner she went to her locker for some instant coffee. Then she waited for the water to boil.

She and Connie had talked late. Sybil noted that not too much of the scotch was gone from the bottle sitting on the desk. There had been more conversation than drinking, which accounted for her clear head even that early in the morning.

A few minutes later, sipping coffee, she stared out into the compound. There was a large pile of sandbags waiting to be filled. The burlap containers were stacked between the nurses' billets and the supply shed. With the war sharply escalating, it was feared the Viet Cong would step up their activities to include strikes inside Long Binh itself. Thus, all buildings were going to be sandbagged for extra protection. Even the windows were going to be provided with reinforced shutters.

Sybil felt terribly sad. For the first time since her arrival she had to admit to homesickness. The thought of curling up in her own bed in the house back in Oklahoma City was so comforting and wonderful, she could feel her eyes watering.

But she knew that was only a cover for her real emotions.

Her heart ached for Brian. Her first love—her only

love. She brought Brian's face to focus in her mind. Sybil could see the square jaw and sharp nose. His close-cropped black hair, green eyes and rugged good looks were as plain to her at that moment as if he'd been standing there.

He was her man—kind, considerate, caring, loving—and he was out somewhere in that terrible war. Maybe deep behind enemy lines involved in that awful guerrilla fighting the Green Berets participated in.

If only he were in a nice safe rear-echelon supply or maintenance unit instead.

But then, if he hadn't been in Special Forces, he wouldn't have know Nicholson. And if he hadn't known Nicholson, he wouldn't have come on the ward to visit him. And if that hadn't happened, he and Sybil would never have met—never have become lovers.

Fate was kind in that instant. Would it stay kind and let them see the fulfillment of the dreams developed from their relationship?

Sybil continued to sip the coffee thoughtfully.

Suddenly she was angry with herself. She was acting like her whole world had been destroyed. Nothing had happened! There was no reason to weep! She had to be strong and get on with things. There were too many wonderful years ahead to worry about their being wiped out of her life.

"I'll go check on little Sai," she said aloud. She set the cup down and went out in the hall.

Noi awoke when she came into the room. The little Vietnamese woman smiled widely at her. "Sybil! I not see you for some days."

Sybil felt a bit ashamed. "I've been very busy."

"Oh, yes! Nurse all the time busy," Noi said.

Sybil walked over and checked the baby. Its breath was shallow and rapid. The bottles of antibiotics and epinephrine solution seemed fairly full. "How long has it been since anyone's seen her?"

"Nurse here one hour ago maybe," Noi answered. "Then Doctor Sedgewick come before dark."

"Did they say anything?"

Noi shook her head. "No. They not say nothing. But doctor tell me Sai same-same very sick." She started to sob.

Sybil put her arms around her and hugged her, pulling her close to her own body. "Don't worry."

"Sybil?" Noi said in a pleading manner. "We pray, okay?"

Sybil looked at her. "Pray?"

"Yes. Okay?"

She thought about it a moment. "Of course, Noi. We'll pray together. How's that?"

Noi crossed herself. "Yes, Sybil. I have rosary. You have?"

Sybil smiled softly and shook her head. "In my religion we don't use them. Let's each do it our own way."

Noi, the rosary between her clasped hands, knelt by the bed. Sybil, her head bowed and eyes closed, stood just behind the worried little mother, murmuring a plea to the Almighty.

Bring some happiness out of all this horror, Sybil prayed. *Have it make some kind of sense, please. And think of my love Brian and me too, Lord. Put things right once and for all. Amen.*

Sybil watched Mike Pullini slowly and carefully

bandage his stumps. She pointed at his efforts. "One more loop around there, and make sure it's tight."

"Right," he said. He gave the wrapping a pull, then followed her directions.

"You're really limber and loose," Sybil marveled. She noted how he was able to easily reach down past his knees while keeping his legs straight.

"Yeah. People don't realize us weightlifters are agile guys," Mike said. "They think we're muscle-bound."

"They do, huh?" Sybil asked, glad to see the change in him.

"Yeah." He laughed. "Can you imagine somebody dumb enough to think you can develop your muscles to the point that you couldn't even move or bend over?"

"A common misconception of your sport, is it?"

"Sure is. Then they think if we quit lifting, our muscles turn to fat."

"That's a physiological impossibility," Sybil said. "As a nurse I know that."

"Right. If a lifter keeps eating a lot after he stops training, then he might get fat as his muscles grow smaller from not working out anymore. But they don't turn to fat." He made the last turn of the bandage and snapped the fastener on it. "So? How's that?"

"Very professional," Sybil said. "Always remember to leave the knee uncovered. You don't want to bind yourself up too tight."

"Okay."

"I haven't had much of a chance to talk to you," Sybil said, gathering up the wrappings he had just discarded before applying the fresh ones. "How's the lifting going?"

"Real good," Mike answered. He hunched his muscular shoulders, then stretched. "Feel like my old self. I'm up to two hundred and fifty without really pushing it. I expect to be around three hundred for the meet."

"Think that'll win it?"

"You bet!" he said with a wink.

Sybil was genuinely pleased with this new attitude. By the time he was back in the VA facilities he would be a real fighter, ready to put on those artificial legs and get on with the rest of his life. Unless he slipped back into his former funk. Only time would tell, and her work with him was far from over.

"You're a winner, Mike. I'll be there to root you on."

He laughed out loud. "Good! I like to show off for a pretty girl."

Sybil, smiling, carried the old bandages over to the laundry hamper and dropped them in.

Connie, sitting in the office, glanced up as she walked in. "How's ol' Mike doing down there, *amigita*?"

"On the rise," Sybil answered. "Let's hope he can keep it up."

"A lot of them that look promising have been known to lose out in the end," Connie reminded her.

"All we can do is our best."

"You're right about that." The phone rang and Connie picked it up. "Convalescent Ward, Lieutenant Montaldo, duty nurse speaking—right—oh—" Her face suddenly paled and she put a hand to her face. "—God! When? Okay, thanks." She hung up and looked at Sybil with a pained expression. "That was from the billets. Noi's baby just died."

"Oh, no!"

Connie's face registered alarm as she looked at Sybil. "Take it easy, okay?"

The same overwhelming feeling of grief she'd experienced when Nellie Simpson died swept through Sybil's emotions. She suddenly bolted, rushing off the ward.

People turned to stare at her as Sybil ran across the compound to the billets. She rushed through the hall down to the room. The door was open and she could see Noi sitting numbly on the edge of the bed. Little Sai was gone, but the intravenous bottles, their tubes now hanging limply in the air, were still slung in their places.

"Noi! Oh, Noi!" Sybil cried. "I'm so sorry!" She sat down and put her arms around the small woman.

Noi didn't respond. Her face was a mask of numbed incomprehension as she stared at the floor.

Sybil, weeping softly, continued to hold her. "It's such a shame. Little Sai—little Sai—"

The quiet was broken by the sudden wheezing on the compound loudspeakers. Then a voice, distorted slightly by the electronics, blared out.

"Incoming wounded! Incoming wounded! All personnel report to alert stations for incoming wounded!"

"Oh, God! Not now! Not now of all times!" Sybil cried. She could hear the sleeping off-duty nurses stirring. At the same time came the ominous sound of helicopters in the distance. Calming down a bit, she looked at Noi. "I have to go, understand? There are hurt soldiers arriving, and I must help them."

Noi said nothing, still gazing dazedly at nothing.

Sybil got off the bed. "Stay here. Wait for me. I'll be back when I can."

After one more glance, she rushed outside.

When Sybil arrived at her proper position on the chopper landing pads, she found Connie, Ernie, and Joe Sampson standing by the ambulance.

Connie walked up to Sybil and took her arm. "How is Noi taking it?"

"It's hard to tell," Sybil answered wiping at her eyes. "She's somewhere between devastated and completely in shock. I left her in the billets and told her to wait for me."

"Yes. That was best," Connie said.

By then the most advanced of the helicopters were hovering in for a landing. Ernie and Joe rushed out to unload the first litter.

It turned into a long afternoon. An entire battalion of infantry had been badly mauled during a battle. They had disembarked on their landing zone in a normal manner, but suddenly all hell had broken loose.

Several helicopters had been blown out of the sky to crash into the troops below. The result had been several bad burn injuries. Sybil could see that a couple of these wounded were stark naked, their uniforms having been burned off, and their massive, charred wounds covered nearly all their bodies. The stench wasn't the worst part of it. What made it so terrible was that they were all classified as expectants.

Sybil and Connie left these doomed victims of the war to others. Their task was to treat those who could survive. Most of these other injuries were not too bad. They were the lucky wounded who had been hit by small arms fire and suffered one or two gunshot wounds that were relatively clean.

The next batch of patients proved to be the most mangled. These were the unfortunates who had been in on the pursuit of the enemy once the ambush was finally broken. The Viet Cong had used prearranged escape routes, heavily booby-trapped and mined, to withdraw. The American soldiers following them had stepped on these explosive charges that turned healthy feet and legs into splintered sticks of shredded flesh and splintered bone.

"Jesus!" Connie said. "More like Mike Pullini."

Sybil nodded a silent agreement as she went through the procedure of examining the suffering burdens on the litters. She instinctively followed the A, B, C of checking out the wounded:

A—Airway. Make sure it is clear and unobstructed.

B—Breathing. Check the wounded man is able to breathe, watch for sucking chest wounds.

C—Circulation. Check the heat and insure there is an adequate volume of circulating blood.

Now and then she looked at the expectants, lying off to the side. The doctors who had verified the unlucky men's condition supervised the administration of painkillers to ease the last hours—or minutes—of life.

Ernie and Joe made no less than a dozen trips back to surgery with the ambulance before the last stretcher had been delivered. When they returned for Sybil and Connie, the two nurses were physically exhausted by the heat and effort of the previous hour and a half.

"Here, ladies," Ernie said handing each a cold canteen of Kool-Aid. "Get in the back and we'll get you back to the billets."

The two wordlessly followed his suggestion and barely noticed the discomfort of the bumpy ride as they returned to their quarters.

"I'll check on Noi," Sybil said sliding out the tailgate of the vehicle.

Ernie and Joe gunned to motor of their ambulance and headed toward the motor pool, while Sybil and Connie went in the building.

"Bring her to our room," Connie said. "I'll be waiting for you there."

"Good idea," Sybil said. "See you in a minute."

She hurried down the hall and checked the impromptu ICU they had set up. But it was empty. A flash of frustrated anger shot through Sybil. She figured that Mother Moorehead must have come and taken Noi away. But she noticed the young woman's pathetic bundle of belongings was still in the corner.

"Noi! Noi!" she called out. She walked quickly down the hall. Sybil went from room to room searching frantically. Then she went outside and checked the immediate area.

A couple of unit medics walked by. Sybil called out to them. "Have you seen a Vietnamese woman around here?"

They laughed. One replied, "Sure, ma'am. Hundreds of 'em."

"Millions!" his companion chortled.

"I wish there was half that many white gals," the first said.

Frustrated, Sybil turned from them. The next logical place to look was the latrine. She rushed there, hitting the door so hard she scraped her arm. She ignored the hurt as she called out Noi's name. Sybil looked into each toilet stall before going into the shower room. When she got there she stopped. "Oh, sweet Lord!"

Noi, her face contorted, swung slowly back and forth. The colorful scarf that was tightly wrapped around her neck had been tied to one of the spigots. The small woman's body wasn't heavy enough to pull the plumbing down. An overturned stool lay beneath her bare feet.

Sybil grabbed Noi's legs and attempted to lift her while screaming at the top of her lungs. "Help me! Help me! For the love of God! Somebody get in here and help me!"

Chapter Sixteen

The nurses in the briefing room stood at attention, their eyes riveted on the front wall where the blackboard stood. Major Moorehead strode to the head of her captive audience, then turned and faced them. Her face was severe and ill-humored. "Take your seats, ladies."

There was a rustle of chairs and feet as the group sat down. Mother set her notes on the podium situated directly in the center of her nurses. "There are a few announcements to be made," she said loudly. "So let's all listen attentively."

Sybil, seated between Connie Montaldo and Penny Darwin, knew she was going to have trouble concentrating. Noi and Sai's double funeral had been only the day before. The Triple-Nickel's Catholic chaplain conducted the services. Because Noi was a war widow, she and her baby were able to be interred in the military cemetery at Long Binh. The nurses chipped in for a simple headstone that was designed for both graves.

Although she felt terrible in a personal way, Sybil was aware that the awful event had affected the other nurses, too. All had taken their turns in caring for the baby, and the useless cruelty of Sai's death, coupled with the tragedy of suicide, had sobered their moods even more than did the influx of badly wounded soldiers.

Sybil didn't know if she would be able to endure much more of the long ride she was taking on an emotional roller coaster. The elation she'd felt over finding Brian, which had been bolstered by Mike Pullini's new attitude, had plummeted after the two deaths and Brian's assignment to active operations. The sudden wiping away of her happiness had left her mentally listless and easily irritated.

Major Moorehead's emergence back into the life of the Triple-Nickel hadn't helped much. Extremely embarrassed and angry, Mother had resumed her duties with a vengeance after the three days it took her to recover from her unintentional bender. She perceived every smile or innocent look in her direction as an insult or act of derision toward her—and the chief of nurses responded accordingly.

Now, eyebrows arched and eyes blazing, she gazed out over the nurses seated before her in the unit briefing hut.

"The first thing on our agenda is security," Mother said. "We all remember the large number of casualties that were brought into our area the other day. Some careless person in that infantry battalion had made a casual remark about their upcoming attack, and the news was overheard by a spy or someone in the employ of the enemy. That communist agent then turned the information over to his superiors. Thus, when those brave American boys went into action, they found themselves trapped in a well-conceived ambush."

Sybil tried to concentrate.

Mother Moorehead went on. "So we want to be very careful about what we say and to whom. Even an innocent comment may prove invaluable to the Viet Cong. An example would be to disclose the location of our headquarters to someone making what seems a casual inquiry. Such comments could give information to a potential bomber—such as the one who struck out in the market area a few weeks back."

Penny Darwin raised her hand. "How are we supposed to identify these spies or whatever they are? All the Vietnamese civilians look alike."

"Then don't talk to any of them," Mother advised.

"But we have to," Penny argued. "The maids who clean our room are Vietnamese. Can't they be trusted?"

"No."

"Good Lord!" Penny exclaimed. "You mean the girl who changes the sheets might slit my throat?"

"Or leave a booby trap in your room while you're on duty," Mother said. "There's also the possibility she reports what she sees and overhears in our garrison to a superior. Or, perhaps, someday in the future, will guide enemy raiders into our midst."

Another nurse, her voice trembling with emotion, stood up. She had only been in Vietnam for a few weeks. "What kind of a war is this?"

"It's a just struggle. But a dirty one," Mother said.

"Waged against a godless communist cause."

"But—but—" The young woman had trouble speaking. "If we can't trust the people in the compound, what are we to do? Simply hope for the best?"

"Yes," Mother said. "Keep in mind what our soldiers are going through out in the field. Sacrifices have to be made in times like these. People are going to die—as you all should well know."

The nurse was angry. "This is not—"

"At ease!" Mother commanded. "That's enough discussion on the subject. Just remember to always be conscious of security requirements. During World War II they had a saying that went: *Loose Lips Sink Ships.* The meaning behind those words is just as important in this struggle. Any questions?"

It was obvious from the silence that Mother's words had dealt a hard blow to their morale. An invisible wave of fear permeated the room.

Mother continued. "Now, item number two involves morals. I've spoken of this before, but evidently it doesn't seem to register with you ladies. There have been many observances of nurses from Long Binh going to the hotel near here with male personnel and spending the night."

Connie raised her hand.

Mother ignored her. "And there have also been cases of nurses sneaking male personnel into the billets to spend the night."

Connes shook her raised hand.

"Ladies, we must guard our own morals," Mother said. "We are here to minister to wounded, not to provide sexual relief to the troops."

Connie stood up. "Ma'am."

Mother sighed. “Yes, Montaldo?”

“I don’t think that’s fair.”

Mother’s eyebrows arched. “Make your point, Montaldo.”

“There’s a double standard here,” Connie said. “It seems it’s perfectly all right for the boys to have their sexual escapades. Everybody laughs about it and cheers them on. Hell, there’s even been commanders that have had whores trucked in for their troops.”

Mother frowned. “The male sex drive—”

“To hell with the male sex drive,” Connie exclaimed. “What about the female sex drive, huh? At least we don’t go out banging hell out of half the population and spreading VD around like a common cold.”

“Montaldo!” Mother warned.

“Connie!” Sybil begged under her breath.

“The girls that have done the things you mentioned only did them with guys they were involved with,” Connie said. “By God, if I like a man I’m—”

“That’s enough!” Mother exclaimed.

“What’s good enough for the boys is good enough for the girls,” Connie insisted.

“At ease!” Mother said.

Connie could see she was getting nowhere. She reluctantly sat down.

Mother glared at her. “You’ll be having a bit of help in maintaining the proper behavior, Montaldo. Effective today, all nurses will have a curfew of twenty-four hundred hours. That means signed in, inside the compound and deep in the interior of the nurses’ billets.”

“What about the male personnel?” Connie asked.

“They are able to remain out as long as they have the proper pass,” Mother said.

Connie leaped back to her feet. "Major Moorehead!"

Sybil grabbed her arm. She shushed her friend, speaking in a whisper. "Give it up, Connie. Sit down—please!"

Connie wisely gave in to her friend's wish and resumed her seat. Mother Moorehead turned back to her notes for some more administrative announcements.

Sybil angrily glared at her friend. "Just knock it off, all right?" she said leaning close.

"The hell if I will!" Connie whispered back.

"All you're going to do is make trouble," Sybil said. "There's nothing to be gained by it."

Connie's eyes flashed. "I'm not taking any crap off her, see?"

"You're in the army!" Sybil said. "Remember what Colonel Sedgewick said."

"That doesn't mean I'm going to get a royal screwing and not say anything," Connie shot back.

"Watkins! Montaldo!" Mother's voice was loud and piercing. "Is it asking too much for you to pay attention?"

"No, ma'am," Sybil said.

"Then see that you do. Particularly since this last announcement is very important to you."

"Yes, ma'am," Sybil said.

"As part of the program to win the hearts and minds of the Vietnamese people, the army is going to provide medical teams to go out to various villages to give examinations and treatment to civilian personnel—particularly children," Mother announced. "The Five fifty-fifth Field Hospital has been chosen to send one such group of people out. The doctor-in-charge will be Captain Anthony Ryder. The medical corpsman assigned to him will be Specialist—change that—*Private First Class* Ernest Kaznowski."

Sybil and Connie looked at each other, then swung their concerned gazes back to Major Moorehead.

"The two nurses posted to the detail are Second Lieutenants Watkins and Montaldo." Mother, almost smirking, looked at them. "Perhaps a few days away from the comforts of this garrison will make you two ladies grateful for what you have here. And you'll show your appreciation by a change in attitudes."

Sybil asked, "Just what are we going to do out there, ma'am?"

"Physical examinations and vaccinations mostly," Mother answered. "And, if time and facilities permit, probably perform some minor surgeries if necessary."

"Yes, ma'am," Sybil acknowledged.

"You'll be out in the countryside where the Viet Cong guerrillas are active," Mother said with a grim smile. "I would advise you to stick close to whatever village you end up in."

Sybil and Connie glanced at each other. Connie winked. "Looks like we're going to war, *amigita*."

Chapter Seventeen

Sybil, buckled into the web seat of the H34 helicopter, gazed out the door down at the greenery of the jungle three thousand feet below.

This was her first ride in a chopper, and the awful noise combined with the shaking, made her feel slightly nauseous. Hot air whipped into the interior of the fuselage adding to her discomfort.

Captain Anthony Ryder sat on her left next to the cockpit. He dozed fitfully with his head resting against the vibrating bulkhead, opening his eyes now and then when the aircraft would react almost violently from either an up- or downdraft. Then, satisfied they weren't about to crash into the trees, he would close his eyes and once again attempt to sleep.

Connie, on the other side, tried to read a magazine she'd brought with her, but the roughness of the flight made it impossible. She was a bit pale, Sybil noticed, and there were beads of perspiration on her forehead.

Ernie, on the other hand, was having a ball. He sat across from them in the wide doorway. He wore a helmet that was plugged into the helicopter's intercom, and chatted over the communications system with the crew chief beside him. The other young soldier was about Ernie's own age.

The kid sat behind a machine gun mounted on the deck. The barrel pointed outward, and he demonstrated to Ernie how he used it. He swung the muzzle around, showing the arc of fire he had, then suddenly pulled the trigger very quickly a couple of times.

The shots sounded dull in the roar of the engine. Sybil could barely discern the reports but could see the flash of the muzzle as the bullets were fired. She saw Ernie speak enthusiastically into the microphone, then the two youngsters changed places.

Now Ernie sat behind the gun. After a couple of experimental swings, he slipped his finger into the trigger guard and fired the weapon a few times. Again, the rapid chug-chug of the firearm sounded dully within the engine's noise.

Sybil vaguely wondered if Ernie had any idea where the bullets were striking down in the jungle canopy below. After a while, Ernie changed back with the crewman. The two returned to their enthusiastic chattering to each other over the intercom.

Sybil glanced at their medical supplies lashed down to the deck toward the rear of the fuselage. There were also some rations and other gear destined for some outlying infantry unit. The gear vibrated with the aircraft, the heavy canvas straps holding the cargo securely in place.

The several boxes that belonged to the medical team

contained vaccines, bandages, medicines, and apparatus to conduct their mission. She and her companions had been told that most of the children in the rural areas suffered from intestinal parasites. For that reason Doctor Ryder had seen to it that there was an ample supply of metronidazole and didohydroxyquin in with the drugs.

There was a sudden change in the pitch of the engine. The horizon outside the door tilted crazily, and Sybil knew they were turning. The feeling in the pit of her stomach also informed her the helicopter was descending.

Ernie waved to attract her attention, then pointed downward enthusiastically. Evidently this was their destination. Sybil leaned forward to see better. In her imagination she had pictured thatched huts arranged in a circle within a jungle clearing. Instead, she saw a system of trenches and what appeared to be piles of sandbags formed into a line that snaked around the area. She reached over to shake Doctor Ryder, but he was already awake, looking out the door.

It seemed to grow a bit warmer as their descent continued. Soon there were clouds of dust outside, then the helicopter bounced a bit, before settling down. After a few moments, the engine's noise ceased, leaving a vacuum of silence that pounded at Sybil's ears as badly as the former roaring she had endured for two hours.

Ernie slipped off the helmet. "We're here, folks," he announced with a grin. He slipped out to the ground, then turned to help Sybil and Connie off.

Sybil's legs felt stiff. Once on the ground she stretched while emitting a loud sigh of relief.

"Ay!" Connie exclaimed. "That isn't exactly the most luxurious form of travel, is it?"

"It beats walking," Sybil said. "But not by much."

Ryder joined them at the same time an American soldier strode up. He wore no rank insignia, only a uniform bearing a camouflage pattern of black and green stripes. His hat, a sloppy, narrow-brimmed affair, sat on the back of his head. A rifle was slung over one broad shoulder. He smiled at them, "Howdy."

Ryder looked uncertainly at him. "Good afternoon. I'm Captain Ryder reporting in with a medic and two nurses to set up a clinic for the village children."

"I'm Lieutenant Coleson, the exec," he said. "What's this about a clinic?"

Sybil, uncertain, glanced around the area. "We've been detailed to give the local youngsters physical exams and limited treatment," she said.

Coleson laughed. "You won't be able to involve yourselves in that kind of activity here. There's no kids around. No civilians at all, as a matter of fact."

"Damn it!" Ryder said in irritation. "We must've landed at the wrong place. We were supposed to go to a village called Ha Khe Nui."

"This is Ha Khe Nui all right, but it ain't a village. We're a fortified hamlet, but there's only military here now," Coleson explained. "There were some people and a militia outfit, but they've been moved further south."

"When was this?" Sybil asked.

"It was before I got here," Coleson said. "Prob'ly three or four months ago."

"Three or four months!" Connie exclaimed. "And the people back at Long Binh didn't know about it?"

"I suppose not," Coleson said.

"Typical army fuck-up," Ernie said.

The helicopter pilot, a young warrant officer, stepped from his machine. He walked cheerfully over to them. "You folks look confused."

"Yeah," Ryder said. "Evidently the people we're supposed to treat aren't here anymore."

"One of these days somebody that knows what he's doin' is gonna take over this war and we'll win it in within a week or two," the pilot said.

Connie crossed her arms. "Just a normal screw-up, right?"

"Well, something's certainly wrong," Ryder said. "My crew and I were supposed to be conducting a kiddie's clinic, but evidently there's no children here."

"Typical, all right," the pilot said. "Listen, I've got another delivery of supplies to make. Why don't you contact your headquarters and get it straightened out? I'll be back in the morning and pick you up."

"You can't wait?" Sybil inquired.

"No, ma'am. I've got to get that other stuff out to the grunts, pronto," the pilot said. "And I'll have to refuel before I do much more flying."

Ryder sighed. "Well, I guess we have no choice." He looked at Coleson. "You have accommodations here for overnight visitors?"

"Sure," the lieutenant said with an easy grin. "They ain't the best, but they're snug and safe. C'mon, I'll take you to the old man."

"We'll get our personal gear out of the chopper," Ryder said. "We can leave the medical supplies aboard since we won't be using them."

"Good idea," the pilot said. He glanced skyward.

"Look at them clouds. The ol' monsoon will be with us soon."

Sybil looked upward. "I hear from the old salts that you haven't seen rain until you've seen the monsoon."

"They're right," the pilot said. "The water comes down in sheets." He motioned to Ernie. "C'mon, let's get your stuff off my chopper so I can haul ass."

Ernie followed the flyer back to his machine and fetched the medical team's bags. They stood back watching as the chopper rattled back to life, then lifted off into the muggy, tropical sky.

"C'mon, folks," Coleson said cheerfully. "I'll take you over to the command post."

As they walked across the hamlet, Sybil took in their new surroundings. There were plenty of gun emplacements and trenches. All were manned by armed troops. Sandbags and barbed wire were everywhere. The men, not on duty, dully watched the group as they walked through them. The staring of so many male eyes made Sybil a bit nervous. She was glad Ernie and Ryder had come along with her and Connie. There were only a few Americans, dressed like Coleson, standing around. Most were South Vietnamese soldiers.

Coleson stopped in front of a dugout. He leaned down and shouted into the interior. "Hey, Skipper. We got some visitors. C'mon out and say howdy."

Within seconds the covering over the door, which was no more than a G.I. poncho, was flung back and a figure emerged.

Sybil gasped. "Brian!"

Brian Mallory, dressed like Coleson, stared at her for one incredulous moment. Then his handsome face broke into a delighted grin and he rushed forward. Without hesitating, he kissed her on the mouth while encircling her with his muscular arms.

Sybil's emotions flipflopped. "My God! Brian!"

"I can't believe it!" he exclaimed.

After the terrible letdown following Noi's and Sai's deaths, then Brian's sudden departure, her spirits suddenly reversed themselves and soared at seeing him. "I'm flabbergasted, darling!" Sybil said. "And that's putting it mildly."

"I'm a bit shaken myself," he conceded happily.

Sybil thought he looked wonderfully, romantically handsome—like a movie star. He was dressed in camouflage fatigues with a pistol belt, complete with holster, around his slim waist. His hat, of the same material as his uniform, was similar to Coleson's, but the brim was turned up at a cocky angle, and he wore it tipped forward on his head in a belligerent, but strangely charming kind of way.

Coleson laughed. "Skipper, that's either the girl you told us you're goin' with, or you're the best make-out artist in Southeast Asia."

Brian broke off the kiss but kept an arm around Sybil's waist. "Sweetheart, this is an old friend of mine and my exec, Jim Coleson. Jim, this is Sybil Watkins."

"Hi, Sybil," Coleson said offering his hand. "I hear you two are real serious."

"Yes," Sybil said. She introduced her three companions.

Ryder shook hands with Brian. "I've seen you before. I believe you were at Colonel Sedgewick's birthday party at Lucky's."

"Right," Brian said. "May I inquire as to the nature

of this unexpected but welcomed visit?"

"We were told there were children here," Sybil said. "The idea was to set up a temporary clinic for vaccinations, treatment of illness, and the like."

"The folks that used to live here are long gone," Brian said. "We've turned this place into a fortified base of operations."

"In other words," Ryder said, "there's no way we can find out where the villagers went either, huh?"

"I'm afraid not," Brian said. He made a gesture toward the entrance to the dugout. "Well, we don't want to stand out here in the hot sun, do we? Let's go into the shade and relax. There's cold beer in there."

"I'll see you later, Skipper," Coleson said. "I'm gonna finish running a check on the perimeter."

Sybil, holding hands with Brian, went down the earthen steps and slipped through the covering. As the others entered, they took seats around a picnic-style table in the center of the dugout.

"Sit down," Brian said. "Who wants a brew?"

"Me!" Ernie shouted.

"That goes without saying, sport," Brian said with a grin. He went to a small refrigerator and took out five beers. "We have a generator to give us a sufficient supply of electricity. We try to use our limited resources for important things." He laughed. "Like keeping our beer cold."

Ryder wiped the sweat trickling from beneath his fatigue cap. "We'd better send word back to Long Binh for further instructions."

"Yeah," Brian said. "We'll drop over to the commo shack and contact your outfit. But there's no rush. The chopper won't be back until tomorrow morning.

So relax and enjoy yourselves."

"What sort of a setup are you involved in here?" Ryder asked taking his can of beer.

"I've got a miniature A-Team," Brian explained. "Normally that would be about a dozen guys. As it is I've only got six besides myself. There's the exec, the operations sergeant, intelligence sergeant, a medic, a commo man, and one weapons leader. I'm working with two reinforced companies of ARVN infantry."

"Those are the South Vietnamese soldiers we saw in the trenches?" Sybil asked.

"Right. We were running counterinsurgency ops against the local VCs, but things have turned nasty," Brian explained further. "The Reds have been built up, and now they control all the surrounding countryside."

Connie took a sip of her beer. "You should ask for reinforcements."

"I have," Brian said. "In every after-action report I send in, I tell 'em Charlie has me outnumbered and outgunned." Brian's voice took on a bitter ring. "Then I add my casualty list. Right now we're pinned down here and can't do a damned thing about it."

"Is the situation impossible?" Ryder asked.

"Not yet," Brian answered. "But it's sure as hell going to be if something isn't done pretty damned quick. The best I can do is send out small night patrols. And even that is dangerous as hell under the circumstances."

"Can I have another beer?" Ernie asked.

"Sure, help yourself." Brian pulled a cigarette from his pocket.

"Do you smoke?" Sybil asked surprised.

"Only out here," Brian said. Then he grinned. "That sort of gives you an idea of how nervous I get."

Ryder seemed concerned. "We won't have any trouble flying out of here, will we?"

"No," Brian answered. "Charlie doesn't have an antiaircraft capability, or we wouldn't even be able to utilize choppers. But I'm waiting for that unhappy event to occur. Then I most certainly will be up that proverbial creek without a paddle."

"Anything we can do?" Sybil asked. "I mean in the way of medical assistance?"

"I'll have my medic come over," Brian said. He walked to a field telephone hanging on the dirt wall. He cranked it three times—two short and one long—then waited. Finally he spoke. "Barney, there's some medical personnel here. Why don't you drop over and see if they can be of some help to you?" He slipped the phone back into place, then resumed his seat. "We may be a bit short supply-wise, but nothing serious. Barney Chapman—that's our medic—hasn't had any real problems. He practices preventive medicine mostly. When there's casualties he just patches up enough for MEDEVAC, then sends 'em to the rear on the next chopper."

A few minutes later the poncho covering rustled. A lanky, slim soldier stepped inside. "These the people, Skipper?"

"Right," Brian said. "Folks, this is Barney Chapman." He introduced each of the visitors in turn. "These are the folks that took care of Gary Nicholson."

"How's my boy Gary doin'?" Chapman asked.

"Not bad," Sybil explained. She found the Special

Forces habit of addressing each other by their first names a refreshing change from the strict following of regulations under Mother and Rafferty back at the Triple-Nickel. "From the last report, it looks like he'll be sent back to duty."

Chapman laughed. "He'll be happy about that. The sumbitch is hardcore all the way. Really loves this army." He walked to the refrigerator and got a beer. "Say, I'm a little short on supplies. Is there any chance you brought somethin' that could be shared with me?"

"We left all our goodies on the chopper," Ryder said. "It didn't dawn on us that you could use any of them."

"Damn!" Chapman swore.

"It's all stuff for physical exams anyhow," Sybil explained. "Probably not much you could use."

"I can use anything, lieutenant," Chapman said. "I got everything here from gunshot wounds to beriberi. If I had some o' the right drugs, I could keep guys here instead o' shippin' 'em back allatime."

Ryder was interested. "Give us a rundown on the operation you've got going in this place."

"Sure, cap'n." Chapman launched into a professional summary of the work he was doing in the camp. He revealed he had a weird assortment of supplies due to the catch-as-catch-can system he worked under. There was plenty of anesthesia and surgical tools, but he was sort of simple antibiotics and bandages—though he had gotten in a rather curious shipment of dozens of field dressings for some reason. Chapman concluded with a quick rundown of the medical care he was providing single-handedly for the troops assigned to the hamlet.

Sybil and Connie were amazed. The medic, while an enlisted man, had received unusual and detailed instructions as a Special Forces medical specialist. In comparison with their own education, they found that he had received even more extensive training in certain areas than they had. He was able to perform emergency surgery and, indeed, had done exactly that on several occasions. The only area he had less training than they, as far as they could see, was in the kind of medicine that could be classified as the sophisticated, complicated procedures that weren't too practical to begin with.

"You have an excellent background on which to base further study," Ryder told him. "You should shoot for medical school when you get out of the army."

"I'm a lifer," Chapman said. "I been in the army twelve years, and I'm gonna stay 'til they throw me out or Charlie puts an end to me."

"Can I have another beer?" Ernie asked. Without waiting for an answer, he went to the refrigerator.

There was another rustle on the poncho entrance. An older American soldier stepped in. His hair was iron-gray and cropped short over his weathered face. Despite the ruggedness of his features, he displayed a friendly smile. "Hi. I heard from Jim we had visitors. Thought I'd drop in and get acquainted."

"How you doin', Top?" Chapman greeted the newcomer. "Want me to fetch you a beer?"

"Sure, thanks." He grinned at Brian. "Well, hell, Skipper. Don't just stand there. Do the honors."

Brian introduced Sybil and her friends. "This is Master Sergeant Top Meyers, the operations sergeant.

He's the senior NCO in the detachment, hence the nickname, Top."

Sybil mentally compared Top Meyers with Sergeant Major Rafferty. Top was obviously what could be described as a soldier's soldier. Tough as nails in appearance, he still seemed to have a human side to him. Sybil decided that the difference between Rafferty and Top was the difference between a commander and a leader.

"Looks like we'll have comp'ny for supper tonight," Top said. "Aside from Colonel Vang, that is."

"Who's Colonel Vang?" Sybil asked.

"He's the commander of these ARVN troops," Brian explained.

"A real asshole," Chapman said.

Connie took a sip of beer. "Bad personality?"

"You might say that," Top said. "He had a villa in the area here before the VC built up their strength and turned nasty. He had to flee from his luxurious accommodations and move in here with us poor folks. One of the reasons that the defenses here are a bit lacking in certain areas is because he took some of our cement to build himself a swimming pool."

"Can he do that?" Sybil asked. "I mean legally?"

Chapman looked at her. "You wouldn't believe how corrupt these ARVN sumbitches are."

"God!" Sybil exclaimed. "I find out that the rich Vietnamese keep their sons out of the army—and now this! The whole situation over here is so wretched and unfair it turns my stomach."

Top nodded his head in agreement. "This is my third war, and definitely the worst."

"Your *third?"* Sybil exclaimed.

"Yeah," he said.

"Top was a paratrooper in Europe in World War II, and again in Korea," Brian said.

Connie stared at him. *"Chihuahua,* Top! Isn't it time you got a nice soft job in the rear echelon?"

Top laughed. "Naw! What would these crazy young bastards do without an old hand like me watching out for them?"

"Amen, Top!" Chapman exclaimed.

Brian checked his watch. "Let's have a couple of more beers. Then it'll be time for dinner."

"I'll drink to that," Ernie said tossing his empty can to the table.

It was dark as Sybil and Brian stood together in the sandbagged emplacement. The position was located between the command post and the outer perimeter.

Brian put his arms around her and drew Sybil close. She tipped her face up and felt his lips brush her nose, then cheek, before finally settling onto her waiting mouth.

"Oh, Brian," she sighed. "I love you so."

"I love you, Sybil." They kept their voices low. He kissed her again, his hands lightly caressing her face. "I can't tell you how wonderful it was to climb out of that dugout and see you standing there."

"I was so ecstatic I thought I was going to burst into tears," Sybil said.

The sound of their voices was barely discernible to each other. This wasn't so much because of their being involved in lover's talk, but due more to the proximity of enemy activity. It was dangerous to speak normally or display any lights. The rule against loud talking was strictly enforced. Thus, the camp had settled into an alert silence as the men on duty strained their ears more than their eyes in trying to detect any unfriendly movement outside the perimeter of their wire.

Sybil stood close to Brian, feeling comforted by the pressure of his unseen arm around her. "How can you fight if they attack you in the dark?" she asked in a whisper.

"We have illuminating rounds at our mortar positions," Brian explained under his breath. "If Charlie hits us, we can turn the area bright as day. It's bad news for him."

"Have you been attacked since you've been here?" she asked nervously.

"Yeah. Twice," Brian said. "But they weren't serious. Charlie was just probing us to see how strong we were. We sustained casualties, but not many. Most of the men who've been hit were wounded out on patrol."

"Maybe you shouldn't have those patrols," Sybil said. She found the thought of Brian's leaving the safety of the hamlet and going out into the dangers of the surrounding jungle made her nearly shiver with fear and apprehension.

"Remember the old saying about the best defense being a good offense?" Brian asked. He didn't wait for an answer. "Anyhow, it keeps Charlie off balance and not so sure of himself. We've hurt him a few times while being out there."

"Let's not talk about it," Sybil said.

"Okay."

"Why do the men call you Skipper?" Sybil said. "Is that your nickname?"

"Not a personal one," Brian answered. "That's what they usually call the commander. The same as referring to the team sergeant as 'Top.' "

"Very interesting. By the way, that was some supper tonight," she said with a smile. "Bacon, kidney beans, tomatoes, and shoestring potatoes. How'd you come up with a combination like that?"

"Five-in-One rations," Brian said. "They come in big cans. Enough in one ration for five men."

"The tomatoes didn't come in a can," Sybil said. "They were fresh."

"We have vegetable gardens to supplement our diet," Brian said. "The ARVN troops used to keep chickens and pigs, but I made them get rid of them."

"Why?"

"Too much noise," Brian answered. "Charlie could hear them in the night and pinpoint the spot for harassing fire."

Sybil laughed softly. "Charlie could probably smell them, too."

"Yeah. What did you think of Colonel Vang?"

Sybil shuddered in the dark. There had been something foreboding about the South Vietnamese officer despite his outward friendliness and courteous conduct toward her and Connie. He was a small, thin man with a wispy moustache. His eyes, lazy and heavy-lidded, had an aura of cruelty about them.

Brian said, "I presume your silence is a sign of disapproval."

"What kind of a man is he?" Sybil asked.

"Well—aside from being a ruthless, cunning, evil sonofabitch, he's not too bad," Brian said.

"I hope you're kidding."

"The normal rank for an officer with his command would be captain, or at most major. He's a full colonel from bribing his superiors for promotions."

"I'm beginning to grow more and more disenchanted with out South Vietnamese allies," Sybil said.

"Well, he's really roughing it now," Brian said. "When he was forced to move in here, he had to send his mistresses back to civilization."

"Mistresses!" Sybil exclaimed. "How many did he have?"

"Two," Brian answered. "He brought one with him, then acquired a village girl later on."

"It's disgusting!"

"Forget it." He took her hand. "Come on. I'll show you where I live."

"I can't wait," Sybil said.

She allowed him to lead her out of the wall of sandbags. They walked slowly through the darkness, his familiarity with the area making it easy for him to find his way. Finally Sybil felt herself being taken down across a deeply slanted bit of ground. There was a rustle of poncho, and she knew they had stepped inside a room. After a bit of fumbling, a weak light switched on.

"Civilian hurricane lamp," Brian explained. "I bought it at our PX in Long Binh." He gestured at the small place. "My home," he said. There was a bunk, a small field table and chair, and a set of shelves made from ammunition boxes. All his belongings and clothes were either stowed or hung on the improvised furniture.

It was extremely hot in the cramped quarters, and perspiration broke out immediately so that Sybil was quickly soaked. "It's like a steam bath."

"We get used to it." Brian embraced her again, then slid his hands around to the front of her uniform, unbuttoning it.

She did likewise for him and within moments the two were naked, their sweating bodies pressed against each other. "Brian, darling, I'm so nervous!"

"There's nothing to be afraid of," he said.

"It's just that things are—well, so close and compact around here," Sybil said. She indicated the absolute silence outside with a nod of her head toward the door.

"We'll have to be very quiet," he said.

Sybil kissed him. "This time we'll just take care of you, okay?"

"If you feel that way, fine," Brian said understanding how the atmosphere was far from romantic. He gently took her to the bed and she lay down on it, facing up toward him. He joined her, kissing her mouth, then neck, before slowly going down to her breasts. He gently sucked the nipples to erection as sweet spasms of passion wafted through her body.

Then Brian moved upward until Sybil could feel him inside her, his gentle movements easy and pleasurable in the warm wetness of her body.

"Brian, sweetheart—" Sybil clasped him tightly, feeling so much in love with him she wanted to cry with happiness. The oneness of this gentle joining made her spasms of joy soar as high as her sexual pleasure.

He whispered in her ear, "Sybil, darling." Brian climaxed, and Sybil could feel the gentle pulsations within her.

The couple lay enjoined for several more moments

before they reluctantly parted. Brian got to his feet. "I have a jerry can of water and a basin here."

Sybil, wrung in both her own perspiration and his, spoke languidly. "Good. I think we could use a bath."

The two lovers sponged each other with the cool water, then toweled themselves off. They finished the simple bath feeling refreshed and fulfilled.

It was nearly ten o'clock when Sybil and Brian stepped in from the darkness and slipped through the poncho of the command post to join the others. All were sweat-soaked and uncomfortable. Ernie, however, was slightly drunk from having consumed so much beer. He would have been even more intoxicated, but the heavy perspiring he was doing kept him from going under.

"Interestin' out there?" he asked Sybil.

"First war zone I've ever seen," she answered.

"It's spooky, that's what it is," Ernie said. "I went over to the latrine and couldn't hear a sound. Jesus, I couldn't see a thing either."

"After a guy's been out here a while, he feels the darkness is his friend," Brian remarked.

"Speaking of darkness," Connie said sitting in the dull glow of a kerosene lantern, holding up her magazine, "how about getting the electricity turned back on? I can't see well enough to read."

"The generator makes too much noise at night," Brian explained. "It would show Charlie its exact location. Then he'd drop a mortar round on it."

Anthony Ryder, sipping a cup of lukewarm coffee, looked at Sybil. "We contacted Long Binh while you were out on your walk. The chopper will pick us up tomorrow and we'll go back to the Triple-Nickel. Our mission of mercy has been aborted."

"Yeah," Ernie said. "Just think. In less than twenty-four hours we'll be back with Mother and Rafferty."

"It could be worse," Brian said. "How'd you like to be stuck out here with us?"

Connie laughed. "I don't think that would bother Sybil one bit, would it, *amigita?*"

Sybil didn't respond. She felt a stab of anger at having to leave Brian so quickly. But her emotions settled down. She should consider herself lucky to have had these few brief moments, she thought looking at him. Then a feeling of foreboding, as strong as it had been when she'd learned he'd returned to the war, swept over her. *Sweet Lord, don't let anything happen to him!*

Chapter Eighteen

An ominous roar of distant thunder rolled across the early morning sky. Overhead, thickening clouds billowed in the pressure of the winds at high altitudes.

"The monsoon is starting for sure," Brian Mallory said. "It'll hit us off and on for a while until the real deluge starts."

Sybil, with Brian's arm around her, stood with her two friends and Dr. Ryder. Their bags were sitting out just off the small helicopter landing pad that lay before them. Top Meyer and Jim Coleson were also there along with Colonel Vang. The ARVN officer, standing beside the taller Americans, seemed even more diminutive than he had at the previous evening's meal. In fact, Sybil noticed, he was about the same height as Connie.

Obviously taken with the Chicana, Vang moved about in a seemingly casual manner until he ended up beside her. "You were a welcomed flower in this field of desolation, *mademoiselle,"* Vang said to the young nurse. "All of us shall miss your company." His English was precise, but heavy with accent.

"Thank you," Connie responded feeling a bit awkward.

"Tell me, *mademoiselle,"* Vang continued. "Would it be possible for me to see you in the event I am able to travel to Long Binh?"

Connie, reddening slightly, cast a quick glance at her friends for moral support. "Uh—I don't think so, colonel." Then she lied desperately. "You see I have, that is, I'm seeing somebody."

Vang, his evil grin still strong on his face, let his eyes travel in an obvious circle between her large breasts and face. "Perhaps the young man wouldn't mind if we engaged in a, ah, *souper innocent* late some evening in a local restaurant."

Connie swallowed, feeling terribly uncomfortable and angry. "Oh, no! We couldn't do that. Scab would be terribly upset."

Vang's eyes widened. "Scab? His name is Scab?"

"Yeah," Ernie interrupted loudly. "A big, mean bastard—with tattoos."

Sybil, afraid Ernie might go too far, entered the conversation. "A very big guy."

"Oh, yes," Connie said. "You see he was in a motorcycle gang before he got drafted."

"I have heard of those organizations," Vang said. "Since he is a conscript, I presume your man friend serves as a soldier rather than an officer."

"That's right," Connie said putting some meaning in her voice. "Why he just hates officers. He's been in the stockade a lot of times for beating them up."

Ernie spoke in a low voice. "I ain't sure but I think he's even killed a couple."

"Co dung khong?" Vang blurted out in Vietnamese. Then he nervously cleared his throat and smiled weakly at Connie. "Yes. Well, perhaps you and Mr. Scab will both join me for a late supper, eh?"

"I'll speak to him about it," Connie said. She moved away from the ARVN colonel and stood close to Sybil. Connie, her face turned away from Vang, rolled her eyes in exasperation.

Top, his craggy face folded into an amiable grin, glanced over at the two nurses. "Well, ladies, like Colonel Vang said, we sure did enjoy your comp'ny."

"We're flattered, Top," Connie said.

"Yeah," Coleson said. "Come back and see us again as soon as you can."

"We'll do that," Sybil promised.

Connie suddenly pointed outward. "Oh, look! In the distance. Is that our chopper?"

Everyone glanced in the direction she indicated. A small dot could be seen. After a few moments it was obvious it was growing larger.

"I'd say that's it," Brian said.

Sybil felt sad at the impending parting that was only minutes away. Her voice was low as she gave Brian's hand a mournful squeeze. "Oh, hell!"

Soon the engine could be heard, the familiar chopping sound echoing off the surrounding countryside. After a bit, the shape of the helicopter could be clearly perceived. It seemed to be on a course running perpendicular to the camp, but eventually it turned and came straight on.

Finally, it was only a few hundred yards away. Suddenly a stream of smoke zipped out of the jungle and streaked toward the aircraft.

The helicopter exploded into a fiery, orange ball.

Then it appeared out of the resultant smoke, falling in pieces into the trees under it. The body of a man, probably the young crew chief, spun lazily down with the wreckage.

Everyone was silent for one second. It was Top Meyer who first spoke. His voice was amazingly calm for having just seen the destruction of the chopper and its crew. "Charlie just blew your ride home all to hell," he said. "Prob'ly used a rocket launcher for antiaircraft."

"Oh, my God! How awful!" Sybil exclaimed.

"Holy shit!" Ernie said echoing her feelings.

"We've been worrying about them getting that capability for a long time now," Brian said. "It looks like they finally did, and a slow moving chopper like that would be easy to hit from that short range."

Suddenly three explosions erupted simultaneously just outside the wire. "Incoming mortar rounds!" Colonel Vang hollered. He immediately bolted for the safer area in the interior of the camp. At the same time, one of the ARVN soldiers began cranking a hand siren to alert the garrison.

"Head for the bunker!" Brian said. He turned, still holding Sybil's hand, and sprinted for cover. Startled, and more than a little confused, the people from the Triple-Nickel didn't hesitate to follow the example set by members of the garrison. They, too, ran for cover.

Other tremendous bursts rocked the area. The men allowed Sybil and Connie to precede them into the dugout. Ernie Kaznowski demanded information.

"What the hell's goin' on around here?"

"We're under attack," Top told him. "Didn't you see them mortar rounds blowin' up all over the place?"

"I didn't know what they was," Ernie said.

"As soon as that barrage is over, the VC foot sloggers are gonna be doin' their damnedest to get over our wire," Top said.

Brian wasted no time. He went directly to the field phone and cranked it to speak with all the subordinate command posts scattered around the perimeter. When he finished the check, he replaced the phone. "We've got several casualties," he said to Ryder. "Looks like we'll need your services. Top hit the nail on the head. From the looks of things, a major attack is underway against us."

"We'll sure help out," Ryder said. He started to speak again, when a tremendous roar of explosives and gunfire rent the air.

When the noise broke for a few moments, Brian shouted further orders. "They're throwing everything at us. You Triple-Nickel folks get down and stay out of the way!"

Several ARVN soldiers, evidently having battle stations in the bunker, arrived. They went to firing slits and began returning fire toward the enemy which had now reached the outer wire.

"Get down I said!" Brian yelled at Sybil and Connie. Ernie and Ryder had already ducked. Their combat training had been more extensive than that of the two nurses.

Both women got on the floor. Brian, his face clearly showing his anger, yelled again. "Goddamn it, Sybil! In a situation like this do exactly as I say the second I say it, understand?"

"All right, Brian." She didn't like the angry tone in his voice, but Sybil immediately complied and crawled to the sandbagged wall beside Top Meyers. The uneven staccato of automatic weapons now chattered throughout the area in brief, but numerous bursts.

Sybil crouched with her back pressed tightly against the sandbags. She grimaced at each blast of shooting. Top, standing up with his M16 rifle pointing out of the firing slit, methodically squeezed the trigger, adding his own contribution to the noise of the battle.

Sybil could smell the acrid, masculine odor of his sweat and the pungent smoky aroma of cookfires and jungle soil that wafted from his unwashed camouflage-pattern fatigues. The expended cartridges from his weapon bounced soundlessly off the earthen floor in the din of the fighting.

Sybil glanced up at Top's face and could make out his features. His expression was almost detached as he returned the fire of the attacking Viet Cong. He squeezed the trigger regularly and nearly rhythmically, sending small swarms of bullets flying out toward the jungle.

The sergeant looked down at Sybil and said something to her with a grin.

Her eardrums, numbed from the thundering concussion of the weapons being fired in the bunker, couldn't make out the words. She shrugged and shook her head at him, indicating she couldn't hear.

He kneeled down and leaned close to her ear. "I was just wondering what the poor folks are doin' today."

Sybil smiled weakly at the humor and went back to hunching against the sounds of the roaring gun battle.

She glanced across the room at Brian who was once again speaking into the telephone, the receiver tight against one ear, his hand clamped over the other in order to keep out as much combat noise as possible.

Suddenly the fighting died down—then stopped.

"Okay," Brian announced. "They've pulled back."

Sybil's hearing was badly affected by the firing. Brian's voice seemed muted. She looked at him. "Is the fighting over?"

"I'm afraid not," he answered. He looked around until he spotted Ryder. "Ready to care for the casualties?"

"In here?" the doctor asked.

"This bunker serves as the hospital, too. I'll shift these ARVN riflemen out of here to other positions," Brian said. "Barney Chapman should show up shortly. He's got some of the ARVN bringing in wounded."

Ryder, confused, looked around. "Where the hell do we perform the operations?"

"Chapman does it on the table there," Brian said pointing.

Ryder's eyes opened in astonishment. "The same one we *ate* on?"

"Yeah," Brian said. He walked over to Sybil and helped her to her feet. "Sorry for snapping at you, but we have a saying that goes: 'There are two kinds of people out here—the quick and the dead.' " He smiled and gently put a hand on her cheek. "You were moving kind of slow."

"I'll do better next time," Sybil said. She appreciated his genuine concern even if he had yelled at her.

At that moment the Special Forces medic made an appearance. He stood at the entrance holding the poncho back so that three wounded ARVN on stretchers could be brought in. As soon as the litters were placed on the dirt floor, he rushed to a footlocker and pulled out several sheets. He threw them on the table and looked at Ryder. "I'll get the surgical kit. Ready to start?"

"Ready," Ryder said. He motioned to Sybil and Connie. "Let's go, ladies."

Ernie, whose face bore an expression halfway between fright and excitement, leaped into action and grabbed one end of the first stretcher while Sybil and Connie grabbed the other. They set the injured soldier on the operating table.

In the meantime, on a small field desk, Chapman was laying out the medical tools along with the several types of anesthesia he had to offer. He was almost apologetic. "No time or place to scrub properly, doc," he said. "And this is all the goodies you're going to have to work with."

"Okay. Stay out of the way of my nurses and me," Ryder remarked nonplussed. "I hope you have some masks and gloves."

"Right there in the big kit. I'm goin' back to check for more casualties," Chapman said. "Can I take your medic with me?" He pointed at Ernie.

"Is he that necessary for your efforts?" Ryder asked.

"I reckon I can use the ARVNs," Chapman answered.

"Then leave Kaznowski with us," Ryder said. "He'll come in handy moving the patients around and doing odd jobs for us."

"Right," Chapman said rushing for the door. "See

you later."

Ryder stood back while Sybil and her two friends eased the wounded soldier off the stretcher and onto the table. Then the litter was tossed over into a corner of the bunker.

The first patient had multiple shrapnel wounds in the upper chest. After cutting away his shirt and checking him out, Ryder inspected the anesthesia. He turned to his nurses. "We have ether here, and a few drugs for locals. I want this guy put to sleep."

"I'm familiar with the open drop, doctor," Sybil said.

"Get the stuff and go at it," Ryder ordered.

After donning mask and gloves, she pulled the necessary items from Chapman's meager surgical kit. Taking a wire frame, she taped two layers of gauze bandage over the top. Then she checked the bottle of ether. The cork in the top was already notched and prepared with the wick in place. She slipped the frame over the soldier's face. He looked up at her, his eyes open wide in anxiety and pain.

Sybil gave him a reassuring smile. "We'll have you good as new before you know it."

The soldier said something in Vietnamese, his voice husky and weak.

"Relax—relax—" Sybil made her voice as soothing as possible as she administered the drug. She automatically checked the patient as he went through the stages of anesthesia.

The man's facial expression relaxed a bit as he went into analgesia. He was still conscious, but the sense of pain had lessened to such a degree he was barely aware of it.

"Right," Sybil said to him. "Just close your eyes and drift away."

Luckily, when he slipped into delirium, he wasn't too physical. The dreams and hallucinations he experienced were not the sort that caused him to thrash, and he continued into the surgical stage showing the easy breathing of lost consciousness.

Ryder, now gloved and masked, probed for the shards of metal that had torn into the man's living flesh. Connie had also joined the team and sponged away the blood that continually seeped into the fresh wounds and got in the way of Ryder's work.

Finally, after a half-hour, the job was done. "Okay. Let's get him over there. Kaznowski, how's your bandaging technique?"

"I'm up to date on it, sir," Ernie answered. "But there ain't too much wrap here." He looked up from the box he was examining. "There's plenty o' field dressin's though."

Sybil looked at Ryder. "Chapman mentioned that yesterday, remember?"

"Yeah." He motioned to Ernie. "Okay. Use what you got."

The patient, with the nurses on one end of the stretcher and Ernie on the other, was removed. Sybil shook her head. "How are we going to treat these guys for shock?"

"What would you do if you were giving them first aid?" Ryder asked.

"Keep them warm and elevate their feet," Sybil answered.

"Then do it," Ryder said. "And let's shake a leg, folks. We're going to have to follow the examples of the best surgeons of the nineteenth century."

"How did the top ones perform their operations, doctor?" Connie wanted to know.

"Fast!" Ryder answered.

The battle, which had slowed, picked up momentum as the day progressed. There were no less then three full-scale attacks before late afternoon.

The casualties came in, pushing the limited medical resources past their already confined limits. Even Chapman, who didn't like to act like anything particularly upset or worried him, admitted that there had never been caseloads like the ones that were growing as the day went on.

Sybil, being able to make brief observations of Chapman when he made quick appearances in the bunker, was very impressed by the devoted skill he demonstrated. The Special Forces medic was untiring and brave. He never hesitated in returning to aid in the evacuation of wounded to the bunker, no matter how severe the fighting was outside. His complete dedication to his military calling was evident in the care he showed the injured. During the rare lulls he could have enjoyed, he rechecked all patients, seeing that those who had been operated on were doing as well as could be expected, and that those who were waiting were kept as comfortable as he could possibly make them.

There were three expectants, and he ministered to them with a tenderness that belied his rugged countenance. But the mercy he showed also had a deadly practicality to it. "Say, doc," he said after checking the dying men, "how much o' that anesthesia can you spare for these guys?"

Ryder was thoughtful for a few moments. "Well—you have a good amount here. There should be plenty to keep them comfortable."

"I mean for takin' em out."

Ryder was angry. "What the hell are you talking about?"

Chapman wasn't backing down. "You know damned well what I'm talkin' about. There's no sense in these poor bastards thrashin' around, goin' to sleep, then wakin' up to thrash around again before gettin' another shot."

"Don't you ever talk to me about terminating a patient!" Ryder shouted. "I'm a doctor, damnit!"

"And I'm a frontline, nose-in-the-dirt, fuckin' Sneaky Pete medic!" Chapman yelled back. "You gotta be realistic at times like this. For all practical purposes, these guys are already dead, and there ain't nothin' we can do to change that."

"Give them shots whenever necessary because of pain," Ryder said. "And that's an order."

Chapman walked over from the wounded. "Lemme tell you somethin', doc. This here's my turf, got it? If I decide it's practical to off some poor, dyin' sumbitch, I'm gonna do it. And don't you say nothin' about it. The only thing I'm inter'sted in is how much o' these drugs you figger you can spare me to do the job."

"Hey!" Sybil said. "We've got enough going on around here without you two arguing."

"Yeah," Connie echoed. "There's too much work right now."

"Sorry," Ryder said turning back to his work.

"Yeah, me, too, Doc," Chapman said. "I gotta get back. Think about what I said. I'll see you later."

Chapman left them, and Ryder looked at Sybil with a nod toward the patient. "Wipe him."

Sybil daubed the wound they were treating, the gauze soaking up the excess blood that had seeped into the wide tear put there by shrapnel. "Chapman has to be practical," she said. "And he figures it's the best way."

"Of course it's the best way," Ryder said. "But I take being a doctor just a bit seriously. I'll never hasten the death of a patient under any circumstances."

"Never?" Connie asked.

"No, never." He nodded toward Sybil. "Wipe him again."

The fighting died off enough that in three hours all the wounded had been treated. The team from the Triple-Nickel had just sat down to relax when Barney Chapman made another one of his appearances. He came into the bunker and went over to Dr. Ryder.

"I got a ARVN out there I ain't sure about movin'," he said.

"What's the problem?" Ryder asked.

"His neck might be busted or somethin'," Chapman said. "Maybe spinal injuries, too. How's about takin' a look at him, doc?"

"Sure," Ryder said.

Sybil, wanting a breath of fresh air, followed them out of the bunker. She stood just outside the entrance and watched the pair walk across the cratered area between the various dugouts.

Suddenly there was an explosion outside the wire. Others rapidly followed the first in a straight line, sending geysers of earth flying into the sky. The final one went up in the exact spot where Ryder and Chapman were walking.

They were there one second, then suddenly disappeared in the flash of the blast. Sybil gasped, then unwisely and instinctively ran to where they had been.

Sybil looked down and could see nothing but a large, smoking hole in the earth.

The doctor and the medic had been instantaneously vaporized into nonexistence.

Chapter Nineteen

Rain fell heavily outside the bunker. The deluge had been drenching the hamlet for the previous several hours, turning the area between the various dugouts into a quagmire.

Sybil and Connie sat together on a bench by the operating table. Both wore green operating-room shirts. The garments looked out of place with the fatigue trousers and boots. But Barney Chapman's mixed bag of supplies had not included any pants to match the tops.

The two nurses were unaware of it, but they were instinctively holding hands. Ernie, nervously smoking a cigarette, squatted near them. Jim Coleson and Top Meyer leaned nonchalantly against the opposite wall, seemingly unperturbed by the circumstances they were in. Colonel Vang, seated in a chair close to them, fidgeted. He wore an American army poncho, the rubberized garment dwarfing his small frame. He smoked a cigarette in the Asian style, holding it between thumb and forefinger. Now and then his heavy-lidded eyes would swing over for a quick perusal of Connie, then go back to empty staring at the opposite wall.

The wounded were lying on the floor of the bunker. They were mostly quiet, though a moan or sigh could be heard from time to time.

Brian Mallory was busy contacting the various control points through which he coordinated the defense of the garrison. After speaking a few terse words into the field telephone, he hung it up. Brian turned and faced the others who were with him within the sanctuary of the sandbags. "Okay, I'm going to level with you," he said. "Here's the skinny on the situation."

Everyone turned their eyes toward him. Sybil and Connie out of nervous apprehension, Ernie because of the excitement he felt, and Top and Jim from professional interest. Whatever was going on was simply a part of the two soldiers' everyday working life. Vang lit a fresh cigarette off the dying one and continued his pensive smoking.

"They've got us hemmed in tight," Brian said. "The only chance we have for relief is an air strike." He looked upward at the sound of the heavy plummet of water on the roof. "But until the weather breaks, that will be impossible. I've been informed that the air force is standing by, so we'll have some ground attack sorties when the situation permits."

Sybil spoke up. "Will we get in some choppers to take the wounded out?"

Brian shook his head. "Sorry. It'll be some time before that's possible. I'm afraid that rates a low priority on our list of things to do."

"A lot of these men will die without proper medical

attention," Sybil said. She was surprised her voice was so calm.

"I realize that," Brian said. "But we'll lose even more if the VC aren't beaten back. Better yet, they should be run off."

Jim Coleson smiled and winked at Brian. "Now I know what Custer felt like."

Brian slowly shook his head. "I hope this situation doesn't deteriorate to that point."

Vang was more blunt. "If the weather does not improve, we are doomed. The Viet Cong will slaughter us."

"Shit!" Ernie said.

"Hey!" Brian said forcefully. "Let's not panic, people, okay? The situation is far from impossible. It's going to get hairy, but if we hang on we'll make it."

"I'm worried about the wounded," Sybil said.

"Me too," Connie said.

"We have to rely on you two—and Ernie now— since Ryder and Barney are dead," Brian said. "I know it's going to be a tough job. All that can be asked of you is your ultimate best. Whatever results come from those efforts will be appreciated by the garrison, believe me."

Sybil cast a worried eye in Ernie's direction, then gave Brian a beseeching look. "I'd rather Ernie stay with us."

Ernie jumped to his feet. "No! I'm takin' Barney's place."

"Doesn't the ARVN have medics?" Sybil answered. "I don't want Ernie going out there in the fighting."

Ernie's face was flushed with anger. "Hey, Sybil, I ain't your little brother. And I ain't no candy-ass either. I'm a medic—a bonafide U.S. of A. Army medic and I'm gonna do my job just like Barney. The ARVN ain't got reg'lar medical corpsman, only aidmen. They'll need me out there."

"Damn straight," Top said showing an open respect for the feisty young Polish-American. "I'll feel a helluva lot better knowin' Ernie's around to look after things."

"I agree a hunnerd percent," Jim Coleson interjected.

Connie had about as much enthusiasm for their friend's going out into the fighting as Sybil. "Oh, Ernie! Don't go getting gung-ho on us, please. You could get killed!"

Ernie blanched a bit, but he grinned in his cocky way. "Gee, thanks. I really needed that." Then, knowing the other men in the room were watching him, he added, "Besides, I'll get buried in Tucson and your ma will put flowers on my grave."

"Ernie!" Sybil cried.

"Never mind all that," Brian said with the cold logic of a combat commander. "Kaznowski is needed as a combat medic. That's what he'll do." He fumbled in his pocket for a cigarette, and brought out a badly bent one. After lighting up, he spoke again. "This lull we're enjoying is going to be over pretty quick. Anybody have any questions? Okay, then. Let's go."

The men quickly left to return to their posts. Ernie was the last one through the poncho. Sybil called out to him, "Ernie! Be careful!"

But he was already gone.

Time meant nothing as the battle progressed. There was neither night nor day. Hours and minutes were no longer the increments used to gauge the earth's rotation through space. The brief span of history in which the fortified hamlet existed was measured by the number of wounded that were brought through the poncho-shrouded door of the hospital bunker.

The injured troops were badly mangled. None of the casualties were from small arms' fire. All had massive trauma and tremendous loss of blood due to incoming mortar rounds and the resultant shrapnel. Without antibiotics, Sybil and Connie could do little more than stop bleeding and drench the injuries with iodine—Barney Chapman had gotten several gallons of the antiseptic from some odd source. The meager supply of bandages had run out, so they used field dressings tightly bound around the wounds. Then, after a shot of benzocain or lidocaine, the soldier was set aside to let his own body's mechanisms make up for the lack of necessary treatment.

Many died within a few hours from massive shock. The ARVN were small men who, after years of malnourishment and living in unsanitary conditions of appalling degree, hadn't much resistance or strength to survive the ordeal. There were a few surprises: a badly mauled soldier hanging on somehow, beating the odds while continuing to breathe in his drug-induced slumber.

But not many.

Ernie had inherited a small staff of Vietnamese aidmen. He supervised their efforts on a demanding level of high energy. Working with the ARVNs, he had picked up the Vietnamese word *mau len*—"quick"—and used it frequently on his stretcher parties.

A morbid routine developed out of the chaos of bringing in the wounded for treatment. The aidmen, after leaving a new patient, would be required to remove a dead one. The corpses, without the time or circumstances for burial, were piled outside the door of the bunker. It was a sight that didn't do much for the morale of the men being brought in for treatment. Although the bodies stacked in the rain were covered with their ponchos, their booted feet were exposed.

Sybil and Connie changed their operating room shirts several times, but finally gave it up. It was taking too much time and effort. Besides, the supply was fast dwindling. So the two worked in blood-soaked garments as they patched their charges, some dying in their arms on the crude table.

All this time, the battle's noise was an intrusive, smothering roar of thundering explosions. Sometimes, when the hunks of metal hit the corrugated-iron roof, it sounded like large handfuls of gravel being thrown violently against it. Neither Sybil nor Connie quite got used to it. Although they paid no attention to mortar eruptions on the other side of the camp, they flinched involuntarily from the ones nearby.

The battle seemed to grow in intensity, until each single explosion, machine-gun fusillade, and individual rifle shot blended into a rolling, unending roar.

Then it stopped.

Sybil looked up from wrapping a field dressing around a thin, young soldier's waist. "What the hell was that?"

Connie smiled mirthlessly. "It's called silence, *amigita.*"

The soldier moaned, looking at them with the fear dancing across his features. Yet there was a look of defiance in his eyes. *"Can-than!"* he said in a weak voice.

"What?" Sybil asked.

He took a deep breath. *"Can-than!"*

"We can't understand you," Connie said. Then she added in Spanish. *"No comprendemos."* She looked over at Sybil. "Now, why in the hell did I say that?"

The soldier was insistent. *"Can-than, can-than!"*

Sybil shrugged. "Sorry, we don't know what you're trying to say." She finished wrapping him up. "This one's going to be hurting. I'm administering fifty milligrams of tetracaine every hour."

"Yeah," Connie agreed. "That's enough for a little guy like him."

"It's a good thing they're all small," Sybil remarked. "Or we wouldn't be able to move them around." She gently took the ARVN's shoulders.

Connie slipped her arms under his legs. "It's bad enough as it is what with carrying these guys. *Chihuahua!* My back is about to break, even from these so-called lightweights."

They slipped the patient on the stretcher that had been placed on the table and took him over and set him among the other treated wounded. Then they picked up the next man and carried him over to the table for an examination and subsequent care.

At that moment Ernie appeared. He was on one end of the litter with an ARVN on the other. Ernie, soaking wet and obviously deeply involved in his work, spoke in an authoritative tone to his partner. *"Can-than!"*

Sybil turned to him. "Hey, we heard that word from the last patient. What does it mean?"

"I just picked it up myself," Ernie said. "It means 'careful.' "

Sybil sighed. "No sweat. We'll be as *can-than* as possible."

"Any stiffs?" Ernie asked.

"Yeah," Sybil answered. "Show him, Connie. I'll get to work on this guy."

Connie pointed out three stretchers. "Take 'em."

"Damn," Ernie said. "There's more'n more."

"How's the rain out there?"

"Not real bad, but the clouds is too low to call in air strikes," Ernie answered. Then he added. "At least that's what Top tole me."

He and his ARVN counterpart carried the first of the dead men out into the heavy drizzle. When they returned for the second, Brian was with them.

Sybil smiled at him. "Hi."

"Hi. How's it going?"

"Awful," Sybil answered. "We've got to get these guys out of here and back to proper care, Brian. We're doing little more than first aid and painkilling."

"If that's all you can do – " He let the statement hang.

"What's going on out there?" Connie asked. "The war over?"

"Merely a lull," Brian said. "I'm not altogether unhappy. We mauled them pretty bad during the last couple of hours. None of the little bastards have managed to get across the wire. Their corpses are piled up out there."

"Perhaps you noticed the entrance to our hospital," Sybil remarked. She talked while working on her patient.

"You might find this hard to believe, but Charlie's catching it worse than we are," Brian said. "And his medical facilities are just as bad, if not worse, than ours."

Connie was shocked. "And they're still fighting? They could get the hell away from here if they wanted to."

Brian sighed. "Yeah, they could. But they won't. That sort of gives you the idea of what we're facing in this war, doesn't it?"

Ernie and his partner returned for the next dead man. "How's it goin', cap'n?"

"We're hanging in there," Brian said. He watched Ernie prepare the corpse for removal. "You're doing a good job. We all appreciate it."

"Yeah," Ernie said. "I'm puttin' in for a medal as soon as we get back. I want Mother Moorehead herself to pin it on my bony chest."

"She'll pin it on you all right," Connie said. "But not on your chest."

The remark wasn't particularly funny, but somehow its timing was right on. the four of them burst into laughter. It lasted for nearly a half minute, before dying down to chuckles. Then the mirth ended as abruptly as it had started.

"Don't take much to make a guy giggle around here," Ernie said wiping at the rainwater that seeped from his hair and down his face. "Well, I gotta get these other stiffs outta here." He looked at the ARVN and pointed to the dead man. *"Mau len!"* Ernie looked at Sybil and Connie. "That means 'quick.' "

The Vietnamese, a veteran who knew only a smattering of English, grinned at him. "Okay, Joe. Okay, Joe. We make *mau len*. But no make *can-than*. Too late for him. Too late." Then he laughed aloud. "Maybe too late for eve'body!"

The lull in the fighting turned out to be longer than anyone expected. The only noise was the steady splatter of water on the bunker roof, and after another four hours of work, Sybil and Connie had managed to treat the last of the wounded.

But during that time, no less than a dozen more of their patients died.

Finally, the bloody sheets taken off the table, the two nurses sat sipping hot C-ration coffee out of canteen cups. Sybil looked over at her friend. "You are a mess."

"You, too," Connie said. "Your hair is stringy and scraggly looking."

Sybil smiled. "There're shadows under your eyes."

"You look like death warmed over," Connie replied with a weak grin. She raised her coffee cup. "But you're one hell of a nurse, Sybil Mae Watkins."

"You, too, Maria Consuelo Montaldo."

Connie took a drink of the coffee. "Did you tell Brian about Noi and Sai?"

"No. I just couldn't."

"Yeah. Understandable," Connie said.

Sybil was silent for several moments. Then she raised her cup. "Here's to us."

They banged their cups together, the metallic clank loud in the confines of the bunker. Sybil laughed out loud.

"What's funny?" Connie asked.

"I was just thinking about how happy you'll be when you get back to Long Binh to see your boyfriend Scab again."

Connie laughed. "I wonder what Colonel Vang would think if he could see me now. Think I ought to go over to his dugout and throw myself at him?"

"Sure. Give the little bastard a big thrill."

"Honey, I'm a Chicana," Connie said with a leer. "I'm more woman than most men can handle—much less a sawed off little runt like him."

"You're that good, huh?"

"I'd break a toreador's back, baby," Connie said.

Sybil laughed again, then fell into a moment's silence before speaking. "Why aren't we crying? We should be sobbing bucketfuls of tears."

"Because we're in shock," Connie answered. "And if we stop laughing, we're going to be weeping for sure."

"No doubt!" Sybil drained her coffee. "We'd better check the patients out. According to my watch there're some shots due."

She had just started to get up when a tremendous explosion split the rainy night air. The concussion of the blast was so great that dust splattered down from the ceiling.

Then the battle erupted again.

Without speaking, the two friends quickly prepared the table for the wounded they knew would soon be arriving. Their assumption was correct. In less than ten minutes, Ernie appeared with a stretcher.

"Here we go again," he shouted to them over the din. "Only it's worse this time."

"What's going on? Are the VC reinforced?" Sybil asked as the patient was laid out for her.

"No," Ernie responded. "But didn't you hear that big explosion?"

"Of course we heard it!" Connie said. "You think we're deaf? What's so bad about it in comparison with all the others?"

Ernie's face was a mask of grimness. "It came from *inside* the camp."

"Inside?" Sybil inquired.

"Yeah," Ernie said. "The cap'n says we got a traitor around here somewhere."

Sybil forgot her patient and grabbed Ernie's arm.

"What in the hell are you talking about?"

"It ain't hard to figger out," he said. "There's some sonofabitch in here with us that works for the VC. And he just blew out the south defenses. The shit's really hit the fan."

"A turncoat? Are you standing there and calmly telling me that there's some traitor in our midst that's doing his best to help those bastards outside kill us?"

Ernie, whose exposure to combat had dulled both his senses and comprehension, nodded. "Yeah. That's it in a bombshell."

"*Nut*shell!" Sybil snapped.

"I think he's right in this instance, *amigita,*" Connie said. "Even if he didn't mean to be."

Sybil looked at her for a second or two more, then burst into hysterical laughter.

Connie joined her, tears streaming from her eyes.

"You two are crazy!" Ernie said.

"You bet!" Sybil said. She turned her attention back to the wounded soldier on the table.

Ernie went to the door but paused by the poncho. He looked at the two nurses. "Hell of a war, ain't it." Then he reached over and grabbed the ARVN who had helped him with the stretcher. "Hey! *Mau len,* goddamnit! *Mau len!*"

Chapter Twenty

The soldier's breath wheezed through the hole in his right lung. Sybil desperately crammed a field dressing into the opening, but the whistling still kept up with each heave of the man's small chest.

"God! God! I'm losing him!" she cried.

Connie pushed another bandage on top of the original. "I'll hold it. Tie it tight."

Sybil pulled the gauze taut and managed to make one twist around the ARVN's body. But he'd stopped breathing. "Oh, hell!"

Connie impulsively bent down to begin CPR, but Sybil pulled her back. Connie glared at her. "Let me go!"

"If you spend that much time on him, we'll lose two or three more," Sybil said. "We have to get him off the table."

"No! No!"

Sybil grabbed Connie and pulled her back, then

shook her hard. "What the hell's the matter with you? He's not breathing anymore!"

"Not breathing," Connie said. "Not breathing—he's not breathing anymore—" She walked away from the table and looked at the other casualties lying close together on the bunker floor.

Sybil also gazed at the stretchers. There were already two dead that had to be removed when the medics made another showing. She suddenly remembered the rich men's sons who were probably dancing in Saigon nightclubs at that very moment. "Godamnit!" she shouted.

Connie, whose nerves had quieted some, was concerned. "Slow down, *amigita*. Take it easy."

"They're out dancing," Sybil said under her breath. "And these poor boys are dying." Suddenly she whirled and screamed out at the top of her lungs. *"They're out dancing! And these poor boys are dying!"*

Connie grabbed her again. This time she slapped Sybil's face—once—twice—then for a third time.

Sybil looked at her, the anger blazing in her eyes. Just as suddenly she calmed down. "Let's get the chest wound off the table. He's dead."

"Right," Connie said. She turned to the corpse, then hesitated. But Connie started to lose control again. She sobbed but continued to try to function. "Grab—his—shoulders—Sybil—"

Sybil slipped her arms around her. "I'm sorry, Connie, dearest. I'm truly sorry."

Connie hugged her back. "Me too."

They stood that way for a long moment, then slowly let each other go.

Connie wiped at the tears in her eyes. "Back to work, hey?"

"Yeah," Sybil said. "Back to work."

The two toiled through several more hours. When, again, the fighting died down, it did so in such a gradual way they didn't notice it.

Ernie, still bringing in casualties, made them aware of the changing situation with a chance remark. "I only got two more to get in here."

Sybil, hollow-eyed and exhausted, looked up at him. "What do you mean?"

"There's only a coupla more out there," Ernie said. He looked at Connie. "Jeez! Do I look as bad as you two?"

"Shut up," Connie said without as much as a glance at him.

"You didn't answer me, Ernie," Sybil said. "Why are there only—" She stopped speaking and listened. The only sound was that of the persistent rain on the iron roof. "No shooting. How long has that been going on?"

"At least a half-hour," Ernie said. "I'll be back with them two guys."

Sybil finished up with the patient on the table. After she and Connie carried him off, they put another in his place. She started to examine him, then stepped back. "Forget it. He's dead."

Connie took a closer look. "Yeah. Let's get him off."

They lugged the cadaver over to the doorway, then turned to the other waiting patients. But they had expired, too. Shock and loss of blood had taken their lives.

"We just don't have the time," Sybil said.

"Yeah," Connie said. "And not enough drugs or equipment. The sanitation around here certainly isn't anything to write home about, either."

"Coffee," Sybil groaned. She walked over to the table that held the small campstove. A battered pot of water sat on top of it. She pumped the handle on the heating device, then turned it on and lit it.

Connie, in the meantime, had retrieved two packets of C-ration coffee from a box in the corner. She picked up their canteen cups and carried them over to the operating table. She looked into the G.I. utensils. "They're dirty."

"Fuck it," Sybil said.

Connie smiled weakly. "You talk like Ernie."

"Yeah." She didn't wait for the water to reach boiling. As soon as it showed a bit of steam coming off the surface, she picked the pot up and emptied it into their cups.

The brew was bitter but strong, the caffeine giving them an instant lift. Connie treated herself to a deep swallow. "This has been the only thing keeping me going."

"Yeah," Sybil replied.

They didn't get to finish the drinks before Ernie and his ARVN stretcher crews showed up with the two casualties. One was a simple leg wound that Ernie treated himself.

The other was a massive stomach injury which exposed the patient's intestines. Connie gave the man a shot while Sybil arranged his entrails as well as she could. Then she covered the trauma with a large hunk of gauze before tying it down with a field dressing.

"Another guy we'll keep doped up," she said.

"Well—let's get him off of here."

Ernie helped them place him with the other wounded. Then he sent his stretcher bearers back outside while he stayed with the two nurses. "How's about lettin' me bum some coffee?"

"Sure, kid," Sybil said.

"It's nice and quiet out there," Connie said.

"Yeah," Ernie said. "By the way, they caught the guy that blew up the south wall."

"When?" Sybil asked.

"About a half-hour ago," Ernie answered. "He was out near the wire makin' some kind o' signal or somethin'. Turned out to be a ARVN sergeant for Chrissake!"

"The bastard!" Connie hissed.

The poncho across the entrance way rustled and Brian joined them. His exhaustion was evident from his stooped shoulders and tired eyes. But his voice was firm and steady. "Looks like everything's under control here."

"I suppose," Sybil conceded without enthusiasm.

Before any more conversation could take place, a sharp scream of pain sounded from outside.

"What was that?" Sybil asked in alarm.

"Vang and his boys are interrogating the turncoat," Brian said. "Did you hear about him?"

"Ernie just told us," Connie said.

Another shriek sounded.

"What the hell are they doin' to him?" Ernie asked.

"He's going through what they call 'talking on the telephone,' " Brian explained. "They've taken a field phone—like the one on the wall there—and have attached the wires to his scrotum."

Ernie grimaced. "Oh, shit!"

"They ask a question, he answers," Brian went on. "If they like his response, they go to the next question. If they don't, they crank the phone and send a charge down the wires."

A high-piercing scream flashed across the hamlet.

"Make them stop!" Sybil cried leaping to her feet.

Brian walked over and gently took her by the shoulders. "It's none of our business," Brian said. "It's Vietnamese against Vietnamese."

"But it's inhuman," Sybil said. "Isn't there enough suffering around here?"

"The man is an enemy agent," Brian said. "I'm not crazy about it either, but I'm powerless to interfere. In fact, if I did, they would consider it an exhibition of weakness on my part."

"Weakness?" Sybil asked. "It seems more like an exhibition of civilized behavior."

Brian shrugged. "By our standards, yes. But right now, they don't count here."

Another long bellow could be heard.

"The bastards!" Connie said.

"They torture prisoners and their rich don't fight," Sybil said dully.

The group of Americans waited expectantly for the next series of screams, but they didn't come. Ernie heated up some more water and prepared coffee.

Vang appeared, throwing aside the poncho door covering. "Captain Mallory. Interrogation is over."

"Learn anything?" Brian asked with interest.

"Oh, yes," Vang said with a smile. "There are plenty of VC out there, but no more with us. The wretch was working alone. We shoot him soon." His eye roved the room until he spotted Connie. "Ah, hello, *mademoiselle*. Are you faring well?"

"Yes, thanks."

"Good." He looked at his wounded men lying around the bunker floor. "Are any of these men able to walk?"

"There might be a couple," Sybil said. "Most have painful wounds."

"No matter. Point them out and we'll take them back to the line," Vang said. "We need every man."

"Just a minute, colonel!" Sybil snapped. "I'm not releasing any of these men for duty."

"You must," Vang said, a humorless smile dancing across his features.

"They're my patients," Sybil said. "According to the ARs, they cannot go back to duty until properly released."

Vang continued to smile, but his eyes were narrowed in anger. "That, of course, is according to U.S. Army regulations. I, my dear *mademoiselle,* along with these men, serve in the South Vietnamese Army."

"Never mind," Brian interjected. "We'll work this out later. Do you have anything else to report other than the prisoner has broken under questioning?"

"Why, yes, Captain Mallory," Vang said. "You might be interested to know that the weather is breaking to the east."

Brian, who had been seated at the bench by the operating table, got to his feet. "How long has it been like that?"

Before he could answer, Jim Coleson rushed into the bunker. "Hey, Skipper, good news. I just come from the commo shack and the word is out that the air force is makin' ready to take to the air. Clear skies is movin' in from the east."

Brian's face fairly exploded into a wide smile. "That's what Colonel Vang said. But he didn't elaborate on how good things looked."

"Want me to handle the air strike?" Coleson asked.

"I'd better do it," Brian said.

Sybil grabbed his arm. "What's going on?"

Brian embraced her and kissed her lips hard but happily. "It means we'll have that air support we need pretty damn quick."

Sybil was stunned. "And—and that means this terrible ordeal will be over?"

"Sure does," Brian said.

Connie was happy but confused. "I don't even know what time it is."

Coleson checked his watch. "Oh-seven hundred hours."

"Seven in the morning?" Connie asked.

"Right," Brian enjoined. "That means you three could be out of here by noon." He kissed Sybil again. "I've got to tend to business and be ready for the flyboys when they show up. See you later, darling."

Sybil, relieved and thankful, kissed him back. "Take care and come back here as soon as you can."

Connie sank down to the bench and crossed herself. "*Gracias a Dios y todos los Santos!*"

Sybil watched Brian leave, then suddenly rushed after him. "Brian! Brian!"

He turned and met her at the top of the steps. "Yeah?"

She put her arms around him. "I'm not kidding. Hurry back, okay?"

"Okay." He kissed her again. "I love you, Sybil."

"I love you."

Sybil watched him make his way through the explosive-packed mud, then turned and went back into the bunker.

The two nurses celebrated the turn of events by brewing up some more of the coffee. Ernie finished his off quickly so he could join them. They were halfway through their first cup when the sounds of fighting again began building up.

Ernie tipped his head back and drained the coffee. "Pardon me, ladies. I have to go to the office." He gave them a little wave, then left the bunker.

Sybil and Connie cringed at the first crumps of the mortar fire. Spasms of machine-gun and rifle volleys sounded between the heavier weapons. It seemed there would be another repeat of the previous fighting, but a new sound entered the tortured atmosphere outside the hospital dugout.

"What the hell was that roaring?" Connie asked with fear in her eyes.

Sybil listened intently, then suddenly smiled. "It's the same sound I used to hear around Tinker Air Base in Oklahoma City. Those are jets."

Connie leaped up, dropping her coffee. "The air force! The beautiful air force!"

Ernie's quick reappearance was so violent he tore the poncho off the door. "Air support!" he yelled happily. "The fuckin' sky's openin' up like a umbrella! The fly-boys are comin' in!"

"Where's Brian?" Sybil wanted to know.

"He's callin' in the strikes," Ernie said. "Christ, ladies! There's napalm and the whole bit. They're knockin' the shit outta the VC out there. The whole fuckin' jungle's burnin'!"

"Surely that's going to put the finishing touches on this awful thing," Sybil said.

"Charlie's attackin' through all that shit, though," Ernie said. "We're takin' some casualties, but it's impossible to evacuate em' right now. Too hot out there. The cap'n sent me down here to stay with you two."

Sybil and Connie felt more relief than happiness. They sat down on the bench by the operating table. "Thank God!" Sybil said.

"*Gracias a Dios!*" Connie reiterated in Spanish.

The air strike continued for an indeterminate amount of time. Finally the noise of the explosions and roar of airplanes stopped as suddenly as it had begun.

The three friends in the bunker strained their ears for sound. The only thing they could hear was the crackling of burning vegetation outside the perimeter where the air force had dropped the napalm.

"Better get the table ready," Ernie said. "I'll get my aidmen to work." He walked to the entrance and started up the dirt steps, but stopped. "Oh, shit!"

Top Meyer walked in heavily burdened. Brian Mallory, limp with his head lolling, lay across the sergeant's brawny arms. Blood flowed from his body and soaked into Top's trousers. The NCO seemed almost apologetic. "He got hit in the last rush. The VC must a picked out the antenna of his radio as a target. He was usin' it to talk to the aircraft."

Sybil looked at Brian for a long second before she reacted. She started to turn panicky but fought to remain calm. "Put him on the table."

"Right." Top laid him down.

Sybil quickly cut his shirt off.

Ernie, looking over her shoulder, gasped. "Jeez!"

A massive wound exposing pink lung tissue and splintered remnants of ribs leaked blood and other internal fluids over the covering. His breath was shallow and rapid.

"Grenade," Top explained in a word.

"We'll use ether," Sybil said. She looked at Connie. "Get fresh masks and gloves."

Connie, tears welling in her eyes, slowly shook her head back and forth. "We're losing him, *amigita*. It's too late."

Sybil walked to the surgical kit and donned a mask. As she slipped into the rubber gloves, she spoke again to Connie. "Better insert some gauze in there to soak up the blood. I'll have to probe for metal in there. The wound is awfully dirty. A liberal dose of iodine and plenty of field dressing afterward."

Connie's voice broke. "Oh – Sybil – "

"We'll evacuate him first when the choppers arrive," Sybil said. "Quickly, Connie, let's get to work." She looked down at Brian, his handsome face pale and drawn. His green eyes were open, appearing listless and dry. Sybil put her arms around him and held him close. "Brian – Brian – "

He stopped breathing.

Sybil continued to hold him until Connie gently pulled her away. Ernie stepped up and took Sybil's arm. She didn't resist as he led her outside.

It was a little before noon, and the sun was high in the clear sky. The only clouds were distant ones over the far horizon that promised more rain that evening or in the night. The moisture from the old storm was now being boiled out of the earth.

Despite the growing humidity, the air seemed fresh and clean to Sybil after the long days and nights in the hospital bunker. "I hear choppers."

Ernie looked skyward. "Yeah. It's a unit outta the the One hundred seventy-third Airborne that's relievin' the garrison here."

"Then we can evacuate the wounded, can't we?"

Connie joined them, and both she and Ernie held Sybil, speaking to her in soothing whispers as the hamlet began preparing for the new arrivals.

Sybil said nothing for a while. When she did finally break her silence, it was in a soft, sad whisper as she spoke but one word:

"Brian."

Chapter Twenty-One

Sybil didn't cry until late the first night back from Ha Khe Nui. When she did finally weep, it was a complete breakdown. Connie at first held her in her arms, gently stroking her friend's hair and letting her pour out her grief on her shoulder.

But eventually Sybil slipped into a mild hysteria, and Connie laid her down on her bunk and saw to it that she received a mild sedative to ease her into sleep. Even then, the slumber was restless and agitated, filled with brief periods of sobbing and the crying out of Brian's name from time to time.

A heartrending routine began that lasted for the next forty-eight hours. Sybil would sleep, then come awake in a groggy state. This produced another period of weeping until Connie administered a further shot.

Sybil ate nothing, and took only an occasional glass of fruit juice or water. Since the two nurses and Ernie had been placed on a seven-day administrative leave by Colonel Sedgewick, Connie was able to devote the necessary time to seeing after her friend.

There had been a memorial service for Captain Anthony Ryder, but Connie thought it best that Sybil not attend.

Late in the evening of the second day, Sybil's anguish went from weeping to a need to talk. There was still some crying, but now she had begun to verbalize her grief, and Connie encouraged her through that part of mourning.

Sybil, a handkerchief clutched in her fist, lay on her bunk and dabbed at her eyes. Connie, seated in a chair beside her, listened while reaching out to touch her now and again.

Sybil's voice was low and subdued. "He was my first love—my only love—" Although she spoke in Connie's presence, it was almost as if she were speaking to herself. "I'll never have another man—his last words were that he loved me—those were my final words to him—I'm glad of that, at least—"

"Of course, *amigita,*" Connie said in a soothing tone. She waited for Sybil to continue.

"We had wonderful plans—all worked out and so lovely—but that's gone—all gone—" She looked up at Connie. "Oh, Connie! It's all over and done with!"

Sybil sank back into her crying spell, and Connie again turned to sedatives to ease her friend through the ordeal. This time, however, Sybil came out of it sooner—and under more control.

By mid-morning on the third day, she had managed to eat a sandwich that Connie fetched from the mess hall. After consuming it, she got up and stood by the window of their room for a long time. Then Sybil turned and looked at her friend. "Want to go for a walk?"

"Sure," Connie said. She decided to push it a bit. "What about going to Lucky's? We could have a beer or soda."

"All right," Sybil said dully.

"Would you like to see Ernie? I can telephone him over at the enlisted billets," Connie suggested. "He'd probably like to go over with us."

"Fine."

Connie made the call, then came back. "He'll meet us like always. Shall we go?"

Sybil walked beside her saying nothing as they left the nurses' quarters and strolled to the gate.

Ernie was waiting in his usual place. He smiled a greeting. "Hi. How you doin', Sybil?"

"Okay."

The three showed their passes and went through the gate. If Sybil remembered anything about Noi and Sai as they passed the renovated peddlers' stalls, she kept it to herself. Ernie and Connie only exchanged a few words between themselves as they continued down the street to the Triple-Nickel's favorite hangout.

The interior of Lucky's was quiet. There were several night-shift personnel sitting around enjoying some quiet beers. Lucky, checking the inventory behind the bar, looked up when Sybil, Connie and Ernie came in. He knew of Sybil's loss, and he left his work and approached them in a subdued way.

Connie smiled at him. "Hi, Lucky."

"Hello, eve'body. Want beer?"

"Just cokes for Sybil and me, okay?" Connie said.

"I'll take a San Miguel," Ernie said.

"Why don't you get something and join us?" Connie asked, thinking that Lucky's presence might be of some benefit in the situation.

"Okay. I do."

Within a couple of minutes, they all sat sipping their drinks. Sybil didn't acknowledge their company. She took occasional sips of her cola, and stared down at the table top. Lucky, not knowing what to say in the situation where an Occidental's grief was involved, displayed a slight smile as he sat with the somber threesome.

There was a sudden noise by the door. It had been caused by Mike Pullini coming through it in a wheelchair. He was dressed in a class-A khaki uniform, the bottoms of the trousers neatly pinned up around his stumps. "Hey!" he called out when he spotted them at the table. Bright-eyed and smiling, he wheeled over. "Look at me," he said loudly. "I'm mobile!"

Connie and Ernie smiled and gave him a greeting.

"I just got orders sending me to Letterman Hospital in San Francisco," he said. "I'm gonna get therapy and a fitting for artificial pins."

"Great," Connie said. "I'll bet you're anxious to get on with it."

"Sure am," Mike said. "I just want to thank you." He looked at Sybil. "Especially you."

Sybil finally acknowledged his presence by glancing his way, but she said nothing.

"You gave me the big push, Lieutenant Watkins," he said. "I'd've been in a real mess if it hadn't been for you. Captain Gavin told me the bench press contest was your idea."

Sybil nodded.

"I won my weight division, by the way," he said with a proud smile. "Blew the competition away."

Sybil finally spoke. "Good."

"Yeah. Well, now I've got it all together," Mike said. "I figure I've lost out on a lot, but I can still realize most of my hopes and ambitions."

Sybil seemed to take an interest. "I'm glad to hear that."

"I won't be in the sixty-eight Olympics of course, but there's no rule says a guy with wooden legs can't be a trainer or a strength coach for football, right?"

Sybil smiled slightly. "Right."

He winked at her. "Besides, I think I can set a world's record in bench press—or bust my ass trying."

"Sure you can," Sybil said.

He checked his watch. "I gotta go. I only borrowed this wheelchair out of Captain Gavin's therapy room. Then it's off to Tan Son Nhut and an airplane back to the world." He paused and looked directly into Sybil's face. "Hey. Thanks a lot. Thanks a hell of a lot." He wheeled forward and kissed her on the cheek. "First time I ever did that to a lieutenant," he said grinning. Then he spun the chair and wheeled toward the exit.

Sybil was silent for a couple of minutes. "I'm glad things are working out so well for Mike."

"Yeah, me too," Connie said.

"You bet!" Ernie said.

There was another disturbance at the door. This time it was Joe Sampson. "Listen up," he called out. "All you off-duty folks are supposed to report back to the hospital. There's incoming wounded. Let's go." He watched as the few night-shift people finished off their drinks and made ready to leave. He signaled over to

Connie and her friends. "That don't include you. Colonel Sedgewick says to leave you alone if I ran into you."

"Okay," Ernie called back happily.

Lucky shook his head. "More hurt soldier. Too bad. Too bad."

"Yes," Sybil said.

They sat in silence for several more minutes. Then suddenly, Sybil stood up and walked to the door.

"Hey," Connie said. "What's up?"

Connie stopped and looked at her. "Didn't you hear? There're incoming wounded. They need nurses. I'm a nurse."

Connie watched her for a moment. "I am too. Wait up!" She hurried after her.

"Where they go?" Lucky asked.

Ernie sighed. "To help out with the wounded. Where else? That pair's a coupla hardcore nurses, believe me."

Ernie stayed in his chair for a few more minutes, then suddenly downed his beer. "I can't let them two go without me. They need a good man to keep an eye on 'em."

He hurried out of the bar. Lucky watched him disappear through the door, then shrugged and stood up, going back to the bar to complete his inventory.